Praise fc

"The central characters in Elmington crackle with complexity and conflicted feelings as they navigate the minefield of end-of-life decision making. As Renee Lehnen's pitch perfect prose animates the fictional town, the tensions simmering just below its gleaming surface emerge. This timely and unforgettable book confronts the most difficult choices a family can be asked to make - and the constraints within which those decisions are forced to unfold."

Judith Harway, author of the memoir *Sundown* and three collections of poetry.

Winner of the Crime Writers of Canada Award of Excellence for Best Unpublished Manuscript in 2022

"Very engaging, great dialogue, great dark humour and social commentary."

– Crime Writers of Canada Judges

ELMINGTON

ELMINGTON

RENEE LEHNEN

Storeylines Press

© 2023 by Renee Lehnen

Cover Illustration © 2023 by Sheila Greenland

All rights reserved. No part of this publication may be reproduced, distributed, or transmitted in any form or by any means, or stored in a database or retrieval system, without the prior written permission of the author.

This is a work of fiction. Names, characters, places, and incidents are the product of the author's imagination or are used fictitiously. Any resemblance to actual events, locales or persons, living or dead, is purely coincidental.

Storeylines Press is the publisher of this work. It holds the sole, perpetual, and exclusive license with respect to this work and any derivatives thereof on a worldwide basis. Therefore, any interest in this work should be directed to the publisher at storeylinespress@gmail.com

Land Acknowledgment

Storeylines Press operates on the lands of the Anishinabek, Haudenosauneega Confederacy, and Anishinaabe, Treaty 29, 1827. As settlers to this area, we acknowledge the rights and importance of the Indigenous people and their importance to this region, nation, and its culture, as well as their unjust treatment by the Canadian government and settlers past and present.

For my Family

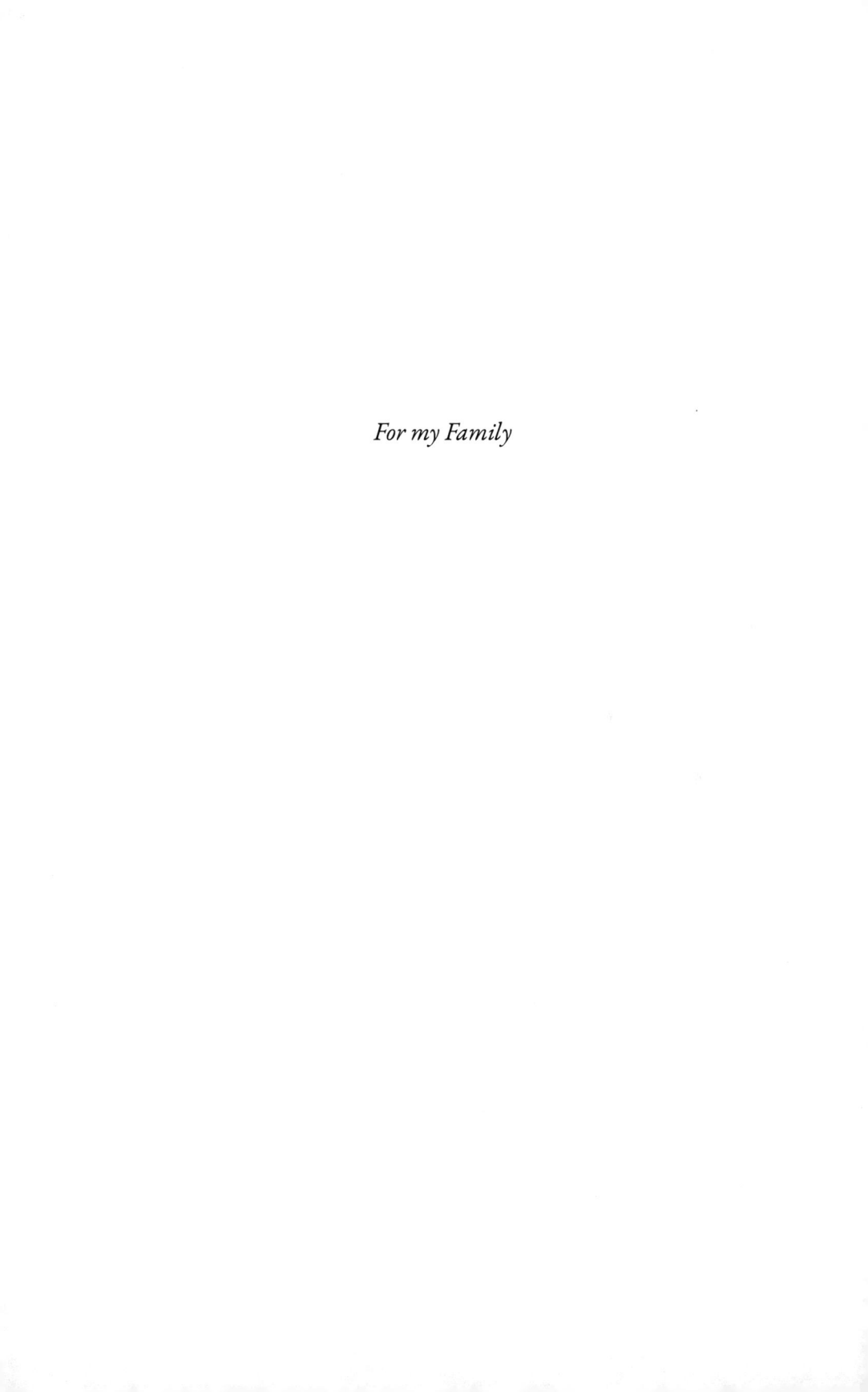

Part I

Wednesday, August 28th, 2019

The first thing Martha Gray had to do was figure out if her father was losing his marbles.

He'd expected her visit, but he hadn't bothered to shave. Sprawled in his recliner, he looked as helpless as a tortoise on its back. A stained singlet covered his bird-cage chest. His feet, swollen with fluid, emerged from grey trackpants. Shove those feet into patent leather pumps with sensible heels and you'd have yourself a textbook pair of church lady cankles. And an oxygen tube snaked from his nostrils to a concentrator hissing and pumping in the corner of the living room. Martha's nose told her he still smoked heavily. Likely as not, he had a pack of Player's "Navy Cut"—a manly, sailor's cigarette—in his pocket.

She hadn't seen her father since Christmas when he was healthy enough to fly to Vancouver. Was he smoking indoors? With his oxygen on? It was too soon in the day, too soon in their visit, to ask him and risk an argument. She scrutinized the old man in his natural habitat with a mixture of pity, curiosity, fear, and guilt. Health-wise he'd skidded sideways into a ditch of misery, but was he okay cognitively?

"Open the drapes, Duchess," wheezed Gordon. "See what's become of your old neighbourhood."

Martha went to the bay window, pulled the heavy, burgundy curtains across the rod, and squinted into sunshine. When she'd arrived by taxi in the night, the haze of streetlights only vaguely outlined the houses on Roselea Drive. She could see alright now. Across the street stood Falstaff in a Zen garden—a half-timbered Jolly Olde English cottage on steroids surrounded by geometric topiary.

"Who lives there, Dad?" asked Martha, pointing.

"Bean counter," said Gordon. "A modern-day Bob Cratchit who toils over ledgers for one of the Bay Street banks."

"Do you know his name?"

"Nope."

"I'll bet he can afford a Christmas turkey."

"Sure," agreed Gordon. "But he probably prefers a thistle salad. His soul is harder than a dried pea. I've only spoken to him once, while he was orchestrating the disgorgement of his belongings from a moving van into that, that . . . house . . . and I knew by the way he treated the box carriers that there was no point in pursuing neighbourly friendship." Gordon waved a liver-spotted hand dismissively, then coughed.

"How about them?" Martha gestured toward the grand Cape Cod style house on their right.

"An advertising exec and his social x-ray wife. Rest in peace, Tom Wolfe. . . ."

"Nice house."

"Yup. I imagine the happy couple inside it, drinking martinis and mending nets by the hurricane lamp."

"Are there any kids in the neighbourhood now?"

"A few, though you never see them. They're ferried about by

SUV, school to sports to elocution classes or whatever kids get up to these days. There's a boy next door, on the left."

"Do you know his name?"

"Ethan. Like the furniture."

Martha smiled. Of course, the old man remembered the boy's name.

"Poor kid will never have a paper route, or play ball hockey, or soap windows on Halloween," wheezed Gordon. "His mother, Joanne, keeps him on a strict schedule. He's fourteen, for crying out loud."

"Who's crying out loud?"

"I am. On the lad's behalf. By the way, how's Joseph?"

"Still incommunicado," replied Martha, voice faintly forlorn. "His community doesn't believe in using modern technology—you know, like telephones—and it's peach season in the Okanagan, so I guess he's too busy to write or get in touch."

"His community or his cult?"

"Take your pick."

Her answer hung in the air while the old man hacked and spat into a Kleenex. She peered through the slanted glass at the home of poor Ethan. The house was reclad in pastel angel stone and stucco and a shiny, black Lincoln Navigator sat on equally black, freshly sealed asphalt.

Her gaze shifted to her father's front yard. The Corolla had come to rest at an odd angle on the crumbling driveway. No doubt the old man had become a menace to pedestrians, cyclists, and other motorists on the broad streets of Elmington. Since her mother's death three years prior, weeds had invaded the flower borders and now lamb's quarter and wild carrot grew among the roses and hostas. The lawn was almost knee-high.

"I'll mow today," said Martha.

"You'll do no such thing," Gordon countered. "I hired a company to do it. It's been a wet summer. They're just behind.

Now I'll thank you for straightening the drapes and bringing me coffee."

"Okay. Coffee."

Martha crossed the shag carpet, passed through a short hallway, and entered the kitchen. The linoleum was sticky under foot. Twin dog bowls, one with dusty kibble, the other empty, graced the corner, although her mother's Pekinese, "Mutsu," had died several months prior. On the counter, dirty spoons and glasses and cups ringed by evaporating liquids awaited a dishwasher who hadn't come. Until now. This was the first chore she'd tackle.

Martha couldn't find coffee beans, but she found a jar of Nescafe. She filled the kettle and set it to boil, then spooned grains of instant coffee into two mugs. She inhaled through her nose, over the open jar. The aroma of coffee, even instant, was a welcome reprieve from the smell of decaying bits of food and crusty, ready-meal packaging.

While Martha waited for the water to boil, she looked through the window over the sink. The kitchen faced northwest, in shadow for much of the day. However, it wasn't the dimness of the room she found depressing, but the absence of three graceful spruces that used to mark the property line behind the house. Now a tall, wooden fence, ugly side out, guarded the lot to the rear and a new monster home dwarfed the bungalow.

She leaned against the counter and considered the old man's circumstances. He was slipping from chronic ill health into advanced decrepitude. Following a weekend conference in Toronto, she'd intended to stay in Elmington for a few days, then fly back to Vancouver for the beginning of the fall term. Plainly that would be impossible. The old man had to be sorted out. At the very least, he needed home care. Better yet, a move to a nursing home, but he'd never agree to that.

The kettle whistled. Martha poured boiling water into the mugs and stirred. The milk in the fridge was curdled sludge.

They'd have to drink their coffee black this morning, bracing and hot. She carried the mugs to the living room and set her father's mug on a tray table piled with books, next to his recliner.

For the first time that morning, he smiled at Martha, revealing a row of yellow teeth that resembled broken doweling. "Thank you, Duchess."

As a young socialist firebrand, she'd hated that nickname. Now she didn't mind it. "You're welcome, Dad." Martha returned his smile.

After coffee, Martha cleaned the kitchen, popped a load of laundry into the washer, transferred the garbage from kitchen to garage, vacuumed the floors, brushed the yellow film from the toilet bowl, and wiped the scum off the bathroom porcelain. To her immense relief, she found no evidence of rodent activity in the two-bedroom home.

Now she rested on the chesterfield with her feet propped on the arm rest and opened her cell phone. A few feet away, her father snored, exhausted from bellowing orders from his recliner followed by a cigarette on the porch and a trip to the bathroom.

Martha emailed the dean of the philosophy department and Daniel, her doctoral student, to explain why she was delaying her return from the symposium and to wiggle out of orientation week. She rebooked her flight to the following weekend and ordered pizza.

"967-11-11," Martha whisper-sang as she poked the number display. Quicker than scrolling through websites. Usually she avoided chain restaurants, but she was tired and no one was judging. She placed the order—Meat Supreme, with a Coke for her father and a Diet Coke for herself. On her way to the restaurant, she'd stop in at Food Basics for a few groceries. That way she could take the Corolla for a test drive and see, in broad daylight, what Elmington had become since her last visit, for her mother's funeral.

Martha found the keys on their usual hook, exited through the front door, and stepped around a folding lawn chair. Cigarette butts covered the soil in a rusting garden urn and lay strewn on the concrete porch. She added "empty makeshift ashtray" to her mental to-do list.

Now midday, the car was as hot as a sauna, so she rolled down the window. The old man's neglect of self and household was not reflected in the automobile. Light streamed through the crystal-clear windshield. Balled up tissues had been deposited in a paper bag taped next to the gear shift. The car purred like a happy kitten. If Gordon could look after his aging Toyota, why couldn't he look after himself?

Best avoid the over-analysis trap. That'd been the purview of her mother, the late Judith Steinman-Gray. Yet the message in this gleaming, well-maintained car was writ unequivocally: wheels mattered. A loss of driving privileges would devastate the old man.

Martha backed onto Roselea Drive, then headed toward Lakeshore Road. Most of the neighbourhood's postwar bungalows had been converted into two-storey homes or knocked down and replaced with mansions. Large lots and modest housing, attractive to couples with children in previous decades, were irresistible to members of the moneyed professional and merchant classes who bought up properties, demolished formerly cherished homes, and rebuilt. There was little sign of residential occupation, yet the neighborhood buzzed with the vehicles of service workers—subcompact cars of Molly Maid, pick-ups hauling lawn tractors and leaf blowers, and vans filled with carpentry and plumbing equipment.

As she pulled up to a stop sign, Martha saw a white-coated woman carrying a massage table into the side door of a house.

When Roselea Park was only a plan on a map, the proletariat worked in factories. Now they kneaded bourgeois flesh.

She turned onto Lakeshore and squeezed into the right lane that ran along a cycling lane delineated by a white stripe. Only the bravest, craziest cyclist would dare a commute on this fast-moving street. Further up, just past an overbuilt Esso station, Martha spotted a liquor store. The steering wheel practically turned itself. The Diet Coke would welcome a splash of gin on a day such as this.

After they'd had pizza and pop, and Gordon had a smoke on the front porch, Martha addressed the miasmic, ever-present elephant in the room, the smell of 1970s bingo hall hovering about the old man.

"Would you like to shower before or after me, Dad?" Martha asked sweetly.

Gordon raised a bushy eyebrow. "Is that a parenting technique you used on Joseph? Give me two options to fool me into thinking I'm making a choice?"

"Well?"

"Well? I asked you a question, Martha."

"No. I'm not trying to trick you. I'm just being polite. I'm sure you want to shower too and I don't want to jump queue if you want to go first."

"You go ahead. I'll see if I feel like it later."

Martha shrugged and headed for the bathroom.

She returned twenty minutes later, towelling her hair. "Okay, your turn, Dad."

"It's too late now," replied Gordon.

"It's three," said Martha.

"I prefer to shower in the morning."

"Then why didn't you?"

"Because we had to catch up . . . have coffee together. I was following your agenda."

"My agenda?" Martha was incredulous. She didn't know if she should push or back off. The old man needed a proper wash and clean clothes, but dirt wasn't fatal. She changed tack. "Okay. If you don't want to shower, how about a nice bath."

"With bubbles, Mummy?" Gordon asked in falsetto. The strain on his vocal cords triggered a coughing fit.

Martha sat on the chesterfield in stony silence.

At last Gordon caught his breath, then looked at his daughter. "You take after your mother, Martha. It's a wonder I've survived without her or you here to tell me what to do."

An oft-played card. Attack her good intentions with accusations of bossiness to avoid addressing the issue. Martha wouldn't fall into the trap. This situation called for direct communication after all, not tact.

"Dad, you stink. You need to wash."

Instantly, Gordon's face sagged, and his eyes met Martha's in an expression of shame. At once, she felt very, very guilty.

"I can't use the shower, Martha. The tub's too slippery for me," Gordon said softly.

"Why didn't you say so? We can fix that."

"I don't think you can—"

"I'll get some of those adhesive strips for the tub . . . and maybe a bath chair. At least have a wash at the sink, Dad. Today."

"In a bit, Duchess. In a bit," said Gordon.

This time, Martha didn't cajole or argue. "Fine," she said. "Reading time?"

"Yes, I think so," replied Gordon.

Martha stood and went to the bookshelf. "What do you recommend?"

"How about *The Secret*?"

"No way," Martha laughed. "You don't have that book, do you Dad?"

"I do. Joanne gave it to me. It's about the law of attraction. She said it would change my life."

"And has it?" asked Martha.

"Not yet," replied Gordon. "You read it and tell me what I'm doing wrong, and then we'll turn my luck around."

CBC News, Journalist's Recording, Thursday, April 9th, 2020

I'm Joanne Kingsworth, neighbour of Gordon Gray, may he rest in everlasting peace. Normally I wouldn't talk to the media, but I think it's important to shine a light in dark places . . . to draw attention to the issue of elder abuse, even during a global crisis. I consider it my personal duty to speak with you today. I'll stand over here. The juniper hedge is a nice backdrop.

How long did I know the Grays? Well, I never met Gordon's wife. She passed away just before my husband, Michael, was transferred to the Elmington office of Eastern Technology Solutions. He's regional vice president. We renovated 24 Roselea to meet the needs of our growing family, registered Ethan Michael at Applegate College, and settled in . . . um . . . three years ago? Yes, three. Time flies for busy mothers.

Gordon Gray was a kindly man, just like Morrie Schwartz in Mitch Albom's book. Mind you, I kept a fire extinguisher by the side door as he had the alarming habit of smoking with his oxygen on. He told me he always took off his oxygen when he lit up, but he was forgetful. And odd. He offered Ethan money to cut his grass and shovel snow. Ethan would've been twelve at the time, a sensitive age, and he accepted. As soon as Ethan told me, I marched over and knocked on Gordon's front door and set him straight. Child labour is simply unacceptable.

And so is abuse and neglect. I'm not surprised the police have charged Martha Gray with murder. Oh, I did my best to reach out to Martha. I invited her to my book club and our annual pool party. To my surprise, she attended both.

Yes, that's correct. She drank more than she should have. I have a BA in psychology, and I could tell from the day that I met her she was socially anxious, painfully introverted, and that she abused substances to cope. I like a glass of wine on occasion too, but Martha's intake was notorious on Roselea Drive.

The first I realized something was amiss was last week when a police cruiser crawled the curb in front of Gordon's house. When they escorted Martha out of the house last night, she didn't look upset at all. Not one iota. She was as calm as an ice queen. It just goes to show—you never know if you're inviting a monster into your midst when you do as Jesus instructed and invite the stranger into your home.

She has a son too, you know. This must be mortifying for him.

Thursday, August 29th, 2019

Martha was roused from deep sleep by the roar of a lawn mower outside her window. She reached up from her narrow, childhood bed and pulled the window shut, then found her cell on the bedside table. 8:17. An ungodly 5:17 in Vancouver. She rolled over and pulled the blanket over her ear, but the surge of adrenaline from waking abruptly brought on a panicked alertness that made sleep impossible. At least the lawn would be short enough to satisfy Elmington's bylaw enforcement officers.

Martha got up and padded into the kitchen for a cup of Nescafe and another stab at *The Secret*. "Ask, believe, receive." This short book, cloaked in a cover photo of parchment with wax seal, elevated consumerism, self-absorption, and fixation on social status into a lofty, esoteric spiritual practice. Rhonda Byrne had written a bible for vacuous, neo-liberal, suburbanite shoppers—basically, for the citizens of Elmington. Martha laid the book on the table and looked through the window at the house behind. Perhaps the neighbours, responsible for the removal of the spruces, had also read it and received their wish for natural light.

The sun was high in the sky, the shadows shortening. The old man liked to sleep in. If she called right at nine, she'd have enough time to enquire about home care services and jot a few notes on *The Secret* as contrast piece for *Das Capital*. Martha had a hunch that she could squeeze a decent article, maybe even a whole book, out of Ms. Byrne and her brethren in the self-help industry.

Over a lunch of leftover pizza, Martha broached the subject of home care. "I told the case manager I was visiting from Vancouver, so she fit us in for an assessment this afternoon. She's coming at 2:30," Martha said nonchalantly.

Gordon bit the point off a slice of pizza as if he was Ozzy Osborne biting the head off a bat and chewed as aggressively as his crumbling teeth would permit.

"The visit won't take long," Martha added brightly. "Less than an hour, I should think."

Gordon swallowed hard and said, "I thought we were going to the library this afternoon."

"We still can," replied Martha. "Tonight . . . or tomorrow. Soon, Dad."

"You should have asked my permission, Martha. You've invited a meddlesome bureaucrat into my home . . . my precious inner sanctum."

"She needn't go any further than the living room." Martha

took a bite of pizza. "Anyway, since when do you hate bureaucrats? You were a bureaucrat."

"Now you're chewing with your mouth full," complained Gordon. "And I wasn't a bureaucrat. I was a public servant. Head librarian. There was nothing bureaucratic about my career."

"Well, I'm sure the case manager regards herself as a public servant too. You need help. She can arrange it. Can't you keep an open mind?"

"My mind is as open as a prostitute's knees."

"That's the spirit," soothed Martha. "Her name's Sonya Tam. She sounded very pleasant on the phone."

"I'll judge her character myself, Martha."

They finished the meal in silence, then Gordon hobbled onto the porch for a cigarette.

Sonya Tam pulled into the driveway at 2:35, apologizing profusely for her tardiness.

"It's just five minutes, lass." Gordon affected a faintly Scottish accent. Martha rolled her eyes. What a faker.

He rose from his lawn chair and extended his hand in greeting as Sonya climbed the porch stairs. After introductions and brief commentary about the fine weather, all three went inside.

"Can we offer you a drink, Sonya?" Gordon wheezed with exertion.

"No, no, I'm fine." She nodded at the pile of books on Gordon's table. "I see you're a reader."

"Oh yes, I've read a library's worth of books in my time. My daughter Martha? Not so much." He tapped his temple, crossed his eyes, and smiled vacantly. "She's struggling through *The Secret* right now."

"That's a fantastic book," enthused Sonya, casting a

sympathetic look at Martha. "Do keep with it. I promise you, Martha, it will be worth it if you read a little every day."

"I will," said Martha, frowning briefly at the old man.

Sonya opened her clip board and addressed Gordon directly. "Do you know why I'm here, Mr. Gray?"

"Please, call me Gordon. Yes. My daughter is a worrier and she is concerned that I'm not managing well—"

"You're not, Dad," Martha broke in. "You're malnourished. You're unkempt. You could fall down and no one would know for days."

"How do you feel you're managing, Gordon?" asked Sonya.

The old man was silent for a moment, as if weighing his options. Finally, he said, "I'm tired. The smallest task seems gargantuan. I shall bow to my daughter's counsel and accept help."

Martha mouthed the words, "Thank God."

"Excellent idea," said Sonya, passing her clip board and pen to Gordon. "First, I need you to sign this consent form, and then we'll begin your assessment."

An hour later, Gordon was signed up for custody of a bath chair, a raised toilet seat, a rollator, Meals on Wheels, a panic button to wear on a lanyard, and weekly assistance with bathing.

As Sonya took her leave at the door, Gordon winked and said, "I hope the care worker is as sweet and pretty as you."

Sonya stiffened. "They're well-trained professionals. You'll be in competent hands."

Martha gently punched Gordon's shoulder as Sonya returned to her car. The old man was utterly oblivious to the preoccupations of the present. Hashtag Me Too wasn't even on his radar.

Toronto Star, Reporter's Cell Phone Recording, Thursday, April 9th, 2020

Yes, correct. I'm Sonya Tam, case manager with the Local Health Integration Network.

Well, I can tell you that Gordon Gray was our client, but I can't comment on any specific case, especially that one. Umm... I really should refer you to our media relations manager, but I suppose a quick word won't violate our confidentiality policy.

Caring for an elder or disabled loved one can be isolating and demanding, especially when the relationship is complicated by complex family dynamics and the caregiver is at an intellectual disadvantage. Informed by client goals, we plan and provide practical strategies and assistance to support the client to live as independently as possible but sometimes resources are strained.

Of course, Gordon Gray's death was a tragic outcome.

He was on and off our caseload and, umm, I'll leave it at that.

Yes, we report abuse whenever we witness it. We do our best under difficult circumstances.

Listen. I can't take any more questions. Call the 800 number and ask for media relations. I have no further comment.

Click.

Thursday, August 29th, 2019

Gordon followed Sonya through the front door, slumped into the lawn chair, and fumbled in his pocket for his cigarette pack. He'd put on a good show, thought Martha. Sharp witted and personable, master of his own affairs, spewing bullshit like a manure spreader. At least Sonya had seen through the act.

Martha found another lawn chair in the garage, carried it to the back yard, and set it among the clumps of hay left by the lawn service. She'd found the name of Gordon's doctor on a Guardian Drugstore bottle and called her number to arrange an appointment. Maybe something could be done about the old man's breathing, his lack of stamina, and the tree trunk legs. Really, he needed a complete overhaul — dentist, barber, new clothes. Baby steps. Doctor first. After navigating through the automated menu, Martha convinced the receptionist to fit them in the following day.

She leaned back in the lawn chair and wiggled her toes in the grass. She was marooned in Elmington, but only for ten days and she'd be so busy that ghosts from the past, specifically in the person of the esteemed Judith Steinman-Gray, would have little opportunity to haunt her. When she went inside a half hour later, Martha found Gordon sprawled in his recliner, reading glasses perched on his nose, a pile of mail on his lap.

"Anything for me?" joked Martha.

"As a matter of fact, there is." Gordon extracted a pink paper from the pile.

Martha accepted the missive, unfolded it, and read aloud,

Happy Labour Day Weekend!! You are cordially invited to the Roselea Drive barbecue on Sunday, September 1st at the home of Joanne, Michael, and Ethan Kingsworth, 3 pm until ??? We'll provide hotdogs, hamburgers, and gluten-free, vegan options. You supply the enthusiasm!!! Let's celebrate the workers who've made

Canada the greatest country in the universe with a pool party!!! Games for the children!! BYOB ~ RSVP.

Martha refolded the paper and handed it back to Gordon, but he raised his palm and said, "Nope. My oxygen tubing and patriotism do not reach as far as Joanne's backyard. You be my emissary, Martha. As a socialist, Labour Day is your special day, and you can mix and mingle at Joanne's party."

"Mix and mingle?" Martha shook her head.

"Yes, mix and mingle," Gordon rasped. "Drink socially instead of furtively from a pop can. Perform a cannonball from the diving board and splash the nouveaux riches. Given the short notice for the party, Joanne probably doesn't expect us to turn up, but Miss Manners and Jesus would disapprove of excluding the shut-in next door. Nothing would please me more than for you to attend in my stead. You know—materialize like Banquo's ghost."

"Absolutely not," declared Martha. She dropped the invitation onto Gordon's book pile.

"Why not?"

"Because I'm allergic to gratuitous displays of cheer, I don't attend events to which I'm invited due to the hostess's sense of duty, and I'm a social cripple."

"Consider this an opportunity for rehabilitation, Martha. You go, then report back to me. All the juicy gossip."

Martha crossed her arms and shook her head. "No, Dad. An event like that is my personal version of hell."

Gordon turned his attention to a Home Hardware flyer.

"Are you giving me the silent treatment?" asked Martha.

"Nope. You're right. Better to stay here and wallow with me. We don't spend enough quality time together." Gordon squinted at an advertisement for plastic compost bins.

Martha collapsed onto the chesterfield and rolled onto her back. Never mind the party. How had he known about the gin in her Diet Coke? Now was not the time to ask. She had to tip-toe through the minefield of discussing the old man's health and informing him about his doctor's appointment. After a few moments of deliberation, she set off through conversational no-man's land, consequences be damned.

"Dad, I've arranged an appointment with Dr. Southey for tomorrow morning." Martha stared at the swirls of plaster in the ceiling and waited for a blast of outrage.

"Why? Are you feeling unwell, Duchess?" Gordon's tone was sweetly unctuous.

He was deliberately misunderstanding her. So annoying. "No, I'm fine. The appointment is for you."

"Me? I'm beyond repair, Martha. You might as well cancel the appointment."

"Dad, you're sick. You wheeze like a broken harmonica. There might be something she can do."

"I have COPD. That's a well-established diagnosis. I'm on puffers, as you're aware since you've been snooping in my medicine cupboard." Gordon scowled indignantly and coughed.

"What about your legs?" challenged Martha. "I googled 'swollen legs.' You could have heart failure, or kidney failure, or cancer."

"Maybe even all three," said Gordon.

"Yes, but then again, maybe not. Why don't we let Dr. Southey figure that out?"

Gordon stared straight ahead in silence. At last he said, "Fine."

"Fine?" asked Martha. "Wonderful—"

"But on one condition."

Martha was immediately suspicious. "What condition?"

"On the condition that you accompany me to Joanne's pool party. I've decided I'd like to attend after all."

Dr. Katherine Southey's Progress Note for Friday, 30 August 2019, 11:45

Gordon Gray, 78-year-old male, presented with daughter, Martha, who lives in Vancouver and is generally uninvolved in patient's care. Daughter expressed concern for patient though his diagnoses are long-standing and chronic.

Situation: "Short of breath, wheezy, swollen feet".

Background: COPD, CHF, A-fib, smoker, 60 plus pack years. Due for quarterly blood work and follow-up in late September. However, shortness of breath subjectively worse. Wife deceased. Patient may be less compliant with medications since loss. Continues to smoke.

Assessment: Dependent on supplemental O2, signs of heart failure including bilateral crackles in lower lung fields, marked peripheral edema. BP: 164/78, HR 84, irregular due to chronic A-fib. Weight 63.5 kilograms, down 1.3 kilos from June. Per daughter, patient lies about amount he is smoking. Cigarette after meals versus pack a day. Unreceptive to joining smoking cessation program.

Plan: Increase Lasix to 60 milligrams daily. Add Symbicort puffer twice daily. Watch weight, fluid balance, malnutrition. "Ensure" meal replacement for protein. Harm reduction: agreed to cut to half a pack daily. Follow-up at routine quarterly appointment.

Re. Daughter: Anxious due to absence and feelings of guilt? "Daughter from California" syndrome? Potential for hostility secondary to unrealistic expectations.

Saturday, August 31st, 2019

The old man had honoured his end of the bargain, so she'd honour hers and attend the Kingsworths' party with him. Martha hadn't packed a bathing suit, but the idea of being stranded on deck by a pool was unthinkable. She loved the water, and as long as she was in it, she wouldn't have to make awkward small talk with the Kingsworths or the other guests. The edge of the pool would form an impenetrable defence against banal conversation.

Martha descended the basement stairs and pulled a chain dangling from a joist to illuminate a naked bulb near some metal shelving. Behind the Christmas decorations, she found a box labelled, "Judith—summer clothes" in her mother's blocky printing.

Martha untucked a cardboard flap and the box sprung open from the pressure of layers and layers of tightly packed cotton blouses, slacks, and skirts. Every garment was tasteful, well-made, and no larger than size ten. She unpacked the box, item by item, searching for Judith's bathing suit. About two thirds in, she found a sensible, brown one piece with a golden metal ring that gathered the nylon fabric at the neckline in graceful folds. The style drew the eye to the stem of the pear, not the fleshy bottom.

Martha took the suit upstairs to her room to try on. She discarded her clothes on the floor and stood before the dresser mirror. As a fifty-three-year-old feminist, she should've made peace with her generous proportions decades ago, yet she winced at the sight of rolls of flesh burying her C-section scar, at her pillow-like thighs. As she turned for a rear view, she remembered Judith's words, biting yet accurate, issued with venom. Martha really did have the morphology of a tailless Tyrannosaurus rex.

Frowning, she dangled the bathing suit from her outstretched arms. It looked small. She was at least a size fourteen. In contrast, Judith had never permitted herself to gain a single pound over her bridal weight. The fabric expanded forgivingly when Martha stretched it. Maybe...

She stepped into the leg holes, pulled the suit up, and shrugged the straps over her shoulders. Nope. There was no way. The suit stretched over her hips, but her buttocks hung below the elasticized bottom like two massive, dimpled cantaloupes. Essentially, she was wearing a thong with shoulder straps. Fashion crime of the century. She'd have to go shopping for a bigger suit to avoid gross indecency.

"Martha?" Gordon's voice pierced through the bedroom door and attacked her eardrums.

She wriggled out of the suit and stuffed it into her top drawer. The suit was stylish and if she lost weight—

"Martha!"

"Yes, Dad?" She called back as she put on her underwear and jeans.

"Martha?!"

He hadn't heard her. He sounded panicked. She left her bra on the floor, pulled on her T-shirt, and rushed to the living room.

Gordon stood at the threshold of the hallway, brandishing an empty pack of Player's. "My cigarettes. I've looked everywhere. Where are they?"

"Tucked away for tomorrow, Dad. You made an agreement with Dr. Southey to cut back to half a pack a day. You're supposed to pace yourself—"

"For crying out loud, Martha." Gordon leaned against the door jamb, wheezing. "I'm not running a goddam marathon."

"Obviously not."

"So, my pace is of no concern to you."

"Dad, you're smoking yourself to death. You have to cut down."

"Why?" Gordon coughed and staggered to the La-Z-Boy to rest.

Why did he always have to play stupid so she had to spell out the obvious? It was an infantile game, cloaked as a weird Socratic debate. "Because."

"Because why?"

Silence.

"So I don't squander your inheritance on cigarettes?" asked Gordon.

"Don't be ridiculous," replied Martha.

"So I'll live longer to contribute my labour to the collective?"

"So you don't suffocate, Dad. Jeez. Listen to yourself." Martha sucked air through her teeth to imitate Gordon's breathing.

"I'm not a living museum specimen, Martha. My goal is contentment, not longevity." Gordon paused to catch his breath. Martha sensed he had more to say and she stood in silence.

"I've been smoking since I was twelve. A pack a day since I was eighteen. I am now seventy-eight. I'll either die from smoking or die from nicotine deprivation. I choose the former."

"Fine," said Martha.

"Yes, fine," said Gordon.

Martha turned on her heel and went to the freezer to fetch the Ziploc of cigarettes she'd hidden behind a box of dried-up chocolate chip ice cream. The old man had every right to smoke himself into oblivion. He wasn't a marionette under her control. It wasn't her job to save him from himself. Tears stung her eyes. At the rate he was going, she wondered if he'd see Christmas. She returned to the living room and flung the Ziploc onto his lap.

"Thank you," said Gordon.

Martha went back to her room, grabbed her wallet and cellphone, then headed through the living room for the front door.

"Where are you going?" asked Gordon.

"Out," said Martha. "For fresh air."

"Don't be like that, Duchess."

"Like what? I'm going shopping." Martha snatched Gordon's car keys from the hook and left without a good-bye.

As she buckled her seatbelt, she realized she wasn't wearing a bra, but if she returned to the house, she'd have to apologize. And she had to find a bathing suit before the Labour Day holiday.

Martha navigated through Saturday afternoon traffic and parked in the vast Elmington Place lot under a spindly locust tree to shade the Corolla's windshield. She walked across a Sahara of asphalt, arms snug to her sides to control the bounce of her wayward boobs, and entered the main foyer of the mall. There she found the business directory, a lit up, technicoloured map with a beige smudge at the tip of the "you are here" arrow.

Martha scanned the list of shops under "Women's Apparel." Bikini Village? Uh, nope. Boldly Beautiful? As in, bathing and fitness apparel for full-figured women? Promising. Located in Two-Blue, second floor near The Bay. Martha boarded the escalator and stood to the right to allow people in a hurry to pass. She crossed her arms and enjoyed the cool breeze of the air conditioning. Now that she'd escaped from Gordon's suffocating house, she'd dawdle.

Boldly Beautiful was a small boutique with a scowling Adele-look-alike mannequin in a tiger stripe tankini in its window. A distorted song from the Buenavista Social Club beckoned from the store's broad doorway, music undoubtedly selected by a marketing team to create a carefree, Caribbean vibe. A mindless consumer and her money were soon parted, but Martha was mindful and wary. She'd buy the cheapest, most conservative suit she could find and refuse to be upsold. Perhaps something dark with flattering, vertical stripes.

Martha nodded to the girl at the cash register, "Claire, Your

Activewear Fashion Expert!" as identified by the tag pinned to her crop top. Above the counter hung a large chart of the Boldly Beautiful sizing scheme, Curvy through Bodacious, and the seasonal corporate slogan, "From thong to aqua burqa, we've got you covered!"

I think I've come to the right place," Martha muttered. She hadn't considered a full body suit.

"May I be of assistance?" asked Claire.

Martha was surprised by the formality of the girl's language, at odds with the store's ambience of forced joie de vivre. "Umm, I'll look first, thanks," Martha replied.

"Of course." Claire returned to her task of clipping bits of fabric to hangers.

A rack of skirted one-pieces caught Martha's eye. She shuffled through suits in a rainbow of colours and sizes — curvy, queenly, generous, Rubenesque, bodacious — and found a navy suit with an ample skirt in "queenly". Martha imagined herself in the suit, a matronly Nancy Kerrigan sitting in a Muskoka chair, removing her skates for a swim. She hung its hanger on her left wrist and continued searching for other candidates. There was no point in disrobing in the change room until she had an array of options.

After a few moments, Claire approached, like a lioness stalking prey, thought Martha.

"I see you've found our 'Barbara Ann' ruffle bottom," said Claire. "That's a popular style. Understated, reserved. We have various maillots with ruffle bottoms in your size."

"Cool," said Martha. "Umm, Claire, I'm confused by the sizing. I've got a 'queenly' and a 'Rubenesque' here, but . . ."

Claire stepped back and appraised Martha's shape from shoulders to knees. "Queenly," judged Claire. "You'd be swimming in anything larger."

"Isn't that the point?" Martha joked in a royally posh English accent. "We wish to swim."

Claire didn't smile, let alone laugh. She shifted hangers on the rack and held up a purple bathing suit with a complicated pattern. "Perhaps something more colourful to try as well?"

"Is that Mount Fuji?" asked Martha.

"It is," confirmed Claire. She cleared her throat and looked up as if preparing to recite a Shakespearean soliloquy. "'The Midori features a boldly colourful print reminiscent of the silk-screen kimono art of Old Edo. It's classic, yet playfully reveals the bather's inner geisha.' Would you like to try it on as well?"

"Hai." Martha bowed. "Why not."

Claire handed Martha the Midori, then found an extravagantly sequined suit. "This is the Tonya. It's cut higher to lengthen the leg and it positively sparkles with bold radiance."

"There isn't much fabric at the bum," said Martha.

"The elastic is reinforced to prevent cleft-creep but it's a daring choice, to be sure," agreed Claire.

"Okay," Martha nodded. "I'll start with these three."

"Very well," Claire gestured toward the back of the store. "This way, please."

Martha was impressed that someone so young could affect the persona of Reginald Jeeves. She followed Claire to the fitting area and entered a large, curtained box with a mirror inside it. After she tugged and twisted within the confines of the box for several minutes, Martha heard Claire's voice.

"How are we progressing?"

"We struggle," replied Martha. "I feel naked and vulnerable in the Tonya and I look like a corpulent parrot in the Midori. Maybe the Barbara Ann."

"May I offer you a second opinion?"

"What, open the curtain?"

"Yes, umm . . ."

"Martha. My name's Martha. No, that's okay, Claire. I think I'll take the Barbara Ann." Martha emerged from behind the curtain and handed Claire the rejected suits.

"We have another line that may interest you, Martha." Claire pointed to a nearby rack of similarly skirted one pieces.

"They look the same as these," said Martha.

"Yes, but those suits have our hidden 'Oprah' feature. It's patented technology that enables the wearer to expand or reduce the garment by a full size using concealed tethers in bust, waist, and hips. The suits are engineered for yoyo dieters."

"I'm not a yoyo dieter, Claire. In fact, I don't think restricting calories is healthy. I'll take the Barbara Ann."

To Martha's dismay, Claire looked crestfallen.

"Perhaps a sarong? To accessorize your outfit for après-pool or beach?" Claire peered shyly from under her bangs at Martha.

Martha didn't want to let Claire down again. "I'd be open to looking," Martha said noncommittally.

Fifteen minutes later, Martha left Boldly Beautiful with a new bathing suit, a "Spirit of Tahiti" sarong, and a Visa charge of $169.85. If Joanne's party was as awful as she expected, she could make a tent with the sarong and a couple of lawn chairs and hide out with a bottle of gin.

The traffic was heavier still when Martha drove back to Roselea Drive. As she turned the corner, she saw a large white van in the driveway with "Practi-Care" in red lettering on its side. A bearded young man was pushing a rollator up the driveway, and Gordon was shouting, "Hurry hard!" from the porch, as if cheering on a curling mate. Martha smiled. Even though the old man was sick, he retained his sense of humour.

She parked at the curb and paused to watch. Gordon could accept delivery of his new safety equipment without her interference.

Entry in the Diary of Claire Posner, Friday, April 10th, 2020

Dear Universe,

    I am utterly gobsmacked. I was at the bank to change euros back into dollars to scrounge up some cash, when I caught a glimpse of a familiar visage on CP-24 which was broadcasting in mute from a television dangling near the vault. The face belonged to one Martha Gray, a client-shopper whom I vividly recall for her strangeness. Evidently, the police are interrogating Martha about the death of her father.

    I remember Martha as a quirky, oddly dressed woman. The first time I met her, she wore an untucked, baggy T-shirt, and she had clunky sandals on her feet. She was turned out like one of the angry females in the Gender Studies department, but she had kind eyes, a nervous laugh, and long, silver hair.

    Diary, I am ashamed to admit it. I twice upsold Martha by exploiting her maternal instincts. From the moment she greeted me, she telegraphed insecurity. Her eyes darted from rack to rack, and she rifled through the maillots and yoga wear as if she were a thief ransacking a closet. First, I gained her trust, and then I played the wounded child to nudge her into purchasing over-priced accessories. If it is proven that Martha Gray murdered her father, my guilt will vanish. However, I hope the police are barking up the wrong tree. She doesn't fit the typical profile of a killer.

    Otherwise, my day was uneventful.

    Wisdom gained today: I may be a poor judge of character despite my interest in forensic psychology.

    Now, I should work on my criminology essay before Jake comes over. I'll update you on the romance file tomorrow, Dear Diary.

Labour Day Weekend, Sunday, September 1st, 2019

Joanne Kingsworth extended her hand, metallic bangles clacking, blood-red nails slicing the air. "Martha!" She gushed like a mall fountain. "Your father has told me so much about you! Aren't we fortunate to have you join us."

Martha shook Joanne's hand and replied, "How do you do?" Jeez. She sounded as if she were at a job interview. Martha quickly retracted her hand and presented a bottle of wine. "It's Zinfandel . . . but not too sweet."

"Thank you, Martha." Joanne accepted the bottle, then looked to Gordon, who grinned like the Cheshire cat, his portable oxygen tank tucked into his rollator basket. He was dressed as if he'd stolen his clothes from Don Cherry's closet—red and white seersucker shirt, beige cargo shorts, and red and white argyle socks with beige sandals. Joanne smiled back at him benevolently and waved toward a lawn chair. "Sit over there, Gordon. That chair's in the shade and away from the pool. You won't get splashed. I'll get you a drink."

Gordon obeyed.

"Martha? I get the first drink for you, then after that it's self serve. Those are the Kingsworth party rules. Watermelon daiquiri?"

It was easier to say "yes" than request a glass of wine, so Martha nodded. There was something about Joanne's erect bearing . . . the bossiness . . . that reminded Martha of—

"Your father's in fine form today." A man's voice.

Martha turned.

"I'm Mike Kingsworth."

"Martha Gray. But you know that." Martha shook hands with Mike. "Thanks for inviting us. I'm afraid Dad is rather isolated these days, and it's such a lovely day to be outdoors."

"Isolated? I wouldn't say that. Joanne has taken him under her wing as a project, and Ethan and your father are chums."

Sure enough. Several kids were calling to Gordon and he was already pushing his rollator to the poolside, probably to judge a fancy diving contest or marshal a race. Martha had a feeling that she'd been tricked into attending this wretched party. "Dad speaks fondly of Ethan," she said.

Mike pointed at a tall, skinny youth in blue and purple trunks. "That's Ethan there. Fourteen going on twenty."

"They grow up quickly these days. . . ." Martha didn't really believe that cliché. In previous decades, adolescents Ethan's age worked in factories and fields, but at parties, banalities tumbled from her lips like rain drops from a thunder cloud. "What grade is Ethan in?" she asked.

"He's going into grade nine," replied Mike. "At Applegate College."

"Private school."

"Yes. Worth every penny," said Mike. "I know some people think private school kids are spoiled, but nothing could be further from the truth. At Applegate the grade tens go on community building projects as part of their civics curriculum. Next year, Ethan will be building a school in Uganda."

Martha couldn't think of anything to say. Mike mistook Martha's blank nod as spellbound approval and continued. "African children need role models, and they look up to the Applegate kids. The program is a win-win, and Ethan's looking forward to swinging a hammer."

Martha imagined small Ugandan kids cowering behind piles of two by fours as Ethan bent nails.

"Martha?" A shrill voice lifted the hairs on Martha arms. "Martha Gray, I heard you were coming. You look great!"

"Sally Dunfield. It's been years." Martha braced herself for Sally's lunge. Sally swung her arms over Martha's shoulders and planted a wet kiss on her cheek. Gross. Had the woman never heard of an air kiss?

"It's been three years, Martha. I attended your mom's

visitation. Oh, there I go being stupid. Dredging up dreadful memories."

"Not so dreadful," Martha said truthfully. "And you're not stupid, Sally. You say what's on your mind . . . except the part about me looking great. I'm more or less average. You look great though."

Sally curtsied, "Thank you, Martha."

"I'll fire up the barbecue," said Mike, escaping from the conversation.

Sally leaned in. "Bit of yoga, bit of Tabata, and some Botox and fillers . . . I have a fantastic colourist."

"Really? I can't tell. You look so natural and young," Martha lied. Sally was as shallow as a wading pool in the Arizona desert, yet fearlessly honest. Just as she'd been in high school.

"In my new business, appearance is essential. You have to look contemporary. Au courante."

"Oh? What business is that?"

"House staging and photography for real estate. It's easier and more lucrative than interior decorating. In the decorating business, people care about function. They're sentimental. Colour and texture matter. The clients are high maintenance, let me tell you. In the staging biz? No one cares. It's all neutrals and conventional furniture, like the Hilton Hotel. I have to show off the houses, but they'll just be redone by the new owners anyway."

Joanne returned with a tray of daiquiris, and Martha and Sally each accepted one before she strode off to a circle of mommies in fashion-forward sundresses.

"Cheers," said Martha as she raised her glass to Joanne's back. She sipped the sweet, pink liquid gratefully, then asked, "How do you know Joanne?"

"Book club. Through Mavis Partridge. You remember Mavis."

"Yes, though I haven't seen her in years."

"She's a friend of Joanne through the Elmington Club. She's 'Mavis Mill' now. Big into real estate. Partners with her husband, Gary Mill, though really it's her business." Sally put a tanned hand to the side of her face, flared her nostrils, and sniffed. "He's a cocaine addict," she whispered.

"That seems old fashioned," said Martha.

"I know, right?" laughed Sally. She lowered her voice again. "As long as Mavis keeps him in drugs, she can run the business her way. It's a bargain compared to divorce. And let me tell you, she's an amazing broker. She sends me a ton of referrals. I'm as busy as I want to be."

Martha swallowed more daiquiri. A lightbulb lit in her skull. So she really had seen Mavis's face plastered on the side of a bus. "I remember now. 'Matching people with property.' That's the slogan, right?"

"Right-e-o, Martha. I get the houses all tarted up for their big dates with the buyers. Though tastefully, of course, in boring beige. And then Mavis takes over as 'matchmaker'." Sally made air quotes.

"That's horridly gimmicky."

"Sure," agreed Sally. "But it's a gimmick that works."

Martha chastised herself for being dismissive of Mavis and corrected course. "Good for Mavis. And you too, Sally. I always knew you two would be successful."

"Really?" Sally frowned and sipped her daiquiri. She was way behind Martha whose glass was nearly empty.

"Do you think we'll see Mavis here today?" Martha asked innocently.

"I don't think so. The market's hot right now, and Labour Day weekend isn't exactly Christmas as far as holidays go. Mavis will be matchmaking all day."

Martha laughed. She was struck by Sally's generosity. Sally could've defended Mavis against Martha's cattiness, but instead she papered over Martha's faux pas with her own small joke.

"How long are you in town, Martha?"

"Until I get Dad sorted out. He's struggling with his COPD."

They both looked at Gordon, who was standing by his rollator, now a climbing apparatus for a kindergarten-age boy. Gordon held up two open hands. A perfect ten for the girl in the polka-dot suit who'd belly flopped off the diving board.

"He looks pretty good today," said Sally.

"But he'll be tired tonight." Martha drained her glass. "Want to dive into the pool and see how we rate?"

"Absolutely," replied Sally. "But I need to change first. I'll meet you in the water."

Martha was already draping her sarong onto the back of a chair. She'd either drink herself into oblivion or swim. At half past four in the afternoon the choice was still easy. As confidently as she could, she walked to the pool in her new Barbara Ann bathing suit and dipped her toe. The water was cool and clean.

"Are you competing?" wheezed Gordon.

"Depends. What's the prize?" asked Martha.

"Umm, free skate sharpening?"

"Then I'm in." Martha joined a short queue of divers in the blinding sunshine.

After two small competitors took their turn, Martha walked to the end of the board, took a hard jump, and dove, arms cutting through the water. She bobbed to the surface and kicked around to face the old man. Sure enough, he held up ten gnarled fingers, another perfect score. The water was glorious, the sun shone merrily, and all around her children were yelling with excitement. On this Labour Day afternoon, in this sliver of time, everything felt right with the world.

Sally sat on the deck with her feet dangling in the water while Martha treaded lazily to the side of the diving board, dreaming about a tall, appealingly bitter G and T. They'd exhausted all of Sally's gossip about old classmates and now they were on to menopause, much to Martha's chagrin.

"I can handle the mood swings and the occasional whisker, but it's the insomnia that's killing me," Sally whined. "I can barely see in the mirror to tweeze my chin, I'm so bloody tired in the morning."

"Have you tried valerian?"

"Valerian?"

"It's an herb. You can make tea from the root. Or use a tincture at bedtime to help you sleep." Martha hadn't used any herbal remedies herself, but maybe suggesting a treatment would end the conversation. "You can buy it at a health food store."

"You always were the smart one, Dr. Gray. You should've studied to be a real doctor."

"Thank you, Sally." An awkward compliment, but Sally meant well.

"Really, Martha. What was that book you wrote? Something about Karl Marx and happiness and Hollywood? I suggested it for book club . . . and there I go with my foggy, change of life brain. You'll have to remind me of the title."

"*Pacifiers for the Proletariat: Celebrity Worship and Professional Sport Fandom.* Did you read it?"

"No. It was vetoed by Joanne. I think we read *Tuesdays with Morrie* that month instead."

"A fine choice." And a book Martha would never read.

Suddenly Sally kicked her feet as if she were a preschooler receiving a present, then squealed, "I have a great idea! You're in town for a week—"

Oh-oh, thought Martha. Here it comes.

"We should have a reunion. Mavis would be thrilled and—"

"Dr. Gray! Dr. Gray!" The voice was high-pitched, then abruptly a husky octave lower, still urgent.

Martha looked over her shoulder. It was Ethan, eyes wide with panic.

"Gordon is sick, Dr. Gray. He needs you now!"

Martha climbed up the pool ladder and jogged behind Ethan to a circle of people on the patio. In the middle, the farmer in the dell, was the old man. He was perched on the edge of his rollator, hands on knees, struggling to catch his breath. Joanne loomed over him, reciting a mantra. "In through the nose, out through the mouth. That's it. . . ."

"Dad?" Martha broke through the circle. "Dad."

Gordon met her eyes. He was slack-jawed with the effort of breathing, but he managed a weak smile.

"He seems to be improving," said Joanne.

"What happened?" asked Martha, crouching in front of the old man.

"He turned blue, really quite suddenly, and he collapsed backward. Ethan managed to push his rollator under him just on time," answered Joanne.

"We should call an ambulance," said a young woman with a toddler on her hip.

Gordon waved his hand limply. "No need, Candace," he puffed. "I'm fine now."

"No talking, Gordon," commanded Joanne. "You'll only tire yourself more."

"Dad, maybe she's right, about the ambulance," said Martha. "You're awfully pale."

"Nope," huffed Gordon. "Just home."

"Okay," Martha agreed. Arguing would only force the old man to expend precious energy.

Sally handed Martha her sarong and whispered, "I'll check in with you tomorrow."

Martha nodded as she tied the sarong around her waist.

"Ethan and I will help you home, Gordon," said Joanne.

Gordon didn't protest. Flanked by Martha and Joanne, Ethan pushed Gordon on his rollator down the driveway of 24 Roselea Drive and up the driveway of number 22 to the porch steps. A few minutes later, Gordon was settled in his La-Z-Boy with a glass of ice water in his hand.

"Thanks, Joanne. And thank you, Ethan." He winked at the boy. "I owe you one."

"Don't mention it, Mr. Gordon," said Ethan, bowing as they took their leave.

Martha saw the Kingsworths out to the driveway and thanked them again.

"Your father tries his best, Martha, but he's not managing well. He could use a lot more help than we can give him," said Joanne as she descended the concrete steps.

The covert scolding punched Martha in the belly. As if she were responsible for her father's condition and circumstances. As if she'd neglected him. Yet Joanne wasn't wrong. The old man had skittered into a mucky, garbage-strewn ditch in her absence.

Before she could respond, Joanne said crisply, "Now, I have guests to take care of. Good night." She turned on her heel and strode down the driveway with Ethan trailing behind.

"Happy Labour Day, Joanne," Martha called back, and then she mouthed, "And fuck you too."

Martha towelled off, hung her sarong and bathing suit over the shower rod, and changed into capris and a T-shirt. By the time she returned to the living room, Gordon was fast asleep. His breathing was noisy yet even, and his cheeks were pink. He'd probably just pushed himself too hard. That was all.

Martha decided to have a tipple of gin over ice to toast the day and soothe her nerves. She went into the back yard with a glass of ice and a bottle of Beefeater and sat in the lawn chair. From the other side of the fence, she heard children playing Marco Polo in the pool, men agreeing to another round of beer, and women giggling. She was grateful to be away from lame jokes, forced hilarity, and disingenuous compliments. The whole yucky ball of yucky, slippery, yucky social wax. And now home—

But not her home. Not for decades. It was Judith's home overlaid with Gordon's recliner, books, and smog. Judith had insisted that Martha remove her belongings and all trace of her childhood when she went to Vancouver for grad school in the 90s.

After several drinks, Martha marvelled at how the arm-like branches of Judith's rose of Sharon cast long shadows across the lawn. Graceful branches that might smack you in the face in a wind or whimsy. Martha lifted her tumbler of gin to her lips, took in the bitter liquid, and squinted at the shrub's silhouette, its shadow self, as real a part of its personality as its ostentatious flowers.

Gulp. Jungian psychological theory imposed on a plant. No question. Martha was drunk now. What would Judith say about that?

"To you, Mommie Dearesht," slurred Martha. She sloshed the last of the gin and melted ice water, raised her glass in mock honour, and belted it back. Dr. Judith Steinman-Gray would not have approved.

Martha pursed her lips, sneered down her nose, and mimicked the tight, nasal tone of her mother. "Martha, I am so disappointed by your weakness. Self control is a muscle and yours is flabby. You are inebriated."

Then, she answered herself in a baby-like voice. "Yes, Mommie Dearesht, I am drunk. But tomorrow I'll be sober, and you'll shtill be a mean, dead bitch."

Monday, September 2nd, 2019

Martha woke, still mildly drunk, prodromal hangover foreshadowing a difficult day. She listened to a glee club of robins and wrens singing in the barest glimmer of dawn. Common songbirds weren't stupid enough to drink themselves senseless and Martha felt oddly jealous for their bird-brained, teetotal joy. Intelligence was a dubious trade-off for human psychiatric ailments such as dipsomania.

Heat rushed from Martha's torso to her scalp and she broke into a sour sweat. Evidently not the first either, for her legs and hips were bound in a twist of sodden linen. Just capital. Menopausal hot flashes and a doozie of a hangover in one nasty, self-delivered package.

Martha opened her right eye to a narrow slit, then clamped it shut again. Time for the checklist:

Turntable bed? Check.

Throbbing temples? Check.

Eyeballs swollen to the size of tennis balls? Check.

Motel carpet tongue? Check.

Queasy, icky stomach, raring to hurl like a burly Scotsman with a log? Check and check.

Achy, breaky joints? Check.

Heart pounding a tattoo of dread? Checkeroo.

There was only one thing to do. Stay as still as possible. Stillness was the balm. Martha eased herself onto her back, turned her pillow under her head, and surveyed her memory of the previous afternoon and evening. Mercifully, she'd saved her debauchery for the solitude of the backyard. She was probably the only person in the whole wide world who knew that she'd tied one on, and with a flouncy, taffeta ribbon at that. Time healed all. If only it would accelerate to warp speed on this wretched morning.

Despite her dehydration, Martha had to pee. But she had to stay still even more. She drifted into a fitful sleep.

"Cock-a-doodle-doo-doo!" A gruff baritone followed by a phlegmy cough. The old man.

Martha rolled onto her side gingerly, as if she were in traction.

Gordon called again from behind the plywood door. "I repeat, 'Cock-a-doodle-doo!'"

"Aggh." She'd have to force herself to speak intelligible words.

"What's that, Duchess?"

"I said, 'Good morning, Dad'."

"It's almost nine, and your friend Sally phoned. Don't worry. I put her off. Told her you were powdering your nose."

"I'll be up in a minute."

"That's the spirit. Anyway, Sally's phoning back soon, so make haste." More coughing.

Martha heard Gordon's heavy clomp as he retreated from her door down the hallway. It was funny, though not hilarious, how a hangover blurred the vision but sharpened one's hearing. She shifted her legs over the side of the bed. Did the old man know of her intemperance? He'd delivered his relentless rooster calls as if they were taunts.

Martha would undertake her ablutions before Sally called again. As she headed for the bathroom, a passive-aggressive clatter of pots and pans pierced her eardrums. Yup. He knew. And she hoped he'd keep his opinions to himself.

True to her word, Sally called just as Martha emerged from the bathroom with her hair fastened in a towel turban. Martha accepted the cordless phone from Gordon and jammed the receiver to her ear, releasing a tumble of wet terry cloth and hair.

"Hello?" said Martha.

"Martha! Good morning!" The voice was an enthusiastic singsong, as if Richard Simmons had undergone sex reassignment and taken up telemarketing. "Guess who!"

"Umm . . ." No witty answer. Martha was seriously compromised.

"Come on?" urged the voice.

"Margaret Thatcher?" ventured Martha.

"No, silly Martha. It's Sally!"

"Sally. Of course. Good morning."

"You don't sound like it's a good morning. Even your dad sounds better than you. Are you okay?"

"Yeah, I'm fine, Sally. I didn't sleep well. That's all." From the corner of her eye, Martha caught Gordon pretending to guzzle from a bottle, then burp. She turned her back to the decrepit Marcel Marceau in the La-Z-Boy chair.

"Probably menopause and jet lag. Vancouver is like what . . . seven, eight hours behind Elmington?"

"Something like that." Martha shrugged and imagined North America extending to the mid-Pacific with a mere strait separating the continent and Hawaii.

"Wacky hormones and time zones. A double whammy."

"Yes, probably, Sally. I think I'd better lay low today," said Martha. There was no point in reminding Sally that she'd been in Ontario for nearly a week.

"Good idea. Rest up. Because you'll never guess what!"

Here we go, guessing again, thought Martha. "No, I suppose I won't."

"Suppose you won't what?" asked Sally.

"I suppose I'll never guess."

Sally giggled. "You don't have to guess, Martha, because I'm about to reveal the surprise. I saw Mavis at yoga-in-the-park this morning, and I told her you're in town. She's dying to meet up."

"Dying," Martha repeated blankly.

"Really, Martha. What on God's green earth is the matter?"

"Nothing's the matter."

"Well, if you say so. Wednesday, twelve sharp, Chez Charles, the new bistro on Lakeshore and Queen. It's upscale, so no Birkenstocks."

"But—"

"No buts, Martha. We hardly see you. Mavis knows Charles and she's already reserved a table."

Before Martha could decline, Sally hung up. At least she'd given Martha a helpful wardrobe tip. If she didn't wiggle out of the occasion, maybe she'd paint her toenails. As she turned to place the receiver on its cradle, Gordon asked, "Nothing planned for tomorrow, I hope?"

"No," replied Martha.

"Excellent," said Gordon. "The library will open at ten and the kids start back to school, so it'll be quiet. You can be my chauffeuse."

Tuesday, September 3rd, 2019

Martha wrestled Gordon's rollator from the trunk, slung a canvas bag of books over her shoulder, and wheeled the rollator to the passenger side of the Corolla. Two swollen feet stuffed into Crocs appeared at the open door and planted themselves on the pavement. Martha pushed the rollator in front of the old man and stuck his oxygen tank into it. The process was a bigger production then wrangling Joseph in and out of his car seat when he was a toddler. They'd have to watch Gordon's oxygen supply.

They entered Elmington Central Library by a side door marked with a blue wheelchair symbol rather than struggling up the stone steps of the main entrance. Martha remembered Joseph as a preschooler climbing similar stairs in Vancouver, as if he were Hillary conquering Everest. He'd refused her hand, though he'd allowed her to sherpa his gigantic Richard Scarry books.

This red sandstone Carnegie library was as sacred as a cathedral to Martha. The vanilla smell of musty paper and old wood; shuffling pages and whispered chatter echoing in the stacks; the benediction of the librarian's stamp—these reassured her. Books offered explanations, advice, and solace—things she seldom found in people.

If the minister's children were poorly behaved, and the drunk's children teetotal, Martha broke the pattern. In this sanctuary, her father was priest—nay, bishop. Gordon Gray, Head Librarian, had served his flock of bibliophiles and knowledge seekers with patience and wit for four decades, and Martha respected him for it.

They entered the elevator and the old man stabbed the M button with his index finger. The gears lurched. Martha caught Gordon's elbow to steady him. This arduous excursion could have been avoided with a few keystrokes and mouse clicks and delivery service for the homebound, yet Martha understood. While he could, Gordon would attend church in person.

They exited the elevator, struggled through the foyer, and entered the adults' level. Rows of computer terminals had replaced much of the reference section but otherwise, the library seemed like a living, breathing, sepia-toned daguerreotype with splashes of incongruous colour. A strangely relevant anachronism.

"Hello, Gordon." A black-haired, corpse-pale woman wearing a man's yoked shirt waved from the circulation desk.

"Imogen! How are you, lass?" That fake Scottish accent again. Ugh.

"Oh, you know . . . holding the line." Imogen saluted and nodded toward a clean-cut man who was frowning at a computer screen. "Simon's running the place like a sergeant major. But he's on budget and prompt with paperwork so the board adores him. Things aren't the same since you left. I'm still adjusting."

"I retired ten years ago, Imogen."

"And I've been aware of every bloody second. Wait—where are my manners? An old codger like you needs a chair."

"No need. I have this contraption." Gordon turned his rollator and sat down heavily.

"Bloody nifty." Imogen's thickly kohled eyes shifted from the rollator to Martha.

"And who have we here? Your granddaughter, I presume?"

Martha's heart melted under the warmth of the ridiculous compliment. "Daughter. I'm Martha."

"Martha the Marxist?" Imogen's pencilled eyebrows rose.

"The one," replied Martha.

"Author of *Pacifiers for the Proletariat*?"

"Correct."

"Well, isn't today our lucky day? We have it on our shelf and it begs for your autograph."

Gordon coughed. Martha wondered whether the old man was clearing phlegm or trying to regain Imogen's attention.

Without breaking her focus on Martha, Imogen withdrew a tissue from a box behind the desk and handed it to Gordon. "Fucking best book I read last year."

"There are better modifiers than that vulgar, unimaginative word," rasped Gordon.

"No, there aren't, Gordon. The book deserves a long, deep, sweaty fuck," said Imogen.

"That's it. I'm reporting you to Simon. Uttering obscenities violates the workplace code of conduct."

"What do you think, Martha? About the use of expletives?" asked Imogen.

"Umm . . . they're expressive words. . . ."

"There you go. They express." Imogen broke her gaze at the very moment Martha began to feel uncomfortable and turned to Gordon. "Have you brought your list for the week, my ancient prude?"

"Yes, impertinent lass," answered Gordon. "But Martha already has it and she can find everything. And we can have a good chat."

"'Good.' Now that's an unimaginative word," said Imogen.

Martha dropped the borrowed books into the return receptacle and left Gordon and Imogen to their flirtation. She wandered to the nonfiction section. Primed with the affectionate recognition of a mother for her child in a class photo, Martha's eyes quickly located the yellow spine of *Pacifiers for the Proletariat* in the 330s. She withdrew it from the shelf. The book was in better condition than she'd hoped it would be. Perhaps Gordon and Imogen had been its only readers. She took a pen from the book bag, flipped open the cover, and wrote her name.

"What do you think you're doing?"

A school principal's rhetorical question. Martha jumped, and the pen ran away from the tail of the "Y" in a flamboyant flourish. Martha turned to face Simon. "Umm, signing this book. It's mine and—"

"It's not yours. It's the property of Elmington Central Library. You are vandalizing a public resource."

"But Imogen requested I sign it. I'm Martha Gray. See?" Martha held up the book and pointed at her name.

"Well, this is most irregular." Simon extended a hand, palm up. "Please show me what you've written."

Martha passed the book to Simon and he scrutinized the offending scrawl. "At least it's only your signature. We couldn't allow anything sentimental to deface library property. We'd have to replace the book."

"There's a policy on that?" Martha asked incredulously.

"Certainly," said Simon. He looked away. Martha felt sure he didn't really know if that were true.

Simon met her eyes again. "You're Gordon Gray's daughter. I thought I saw your father at the circulation desk."

"Yes. He's visiting Imogen while I gather books for him," said Martha, relieved that Simon had decided not to expel her or issue a ticket for a library infraction or whatever policy dictated.

"Imogen." Simon's perma-frown deepened. "Perhaps she should be assisting you rather than indulging in idle chit chat."

"I'm fine." Martha waved dismissively. "I can find everything myself."

Simon nodded and strode off toward the circulation desk with the book tucked under his arm.

Martha sighed and pulled Gordon's list from the bag. As always, his writing raced forward in spikes and angles, as if his pen were sprinting, but there was an unfamiliar quivering quality as well, the penmanship of a tremulous, weak hand. Martha had forgotten her reading glasses, so she squinted at the titles.

Hitchens, C. Mortality.
Richler, M. Barney's Version.
Sacks, O. Gratitude.
Vonnegut, K. God Bless You, Dr. Kevorkian.
And some decent poetry. Surprise me, Duchess.

Martha swallowed hard. The authors were dead birds of a feather, an alphabetized murder of literary crows. The old man was giving up on living writers and turning to late, kindred spirits. This was the reading list of a dying atheist. Gordon was behaving like his usual, radically extroverted self to the extent he was able, yet inwardly he was turning toward death.

Some decent poetry. The old man's requests reflected his preoccupations. Was he challenging her to jar him out of them by asking her to choose poetry? What did "decent" mean?

Something life-affirming? Or cheery? Aside from nursery rhyme, was poetry ever cheery? Martha emerged from the stacks. Gordon and Imogen were snickering like a pair of juvenile delinquents as Simon stalked off. Maybe a book of dirty limericks? No. Inappropriate for a daughter to choose for her father. She had to decide. Would she receive Gordon's message and acknowledge it, or avert her eyes and find a book of benign poetry about daffodils and lonely clouds?

Martha headed for the 800s. The old man could do with some Poe. *The Raven* for sure. And some Blake and Thomas. Gordon might be terminally ill, but surely he could be inspired to rage against the dying of the light. She'd search for a poetry anthology of dead, white males and she'd throw in some Dickinson, Plath, Angelou, Oliver, and Bishop for gender balance.

They returned to Roselea Drive with a quarter tank of oxygen and a sack-load of books. Martha left Gordon on the porch for a smoke. She desperately needed a tall glass of water and a couple of Tylenol.

The answering machine was flashing and it irritated her, a gross overreaction to a minor stimulus. Martha pressed play to extinguish its pulsing strobe light. Obscured by static, an accented male voice echoed in the hallway:

"Hello. I am Angelo from Quality Home Care. This message is for Mr. Gordon Gray. I am giving you a bath or shower tomorrow at nine o'clock. If this is no good, please call to Quality Home Care office." Click.

"Great," muttered Martha. "The old man can keep his Canadian accent for his bath."

As Martha drank her water, she glanced at the Guardian Pharmacy calendar hanging on the kitchen wall. She'd arranged her flight for Saturday. Four more days in suburban purgatory. Yet Martha dreaded the moment the Airporter would pick her up. The old man was unravelling, and four days was scarcely enough time to weave the strands of his life together.

Morning Page from the Long Hand Notebook of Imogen S. Wallis, Thursday, April 9th, 2020

Jesus H. Christ on a bike and his Simpering, Fornicating Mother in the sidecar. I have no words for my horror, but I'm supposed to write three bloody pages every morning. Julia Cameron, you're a bitch. Brilliant, but a bitch. I can't write when I'm in the depths of despair, but I can't break my streak. A fucking dilemma. So one page Ms. Cameron. That's all you're getting today.

Last night they arrested Martha. She went with the cops willingly, not kicking and scratching like I would've. She called from jail with her one precious phone call.

This is what I know: Gordon was very sick. End stage COPD, then the stroke, and that's an ugly way to live. Gasping like a guppy on hot sand, night and day. He told everyone that he wanted to die, and no one listened except Martha. It was all, "Oh Gordon, you look so fucking swell." Meanwhile his face was the colour of a ripe plum and his chest went up and down like a goddamn accordion, and he was helpless. Whatever Martha did or didn't do, she always put Gordon first. Martha loved her father and that's the plain truth.

And I love Martha. From the first time I saw her when she walked up to the circulation desk. I saw those intelligent hazel eyes and her long silver hair. And her fat peach of an ass when she walked away to get some books for her dad. When she returned with a compilation of feminist poetry for the codger, among the books he'd actually read, I was well and truly smitten.

I'm still not sure if she's actually a dyke, but I love her, heart and soul. I can't stand to see her tried and convicted in the court of public opinion. The media vultures are gobbling her up. She provides a sensational break from all the tedious COVID pandemic hysteria. They've got the story all wrong, but they don't care as long as they get a shit load of clicks on their so-called news pages.

Be strong, Martha. I'll bake a cake and stick a fucking file in it. We'll bust you out. You'll see.

Wednesday, September 4th, 2019

Gordon watched the clock as if he were awaiting the arrival of a blind date. "A bonny lass to scrub my back and see that I'm decent," he crowed, a faint brogue inflecting his words once more. "As you said at supper, Duchess, sometimes a man must accept what help is offered."

Martha nodded and concurred, "There's nothing like a thorough shower, Dad. You'll feel like a new person."

When the doorbell rang at five to nine, Martha watched Gordon from her vantage on the chesterfield. A smirk invaded her face as the old man hobbled to the door in a manner the condescending observer would describe as "sprightly."

Gordon finger combed his hair into greasy furrows and opened the door. At once, his shoulders slumped, and he stepped back, silent.

"Good morning. Mr. Gordon?" The live version of the voice on the answering machine.

"Yes, yes. I'm Gordon Gray," stammered the old man. "My daughter didn't tell me—"

"If it is not convenient time, I can coming another time."

"No, that's okay," Gordon said gruffly. He gripped his

rollator and squared his shoulders, telecasting that he would take no pleasure in his shower, or in another man seeing him naked. "I'm sure you can scrub my back as well as anyone. Come in."

"Thank you." A young Asian man with the physique of a wrestler stepped over the threshold. "I am Angelo," he said.

Gordon tilted his head back and appraised his personal support worker, eye to eye. "Angelo? Call me 'Gordon.' Martha —that's my daughter—has put everything out in the bathroom. We might as well get down to brass tacks."

"I'm sorry?"

"The business at hand." Gordon gestured with a manly karate chop toward the hall. "Bathroom's through there. Mind my tubing."

"Yes, Mr. Gordon."

As he followed Gordon toward the hall, Angelo nodded a sombre greeting and Martha smiled back, for encouragement.

She bit her lip to stifle laughter and turned to the small pile of self-help books she'd borrowed on the old man's library card. *The Secret* had lured Martha into the smoke and mirrors world of self-help for status seekers and the question of what Karl Marx would make of the genre had he been born a century and a half later. She'd survey the best-sellers chronologically. *Think and Grow Rich* sat on the top of the stack. Martha typed the book's publication date, author, and chapter headings into a spreadsheet she'd labelled "Bourgeois Religious Literature."

As Martha scanned Napoleon Hill's musings on desire and wealth, laughter punctuated by gut-deep coughing echoed from behind the bathroom door.

A quarter of an hour later, Gordon emerged in a billow of mist, skin pink, hair combed into a pompadour, the lines on his forehead softened in tired contentment. Martha watched with curiosity as Angelo escorted his charge to the La-Z-Boy and assisted him to recline.

"I just go and clean up now," said Angelo.

"Don't bother, Angelo. We'll do it," wheezed Gordon. "You've worked hard enough, and you have to get to your next client."

"Are you sure?"

"Sure, I'm sure." Gordon reached for his wallet. "I feel like a million bucks. Thank you."

Angelo shook his head. "No need, Mr. Gordon."

"Not even a small tip?"

"We can't take any money." Angelo produced a piece of paper and a pen from his pocket. "Just sign that I am here. That is all that is needed."

"With pleasure." Gordon signed and returned the paper. "Angelo, I forgot to introduce you to my daughter, Martha."

"Martha," repeated Angelo, bowing slightly.

Martha rose and extended her hand. "Thank you for helping Dad."

"No problem," said Angelo as he shook Martha's hand. "Your father, he's a very kind man."

"No. You're the kind one," rasped Gordon.

Angelo smiled bashfully and shook his head.

"Next week. Same time, same place?" asked Gordon.

"You bet, Mr. Gordon."

Martha watched the young man back through the front door and hurry down the driveway to a battered Kia Rio. "Nice fellow," she said.

"Bland words, Duchess. He is his name," said Gordon. "Angelo, the angel."

"Oh?"

"Oh indeed. You know, he works two jobs and sends most of his income back to his family in Manila? He hasn't seen his kids in a year."

"It's an unjust world."

"'Unjust' says the champagne socialist with her pile of capitalist propaganda."

"Jeez, Dad. I agree with you. His situation sucks."

"That's more like it."

"If I'm not mistaken, a half hour ago you were expecting a young wench to scrub your back and anoint your feet with perfumed oils."

"I used the word 'lass' if memory serves. 'Wench' has unfortunate overtones," squawked Gordon. "And the feet would've been optional."

"If Angelo were an Angela, would you worry about exploitation?"

"You have to admit, Martha, it's unusual work for a man."

"The world revolves and evolves." Martha shrugged and glanced at the clock. "Guess it's my turn for the bathroom."

"Lunch with the ladies?"

"Yup. The prodigal daughter returns to feast on the fatted calf. That should make the ordeal bearable."

"Friendship is a beautiful thing, Duchess." Gordon patted his pocket to check for his cigarettes. "And you can't go wrong with a thick steak, medium rare."

Text Messages, Friday, April 10th, 2020

> OMG Joy! Did u see the news? Says daughter murdered Gordon Gray

> What! The guy on O2 on Roselea? The one I saw for you in November

> Yes.

> Murder? What did she do? Stand on his oxygen tubing?

> Not funny. They were nice people

> He was creepy

> Papa Gordon? No way

> Papa Gordon was not a creeper

> Your a man Angelo. You don't know

> What r u doing tonight

> Same as u. Nothing. Maybe skype with fam

> K. Stay safe. It's a crazy world 😊

> U2

Wednesday, September 4th, 2019

Martha eased the Corolla into a spot between two SUVs on Lakeshore Road. She was meeting old friends, yet she felt nauseous and dizzy, a hair's breadth away from a full-blown panic attack. Blinding sunshine beat through the windshield and beads of sweat trickled between her shoulder blades. Best leave the windows open a crack.

As her Birkenstock slapped the pavement under her left foot, she felt a pang of embarrassment. She'd rejected Judith's sandals due to the height of the heels and she refused to shop for new ones. Now, against Sally's advice, Martha was turning up in therapeutic footwear to meet the cool girls.

Silly. Chez Charles wasn't Elmington Collegiate. The

Birkenstocks were fine. It was her confidence that was lacking. She thrived in the rarified air of the ivory tower, but she couldn't catch her breath in the sea-level atmosphere of an ordinary bistro in an ordinary suburb among ordinary middle-aged women.

Martha locked the car door and pocketed the key. Survival was a matter of adaptation. Chez Charles was two blocks away. As she walked, she coaxed herself from a state of dread into curiosity, to regain her sense of aloof superiority. She resolved to examine Sally and Mavis as if they were sources of qualitative data for field research rather than members of a cool girl clique to which she'd never quite belonged.

Martha spotted Sally and Mavis at a table under a canvas umbrella before they saw her. Both were blonde, tanned, and wearing oversized sunglasses and fitted sundresses. They resembled twin praying mantises. Martha took a deep breath and crossed the patio to the table.

After loose hugs, air kisses, and several rounds of blousy flattery, they sat down on austere, wooden stools in the shade of the umbrella. A waiter dressed like Johnny Cash brought a pitcher of sangria and a platter of tapas. Gratis, according to Mavis, because she'd found the perfect house for Charles, a match made in heaven, and sold his condo well over asking.

"She's amazing at real estate, Martha," bragged Sally. "You should see for yourself."

Mavis took off her sunglasses, closed her eyes, and placed a professionally manicured hand on Martha's shoulder. "Martha darling," she drawled. "I sense rugged spruces, water . . . hmm . . . interesting. Homespun yet cerebral . . . bookcases . . . A saltbox?" Mavis opened her eyes and fixed them on Martha. "You'd fall hard for the Cape Cod cutie I'm listing tonight."

"Really," sputtered Martha. "Wow. I do love the simplicity of that style. You nailed me."

"Of course, I use more than intuition. I refine my initial judgement with your astrological chart, a questionnaire, and practical matters such as financing to achieve the perfect match. Every time. The process combines emotional data, psychological science, and spiritual technology."

"Still, well done, Mavis," said Martha as she made a mental note to google "spiritual technology".

"She's a genius, isn't she, Martha?" said Sally. "Anything she lists ends up in a bidding war. I swear, she could sell a tar paper shack by the train tracks for a million bucks."

Mavis laid her hand on Sally's forearm. "I hire the best. You're a very capable stager."

Sally whispered, "Thank you, Mavis," and took a demure sip of sangria.

Martha stabbed an olive with her fork and popped it in her mouth. She longed for a belt of sangria, but she'd have to drive, and anyway, it was unbecoming to lose control.

"Wait a sec," said Sally. "I have an idea."

"Ooh, do tell," Mavis encouraged. "Ideas are the aggregate of emotion, creativity, and intellect."

Martha chewed on her olive without tasting it, and wondered if what Mavis said was true, and if so, what sort of idea Sally's feather brain would generate.

"Well . . . it's a seller's market right now. And, well, your dad, Martha. I think he needs a nursing home, pronto. Roselea Drive is a hot location. The original owners are mostly gone. That is, except your dad. And that bungalow . . . it would fetch a good price even in the condition it's in. I mean, if you had Mavis to help you."

At once Martha washed the olive down with a belt of sangria. She felt defensive for the house and the man in it.

Mavis bestowed a benevolent smile on her middle-aged protégé, then spoke to Martha. "Sally's suggestion is, umm, indelicate but bears consideration, Martha. The comparables on that street are just under a million. For the lot, mind you. There aren't buyers for post-war bungalows. People want second and third bathrooms and great rooms . . . open concept. Those sweet, older homes just aren't adaptable, unfortunately."

"You wouldn't need to stage it, Martha. Everyone knows the house is a teardown," said Sally.

Martha's face burned. No, everyone didn't know that. The old man didn't. And he had help so he didn't need to move. Angelo. A rollator and bath chair, and soon, Meals on Wheels and a panic button on a lanyard. Everything on one level, no stairs aside from the porch. Why would Sally even utter the words 'nursing home'?"

Mavis shot Sally a Botox-subtle frown, then softened her expression and said to Martha, "Sally's not wrong. The wait lists for good nursing homes are months long, if not years. Your dear father may be fine now, but perhaps it's prudent to think ahead, to the future. In the meantime, I'm sure his home is a perfect match for his personality and needs."

Martha imagined Gordon snoozing in his La-Z-Boy, a John Irving novel or some such turned over on his chest to keep his page. A faded twentieth century man in a fading mid-century bungalow. Soon the curtains would close, but not yet. Martha said, "He seems content."

"Content. It's the best we can hope for, isn't it?" Mavis smiled. "We moved my mother into Valhalla Terrace last year and she couldn't be happier. At eighty-eight, she's learning chair yoga, bless her. She's put on weight and made new friends. And my brothers and I have peace of mind knowing she's safe. No more pots to boil dry. Or telemarketers to trick her into buying things she doesn't need."

"Did she raise a fuss when you broached the subject? Of moving?" Martha asked, genuinely curious.

"Not exactly. We told her she was going to a spa and we left her in the beauty parlour on the main floor. Then, we went to her room, unpacked her suitcases, and got out of Dodge. After her wash and set, they showed her to her room. I won't lie to you.

Apparently, there was an ugly scene. But she settled in, like a child in kindergarten. You drop them off and leave. They adjust faster that way. It's for their own good."

"So, it's a suitable match?" asked Martha.

"Darling, it's a perfect match," Mavis crooned and raised her glass triumphantly.

The conversation shifted to late-blooming offspring, semi-retired husbands, and fall fashion. Martha's boredom eclipsed her social anxiety, and she was about to make her excuses and "get out of Dodge" herself when Sally asked if she was working on another book.

"As a matter of fact, I am, although I've only got a rough outline," said Martha. "I haven't even written a proposal yet. I just came up with the theme a few days ago."

"So, are we the first to know about it?" asked Sally.

"Yes. I suppose you are," replied Martha, puzzled by why she spilled secrets in the company of other women. A waterboarding interrogator had nothing on a klatch of women for extracting information from the tight-lipped.

"Well now you have to tell us about it," urged Sally.

"Yes, do tell," said Mavis. "I quite enjoyed your last book, though of course, it was untethered from the realities of the modern economy."

"Untethered?" questioned Martha.

"Yes. Untethered. Obviously, it wasn't geared to entrepreneurs, Martha. It was theoretical rather than practical. I read it hoping to glean information on how to pacify my staff with their tiresome complaints and petty squabbles, but you presented no takeaway points . . . no tips. Not even any words of inspiration."

"That was rather the point, Mavis. The proletariat have legitimate complaints, but they're soothed away by spectacle—Royal watching and the Superbowl and the Kardashians' wardrobe choices—psychological baubles and trinkets to distract them from the injustices perpetrated on them. *Pacifiers* isn't a how-to manual. It's a Marxist analysis of the dynamics of economic injustice and the entertainment industry's role in exploiting the working class."

Sally started playing peek-a-boo with a toddler in a stroller at the next table, but Mavis leaned in. "I don't flick on 'Love Island' to distract my employees if they come to me for a raise, so obviously your book didn't capture the whole picture."

Mavis was deliberately misunderstanding the book. They dwelled in different realms, on islands isolated by vast waters. Martha paused to chew on a piece of battered squid and find a bridge.

She swallowed and said, "That's true, Mavis. As you said, the book is theoretical. You know the boots-on-the-ground world of business. What books have you found helpful?"

Mavis sighed and gazed upward, as if hoping to find a ready answer in the fabric of the umbrella. "When I was starting out as a realtor in the 90s, I read *The Seven Habits of Highly Effective People*. And I read every real estate book I can get my hands on. No matter how poorly written, I always find some nugget of wisdom."

They both watched Sally and her new friend for a moment, then Mavis asked, "So what *is* your new book about, Martha?"

"The self-help industry," she answered. "Working title? *It's All Your Fault, Loser.*"

"Catchy," said Mavis, checking her watch. "A dose of socialist tough love for underachievers?"

"You might say that," said Martha.

After Mavis thanked Charles and generously tipped the waiter in cash, they exchanged promises to keep in touch and hugs on the sidewalk. Martha hurried away, leaving Mavis and Sally to their obligatory post-mortem of the reunion.

As soon as Martha was out of ear shot, Sally said, "You can see she's tired, Mavis. She's not taking care of herself. I saw that immediately at Joanne's party."

"And she doesn't even try to hide it. No makeup. Not even a touch of concealer on that dark eye baggage. That sack of a T-shirt. Those sandals," said Mavis, shaking her head with dismay.

"I told her not to wear them. She's never been into fashion, but Birkenstocks are criminal, even on Martha's feet," added Sally.

"She did apply nail polish though," Mavis laughed. "As red as Mao's little book."

"What?"

"Never mind. Just a joke. Seriously though, Sally, I agree with you. She's clearly unhappy and stressed out. Divorced and alone for years, a sick father who ought to be in a nursing home when she's so far away, a son who's dropped out of school. And she's eating too many carbs. That's probably her way of coping."

"I know, right? Did you see how she attacked the bread, Mavis? If I were struggling with my weight, bread is the last thing I'd eat."

"I wanted to move the plate away. It's painful to see her like that."

"But what can we do? She's flying back to Vancouver on Saturday."

Mavis pressed a finger to her lips to signal she was thinking. After a moment, she clasped Sally's elbow and said, "Self help. Martha says she's researching the self-help industry as an academic, but she seemed really interested in books we'd read and would recommend."

"Okay?" Sally stared vacantly, as if her eyes couldn't focus while her brain strived for understanding.

"It's an old ploy." Mavis made air quotes. "Like 'asking for a friend.' Feigning disinterest. She pretends she's reading pop-psychology as if she were an anthropologist studying some Amazonian tribe, but I ask you, did Masters and Johnson never find their research a turn-on?"

"Okay?" Sally drew out the word to prompt elaboration.

"Sally, it's a cry for help. We can answer Martha's cry by throwing her a lifeline. You read that stuff. If you were suffering, and I mean really, really struggling, what would you read?"

Sally's stare intensified, and then she looked at her friend, eyes wide. "Oh Mavis. I've got a good one on my bedside table now. It's called *You Are a Badass*."

"Perfect. She *is* a badass. I think she'd appreciate the directness. Let's give it to her, to show her we care and give her a pep talk."

"Do we buy her a new copy, or give her mine?"

"Hmm. Let's give her yours. A casual gift, no pressure to repay in kind. I think it's better if you deliver it on your own. We don't want it to seem like we're staging an intervention."

"Deal. Should I write a short message in it? You know, to personalize it and give her some encouragement?"

"Yes. How about, 'Darling Martha. For your research and your very bright future. Love, Mavis and Sally'."

As Martha drove along Lakeshore Road, she reflected on her friendship with Sally and Mavis. She'd always been the odd one out, and today was no exception. She and Mavis valued different things, but they were equals intellectually and Martha assumed that was why Mavis tolerated her eccentricity in high school. Although Mavis led a posse of female friends, they bored her, and Martha didn't. On the other hand, Sally compensated for her lack of wit with kindness and sociability. She was the crazy glue who held people together. She had fibrefill for brains, but she wasn't a snob. Martha couldn't say the same about herself.

Undoubtedly, Mavis and Sally started gossiping about her before she'd even walked to the corner. 'Twas ever so and there was no point in dwelling on it. As Martha turned onto Roselea Drive, her mind retreated into the work-a-day world of academia and other pressing concerns. She'd go through her email, follow up with Daniel, read the minutes from the department meeting, and check if Joseph had returned any of her messages. Then she'd take a siesta. Meals on Wheels wouldn't begin delivery until the following week, so she'd have to prepare the old man's supper, even if he ate barely any of it.

The theme for CBC Toronto's drive-home show, "Here and Now," played on the car radio as Martha pulled into the driveway. Three o'clock. Plenty of time.

Gordon wasn't keeping sentry on the porch as he usually did on pleasant days. Martha entered the house and hung the car keys on the hook. He wasn't in his recliner either.

"Dad, I'm back," she called.

The oxygen concentrator hummed and hissed in the corner. Otherwise, the house was silent.

"Dad?" Martha called more loudly. "That's odd," she muttered. She followed the oxygen tubing from the concentrator through the hallway and into the backyard.

She saw the overturned rollator before she saw Gordon, seated on the patio against the railway ties of Judith's elevated herb garden. "Dad!"

"Duchess," wheezed Gordon. "How was your luncheon?" The old man held his hand against his forehead, blood oozing between his fingers.

"What happened?" exclaimed Martha as she rushed to his side and crouched.

"Tripped. My Croc caught the edge of a patio stone. I flew,

ass over tea kettle." He caught his breath while Martha retrieved his rollator. "It was spectacular."

"How long have you been out here?"

"Not long. A half hour or so."

"Do you think you can stand up?"

"With help," wheezed Gordon.

The old man was skinny and pulling him up to his feet was an easy matter, using her own bulk for leverage. Martha steadied the old man by his elbow, but he immediately yanked his arm away.

"I'm okay, Martha. It was a garden variety trip-and-fall incident. Could've happened to anyone. Including you," rasped Gordon.

"You're not dizzy or anything?"

"Nah. Just shaken, like a vodka martini."

They proceeded to the bathroom where Martha washed Gordon's forehead, hands, and rollator. The wound clotted atop a bruised goose egg.

"My third eye," wisecracked Gordon.

"No, a serious head injury," Martha countered. "What were you doing on the back patio? You never go out there."

"I was trying to get into the garage. You had the car and thus the garage door opener. The damn door's too heavy to open myself so I decided to go through the back door."

"But why?"

"I needed something."

The old man was being cagey. She asked, "Can I get you whatever it is you're looking for now?"

"No. No need. All I want now is a smoke." He pushed his rollator past Martha to the front door.

The old man walked like a rusty robot, but he didn't look as if he'd suffered any permanent damage to head or limb. "I'll get you some ice. For the bruising," she called after him.

"What, and take away this fabulous Fabergé egg on my forehead? Nothing doing, Duchess," he said as he left the house.

"Then I'll plan supper," murmured Martha. She flopped onto the chesterfield to gather her thoughts. She'd have to check on him over night. Head injuries could be devastating for the elderly. She'd make sure he had his panic button and reconfirm the Meals on Wheels arrangements before she left on Saturday. Phone calls to Joanne and Imogen, thanking them for watching out for the old man and giving them her contact info, wouldn't hurt either.

She drifted into dreamland. Joanne, Mavis, and Sally, prim in military green, stood before her, epaulette to epaulette, like a firing squad. Their voices reverberated through her skull. *He could use a lot more help than we can give him.... The waitlists for good nursing homes are months long.... It's prudent to think ahead.... Your dad needs a nursing home—Pronto!*

After supper, Gordon donned a frayed cardigan against the evening chill and went out to the porch for a cigarette. Martha washed the dishes, a task she found calming. The goal was simple. Scrub away supper and organize dishes on a rack. First glasses, then plates, then silverware and gadgets, and finally, bowls, pots, and pans. The unchanging method unshackled one's mind. You could sit on a plank in a zendo, back screaming for mercy, legs anaesthetized by contortion, or immerse your hands in sudsy water. The outcome was the same psychologically.

As Martha pulled the plug, she heard Sally through the storm door.

"Good evening, Gordon."

"Sally. Always a pleasure." Martha imagined the old man grinning like a jack-o'-lantern.

"I didn't call ahead. I hope this isn't a bad time...."

"It's never a bad time when you visit, lass. Martha's inside, likely alphabetizing the spices or something." Gordon pulled the door open from his lawn chair and shouted, "Martha?"

Martha dried her hands on a tea towel and, feigning happy surprise, met Sally at the front door. "Sally! Come in. Have a seat."

Sally shook her head. "Martha, I won't stay because I have to go by the new listing. I'm just dropping in to bring you a book. For your research." She passed an item wrapped in green tissue paper to Martha.

"Oh?"

"Well, open it, silly."

Martha did as she was bid and read aloud, "*You Are a Badass. How to Stop Doubting Your Greatness and Start Living an Awesome Life.*" An encircled R symbol graced the first part of the title. Had the author trademarked a new compound word? "Badass" versus "bad ass"?

"Well?" prompted Sally.

"Thank you, Sally," said Martha. "It's a great example of the self-help genre. For my book."

"And for you too." Sally winked. "This book will change your life."

"Does my life need to change?" asked Martha.

Sally reddened, and quickly answered, "Only if you want it to. And if you do, 'there's nothing as unstoppable as a freight train full of fuck-yeah.' That's a quote from the book."

"Provocative," said Martha.

"Isn't it? I keep that particular quote taped on the sun visor of my car. I can flip it up and hide it if I'm driving with a passenger, but I know it's there, coaching me. You know . . . the F-word. I have to be careful. I've memorized a few of her quotes. Do you want some more?"

"That's okay, Sally. I'll read them." Martha examined the cover again. "Jen Sincero."

"That's her. The author. She's a genius."

Martha was touched that Sally went out of her way to deliver the gift even if, belying the proverb, Martha could judge that she'd detest the book solely by its cover. She clasped it to her chest. "Thank you, Sally. You are really, very kind."

"And you are a badass, Martha. Promise you'll call Mavis and me when you're home in Elmington again?"

"I promise," Martha declared, though mentally she crossed her fingers behind her back.

Sally flashed her ten-thousand-dollar smile, hugged Martha, and vanished into the night.

Thursday, September 5th, 2019

"Are you calling her, or am I?" Martha asked, dreading the old man's inevitable reply.

"You are. So you can give her your contact info." Gordon's eyes narrowed as he zeroed in on Martha's issue. "She doesn't bite."

"I'll wash the dishes first."

"If you do that, you'll miss her, Martha. Joanne's a busy woman. The club, yoga, the Applegate Parents and Mentors Association, and Mothers Against—what is it the kids do on their phones these days? Send each other naked pictures . . . declare their undying lust for one another—"

"Sexting?"

"That's it. Mothers Against Sexting. Joanne's the chairlady of the Elmington chapter."

Martha scraped the remnants of a poached egg into the garbage can with a crust of toast.

"I'm feeling chipper today," continued Gordon with a contradictory wheeze. "I'll do the dishes."

Martha recognized that she was cornered. "Okay, Jeez," she mumbled.

"Okay," echoed Gordon. "Number's on the wall by the phone."

"I know, Dad."

"Or you could just ring her doorbell. Chimes like Big Ben."

"I'll call." Martha went to the hall, picked up the receiver, and punched the numbers on the keypad, hoping to reach the Kingsworths' voice mail.

Joanne answered on the third ring. "Good morning. Kingsworths." As if they were a law firm.

"Hello, Joanne? This is Martha Gray. Gordon's daughter."

"Martha. How lovely."

How unctuous. "Umm, thank you for the wonderful party last Sunday, Joanne. Dad and I had a great time. It was nice to meet you and Mike and Ethan." Platitudes piling like platters.

"You're welcome. How's your father?"

"Fine, fine. That's actually why I'm calling."

"Oh?"

"Umm, Dad's getting a Lifeline button. To keep with him at all times. He'll press it if he needs help. If he falls, or gets short of breath and can't make it to the phone, or—"

"For emergencies," Joanne clarified.

"Yes. I hate to trouble you, but would it be possible to list you as an emergency contact on the Lifeline system?"

"Martha, it shall be my honour. You are absent and incapable of assisting; I am present and prepared."

Prepared like a perimenopausal Girl Guide, but who was doing whom the favour? "I'm so grateful, Joanne," said Martha. "We already have your contact info, so we're all set. And can I give you my contact info as well?"

"Yes, you may."

Joanne received Martha's dictation and read it back. Martha was about to say a hasty good-bye when Joanne broke in again. "Have you spoken about the future with your father?"

"Umm, no," Martha admitted.

"Advance directives? Resuscitation? What inevitably must be confronted? How long can he manage alone in his semi-dependent state?"

Martha struggled to respond. The carpet felt like quicksand beneath the soles of her feet.

"May I give you some advice, Martha?"

No. "Yes, Joanne. I'm all ears."

"Have that all-important conversation. Open the channels of communication. Take the reins."

"Umm, that's good advice. Thank you, Joanne."

"You're welcome."

Martha completed the call as fast as she gracefully could and returned to the kitchen. Gordon sat, elbows on the table, fighting to regain his breath. A pair of plates and mugs dribbled sudsy water on the rack, unrinsed, and the rest of the dishes soaked in the sink. Martha took a chair opposite Gordon and grasped his hand.

"Almost done, Duchess," he wheezed.

"I'll finish them, Dad."

"Mission accomplished?"

"Roger. Payload delivered. She's honoured to be your Lifeline."

Martha watched the old man's shoulders, broad and bony like a sawhorse, rising and falling with his breath. Joanne was right. They had to have The Talk. A conversation more excruciatingly fraught than discussing sex and puberty with a preteen Joseph so many years ago. Martha struggled to find an appropriate entry. She released Gordon's hand and rose to finish the dishes, to buy time.

A few moments later, as she put the steel wool back in its

dish, Martha asked, "Dad, if you got very sick, what would you want for yourself?"

"A miracle. On the scale of Lazarus," answered Gordon. "Basically, everlasting life in the body of a twenty-five-year-old NHL player."

Martha sat down again. "And if that didn't happen?"

"A good vet. Your mother was in so much pain at the end. When the cancer got into her bones, nothing helped. We treat old horses better than old, sick people. Find me a country vet with a lethal dose of tranquilizer in a syringe the size of a turkey baster."

"Dad, I'm sorry I wasn't here when—"

"Don't be, Duchess. She wouldn't have wanted to interrupt your work and, well, you know what she was like."

"I could've helped you though."

"Me? Oh no." Gordon shook his head. "I managed. Aunt Becky was here with us. Martha, you didn't choose to be her daughter, but I did choose to be her husband. A half century roller-coaster ride with the most interesting woman on earth. She was my responsibility. Till death did us part."

Silence cloaked the kitchen. At last, Gordon cleared his throat and continued. "I don't expect you to interrupt your work either . . . you know . . . when I get worse."

"You might get better."

"Jesus, Martha. COPD and heart failure don't get better. I want to stay here, no heroics, and fade away."

Martha looked into the old man's eyes. Hazel like her own, pleading for understanding. He was an open book with a magnifying glass on top of it. *See me. I am dying. I don't want to be alone.* She forced herself to say what he needed to hear and to confront what she'd avoided. Voice scarcely above a whisper, she promised, "I'll come back. I'll stay with you at the end."

"Thank you," said Gordon." This time, he looked at Martha

through the corners of his eyes, an invitation to levity. "If it's not inconvenient...."

"Gee, Dad, it's terribly inconvenient. Between grading appalling essays hashed together minutes before deadline and dull faculty meetings, I dunno... I suppose I could take a chance on your party."

"You're on." Gordon smiled, and this time he squeezed Martha's hand. "I'll lay in some gin and throw a Tom Jones LP on the hi-fi."

Friday, September 6th, 2019

"Self-consciously edgy," muttered Martha. She folded the corner of the page she'd been reading to mark her place and tossed the book onto the coffee table.

"If you call the abuse of books 'edgy,' Duchess," Gordon commented from his recliner.

"Use, abuse; tomaito, tomahto. I speak of the sub-genre of self help, 'coaching with expletives,' vowels replaced by asterisks in the taboo words that are liberally sprinkled through the text. Here's another." Martha held up *the life-changing magic of NOT GIVING A F*CK*.

"Hmm. I see what you mean," said Gordon. "The title assaults the reader's eyes, yet in a benign way, and annoys with novel use of capitals and lower case."

"Exactly."

"Duchess, I'm afraid you're getting old. I lost my sense of whimsy when I was in my fifties. Don't despair. As one ages, one takes things less seriously."

"That's something to look forward to," Martha deadpanned.

"In my senescence, there are very few," Gordon said solemnly.

"More coffee?"

"No, thank you, Duchess. I don't want to be caught short when the Lifeline people visit."

"Okay. Dad, would it be alright if you handled them on your own? I'd like to return all these books to the library. I've got enough material for an outline now."

"I've managed for three years without a babysitter. I'm quite certain I can accept a panic button from a friendly stranger all by myself."

Martha looked at the clock. "It's ten now. I'll be back well before lunch."

"Take your time."

"Can I borrow anything for you?" asked Martha.

"No, that's okay." Gordon patted the stack of books on his tray table. "I've enough literary consolation here to see me through another week."

Martha could have deposited the books in the return receptacle without entering the library, but she wanted to speak with Imogen. As Martha exited the stairwell, she spotted her, presiding over the circulation desk like a cross-dressing Victorian undertaker in black serge.

Imogen's face lit up. "Martha the Marxist! Good morning!"

"Good morning, Imogen," Martha smiled back.

"Unburden yourself, my dear," ordered Imogen. "What have you done with the ancient one?"

"Dad's at home, waiting for a Lifeline panic button."

"Ooo, some glamourous bling, eh? He'll cut a dashing figure in those bloody awful sweater vests he wears every winter. Now, how did we make out with all of this Agony Aunt material? Have you awoken the tiresome giant within and unfucked yourself?"

"No, I'm afraid not, Imogen. I'm still a scared, fat mouse,

apologizing for existing. But I've read enough in a few hours to realize that there's a book in all of this." Martha brushed her hand condescendingly over the tower she'd built on the counter.

"Amen sister. You can call it, 'Stop Reading B-U-L-L-S-H-asterisk-T'."

"That sounds ironically derivative."

"I'd enjoy such a book."

"Hmm. Actually, I'm thinking of focusing on the neoliberal definition of success, and how self-help promotes consumerism, status-seeking, and a perverse conformity of purpose that reinforces the capitalist agenda. Basically, how self-help transforms people into tools."

"Tools with inspirational tattoos," Imogen riffed. "Empowered to be screwed."

"Empowered to be screwed. Yes. That's perfect. Could I use that, Imogen?"

"It's yours, baby." She blew Martha a kiss.

Martha looked away shyly. "Aside from gathering your insights, I was wondering if I could ask a favour of you."

"The answer's 'yes,' Martha. But what is it?"

"Look out for my dad. I'm flying back to Vancouver on Saturday morning, and I'm afraid for his safety. He shouldn't be driving, but he still has his licence and car. He staggers around the house with his rollator taking stupid risks." Martha's voice quivered with emotion. "Two days ago he fell...."

"Say no more, my dear. I already do look out for him. Hold on." Imogen pounded several times on the bell and hollered, "Simon?!"

Simon emerged from an office behind the circulation desk. "There is no need for noise. What is it?" he asked impatiently.

"Oh, there you are. I thought you were off assisting customers."

"Patrons," corrected Simon. "Advising patrons."

"Servicing clients?" suggested Imogen, expression helpful.

Simon stiffened and steadied himself, as if struck by a blast of Arctic wind, and repeated, "Patrons."

"Whatevs," Imogen said flatly.

Martha forgot her worry and stood transfixed as Imogen pressed Simon's buttons.

Picking up a travel mug emblazoned with the Jolly Roger, Imogen spoke again, this time honey sweet. "Simon, me and my bestie need to chitty-chat. It's high time for my breaky-poo, so would you be so kind as to replace me at the desk for the interval stipulated in the collective agreement?"

Simon sighed heavily and agreed. "Yes, Imogen. I will spare fifteen minutes of my severely limited time. Don't be late."

Martha and Imogen sat on a metal bench under a maple tree. Imogen had refilled her travel mug, and Martha held a cup of tea, smuggled openly from the library's kitchenette. Martha glanced at her cell phone. "It's nearly eleven. Shouldn't you be getting back?"

Imogen stretched like a drowsy cat, exposing slender, ghost-white wrists at the ends of her sleeves. "No rush. Simon doesn't go into critical melt-down until the twenty-five-minute mark. I still have ten minutes."

"You're sure?"

"Aye, Martha. Gordon's wellbeing is infinitely more important to me than Simon's fragile gaskets. Whenever the boss fusses, I find some arcane clause in the collective agreement and file a grievance of contravention. He hates breaking rules, even when they're totally impractical."

"The union makes us strong?" asked Martha.

"Uh huh," Imogen nodded. "And Simon's high personal standards make him weak."

"Imogen, you are self-help's anti-Christ."

"Thank you," said Imogen. "Let me be your muse. . . ." A dreamy expression washed over her face.

Martha shuffled her feet in the mulch under the bench.

"Now, back to the ancient one," said Imogen. "Once you're out of the picture, I'll deal with him mano a mano. Remember, he's my former boss and I have insider knowledge on what makes him tick."

Martha felt mildly nauseous as she imagined the old man behaving in ways that would see him fired if he were still working. The colour rose in her cheeks.

Imogen noticed and laid her hand on Martha's forearm. "Martha, your dad and I got on like a house on fire. I laughed at his salty jokes and innocuous flirtation, and he let me run the brats' programming with no interference. He was a hands-off, perfect gentleman."

Martha smiled weakly, then sipped her tea.

"Anyhoo, we're reviewing strategy," Imogen continued. "Point one. Martha's goal is Gordon's safety. Keep the codger preserved like a dill pickle till Christmas."

"Yes. I'm hoping Joseph can join us. It could be our last family Christmas," Martha said wistfully.

"Point two. Gordon's goal is also self-preservation." Imogen talked over Martha as she started to object. "He's following your rules, Martha. Panic button, walker, food delivery. He's as compliant as a lump of wet clay."

"But the driver's licence," Martha broke in.

"Driver's license, fucking shmiver's licence. I'll ramp up the home visits and, if necessary, steal the goddamn keys. You leave this in Mistress Imogen's capable hands, my dear."

"Okay." Martha hesitated. "I'm not imposing?"

"Fuck no. Gordon's like a foster dad to me. I'll send you regular updates by text. Deal?"

"Deal."

"Listen, Martha. I love Gordon too. For fuck sakes, stop

worrying and tell me all about yourself for the next seven minutes. Seeing as we're sisters now."

To her own utter surprise, Martha began to prattle, as compliant as a lump of clay in the hands of Mistress Imogen.

Saturday, September 7th, 2019

Martha woke at 6:30 am. She'd showered and packed her bag the night before in anticipation of the early start. She dressed, made the bed, and went to the old man's room to say good-bye. The airporter was due at 6:45.

She opened the door just enough to see Gordon in the dim light, snoring, mouth agape, a rivulet of drool trickling down his cheek. She hated good-byes. The decision was easy. She expressed herself more naturally in writing anyway.

She tip-toed to the kitchen table, tore a piece of paper from her notebook, and wrote:

Dad,

You were sound asleep, and I didn't want to disturb you. Anyway, you know how much I hate good-byes. Please, please take care of yourself. Don't smoke with your oxygen on. Use your rollator. Eat properly. Stay out of trouble. Don't burn down the house.

I've charged your iPad so we can email – or you can call me – <u>anytime</u>.

Dad, I know I'm reserved, bottled-up, cowardly? – sneaking away like this – but I just want to say – You're a wonderful father. I'm counting on you being reasonably healthy when I come back to Elmington for Christmas. That's only about three months away, for crying out loud.

Love,
Martha, Duchess of Arcadia, Kingdom of Baltia

Martha pushed the note to the middle of the table and set a pack of cigarettes on top of it so Gordon wouldn't fail to find it. Then, she picked up her bag, slipped out of the house, and stood on the porch to watch for the airporter. It arrived at quarter to seven.

Gordon's eyes blinked open. White light leaked around the edges of the blind. The house was quiet. Silent. The girl had done it again—pulled a runner. Martha hated good-byes, but she'd probably left a note.

Gordon propped himself up on his elbows and looked at the clock radio. 7:28 according to the red digital display, colon blinking like a set of sideways snake eyes between the numbers. Wincing, he eased his feet over the side of the bed, then sat. The light-headedness passed as his heart beat harder and shifted blood to his brain.

Once upon a time, his mind and body were indivisible, a formidable unit. He was intention and action as a hand in a glove, whim governing muscle. Now his body disobeyed his mind, like a piece of broken machinery under the direction of a frustrated operator and there were no spare parts for repair.

He hacked up a wad of phlegm and spat into a Kleenex. Different morning, same sick music.

Then he pulled himself up with the rollator, a clumsy yet handy sidekick he'd secretly nicknamed "Sancho". He hadn't admitted to Martha that he'd come to rely on this faithful, practical wheeled servant.

Gordon found Martha's note and decided to savour it with the first cigarette of the day on the porch. Christmas, for crying out loud! A decade away in old dog years. She'd only been home for a week and a half and gone for a couple hours, but Gordon already missed the girl's help, their banter, her convivial presence.

He longed to hug her good-bye. He crushed out his cigarette, took the oxygen tubing off the railing, stuck the plastic prongs in his nose, and inhaled several times, then removed the tubing, and lit another cigarette.

Martha, Duchess of Arcadia, Kingdom of Baltia. Once upon a time, he made up many bedtime stories about that courageous, justice-loving, super-smart female protagonist who happened to have exactly the same birthdate as one Martha Elizabeth Gray of Elmington, Ontario. Why, both girls had long, straight brown hair, hazel eyes, and crescent-shaped scars on their right knees from bicycle accidents!

Judith complained that Gordon's stories were inflating Martha's sense of self, that his "pandering parenting style" was producing a female Icarus with wings of hubris, destined for free fall under the heat of reality. In fact, he was mitigating damage. Perhaps another child would've softened Judith's brutality, but she'd wanted only one. She'd read Ehrlich's *Population Time Bomb* shortly after Martha's birth, then informed Gordon that humanity faced a future of mass starvation if people didn't control themselves. "Control." The key word. Judith believed fervently in control. Children were wild subversives. She'd tame one and no more. She'd serve the child balanced meals, impose routine, and nip misbehaviour in the bud, as if Martha were a potted bonsai.

Gordon had fallen in love with bookish, earnest Judy Steinman but married the severe Dr. Judith Steinman-Gray.

Judith didn't correct people when they assumed she was an urban Jewish intellectual. In fact, her roots lay deep in the loam of a Waterloo County farm, her asceticism forged in the pews of the Mennonite church. She enrolled in university to become a teacher, discovered psychoanalysis and a new identity, and never returned. Martha adored her exuberant cousins, but Judith confined their visits to weddings, funerals, and other occasions of constraining formality.

Was it any wonder that Martha couldn't handle good-byes? That she intellectualized everything that made her feel vulnerable? That she found a fleeting freedom in the bottom of a shot glass?

Gordon took a final drag on the stub of his cigarette and coughed. At least Martha didn't smoke. If he was going to see Christmas, he'd have to ease up. They had unfinished business. At the very least, Gordon owed Martha an apology for—

"Nice day, Gordon." A deep voice from thin air.

Gordon saw the dogs first. A beagle, a chocolate Lab, a whippet, and a white, wire-haired toaster on four paws.

"Lewis. A fine day indeed," Gordon called across the lawn. "Class behaving today?"

"Oh, you know . . . quick ones and slow ones. Heading to the off-leash so they can find their own pace. It's a living." The Lab strained on his lead while the beagle sniffed the base of the linden tree. "Looks like Reuben is getting anxious." Lewis nodded toward the Lab.

"Anxious? He's a dog, for crying out loud," said Gordon.

"A dog who will have cognitive behavioural therapy after playgroup this morning."

"Playgroup?"

"Yes. Playgroup. I can charge double over the basic walk if I throw in a session of fetch."

"Lewis, you're a shyster," wheezed Gordon.

"You wound me, Gordon. I'm an entrepreneur," said Lewis. The whippet paced round Lewis's legs, tangling the leashes. "Class needs redirection. Gotta go."

"Whoof!" Gordon's bark triggered a coughing fit, so he waved good-bye to send man and beasts on their way.

Part II

Saturday, September 7th, 2019

Martha stuffed her bag into the overhead bin, shuffled across the vacant row, and squeezed into the window seat for the five-hour flight to Vancouver. She slid her feet from her sandals and fished her phone from her pocket to turn it off. The screen lit with an email notification. Joseph. Her heart somersaulted.

Hi Mom. Got your emails. You're prolific. This morning's my turn to use the computer. I only have a few minutes till meditation to handle all my business. How's Grandpa?

Martha looked up. The fasten seatbelt sign flashed. A tall man in business casual was folding himself into the aisle seat. Maybe there was still time to reply. No demands, no interrogation, no "why in hell's name haven't you replied all summer?" She sent an arms-open message right back:

Joe! Grandpa's okay. Old and crumbly. Me too. On plane to Vancouver. You're up early. How's paradise?

Martha tapped send and immediately regretted it. Would he think she was laying a guilt trip with "old and crumbly"? After all these months, was the message too cool? Or suffocating? Or flippant? She peered at the display, analyzing their exchange.

Joseph replied a moment later.

Paradise is bliss. I'm allowed two computer sessions a month and Master Garuda reads everything to make sure we're offering and receiving Right Speech. I have some big news. I'll call you after grape harvest. Love and peace to you and Grandpa

An announcement crackled overhead, and the plane lurched backward. Martha typed as quickly as she could.

Call me as soon as you can and reverse the charges. I'd love to hear your news. If you need anything – a bus ticket, money, whatever – you only need ask, Joe. I love you. Mom xoxoxo

"Ma'am, ma'am?" The stern female voice hit Martha like a slap. "We must ask that you turn off your device now. We're about to take off."

Martha mumbled an apology, set her phone to airplane mode, and pushed it back into her pocket.

The tall man glared across the empty seat, as if he'd never witnessed such brazen irresponsibility in a fellow traveller.

"That was my son," she stammered. "He's twenty-four. Working on a farm. Hardly ever gets a chance to write...."

The man straightened his jacket by its lapels and looked forward.

Martha shrugged and looked forward as well, but all she could see was the seat in front of her. She was too confused to feel embarrassed over the public scolding. She sighed and closed her eyes. If only she could use her phone to google when the Okanagan grape harvest would finish . . . review their conversation . . . check her email in case. Now she felt hollow, a Joseph-sized hole gaping in her chest.

He wouldn't have answered anyway. Evidently, at Agape Ecovillage computer time was as precious as a genie's wish, bestowed by the master, and Joseph said *after grape harvest* even though he had *big news*. Martha tried to recreate their exchange in her head, to read between the lines, but there were too few lines.

Why would Joseph submit to an authoritarian creep like Master Garuda anyway? What kind of tyrant vetted other people's messages? Perhaps he was a father figure to Joe. Brian sent Christmas and birthday cards with cheques enclosed, but otherwise excused himself from the joys and responsibilities of fatherhood. Gordon had filled the vacuum of Brian's departure during school holidays. Judith railed against "enablement of unaddressed familial dysfunction," but Gordon took Joseph fishing anyway. What if they'd never left Ontario? Was tenure and distance from Judith worth the cross-country separation of grandson and grandfather? There were only the three of them now and they were scattered across the country likes leaves in the wind, finding substitute families wherever they landed.

She needed a do-over with Joseph. She had to tell him that his grandfather's time was running out. She imagined Master Garuda reading her email, then sermonizing on the turning of wheels and discarded meat containers and other nonsensical garbage about illness and death. What did Joseph think of death? Bardo and rainbows or annihilation and worms? At Judith's funeral they'd all joked that the deceased was probably psychoanalyzing St. Peter himself. Martha assumed Joseph shared her belief that human life is finite and dependent on the function of the physical body, but now she wasn't so sure. She didn't know her son anymore.

She would email Joseph again when they landed and hope he got her message. Low-key, nonthreatening, nary a whisper of coercion, the plain truth. "Hey Joe, BTW, Grandpa's sick and he might die soon." She had hours to get the words right. Her message had to pass by the lofty eyeballs of the censor-in-chief, Master Garuda himself. She'd google "Right Speech" and edit accordingly before hitting send.

And she'd call the old man and check in.

Martha craned her neck to see over the seat. Further up the aisle the flight attendants were pouring coffee into Styrofoam cups, placing ice into plastic glasses with tongs. She couldn't hear their voices for the hum of the engines, but she anticipated their question. "Something to drink, *quelque chose à boire, madame*?" Delivered robotically, English running into French.

Oui. Un gros gin tonic, si vous plait. With extra gin, skip the tonic, thought Martha. That'd give tall, judgy-pants man in the aisle seat something to frown about. She could use a drink to soothe her nerves. But it was morning, no one else was ordering booze, and she didn't want to face Vancouver in a sloppy state. Martha requested orange juice.

By the time she parked in the basement lot of her shoebox condo, it was afternoon. She unlocked the door of her unit and toed it open, hands occupied by keys, two weeks' worth of mail, her bag, and groceries she'd bought en route from YVR. Stale air flooded her nostrils—an odour of empty apartment, lemon cleaner, and damp wool. Martha kicked off her sandals, crossed the dusty laminate floor, hoisted her bags onto the kitchen table, and slid the balcony door open. A sea breeze lifted the curtains. It was good to be home.

She had to attend to university business, but that could wait till she'd mixed a restorative G and T. Besides, "Family first." In the recurring tug of war between work and family, she'd repeated that motto like a mantra, though work was oft the victor.

Martha carried her drink to the table, flipped her laptop open, and googled "Right Speech". Hmm "no lying, no slander, no gossip, no chatter, no taletelling . . . abstinence from false, harsh, or vain talk."

"Well, now I know what it isn't," muttered Martha as she imagined the tedium of the Agape dining hall. Lying and slander were beyond the pale, but what of gossip, chatter, and taletelling? No meandering jokes beginning with the protagonist's entry into a bar. No sly imitations of Master Garuda followed by stifled giggles. No speculation on who was into whom. Perhaps the eco-villagers discussed the price of turnips over their vegan gruel.

Martha clicked through more pages and found a test to determine the rightness of one's speech. "Is it true? Is it pleasing? Is it helpful? Is it timely?" Pleasing would be a stretch, but she could hit the ball out of the park on true and timely.

After composing and deleting several times, she sent her message.

Hello Master Garuda. This message is for Joseph Keys. Hi Joe – I didn't want you to worry, but I realize now I should have told you – Grandpa is quite sick. His heart and lungs are failing and he's on oxygen. He's still living in his house but it's only a matter of time till he ends up in hospital or worse. You may want to find a way to visit him before it's too late. I can help if you need a ticket or something. My phone is always with me. Call when you can. Love, Mom.

Message sent. Someone would read it. Martha took a gulp from her glass. She suddenly felt weary—from trying to reach Joseph through the ether, from transcontinental travel, from ten days in the service of the old man who was, fundamentally, a very demanding individual. Weary, weary, weary.

Martha's phone rang. Could it be Joe? Nope. A 905-area code with her childhood number. The old man.

"Hello?" Martha clutched the phone to her ear and carried her drink to the living room. She sat in an armchair and propped her feet on the ottoman.

"Hello," rasped Gordon. "I was polishing the silver for my Tupperware party, and I'm missing the dessert forks. Just wondered if you packed them in your luggage."

"Tupperware, eh?" Martha laughed at the absurdity. "No. I

didn't steal your silver. Perhaps Joanne has taken the forks. She entertains a lot. I wouldn't put it past her."

"Well, you can forgive me for being suspicious. You snuck away like a burglar."

"I'm sorry, Dad. You were asleep and—"

"That's okay, Duchess. How was your flight?"

"Uneventful."

"That's fortunate. You dodged the ancient Chinese curse."

"What's that? 'May you have an eventful flight?'"

Gordon coughed instead of replying.

"Dad?"

Gordon made a god-awful sound and said, "Sorry, Duchess. Frog or some other manner of beast in my throat. Just thought I'd call and make sure you landed safely."

"I did," said Martha. "And I'm glad you called. If you need anything—"

"Just those damn forks. Return them as soon as you can, okay?"

Martha smiled. Then she remembered. "Umm, Dad? Joe emailed me. Finally."

"Oh? And how is the lad?" Gordon's voice rose half an octave.

"I'm not sure. He's only allowed to use the computer at certain times, and he said he'd call back with news after the grape harvest."

"Allowed," repeated Gordon. "Who's the 'allower,' for crying out loud?"

"Master Garuda. He's their spiritual leader. At the farm."

"Sounds like a horrible old bird. Literally. Unblinking eyes . . . beak of a nose . . . pecking away . . ."

"I think so too, but he also censors the messages so I can't say anything negative."

"And you shouldn't, Martha. If you criticize someone Joe

respects, you'll only push the boy away. They're sensitive at that age."

"At twenty-four?"

"And at fifty-three. Joe's got a rebellious streak. Comes by it honestly. You can't tell him a damn thing."

"I didn't."

"Good. He'll come around, Duchess. He knows who his family is."

"I hope so," said Martha.

"And I know so," Gordon declared.

Monday, September 9th, 2019

A beige Dodge Caravan careened round the corner and slammed to a halt in the driveway, grazing the Corolla's rear bumper. Gordon took a final drag on his cigarette and crushed it out. He didn't recognize the vehicle, and it wouldn't do to greet a stranger, friendly or hostile, with a cigarette in hand in this touchy day and age.

A skinny woman in a yoga outfit jumped out of the van and called from behind the open driver's door, "Gordon Gray?"

"Yes, lass," Gordon called back.

"M.O.W." shouted the woman.

"M.O.W. Mow? Mow . . ." Gordon scratched the stubble on his chin and frowned. M.O.W A perplexing initialism. Perhaps a code. . . .

"Meals on Wheels. Mondays and Thursdays. Gordon Gray, 22 Roselea?"

"Yes, that's right. Now I get it. M.O.W. is Meals on Wheels," Gordon squawked. Why bother with initials for three, single-syllable words? It wasn't efficient. Especially the W. It was a three for one substitution.

The woman turned and opened the van's sliding door. She pulled a navy vinyl sack from the top of a stack of identical sacks and carried it up the driveway, like Balthazar presenting myrrh to the baby Jesus.

Gordon stuck his oxygen on, struggled to his feet, and extended his arms to relieve the woman of her burden. To his surprise, the woman was as old as Balthazar himself. A female magus, elderly on a biblical scale, face creased and puckered as a dried apple doll, but her body! She was as wiry as a gymnast.

She dashed up the steps and spoke with haste. "Never mind, Gordon. Just open the door for me please. I'll put everything in the kitchen for you."

Gordon did as he was bid and followed her into the house.

"Six meals. Three lunches and three suppers." The woman plunked a stack of compartmentalized containers on the counter.

"Two meals for three days. Six in total. Got it," wheezed Gordon. "And you are?"

"Sarah."

"Sarah," repeated Gordon as he extended his hand. "Call me 'Abraham.' It's short for Gordon."

To Gordon's utter delight, the woman laughed and shook his hand as if she were priming a pump. "You fresh old goat. Don't think I don't know what you're about. Here's the menu and instructions for heating." She pulled a leaflet from the bag, waved it like a flag, and placed it on the counter. "Mind you keep everything cold until you want it. We had a fellow on service who was hospitalized with food poisoning because he didn't follow the instructions."

"How is he now?"

"Dead." Sarah smirked.

"For crying out loud," sputtered Gordon.

"Indeed." Sarah zipped up the vinyl bag and stepped toward the doorway. "The chicken Kiev is very good, and it's still warm from the oven. That'll make a nice lunch."

"Thank you," called Gordon. He tried to see her off properly, but Sarah was already gone. He dropped onto a kitchen chair to catch his breath. The clock on the wall indicated ten to twelve.

If Martha were still in Elmington, the chicken Kiev would sit proudly on a proper plate, but Gordon could only muster enough energy to procure a fork and knife from the drawer and transfer the container from counter to table. He couldn't see the contents for the condensation on the inside of the lid. He popped the lid off and set it wet-side-up next to the plastic dish. A brown torpedo lay in the largest compartment and a mound of mashed potato and a heap of elf-sized carrot logs occupied the smaller compartments.

Gordon started sawing. A blob of green goo spilled from a breech in the chicken flesh. He scooped a bit of green with the tine of his fork and tasted it. Parsley. An economical, nourishing herb and one of the few he disliked. So this was the famous chicken Kiev. A peasant dish tarted up in a fancy, crumb robe. He scraped the green away and cut and chewed through a third of the chicken breast, a couple of carrots, and half the potato. Full.

And tired. Too tired. A wave of loneliness swept through Gordon's being. What was the point of eating if you couldn't complain about parsley to another soul? He'd need a smoke and a nap before he transferred the other containers into the fridge. If only he could teleport to the porch. He'd count to three, then hoist himself up.

Or would he? Really, what was the point of it? Once upon a time, king in his suburban castle, he'd smoked in his La-Z-Boy while reading the Saturday *Star*. A happy memory from a simpler time. Gordon recalled the day that Judith, brandishing an article on the carcinogenicity of second-hand smoke, chased him outdoors as if he were an incontinent cocker spaniel, and he'd complied with her rule out of concern for Martha. He still complied, for crying out loud. Yet why toe the line when there was nothing on the end of it?

Why not live as if it were 1972, ashtray at hand, chips in a bowl, TV tuned to a Bond movie? An old one with Sean Connery. Then a man could flirt with a girl without a litigious kick in the nuts. Or tell a joke without causing hurt feelings and hairy conniptions, stern reprobation, and sensitivity training. Harmless fun.

Gordon pulled the Player's package from his pocket and turned it in his hands, considering. Over the years the label had changed. The wholesome sailor had been replaced by an unfortunate girl with a terrible mouth, but the feel and smell of the package were the same. He took off his oxygen, stuck a cigarette between his lips, flicked his lighter, and inhaled contentment. The king was back in his castle.

Imogen dropped by unexpectedly in the afternoon. Gordon was glad to see her cross the threshold, but he was instantly suspicious of her motive. Was she performing a spot check on an elderly adolescent whose parental unit had returned to the west coast?

"For fuck sake, old man. It's like a bingo hall in here." Imogen windmilled her arms to clear the air.

"Fantastic, isn't it? A winning atmosphere," replied Gordon. He cupped his hand over his mouth and deepened his voice. "O-69."

"Bingo," said Imogen. "I haven't brought you any books because you haven't emailed me your list."

"So why in tarnation are you here?" asked Gordon with mock hostility.

"To cry on your bloody shoulder. My new bestie went to Vancouver, so you'll have to do."

"Sit down, sit down. Your agony uncle is in." Gordon gestured to the chesterfield.

"I'll open a window first." Imogen turned the handle on the side pane of the bay window. "I don't want to end up on oxygen too."

Gordon coughed and spat into a Kleenex while Imogen side-stepped behind the coffee table and settled on the chesterfield.

"Well?"

"Well."

"Well, you're the one with the problem."

"Yes." Imogen crossed her legs. "May I ask you a question, Gordon?"

"Shoot." Gordon saw the worry in Imogen's face and softened his expression.

"Do you feel safe around me?" asked Imogen.

"Pardon?"

"Do you feel safe in my company?"

"Lass, I feel as safe as the Christ-child at the bosom of the Blessed Virgin herself. Why do you ask?"

"Apparently our new intern does not. She's been keeping notes on her phone, a log of my transgressions, and she's reported me to Simon. The City of Elmington has a zero-tolerance policy on workplace violence."

"Violence. Surely you haven't beaten the poor girl, have you?"

"No, of course not," said Imogen, deliberately missing Gordon's joke. "My job's on the line because of my alleged inappropriate language. I've been told that my speech is a bloody act of violence. On Thursday, Cassidy recorded that I used the word 'bitch' three times, 'fuck' or some variation of same ten times, and 'bloody hell' five times. Also 'pussy' though she knew full well that I was discussing varieties of willow with a patron."

Gordon wanted a cigarette to help him consider what Imogen was saying, but he didn't dare smoke now.

Imogen uncrossed her legs and sat forward. "Simon called me into his office this morning and read from what he called his 'bible'. 'The City of Elmington's Workplace Code of Conduct'."

"His bible, eh?" Puke. Policy manuals were the refuge of lily-livered, puny-minded administrators. Devoid of nuance and space for wisdom. Gordon rubbed his chin thoughtfully.

"Gordon, he told me he's thinking of suspending me pending investigation of my alleged violations."

"Did you have your union rep there?"

"Kendra? But it's all so fucking embarrassing I didn't think I should."

"Imogen, next time, and there will be a next time, make sure she's there. That's basic."

"But she'll also hear about — Oh, never mind. Forget it."

"Forget what, lass?"

Imogen crossed her legs again and looked out the window. The silence hung as heavy as the smoke in the room. She sighed with resignation. "I might as well tell you. I write lesbian erotica. It's a lucrative side hustle. I'm more creative in longhand, so I write on my lunch breaks and transcribe to my blog when I'm home in the evening."

"Oo-lah-lah," Gordon mocked in falsetto as he fanned his face demurely. Then he coughed helplessly.

"I make bloody good money at it, old man."

"I don't doubt it, lass. You're clever with words. But creative writing doesn't get you fired. What happened?"

"I left my notebook on the counter. Bloody stupid of me. Cassidy found it, read it, and thought I was writing about her. An explicit, wet cunt passage."

"And was it? About her?"

"Bloody hell, old man. Of course not. I'm not a fucking pedophile."

"I believe you, but does Simon?"

"Yes, I think so. But he doesn't have to admit to that, does he?"

"I see what you mean," said Gordon. "You've left a convenient opening for him to be rid of you. Or at least make your life difficult."

"King and queen, both in jeopardy," said Imogen.

"Mate in two," Gordon finished.

"So, what do I do now?"

"Stay as far away from Cassidy as you reasonably can. Wash your mouth out with soap. Refrain from the devil-speech, at least at the library, and write at home for crying out loud. Better yet, write here. I wouldn't mind critiquing your work." Gordon winked.

"Seriously?"

"Seriously. This dreadful business will likely blow over if you keep your nose clean. Think of this as an opportunity to grow. To expand your facility with language beyond your default, shock-collar mode."

"Okay." Imogen leaned forward. "Are you serious about critiquing my work?"

"Sure, I'm serious. It'd get my blood up. Help me feel useful."

Imogen smiled.

Gordon stretched his legs and spoke again. "I desperately need a smoke with all this sex talk."

"Outside?" Imogen pleaded.

"Okay. On one condition."

"What's that, old man?"

"You join me for supper. I have a lovely mac and cheese with string beans, ready for two. Forget about Simon, Cassidy, and the rest of those hyper-sensitive, humourless snowmen."

"Snowflakes."

"Very well. Snowflakes. By the way, what's your nom de plume?"

"Lady Delarosa."

"Lady Delarosa. Enchantée."

"You're a dirty old man," laughed Imogen as she offered her hand.

"Indeed, I am," agreed Gordon.

"And I love you for it," she said as she pulled Gordon to his feet.

Wednesday, September 11th, 2019

Gordon sat on the porch smoking and watching for Angelo. He needed a shower. His hair formed a greasy barcode over his skull. His armpits smelled as if a family of skunks had burrowed into their darkness. His balls itched.

To pass the time, Gordon tried to rank the deprivations of life in an imaginary gulag by discomfort level. Obviously, lack of food and water would come first. You didn't need to study Maslow's pyramid to draw that common-sense conclusion. Then what? A proper bed? Sleeping on boards under a scrap of burlap would suck. Worse if you shared with a blanket hog. Would that tie with threadbare clothes? Surely that depended on the season. Shelter would equal both of those in winter.

And which was harder to bear: longing for family or the lack of a shower? That was easy. Having family by your side made everything better, including lousy hygiene. You could hunt for lice in each other's hair and commiserate. Now Gordon felt itchy all over. He absently wiggled a finger in his ear and considered rats.

Would you try to befriend them or hunt them for food? At this moment, if a rat materialized before him, he'd try to make friends with it. Gordon had promised Martha he wouldn't drive, so he was marooned at 22 Roselea, like Tom Hanks on that desert island. Tom had the volleyball and he'd have ratty. He'd call him "Dave" and they'd share the Meals that arrived on Wheels. Maybe compose an ad together for sale of the Corolla on the Autotrader....

No two ways around it, Gordon felt blue. As he fumbled for his cigarettes, Angelo pulled up in his little Korean car. At last.

"Sorry I'm late, Mr. Gordon," Angelo said as he mounted the porch steps. "The last lady, she weighing a ton and she got stuck in the bathtub."

Gordon raised an eyebrow. "There's a story."

"Yes. A sad one."

"Go on."

Angelo clicked his tongue disapprovingly. "Confidential, Mr. Gordon."

"Understood, Angelo. I won't press you."

"The lady, she all alone and she eats take-out and watches TV to fill her time. I think she have Skip the Dishes app on her phone. Pizza, curry, noodles, KFC, you name it. She so fat, her bath chair broke. I have to call 911 to get her up."

"Is she okay?"

"Yes. Just a broken heart."

Gordon felt a stab of kinship with the nameless woman. Alcohol, fast food, crack cocaine, compulsive gambling . . . humans found so many ways to plaster their emotional cracks. You could hide a porn addiction, but you couldn't hide the sins of the table . . . or Barcalounger with super-size drink holder. Gordon stuffed his cigarettes back in his pocket and allowed Angelo to help him up.

Safely installed on the bath chair, Gordon revelled in the sensation of warm water passing over his skin, of the washcloth under Angelo's firm hand. How he'd missed the touch of another human being. Even in her final days, Judith and he snuggled under quilts, sharing comfort. He'd held her, nuzzled the nape of her neck, stroked her thigh to remind her he was there. Savoured her presence.

"You give a fine shower, Angelo," said Gordon.

"Thank you," replied Angelo, as he squirted shampoo into his palm.

"By the way, how are your kids?"

"Great! Marisol started school in June and she learning her ABCs already. Pedro, he climbing on everything, very active and strong. My father made a climbing gym for him."

"Your kids take after their father." Gordon squeezed his eyes closed as Angelo lathered his scalp.

"No, no. Marisol is smart and pretty like her mom, and Pedro, he more like his grandpa." A moment later, Angelo aimed the shower head over Gordon, crown to tail, to rinse away the suds.

"Do you have any pictures of them?" asked Gordon.

"Yes, on my phone," said Angelo. "I show you."

Gordon grasped Angelo's arm and transferred from the tub to the towel-covered toilet lid. Gordon put his hands on his knees to settle his breathing while Angelo attacked Gordon's wet skin with another towel.

Gordon realized that Angelo was rushing. "I know you're in a hurry. Show me your pictures next week," wheezed Gordon.

"Okay Mr. Gordon." Angelo smiled. "Next week."

Angelo fetched a T-shirt, underwear, and jeans from Gordon's dresser. Five minutes later, Gordon rested in his La-Z-Boy, freshly clothed, exhausted, and content.

"Thank you is not enough, Angelo," said Gordon. "I really appreciate the help you give me."

"No problem," said Angelo as he turned the knob on the front door. "See you next week." He hurried away.

Gordon closed his eyes, breathed through his nose, and exhaled through his mouth. Was it paranoia or was he more tired after his shower than he'd been the previous week? His quarterly date with Dr. Southey loomed on the calendar. She'd give him the what's what.

He pushed his rumination aside and woke his iPad with a clumsy tap. It was high time he made himself useful. He removed his oxygen, lit a cigarette, and opened the file that Imogen had sent him.

Disciplinary Action by Lady Delarosa *(Tabitha Sweet, an innocent prairie girl, attends a tantric yoga retreat and finds herself in hot water with the Priestess)*

"Clobber me with a double entendre sledgehammer," muttered Gordon. "I think we're in for some hot tubbing."

The young women assembled in the hall under the hungry gaze of the Priestess.

"Hungry?" There had to be a better adjective to describe the gaze of a horny religious leader. Maybe "eager" or "lascivious" or "libidinous"—

Tabitha Sweet stood nervously on her yoga mat among the other women. As a good Catholic girl from a small prairie village, she had never experienced yoga before. But she was excited too. Excited to learn about her body and how to get in touch with her innermost feelings, long repressed by her Catholic upbringing. Tabitha wore a black leotard that revealed the swell of her ample breasts and her fleshy thighs.

An image of a roast turkey in stretchy pants invaded Gordon's mind. He tried to edit the document, but the iPad wouldn't cooperate with his fingers. He'd ask Imogen to give him a paper copy.

Gordon checked the status bar for the word count. Fifteen thousand, four hundred, and twenty-three words! Over sixty pages, for crying out loud. If he read the whole story in one go, he'd be as tired as Tabitha Sweet at the end of an all-night orgy with a cheerleading squad from a prairie college. Gordon took a drag on his cigarette, set it on the ashtray, and braced himself for a pornographic roller coaster ride with a dubious set-up.

Tuesday, September 24th, 2019

Gordon sat in a utilitarian chair engineered for maximal discomfort and tried to peer over Dr. Southey's shoulder as she scrolled through his particulars on her computer screen.

"Hmm. BP okay . . . O-two sat 92 percent with your oxygen on. Acceptable. What do you have your stroller set at, Gordon?"

"Three litres."

"Right. So no change there. And your blood work's not bad."

"A gold star, Katherine?" Gordon hoped his predictable joke would encourage the woman to swivel her chair to face him, human to human.

"If sticking a star on your chart will help you adhere to our smoking contract," Katherine said to the screen. "Let's see . . . you agreed to no more than half a pack daily."

Gordon said nothing. If she pressed him on his consumption, he'd be honest. She didn't.

"Last time you were here, we started you on Symbicort and increased your Lasix," she murmured.

"Can't say the inhaler's helping, but I'm peeing like a horse," wheezed Gordon.

"Good. That's the point of it. Gives the kidney's a kick to clear the fluid. Hmm, let's take a look at you." She turned her chair around, rose, put on her stethoscope, and stuck the bell between Gordon's shoulder blades. "Deep breaths please, Gordon."

He did as he was told. The effort provoked a bone-shaking cough and a mouthful of sour phlegm, which he swallowed.

"Right. A bit crackly in the bases . . . and wheezy." She bent, lifted his trouser cuffs, pressed her fingertips into the tops of his feet, and squeezed his ankles. "Still swollen. Well, no surprise there, all things considered. . . ."

"Such as?" asked Gordon.

"Your heart," Katherine replied. "You're holding your own, but the smoking isn't doing your heart and lungs any favours. How are you feeling?"

"Tired," admitted Gordon. "I get winded just getting dressed or making a coffee."

"I don't see what else we can do in terms of treatment, aside from help with smoking cessation."

"I'm not complaining, Katherine. You asked and I'm stating the facts. Truth be told, my fatigue is worsening."

"Do you feel that you're getting enough help in the home?"

What a weird way to put the question. "My home?" asked Gordon. "Yes, I think so. Meals on Wheels, a weekly shower, my neighbour drove me here. I'm coping. But—" He noticed that she'd shifted her focus to her watch.

"But?" Katherine's eyes flashed back to Gordon's. Obviously, she knew better than to appear pressed for time.

"I think my days are numbered. I doubt I'll be alive in a year."

She nodded slowly. She didn't say anything.

"Do you think I'll be alive in a year, Katherine?"

"I don't know. No one can predict something like that. Gordon, I'll be frank with you. You're quite unwell. Every day you're alive is a gift."

"Or a curse."

"Are you depressed?"

"No, of course not. I'm realistic."

"In that case, it would be wise to plan. Think about what you would want if you were to decline further. Perhaps we should be considering placement in long-term care."

"Or a cyanide pill."

"Gordon?"

"I don't want to go into a nursing home. I don't want to be kept alive with machines or have pablum spooned into my mouth."

"Noted," Katherine said flatly. "For now, you're stable. Make another appointment and we can discuss options."

Discuss options. As if they'd choose a colour for the upholstery in a new car or upgrade the kitchen counters from Formica to granite. "Okay," Gordon nodded. The conversation was over. She climbed off the tree when he'd ventured onto an existential limb and there he'd hang.

"Mid-October? Take a couple of weeks to write down your thoughts and your questions, and then we'll meet."

"Thanks, Katherine."

"Take care, Gordon," she replied as she dashed from the room.

He stared at the closed door, collecting his thoughts, mustering energy. After a few moments, he gripped his rollator, and limped out of the exam room, down a busy corridor, and into the waiting room.

Joanne spotted him before he saw her and caught his eye with a brisk wave. Gordon nodded back. They met at the reception desk. After they'd scheduled another appointment, Gordon followed Joanne from the clinic into the weak autumn sunshine.

"I don't have to pick up Ethan till four. Shall we have a coffee or something? If you have enough oxygen," suggested Joanne.

Gordon checked his tank. "Sure. My treat."

Ensconced in a booth in a 50s-style diner, Gordon stirred a packet of sugar into his milky brew, and Joanne swirled her teabag through her tea.

"Swishing your teabag will make the tea bitter," wheezed Gordon. "That's what Judith used to say."

"And your drink is deadly. Sugar is the new nicotine," countered Joanne.

"So, I'm a junkie," shrugged Gordon.

"Addiction is a choice." Joanne smiled at Gordon in a patronizing way and spooned the teabag onto her saucer. "How was your visit with Dr. Southey?"

"Fine." Gordon stared at the creamy bubbles on his coffee.

"Oh?"

"Not fine. She told me that every day I'm alive is a gift. A gift to whom she did not say."

Joanne didn't have a ready response as she usually did. He peered at her across the expanse of the table, her eyes uncharacteristically soft, the smile gone, forehead struggling to frown. Joanne was trying to empathize. Weird.

"Surely she meant the world, Gordon," tried Joanne. "You're a gift to the world."

"Yeah? Maybe the booby prize."

"Do you know what your trouble is?"

"End-stage COPD and a knackered heart."

"No, Gordon. Those are mere symptoms. Dig deeper. The problem that underlies all your other problems."

Now she sounded like a daytime TV guru. A smug, female version of Dr. Phil . . . or Dr. Judith Steinman-Gray when she was off her game. Okay. Fine. He'd play along. Any conversation was better than no conversation.

"Smoking?" ventured Gordon. "They don't call them coffin nails for nothing."

"You're getting closer. Dig deeper."

"Umm, not quitting smoking?"

"Gordon, I'm disappointed. Smoking is the same as not quitting. You've given the same answer twice. You have to go beyond intellect and habit, into your underlying state." She placed her closed fist over her solar plexus. "Here. In the gut."

"Yes. I do have discomfort there after heavy meals. Always have. Dyspepsia."

"Gordon, for goodness' sake," Joanne scolded. "We're talking about your emotional state, not your digestion. How you think and feel is how you manifest. Your emotions, originating in your chakras, drive your habits. Your habits drive your thoughts and your thoughts drive your life. Your life influences your emotions and chakras. It's a loop that either manifests in vibrant well-being and high productivity or in sickness and despair."

"A loop?"

"Basically. What is your cardinal emotion? Your default mode?"

"I don't know, Joanne. I suppose I'm sometimes bored, sometimes lonely, sometimes anxious."

"Those are all negative emotions. Do you see now? You have to make friends with them one by one and transform them into positive emotions."

Gordon drank his coffee. Crazy advice was in the offing and Joanne did not let him down.

"When your default mode is positive, energy will flow from each chakra and your health will improve. I'll give you a poster of Vedic physiology and we'll hang it across from your recliner. Read it, meditate on it, internalize and process the information."

"Okay," said Gordon.

"Okay?" Joanne shook her head. "No, Gordon. Not good enough. Any healer worth their salt can easily diagnose that your heart chakra is blocked. You're like Ethan, telling me he's doing his homework when he's really playing Fortnite. You're closed off, telling fibs to avoid healthy change."

"But—"

"No buts." Joanne slapped the table like Judge Judy calling order with a gavel. "We have work to do. You're embarking on a journey. We have to pry open the gates that are holding you back from your highest energy level and purpose."

Dismayed by Joanne's enthusiasm, Gordon decided to harness an old workhorse—conversational redirection. "What's Fortnite?"

"An online game," sighed Joanne. "I'm afraid it's rather addictive. Ethan is very talented with computers, but I'm concerned that his lifestyle is out of balance."

"Bright kids are often out of balance. It's a sign of originality and imagination," soothed Gordon. "Perhaps the lad is playing Fortnite to develop his talents."

"Perhaps." Joanne sipped her tea thoughtfully. "It's challenging to raise a gifted child. They're sensitive, like orchids. Kids like Ethan need specialized parenting to blossom to their full potential."

"It's fate," declared Gordon. "Fate made you Ethan's mother."

Joanne closed her eyes and smiled as if she'd just had a satisfying bowel movement. Then she opened her eyes, looked at Gordon with tractor-beam focus, and spoke in a grave tone. "Thank you, Gordon. Your words empower. If I manifest in my role as a mother of excellence, Ethan will manifest as a computer genius."

"Is it soon time to pick up the genius?" asked Gordon.

"Yes, but I should drive you home first," replied Joanne. "You'll have an empty oxygen tank if we're not mindful of time."

Gordon waved for the bill.

Friday, September 27th, 2019

Imogen inspected the poster as if she were admiring a Hockney in MOMA. "There are worse things to have on your wall than a woman sitting cross legged with a red flower in her crotch," she said.

"That's not her crotch. That's her Root chakra. You should know that, lass. You sent Tabitha Sweet on a tantric yoga retreat."

Imogen turned to Gordon, who was sprawled in his recliner. She batted her lashes, heavy with black mascara, and spoke in a breathy voice. "Tabitha was a naughty pupil. She flunked mumbo-jumbo 101. She needed discipline and remedial lessons."

"True," Gordon agreed.

"I only have to know as much as my protagonist." Imogen's eyes narrowed. "Bloody hell. You're blushing, Gordon."

"No, I'm not. It's warm in here."

"It is not, you ancient prude. I opened the window. You look like a spinster who found a copy of *Penthouse* among the United Church *Observers*."

"I told you I'd critique the thing and I have."

"And?"

"Despite the intense action, the plot is weak, ironically."

"It's erotica, old man. It's set up, foreplay, hot sex, climax, rest, repeat. The story arc is like a primal drum beat thumping through the jungle."

"Throbbing."

"So you *do* get it. You still haven't told me what you think of it."

"It's provocative. As a reader, I feel it has changed my life." Gordon gestured for Imogen to come nearer, and then he put his hand by his face, expression earnest, and whispered, "Lass, I think I might be a lesbian."

Imogen laughed. "You probably are, Gordon. An honorary dyke."

When they stopped laughing, and Gordon's breathing finally settled, Imogen asked again for an honest critique.

"Honest?" asked Gordon. "Okay. Honestly, I don't know enough about the genre to say whether it's good or bad. It's a page turner. People pay money to download it. *The Malahat Review* would never publish it, but no one reads literary magazines anyway. Your Lady Delarosa fans are your best critics and they love it."

"But what do *you* think, old man?"

"I think it's trashy, but that's the point, isn't it? If I had to choose between *Disciplinary Action* and *Moby Dick*, I'd choose the former, hands down."

"Damned with faint praise."

"Imogen, you asked for honesty. It's fun. It's irreverent. It won't win the Man Booker. Who cares? You shouldn't. I corrected a few typos and jotted some comments in the margins. If you make me read more, I'll have a heart attack."

"I have some poetry . . . a collection of haiku . . ."

"Don't make me read haiku either."

"Holy fuck, Gordon. I think your Third Eye chakra has a bloody cataract. I'm joking."

"All my chakras are blocked," Gordon said wistfully.

"Yeah, I know, old man. And it sucks." Imogen sat on the coffee table. "Time for a scotch?"

"Okay, but I might not have any ice."

"Neat."

"I guess."

Imogen extracted a half bottle of Glenlivet from her canvas rucksack and went to the kitchen to pour the drinks. "There's ice," she called.

She returned and handed Gordon his glass.

"Cheers," said Imogen, clinking Gordon's glass with hers.

"To you, bonny lass," replied Gordon. He sipped the amber liquid. "I thought you'd given up the drink."

"I have, but I make exceptions. My mom put my dad on a program and she's giving his bottles away. Waste not, want not."

"Then to your father too," said Gordon, raising his glass again. "Mind if I smoke?"

"Not at all. Window's open for a reason," said Imogen. "To

my dad," she toasted in reply, "Who'd be fucking jealous if he knew where his scotch went."

Martha was leaving the lecture room when her phone pinged. Once upon a time, she'd have let the phone wait and checked messages in her office. Now she dropped everything in case it was Joseph or news of the old man. She found a low bench near a bank of vending machines and dug the phone from her satchel.

A text from Imogen Wallis.

> Hi Martha. Just visited your dad. He's fine. Car hasn't budged from the driveway. He's eating his ready meals. Smoking indoors but takes oxygen off. 2 out of 3 ain't bad.

"Smoking indoors." Stupid, stupid, unforgivably stupid old man. If he didn't succumb to COPD or a coronary, he'd self-immolate. Jeez. Her fingers flew over the tiny keyboard.

> Thank you, Imogen! Smoking indoors with O2 is very dangerous. What should we do?

> Nothing. He's an adult with all his marbles. We can't do anything except try not to worry.

> He's going to burn the house down!

> Maybe. He'll be infamous. A dramatic end in that stuffy neighbourhood. I'm joking. I'm scared too.

> How's his breathing?

> The same.

> When are you visiting him again?

> Surprise check-in sometime later this week. I like to catch the animal in his natural state to see how he really lives. I'll call you after.

> Sounds good. Thank you, Imogen!!

> Ten-four. Over and out. XO

Martha dropped the phone back into her satchel and gazed vacantly across the foyer. So many young, healthy, fit people, giggling in circles, holding hands in pairs, scurrying to class. Not a single rollator-pushing, oxygen-dependent geezer in sight. Maybe it would be better if Imogen didn't tell her what was happening. She could call the old man once a week, listen to his bullshit, pretend he was safe and live in denial in a scholar's Eden.

Yet once you knew something like this, you couldn't unknow it and you had to confront it. If she called to lecture the old man on fire safety, he'd know that she and Imogen were, in his words, "in cahoots." Diplomacy would be essential.

Lecture room doors were closing, and the crowd was dwindling. The noise in the foyer fell from a roar to a hum. Time to organize her notes on *The Purpose Driven Life* and then head home for a G and T and a phone call to the elderly delinquent in Elmington, Ontario.

Gordon answered on the eighth ring with a gruff "Hello?"

"Hi, Dad. It's Martha."

"Martha. Wait. I'm putting you down for a minute." Martha

heard muffled shuffling, like a misdialled cell in the pocket of a jumping jack enthusiast, and then a breathless, "I'm back."

"You sound out of breath."

"Obviously."

One word. From a lonely man who loved to talk. "Okay. I'll do the talking while you catch your breath."

No reply. Only ragged breathing.

"The weather's good here," Martha continued. "The chrysanthemums are blooming. Amazing colours, though BC doesn't compete with Ontario for fall foliage. Work is fine. My saintly doctoral student, Daniel, is teaching the intro course, so I've had time to read lots of self-help. Not for me of course . . . research for the book. I haven't heard from Joe or the esteemed censor, Master Garuda, for that matter. If there was an emergency, I think I'd have to call the police to reach him. Are you alright now?"

"Yes, Duchess. Fit as a Stradivarius."

"Good. How are the Meals on Wheels?"

"Fine. Sarah delivers them. A pleasant woman. She's my age, a widow with three teenage grandchildren and a parrot named 'Medusa,' though it's probably a male. She runs around like Usain Bolt with a jet pack. Sarah, not the parrot."

"Yes, you've mentioned her before, Dad. Sarah sounds impressive. And the food this week?"

"Salmon with some manner of dill sauce for lunch."

"Was it good?"

"I ate it. My taste buds are dull these days so I can't judge."

"How's the weather?"

"Crisp. It's fall."

"You'll need a warm jacket to smoke on the porch."

"I have one."

"Are you wearing it?"

"Not now."

"Do you wear it?"

"On occasion."

Gotcha.

"I'm worried that you'll catch a chill, Dad. What are you wearing to smoke?"

"My velvet smoking jacket with paisley cravat and silk pocket square. As ever."

"Smoking inside is extremely dangerous. You have to smoke outside."

"Has someone told you I don't?"

Now she'd blown it. Martha recrossed her legs on the ottoman and tried to think quickly. No lies. "You know Imogen and I are friends too, and she might've mentioned it in passing."

"Today?"

A one-word question delivered with righteous indignation to gain advantage. She'd watched the elderly Great One stick-handle around Judith's relentless needling for years. Evade, then redirect, turn challenger into defender.

"I'm emailing you some clear fire safety guidelines, Dad. How's Angelo?"

"Angelic. He showed me photos of his cherubs. Marisol is five. . . ."

They were back on conversational terra firma. Martha felt her shoulders drop as she sank into her armchair for a detailed account of the cleverness of children she'd never meet.

Thursday, October 24th, 2019

"Do you want me to go in with you?" Joanne asked.

"Why? Do I need a chaperone?" Gordon shot back.

"No, Gordon, but it might help to have another pair of ears to remember things the doctor says, just in case."

"In case I come down with amnesia?"

"Fine. I'll wait here."

Joanne opened her magazine to an ad for herbal supplements. Gordon had expected her to push back against his resistance instead of pretending to read, and he felt adrift.

"Gray?" His name rang like a dinner bell across the crowded waiting room.

He struggled to his feet then looked back at Joanne. "Aren't you coming?"

"Only if you think I'd be of help." Joanne was already rolling up her magazine and stuffing it into her purse.

Dr. Southey didn't keep them waiting long.

"Katherine, I've brought my neighbour, Joanne, with me, as another pair of ears. Please regard her as a human tape recorder. We may speak frankly in her presence," Gordon wheezed.

"Joanne. Thanks for coming." Katherine perched on the edge of her swivel chair, turned, and tapped on her keyboard. "If memory serves, we planned to discuss options for the future, in case you get sicker," she said to the monitor.

"That's right. Euthanasia or suicide. Plan A or Plan B," said Gordon.

Joanne stiffened in her chair.

Katherine spun around to face them again. "Aren't we putting the cart before the horse, Gordon? Long-term care is also an option if you're not managing in your home. Many people get a new lease on life with more help . . . a chance to make new friends and join activities without the pressure of keeping a household."

"Thanks, but no thanks, Katherine." Gordon raised his hand from his knee, as if refusing a second helping of dessert. "I want to die in my own bed, when I'm good and ready, and not a moment later."

"Let's back up a bit and revisit your advance directives."

"Okay," agreed Gordon. She'd granted him twenty seconds

of attention, and now he was staring at her posture-perfect back again.

"You've expressed a wish to not be resuscitated if your heart stops beating. No ICU, no tubes, no CPR, no defibrillation. Any change there?"

"No. You can add 'no feeding, no diapering, and no admission to hospital or institution' to the list. I'll be getting off the trolley soon, and I only want help disembarking. Failing that, I'll throw myself off."

Katherine's slender fingers fluttered over the keyboard for a moment, then she turned and scrutinized Gordon as if she were appraising the value of an antique cabinet. "Have you discussed your wishes with anyone . . . besides me?"

Joanne shook her head.

"Obliquely, with my daughter Martha," replied Gordon. "She's my POA. I believe she understands my wishes."

"I see," said Katherine. "Gordon, before I'd even consider a referral for assisted dying, way down the road, I'd want assurance that you're not harbouring a misplaced reluctance to contemplate alternatives. And that you're not depressed or confused."

"I'm neither," objected Gordon. "I'm joyfully compos mentis and I know what I want."

"Still, I'd feel more comfortable advising you if we had a fuller picture of your mental state. Before we make big decisions. I'll refer you to our nurse to test your cognition and screen you for depression."

"But—"

"And I'd like to give you some homework."

Gordon stared blankly at nothing in particular, not deigning to respond.

Joanne straightened in her chair. Like a keen A-plus pupil puckering up to kiss the ass of her favourite teacher, thought

Gordon. She said brightly to Katherine, "If there's anything I can do . . ."

"There is, thank you . . . urr—"

"Joanne. Joanne Kingsworth."

"Joanne. Right. I'd like for Gordon to tour some long-term care homes. At least two or three to help him understand that moving into a well-run facility can bring shine to the golden years. Sometimes we fear things out of ignorance."

"Certainly. We can manage that, can't we, Gordon?" asked Joanne.

Gordon didn't answer. Angry adrenaline surged through his vessels and he was already pushing his rollator toward the door.

Katherine spoke quietly to Joanne. "I'll line up the tests with the nurse. Reception will give you the appointment as you leave."

"Thank you, Dr. Southey," Joanne gushed.

"This isn't our usual route home," said Gordon as Joanne turned her Navigator onto Sheridan Street.

"No, you're right. I have some time before my Mothers Against Sexting meeting, and you have plenty of oxygen in your tank because Dr. Southey saw us quickly. I thought we'd take a little detour, past Valhalla Terrace."

"For crying out loud."

"There's no harm in taking a peek."

"Yes, there is. The place gives me the creeps. I visited Don Schwarz, my old fishing buddy, in the Terrace after his stroke. They had him tied up in a wheelchair, bib around his neck to catch the drool, plaid horse blanket over his lap. Place smelled like fecal matter with top notes of Lysol. Depressing."

"Maybe you went on a bad day." Joanne glanced in her mirrors and signalled to change lanes.

"Every day is a bad day in a nursing home," said Gordon.

They fell into silence as they sped down the left lane. Joanne steered through an advanced green, onto a secondary street.

"I'm not going in," Gordon declared.

"Well, I am," said Joanne. "I'll see for myself . . . and pick up information for you. Knowledge — it really is the key to self-empowerment." She parked in a space reserved for visitors, climbed out, and called, "Last chance," through the open door.

"I'm having terrifying flashbacks of poor Don," said Gordon as he glared straight through the windshield at a cedar shrub.

"You create your reality." Joanne slammed the driver's door closed.

Gordon watched her stalk across the parking lot. He should've pleaded fatigue instead of revulsion. She would've sympathized.

A few minutes later, Joanne returned with a fan of brochures that she dropped onto Gordon's lap. "I spoke with the receptionist and she let me see the main living room, the dining room, and the chapel. They even have a library. You'd like that, Gordon."

He imagined a stuffy room, chock-a-block with cast-off bodice rippers, spy novels, a long shelf of Louis L'Amour, perhaps some *National Geographics* from the 80s and 90s. He shivered.

"I should've left the engine running, to keep you warm," said Joanne.

"Me and the atmosphere." Gordon immediately regretted the comment. Joanne meant to reconcile, and he was behaving disgracefully. "Thanks for the brochures," he said quietly.

"You're welcome," said Joanne. "Shall we check out Oakview Lodge?"

"I decline. Thanks anyway," answered Gordon. "Really and truly, thank you," he whispered.

Having addressed the necessities of toilet and cigarette, Gordon collapsed into his recliner. Joanne had scooped up the brochures that he'd left on the passenger seat and put them on his tray table when she'd escorted him into the house. There they lay.

After he recovered his breath, he removed his oxygen, lit another cigarette, and shuffled through them. "Knowledge . . . it really is the key to self-empowerment," he murmured. "By reinforcing my negative opinion of the whole barrel of worms."

The first brochure was titled "Is it Time for Long-Term Care?" A woman with a tight perm and dazzling white dentures smiled quizzically at Gordon. "Nope, never," he muttered.

He examined the next brochure. "Valhalla Terrace: Welcome to our Family" adorned its front in a wholesome, Rockwellian font. Below the title, an over-nourished, bald man sat in an armchair surrounded by his multigenerational, multiracial family. A baby resembling a Cabbage Patch Kid slept in his arms. An improbably perfect tableau.

Gordon opened the brochure and discovered that Valhalla boasted single and double occupancy rooms, a swimming pool, chapel, library, theatre, and gardens, as well as daily activities such as crafts, choral singing, and bus excursions. Hotel California 2.0. Hell masquerading as heaven. The photos of domestic bliss inside the brochure were equally unconvincing.

The third brochure was a simply worded, plainly formatted outline of the "Residents' Bill of Rights." Fake news. Anyone with a modicum of sense knew the rights of the elderly were violated at every turn.

As he pushed the brochures aside, the phone rang. Thank God he hadn't returned the receiver to its charging cradle.

"Hello?"

"Hello, Gordon. It's Imogen."

"How are you, lass?"

"Better than you. You sound awful."

"I've had a rough day," Gordon admitted.

"Oh . . . wasn't today your doctor's appointment?"

"Correct."

"You didn't get . . . uh . . . bad news or anything?"

"Not as such."

"Okay. Then why are you—"

"Why am I what, for crying out loud?"

"You know—"

"Crazy? Confused?" Gordon interrupted.

"No, I don't mean that," Imogen replied quickly.

"Demented?"

"No, Gordon. Depressed. And hostile."

"Hostile, lass?"

"Yes, hostile. You're not nuts and you're not senile. On the other hand, you're fucking grumpy and your sense of humour has decamped and moved to Idaho. What's wrong?"

Gordon breathed heavily for a moment then answered, "Number one: I'm old and sick. Number two: Katherine Southey seems to believe that my being old and sick means that I'm mentally incapacitated. Number three: she's signed me up for cognitive testing and she's angling to put me in long-term care."

"She can't do that."

"No, I suppose not. I'm likely catastrophizing."

"If you're not getting along with your doctor, you should find a different one," Imogen suggested lightly.

"Oh? And where would I find such a creature? Even healthy people languish on waiting lists for doctors. No one would take me on as a patient. I'm stuck with Dr. Katherine Let-Me-Check-the-Computer Southey for the rest of my God-forsaken days. The woman has no common sense."

"Hmm . . ."

"That's it? Please swear a blue streak on my behalf, Imogen. I need your outrage."

"You try it, my old prudish friend. It's cathartic. It'll do you good."

Gordon thought for several seconds. "Damn it. I'm angry," he tried.

"Really? I'm not convinced," said Imogen. "You sound mildly perturbed. As if someone forgot to change the toilet paper roll."

"Umm . . ."

"How about, 'Take your fucking tests and shove them up your ass, Dr. Bitch Head'," suggested Imogen.

"That's very vulgar," said Gordon.

"But saying it feels fucking fantastic. Come on, Gordon. Find your shadow and work it."

"Umm . . . put your tests in your poop hole, Dr. Stupid Head."

"Well done, Gordon," said Imogen. "Feel better now?"

"A little," conceded Gordon. He threw the brochures into the wastepaper basket and asked after Simon and the intern. Listening to Imogen's litany of problems usually helped him feel better too.

Friday, November 15th, 2019

"Do I pass?" asked Gordon.

"Yes. Normal cognition. Twenty-nine out of thirty," Tanice replied, Jamaican accent rich as butter.

"Where did I lose the point, lass?"

"On things that measure. A watch and a ruler both measure. You said they have numbers on them."

"But I'm right, aren't I?"

"Yes, but not right enough, Gordon. Don't fret. Your mind's as sharp as a tack and I'll tell Dr. Southey just that." Tanice turned her papers face down on her desk and looked Gordon in the eye. "Are you worried about your memory?"

"No. I'm worried about not being taken seriously. About being dismissed with a few keystrokes and winding up on a waiting list for Valhalla Terrace . . . which is no Viking paradise, for crying out loud." Gordon put his hands on his knees and leaned forward to catch his breath.

"You're competent. You decide where you live. Simple as that," shrugged Tanice.

"And the depression quiz?"

"Ah, yes. Well, that's more . . . um . . . complicated. Your score suggests that you are depressed."

"Wouldn't anyone in my situation be depressed? Just look at me, Tanice."

"I'm looking."

"Yes, you are, and I thank you for that. It would be odd if I weren't depressed. I live alone. I've given up driving. I'm tired."

Tanice nodded.

"Why bother diagnosing depression when it's situational and there's no remedy?" Gordon asked rhetorically.

"I see," said Tanice. "You feel that you're beyond help."

"I suppose." Gordon hesitated. "Actually, I'm concerned that my wishes will be dismissed with the excuse that I'm 'depressed'." Gordon tapped weak air quotes on his knees. "And if I'm 'depressed,' as you say I am, it's because I'm realistic . . . and sane."

"Are you depressed enough to hurt yourself?"

"No, no. Nothing like that. I'm mentally stable. Just sad because I'm old and sick."

"Well, depression can be treated. Psychotherapy, medication, even lifestyle changes might help."

"You're missing my point."

"Alright, Gordon. What is your point?" A probing question issued with disarming gentleness.

"I don't want therapy or pills," replied Gordon. "I want control over my future. I want to have the ultimate choice of whether I live or die. Of when I die. That would make all the difference to me."

"You want access to medical assistance in dying. MAID for short," Tanice clarified.

"Yes. But first I'd like more information . . . to plan."

"Information? Okay. Basically, we can refer you for MAID if you are of sound mind, terminally ill, and your natural death is foreseeable. Some doctors, including Dr. Southey, may insist that your depression be treated in case that's the reason you want MAID, rather than for . . . um . . . physical suffering. Before they make a referral."

"Existential suffering doesn't count?"

"It's not as compelling a reason."

"In that case, could you redo my depression assessment?"

"Gordon." Tanice looked shocked by the request. "I couldn't do that."

"Why not?"

"That's not ethical."

Gordon slumped in his chair. "Do you think I'm a candidate for MAID?"

Tanice leaned forward, took Gordon's hand in hers, and said, "Yes, probably. But what's your rush? Make this decision on island time, Gordon. You mentioned that Martha's coming home for Christmas. Enjoy that precious holiday with her. Squeeze out every drop of pleasure you can. We can redo your depression assessment in the winter. The Lord above will whisper in your ear when the time is right for MAID."

"He'll speak to an old atheist like me?"

Tanice squeezed Gordon's hand and winked. "Yes, especially you. Saints and sinners. He loves us all."

Tuesday, November 29th, 2019

Martha had offered to grade essays so Daniel could work on his dissertation, but she already regretted the kindness. The unmarked stack was a foot high if an inch, and the marked stack was a bare three inches. As usual, writing quality varied. Red pen in hand, she flipped over a cover page and read:

Origins of Karl Marx's Ideas about Capital
By Catarina Dench

Karl Marx was born in Germany in 1818 except it wasn't called Germany then because it was still called Prussia. Since he grew up poor with many brothers and sisters, Marx understood that some people were experts at accumulating money or capital (the bourgeoisie) and some people were destined to be exploited by them (the proletariat). Marx also understood that he was like the proletariat and his friend, Friedrich Engels, was like the bourgeoisie because Engels was wealthy and supported Marx while he did all the labour of writing "The Communist Manifesto" and other important books even though they both took the credit. Therefore, lacking capital of his own because of poverty and being unfairly exploited was the foremost, major, primary, early influence on Marx.

As many important theorists, economists, thinkers, and philosophers agree, to comprehend power all you have to do is follow the money and . . .

Classic belt and braces writing to increase the word count of an essay. Martha's eyes wandered from the page to a ribbon of water running down the windowpane. It was an afternoon that Ms. Dench would surely describe as dull, grey, unremarkable, boring, tedious, and monotonous. As Martha willed herself to read about the oppressed Marx, the rapacious Engels, and forensic accounting, her phone pinged with a text. Escape. It was Imogen.

> You have time to talk?

Sure. Skype? Martha tapped back.

> Warming up my far-talker.

Martha woke up her laptop, opened Skype, and clicked on "Imogen Wallis". By twenty-first-century magic, Imogen appeared like a ghost in Victorian widow's weeds from half a continent away.

"Martha! I see you. Can you see me?"

"Yes, Imogen. You look fetching today."

"Thank you! Ten bucks at Value Village." Imogen flicked the lacy edge of a shawl in front of her screen with a dramatic flourish. "I fell in love with the colour."

"It's black."

"Yes, Madame Obvious. So it is. Now tell me about your day."

"I'm marking papers. It's boring. The end."

"Is it true that profs throw the papers down the stairs and assign grades by where they land?"

"Nearly true. We're required to mark using a rubric. Alas, the best essay I've read so far will only get a C."

"You're bloody strict, Dr. Gray."

"Au contraire, Imogen. I'm lenient. 'Imagining Lenin as an Instagram Influencer' does not conform to the rubric, though the paper was brilliant. The mediocre, predictable ones score better." Martha picked up the pile of unread essays and showed them to the screen. "This is what I have to read by Friday."

"Oh, poor proletarian widget reader!" Imogen whined mockingly.

"Crushed into submission by the jackboot of the university industrial complex, wearing away my retinas with exploitive toil," Martha finished.

"Retinae?" corrected Imogen.

"I suppose you're right. Anyway, a liberal arts education ain't what it used to be. Now you tell me about your day."

Imogen's expression darkened. "It bit a shitty biscuit. Simon has decided that all library materials must be vetted for safety and today he started in the children's section. If he deems an item unsuitable by his arcane, frankly weird standard, he slaps a warning sticker on it."

"At least he's not censoring outright."

"Oh, my dear, naïve Martha. Fucking right he's censoring. Huck Finn has been branded with a 'racist' sticker and he's banished from the children's section. Mark Twain is on a permanent time-out on the naughty shelf. Ditto *Tin Tin*."

Martha was speechless. She thought of all the books she'd read to Joseph that could be judged problematic.

Imogen seemed to read her mind. "It's bloody Orwellian, Martha. *Captain Underpants?* Inappropriate language. *Lost in the Barrens?* Cultural appropriation. Anything by Judy Blume? Sexual content. Nothing's off limits."

"Is this something parents want?"

"They haven't been asked."

Martha thought of the old man and his free-range attitude to children's literature. The more frightening the fairy tale, the more enthusiastically he'd read it, even at bedtime, once upon a time. "Have you told Dad about this?"

"No. And I might not. It'd break his heart," Imogen replied. "He's got enough on his plate just existing."

"What are you going to do? About Simon?"

"Nothing."

"Really?" Martha's eyebrows shot up.

"Well, nothing confrontational. I'm on thin ice since the

Cassidy incident. I performed some covert sticker removal here and there while Simon was in a meeting."

"Be careful, Imogen."

"Fucking right I am, Martha. Two condoms at all times."

Martha laughed at Imogen's silliness.

"By the way, have you heard from your son?" asked Imogen.

"Yes, as a matter of fact I have," answered Martha. "Joe emailed that he's probably coming to Elmington for Christmas. He also has big news, but he wants to tell it in person now."

"The Second Coming of the Messiah," exclaimed Imogen.

"Hallelujah," echoed Martha. "I haven't told Dad yet. I'll let him know when Joe has actually bought a plane ticket."

"And when are you coming back, Martha?"

"Mid-December. As soon as the grades are submitted and I've finished my book proposal."

"Pull a Sheryl Sandberg and *Lean In*," ordered Imogen. "Because I've missed you terribly."

Martha nodded. She looked forward to seeing Imogen too, though she felt as if she were peering through a doorway to a forbidden room whenever they communicated.

Martha heard a shrill, off-screen meow from Imogen's chronically hungry Persian cat. Imogen blew Martha a kiss and ended the call.

Imogen scooped up Twinkle, the most fucking annoying cat on the planet, and squeezed her affectionately. Twinkle squirmed free, jumped to the floor, and stood by her empty bowl, whiskers twitching with imperial impatience.

"Feed me, vassal, for I am Queen," Imogen interpreted aloud. As she shook kibble into the bowl, she asked Twinkle, "Do you think Martha is a dog or a cat person?"

Twinkle sniffed the contents of her bowl.

Part III

*Friday, December 20*th*, 2019*

Martha stood in the arrivals concourse as holiday travellers streamed through the sliding doors and met their greeting parties. The Air Canada flight from Calgary had landed a half hour earlier, though she'd been waiting over an hour. Martha squinted at the people surrounding the luggage carousels beyond the doors and tried to pick out Joseph. There were several dark haired young men of medium height, but they didn't move like he did. People's actions were as unique as fingerprints and a mother could recognize her son in an instant by the way he stood or walked.

At last, he strode toward her with an endearingly lopsided grin on his face, a large knapsack slung over his shoulder. Martha's face lit up with a huge smile and she rushed forward, open armed. Who was the pony-tailed girl, just a little behind him, jogging as if trying to keep up?

Martha threw her arms around her boy. So long since she'd

hugged him. A year in fact. A wave of love and happiness washed over her.

They stepped apart, and Joe spoke first. "Mom, this is my wife, Tayana."

Wife. Jesus. So that was the big news. Martha extended her hand to the girl and they shook formally, the autopilot of decent manners replacing words that abandoned her.

"Tayana, this is my mother, Martha Gray. You can call her 'Mom' or 'Martha.' She'll be cool with either one," said Joe, tender eyes cast upon the girl.

"Umm . . . Martha is fine . . . umm . . . Tayana," Martha stammered. "Wife. So . . . I'm a mother-in-law?"

"I guess so," said Joe, grinning again.

The girl smiled proudly at Joe and said, "We're Mr. and Mrs. Joseph Keys. Master Garuda married us in November."

"Two hearts and souls entwined in one identity and destiny," added Joe. "And a Christmas surprise for you and Grandpa."

Martha swallowed hard to regain composure. "It's definitely a surprise. Welcome to the family, Tayana."

"Thank you, Martha." Tayana peered at Martha, then at Joseph, and back at Martha, as if establishing the bottom line in a business deal. Martha wondered what Joe had said about her.

"Shall we?" Martha gestured toward the exit.

They slalomed through the crowded terminal to Gordon's Corolla, parked in the massive concrete garage of Terminal One. Martha longed to interrogate the newlyweds, but their conversation fell into banalities of weather and holiday travel.

As Martha steered the car through the twists and turns of the garage, Joseph read signs and pointed out hazards from the front passenger seat while Tayana yawned and stretched in the back. They merged into thick Toronto traffic and several white-knuckled minutes later, eased into a relatively tame slot in the slow lane of the 403. Tayana was fast asleep. Martha stole a quick glance at Joe. "Tell me everything."

"Everything?" repeated Joe.

"The whole year," said Martha. "Tell me about your year." Probing conversations were less fraught while driving, eyes focused on the road.

"I will. We will," promised Joe. "I know I've been out of reach, Mom, and I'm sorry about that. First you have to tell me about Grandpa."

"Okay, Joe. Fair enough. Well, Grandpa's extremely tired. He has a hard time getting around and he needs a walker and oxygen. He's lost a lot of weight — probably forty pounds or more. You may be shocked when you see him."

"Is he still smoking?"

"Yes."

"We'll have to help him quit."

"Joe—"

"Tayana can mix some herbal remedies to help with the cravings. She's an amazing healer."

"He doesn't want to quit."

"Of course he wants to quit. It's the only way he'll get better."

"Joe. Grandpa has given up. He's decided to enjoy Christmas, probably his last, with us and his closest friends . . . including his cigarettes."

"I can't imagine Grandpa giving up on anything, especially life. He's not a quitter."

"Precisely," Martha deadpanned. She glanced at Joe, who stared straight forward, eyes fixed on the tailgate of the vanity pickup a few car lengths in front of them.

They fell into a dense silence for a kilometer until Martha broke it. "You and Tayana will raise Grandpa's spirits. You know how much he loves Christmas."

"The life of the office party," Joe said flatly.

Flurries twisted and swirled across the frozen asphalt, and Martha thanked herself for provisioning the house before Joe's arrival. "I bought a tree, a Scotch pine, but I haven't put it up yet," said Martha.

"We'll do it," said Joe.

"This is your first Christmas together. You and Tayana. You look so happy."

"We are, Mom, so don't worry."

"Who said I'm worried?"

Joe's dark eyes narrowed, wordlessly dismissing her question.

"You're only twenty-four, but I suppose that's old enough to—"

"Mom, it's definitely old enough. And Tayana's twenty-five. I don't need your permission to make a decision like this."

"I wasn't implying that you do. I'm just trying to process this big change. I'm wrapping my head around it. Tayana seems like a nice girl."

"Of course she is. I wouldn't marry a witch."

Martha signalled as they approached the off-ramp. Silence again. As they waited at a red light, Martha said, "You mentioned Tayana's a healer."

"Yes. She's gifted that way. She grew up in Winnipeg, but her parents separated this year, so their Christmas is cancelled. She has two older brothers and she learned about herbs from her Ukrainian grandmother."

Martha drove through the streets of early rush hour and listened as Joe expounded on the wondrous qualities of the goddess sleeping in the back seat until they pulled into the driveway of 22 Roselea.

Gordon rested in his recliner, mustering his strength for Joe's homecoming. He'd asked Martha to dig out his Santa hat and Christmas sweater from a box she'd retrieved from the basement. There would be no spoiling Christmas with lamentation. They'd be together, a tiny family of three. Though small in number, he'd make sure they sang carols, played board games, and argued about politics and books. They'd remember this Christmas fondly . . . forever. Martha hadn't wanted to bother with a tree, but he'd insisted.

He heard the Corolla pull into the driveway. Showtime! Gordon pulled himself up, limped to the front door, and opened it. The trunk was open—wait—who was that? A girl! For crying out loud. And Joe beside her, broad shouldered from farm labour, a healthy lad. Four for Christmas!

He called, "Merry Christmas," and started coughing. Not part of the plan. He had to stifle the cough . . . gain control . . . breathe in through the nose and out through the mouth. Steady.

"Grandpa!"

The boy had already gained the stairs even under the burden of a heavy bag. Gordon fell into Joseph's arms, melted into the hug. Joe was home.

After an evening of food, drink, and tree decorating, they lay in their beds holding hands, Joe in a camp cot and Tayana in the single bed in Martha's room. Midnight in Ontario, a boy scout-early nine pm in BC. Neither could sleep, though they heard Gordon snoring in his own room and Martha tossing and turning on the chesterfield in the living room. Gordon had insisted they take his queen-size bed, "in the honeymoon suite," he'd joked, but he was overruled three to one.

"I'm not sure your mother likes me," Tayana whispered.

"Of course she likes you," Joe whispered back. "Move over. I'm squeezing in."

They cuddled under the quilts, Joe's breath lifting the whisps of hair over Tayana's forehead. "Why do you think Mom doesn't like you?" he asked gently.

"I don't know ... vibes."

"She's shy. That's all. And she's worried about Grandpa. She buzzes around, cooking and washing dishes and stuff to keep from crying."

"I guess. Tomorrow I'll help her more. Win her over."

"You don't have to win her over, Tayana. You're fine. She's like that with everybody. Cool."

"I'm not so sure. But your Grandpa, on the other hand ... what a sweetie."

"He's a character."

"He's so sick, but he still decorated his walker and found an old sock for me to pin up with your stocking. Gross, though I appreciate the thought. What was he like when he was healthy?"

"I don't know ... the same times a hundred."

"And your grandma?"

"She was different. Hard and cold but very smart. She showed she cared by correcting my manners and paying for my violin lessons. I was scared of her when I was a kid."

"She sounds awful."

"We're not supposed to speak ill of the dead, but she used to go on and on about the neuroses of the only child to me and Mom and by the time I realized that it was subtle psychological abuse, Dad was out of the picture."

"And who do you think you take after most? Your grandma, your mom, or your grandpa?"

"Grandpa?"

"Yes. Your grandpa. You turned out fine. Master Garuda says we can learn from everyone, bodhisattvas and hungry ghosts alike. You did that. But whatever you do, don't start smoking."

Joe laughed weakly. "Tayana?"

"Yes, Joe."

"Promise me we'll die together. That we'll never be apart."

"I'm here, aren't I? Right beside you. What a weird thing to say. Are you okay?"

"Yeah. I guess I'm freaked out about Grandpa. He looks like a skeleton. And his colour — he's suffering."

"He's pretty sick." Tayana rolled from her back to her side to face Joe, silent in the darkness. "What would Master Garuda say? In this situation."

"Offer loving kindness and let karma take care of the rest."

"That's right. Help him. That's your only duty. Simple."

Joe drew Tayana even closer in the stillness of the night. The furnace rumbled below them for several minutes, then clicked off, leaving the house in stillness.

"I think they're both asleep," whispered Joe.

"Yeah. Happy winter solstice, husband," Tayana whispered back.

Joe slipped his hand over Tayana's hip and kissed her and they, very quietly, slipped into the physical nature of newly-wedded love.

Sunday, December 22nd, 2019

"Come for Secret Santa, Mom," urged Joe.

"I was going to refill cups first," protested Martha.

"I've still got a full cup," said Imogen.

Gordon and Tayana echoed Imogen, so Martha put the coffee pot on the counter and returned to the living room. She always felt anxious about gifts. Did the recipient really like what she'd chosen? Did she demonstrate enough delight and gratitude to ease the giver's fears about her feelings? The custom sucked.

Obviously not everyone felt the same way. Imogen and Gordon were pestering again.

Imogen patted the cushion next to her on the chesterfield. "Sit your ass down, Martha. It's only books, for Christ's sake. It's not even real present day yet."

After Martha was seated, Gordon took up a set of jingle bells arranged like brass knuckles on a leather strap and shook them. "Ladies and young gentleman," he wheezed. "For the uninitiated, I introduce to you a Gray family tradition. Every year at Christmas, we each offer a book that has touched us in the past so that another member of the family might find some solace, or words of wisdom, or benefit in some way by receiving it."

The old man paused to catch his breath under the concerned eyes of the assembled, then cleared his throat and said, "This year, we have two new members in our circle. First, my dear friend, Imogen Wallis. Imogen, you're like a daughter to me and a sister to Martha, though you've only known each other a short time. I expect you'll be pulling Martha's hair and stealing from her closet soon. And now you're Joe and Tayana's crazy aunt. Go easy on them, lass."

Imogen smiled broadly and nodded to Gordon, and he continued. "Tayana Keys. My beautiful, kind granddaughter. Joe's a lucky son of a gun. We all are. Welcome to the family."

From her spot on the floor, Tayana reached and patted Gordon's knee. "I'm the lucky one, Grandpa."

Gordon shook the bells again; whether to signal he was finished talking or merely to make noise, Martha wasn't certain.

"Does everyone have a book?" Gordon's tone was imperious now.

"Yes, Grandpa," answered Joe. "Tayana and I went to Centurion Used Books yesterday, so we're all set."

"Imogen?" asked Gordon.

"Affirmative. Bloody good selection at the Friends of the Library sale."

"Martha?"

"Yes. Mine should be . . . umm . . . helpful."

"And I have a classic from my personal library. Books on the coffee table please," commanded Gordon.

In an instant, five books wrapped in garish red, green, silver, and gold paper lay in a loose pile. Gordon slouched in his recliner. "Martha, could you outline the rules?" he wheezed.

"Okay," said Martha, warming to the game. "The most important rule is that you can't wind up with the book you contributed. We each choose, youngest to oldest, and open our presents one by one. Then we can trade, oldest to youngest, and trades are final. Got it?"

"Bring it on!" Imogen hollered.

After a waffle brunch, Gordon had a smoke and went for a nap in his room. Joe and Tayana bundled up and headed out for a walk in the river valley to find pinecones and sprigs of greenery for Christmas décor. Martha and Imogen sipped rum punch. On their second drink, Martha still sat vertically, but Imogen lay sprawled with her head on a pillow and her feet across Martha's lap.

"That was a fun twist on Secret Santa," said Imogen. "How did your old man manage to keep a copy of *The Happy Hooker* hidden from you and your mom for all those years? It's a fucking classic. I'll treasure it forever."

"Then it found the right home," said Martha. "Joe turned fifty shades of red when he ripped the paper off. It's not the sort of book you'd admit to wanting to read. Anyway, Dad intended for you the get the porn book, as inspiration for your fiction."

"It was a nice trade. Joe has a better book for a young man."

"I think he'll enjoy *Meditations*," agreed Martha. "Some ancient Stoic philosophy to balance the pensées of Master Garuda."

"Motherly propaganda. Well done."

"There was no way that Tayana was going to part with Joe's gift," added Martha. "I'd like to read *The Power of Now* myself. Maybe she'll let me borrow it for notes."

"Don't you like my book?" Imogen pouted.

"I love it," Martha beamed. "*Is God in Your Bedroom?* I can't wait to find out. If He's ever there, I expect He's bored to death. How did that book slip by the elderly curators at Friends of the Library?"

"Probably by that bland cover photo. With all those fancy pillows and ruffles, that bed doesn't look like it sees any action."

Martha picked up the softcover and riffled through the pages, reading here and there. "God seems to go in for married, heterosexual sex. Even 'self-abuse' is out."

"He's a moralizing porn director and He's there to assist," said Imogen. "I hope to see this book mentioned in your self-help critique—and my name in the acknowledgements, Martha."

"That's a tall order, Imogen. First, I have to write it and convince an agent and publisher that it's worth the ink. If all that happens, you'll get a big mention, in black and white."

Imogen took a swig of punch and stared at the Christmas tree, as if finding courage. "I was very touched by your dad saying I'm like a daughter to him."

"I was too. He spoke from the heart."

"Trouble is, I don't feel like your sister. I feel something else." Imogen sat up, cross-legged, facing Martha.

"I know that." Martha turned to face Imogen. "But I don't know what to do about it. This is terra incognita for me."

Imogen leaned over and kissed Martha softly, lips on lips. A semi-chaste, quick kiss. She leaned back again, and Martha saw the pleading in her eyes.

"Well?" Imogen asked.

Martha felt an unmistakable pull, but she swiftly rejected it. "I don't know. I need to think, Imogen."

"That's the trouble with you, fucking Martha Gray. You think too much. But I'm not going anywhere. I'll be here when you're ready."

Martha set her drink on the coffee table. "A walk to sober up?"

"Sure. I could use some fresh air," Imogen agreed breezily, pretending not to be disappointed in the outcome of her risky proposition.

Gordon woke to a quiet house. Was he alone? There wasn't a single sound aside from the wind in the trees. He hoisted himself up and pushed his rollator into the living room. Alone. Good. No one to babysit him. No one to usher him outside and look disappointed when he smoked. The kids were the worst. He flopped into the La-Z-Boy, and after he caught his breath, he removed his oxygen and lit a cigarette. "Merry Christmas, old friend," he murmured.

He picked up his book, *Eat, Pray, Love*, flipped the cover over, and read the round, feminine printing: *Merry Christmas to ??? I hope you like my favourite book. Love, Tayana.*

Eat, Pray, Love wouldn't have been his first choice—he'd eyed *Meditations* with mild jealousy—but protecting the feelings of the giver mattered more. He took a slow draw on his cigarette and started reading the book. Sooner started, sooner finished.

Monday, December 23rd, 2019

Martha usually paid for gas at the pump to avoid small talk at the till, but today she had to buy cigarettes, so she entered the Circle K convenience store. Since giving up driving, the old man had to convince others to do his lousy shopping—Imogen, Lewis-the-dog-walker, even Angelo, who was induced with a bribe "for the sweeties in Manilla." Today was her turn.

"Pump three," she said to the turbaned man at the register. A small, plastic tree decked with candy, fake lottery tickets, and tinsel stood incongruously beside him. The store was a riot of clashing colours. Over the speakers, a tinny George Michael whined about the previous Christmas.

"Thirty-four dollars for the gas, ma'am. Anything else?"

"And three cartons of Players," Martha mumbled, as sheepish as a teenage boy buying condoms. "Not for me . . . for my father. He's the smoker."

"I never judge my customers," said the clerk as he placed the cartons on the counter. "Perhaps a lotto ticket? As a stocking stuffer? Not for you," he smiled. Or was he smirking?

Martha thought fast. She didn't play the lotto. The house profited in the business of gambling, not the nitwit players, but this man, who claimed not to judge, was throwing her a lifeline and saving her from the mall. "Sure. For stocking stuffers," she agreed. "What do you suggest?"

"Lotto Max has an eight-digit jackpot and the draw's tomorrow. Christmas Eve." He waved toward the display like a masculine Vanna White.

"Three please. And I'll take these three packs of gum too," said Martha. "No bag," she added, hoping her environmentalism marked the purchases as exceptional. She completed the transaction, gathered the cigarettes and stocking stuffers, and turned to a growing line-up behind her.

"Martha?"

Sally Dunfield. Two customers back. "Merry Christmas, Sally," said Martha.

"Wait by the door," Sally ordered. "I'll be there in a sec."

Martha obeyed and watched as Sally, felt antler tiara bobbing, tapped her card and laughed with the clerk. Evidently some people preferred interaction with a stranger to the efficiency of a machine when they paid for gas. It beggared the mind.

"I won't take no for an answer," said Sally as she approached Martha.

"I don't know the question yet," said Martha.

"Eggnog. My place. Now."

"That's not a question," Martha protested as Sally scrawled the directions to her home on the back of her receipt.

The Dunfield family home was festooned with kitsch, from the "Santa, please stop here!!" sign on the porch to the garlands and brightly painted ceramic nativity scene on the mantle in the drawing room, as Sally called that enormous space. A tall, artificial tree standing in a foyer worthy of a downtown hotel blinked through the double doorway, and Martha was thankful she didn't suffer from a seizure disorder when she pretended to admire it.

"It looks so real."

"Thank you. We switched to artificial because I like to put the tree up in mid-November. The real ones drop needles and I hate the mess," said Sally. She sat in a leather chair resembling a medieval throne, her legs curled under her, and raised her glass. "Happy holidays!"

"Happy holidays," Martha toasted from her vantage on an equally gigantic rocking chair.

"When did you fly in?"

"About a week ago," replied Martha. A cool sensation on her top lip warned her she had an eggnog mustache and she tried to wipe it away casually with the back of her hand.

Sally handed Martha a tissue box and said, "You promised you'd tell Mavis and me when you were coming back."

"I know, Sally, but Dad isn't well, and I got busy sorting him out and—"

"Say no more." Sally's expression morphed from mock scowl to earnest concern. "How is your dad?"

"Getting by with a little help from his friends. You know — the support worker, the Meals on Wheels lady, the pharmacist, his doctor, the neighbours..."

"He's such a sweet man."

"I suppose." Martha pictured the old man ringing his jingle bells, impatient for a mug of coffee.

"And Joseph? Is he home too?"

"Yes, as a matter of fact he is," replied Martha with unconcealed pride. "And he's a newlywed. His wife, Tayana, has joined us this year."

"You never mentioned he was engaged. A fall wedding?"

Martha nodded.

"I'll bet it was beautiful," said Sally.

"Well... I think it was," Martha shrugged.

"Tayana. Tayana." Sally tested the name. "That's pretty. And uncommon. Is she Asian?"

"No. Her family is mostly of Ukrainian descent, and she was born and raised in Winnipeg. Joe told me her given name was Tiffany."

"Like the lamps?"

"Yes, exactly, and maybe too suburban, middle class for her liking, so she changed it." Sally had a bloodhound's nose for gossip, and Martha thought she saw her nostrils twitch. At once Martha felt catty and disloyal to Tayana. "Anyway, she's a lovely girl," Martha added quickly. "She gave Dad a copy of *Eat, Pray, Love* for Christmas."

If Sally thought the memoir an absurd gift for an elderly man, she didn't show it, but Martha's face burned anyway.

"Oh, I love a good wedding," Sally said with relish. "Then again, all weddings are fun, aren't they?"

"I suppose," Martha said vaguely. She sipped her eggnog.

"Do you have any photos of the big day?"

"No, I don't. Not with me." Martha gestured toward Sally's photo collection, arrayed on a shiny, walnut table among several pine-scented candles. "Is that Benjamin? And Emma, in the gilt frame?"

"Yes, indeed," answered Sally. "Ben's home from Western. He's doing his MBA there. And Emma should graduate this April. Fine Arts, specializing in film. She has a boyfriend, also a film student, and I might be mother of the bride myself this summer if Sam pops the question. It's Christmas, so fingers crossed."

"Fingers crossed."

"Any advice for a rookie mother-in-law, Martha?"

"Just be yourself, Sally, and Sam will feel as if he's part of the family."

"He *is* part of the family," Sally giggled.

"There you go. He probably calls you 'Mom' already and you don't think it's weird. You could write a self-help book on navigating in-law relationships. And teach me."

"Martha, you say the strangest things," laughed Sally. "By the way, what are you doing for New Year's Eve?"

"I'll probably have a quiet evening at home with Dad."

Sally shook her head. "I don't think so, Martha. We're having a party and you're invited. Nothing fancy. Mavis and Gary are coming. And a few others, mostly neighbours and real estate people. A cocktail dress will do."

"But I'm heading back to Vancouver on the third."

"Then you'll have ample time to recover from the first party of the new decade before your flight."

Martha smiled weakly, polished off her drink, and thought of several excuses she could use to escape the occasion.

Martha pulled into the driveway as Joanne and Ethan descended the porch steps. They both waved, then Ethan cut across the yard to the Kingsworth home while Joanne walked toward the driver's side of the car. With no route of escape, Martha got out and wished Joanne a merry Christmas.

"Merry Christmas to you too, Martha," said Joanne. "We've been baking. Nothing much. Just gingerbread, shortbread, and fruitcake, sugar cookies, and some squares. We figured your father could use cheering up, so we dropped off a platter of treats."

"That's very kind of you. Thank you, Joanne," said Martha.

"And we met your son and his lovely wife. Tayana had to stop Joseph from inhaling the platter. He told us you don't bake very well, so I'm glad we could do a little something to make your Christmas merry."

"Joe said that?"

"Yes. He said you're totally stressed out and you could use a brownie or three yourself."

"Stressed out?"

"Martha, if you don't mind a simple observation? As an intuitive, I do sense tension. Here, around your shoulders and jaw." Joanne balled her hands into fists and clenched her teeth, imitating Martha. "It's a sacred holiday, but some of us moms have our challenges . . . with organization . . . and managing the demands. And aligning our attitude with the spirit of the season."

"I'll relax with a stiff G and T and a half dozen brownies," said Martha. Joanne looked as if she were about to offer advice, so Martha quickly cut in. "Thanks again, Joanne. Have a wonderful Christmas. You, Ethan, and Mike."

Joanne gave her warm wishes in return and added, "We'll be away after Christmas for ten days—recharging our batteries at an all-inclusive in Punta Cana, soaking up some vitamin D. We have an alarm system, but one can't be too careful. Could you be a darling, Martha, and watch the house for us?"

Martha agreed she could. After Joanne left, she stood for a while in the crisp cold of late afternoon, surveying the scene of the old man's bungalow. Tayana's homemade wreath adorned the front door. Small piles of snow edged the pavement where Joe had shovelled. There were grassy snow angels, one Joe-sized and one Tayana-sized, on the lawn. Martha heard a carol, faint and ephemeral, in the winter air. The bay window cast a warm, golden glow.

She took a deep, bracing breath. She felt like Ebenezer Scrooge peeking through the curtains of Christmas Present. Since returning to Ontario, she'd been impatient with the old man, stiffly formal with Tayana, dishonest with Sally, evasive with Imogen, and dismissive of Joanne. She was papering over her insecurities with hostility and behaving much as Judith had in Christmas past. Jeez, that very afternoon, she couldn't even manage a friendly transaction with a helpful gas station clerk.

Other people looked forward to the holiday season; Martha dreaded it. Cheerful people would be a lot less happy if they stopped drinking the eggnog soma and faced reality—the world sucked, especially at Christmas. Consumerism was killing the planet. Little kids went hungry while their peers played with shiny, new toys made by other kids half a world away. Even that appalling colour combination, red and green, was a poke in the eye.

Yet maybe, just maybe, she was the one who wasn't facing reality.

While she sulked on the driveway, Joseph, Tayana, and the old man were probably singing along with Bing Crosby and playing Monopoly, and all the while everyone was hurtling toward death, the fate of all human beings. Being grumpy squandered valuable time. Martha took another deep breath, climbed the steps, and entered the house.

"Mom! I thought I heard the car in the driveway," smiled Joseph.

"You're just on time for Scrabble," wheezed Gordon.

"Elvis or Peanuts?" Tayana held up two CDs.

"Elvis," replied Martha. "And a cookie if there are any left. I'll need the energy to beat you three at Scrabble."

Wednesday, December 25th, 2019

And so it was Christmas, though not the Christmas Martha had dreaded. It was far worse. During the night, as parents across western Christendom put gifts under trees and ate snacks meant for Santa, Gordon developed a walloping cough that left him breathless and blue. He huffed and puffed and shook his head "no" when Martha suggested they take him to emergency, but he was overruled by the Telehealth nurse.

"It will probably be quieter than usual," she predicted. "Folks usually hold it together for the big day, then turn up to ER on Boxing Day. Go while the getting's good," she advised. Martha stuck the phone receiver against Gordon's ear so the nurse could repeat the advice to the recalcitrant patient. He gave a single, limp nod. Permission granted.

Joseph carried Gordon to the car, Tayana trailing with an oxygen tank and Martha with the old man's ID. After a hurried journey by car and hospital porter chair and a brief assessment by the triage nurse, Gordon was whisked onto a stretcher for Ventolin, high flow oxygen, and tests. Now they waited in a curtained bay, bleary eyed and pasty skinned under the fluorescent light.

Gordon squirmed on his wheeled bed. "I can't get comfortable," he complained.

"At least you can speak a whole sentence again," said Martha as she tried to beat a plank of semi-inflated plastic into pillow form. "Try this behind your shoulders."

"Marginally better," he wheezed. "What time is it?"

"3:45," said Joe.

Tayana yawned, and seconds later they all yawned.

"I'll wait with Grandpa. You two go home and get some rest," said Martha.

"But we should stay for the doctor," Joe protested as Tayana handed him his coat.

"Listen to Tayana," said Martha.

"She hasn't said anything," said Joe.

Martha raised an eyebrow. "We have no idea when the doctor will come. Grandpa is okay now. You might as well go home, sleep, and come back later. That way, we'll save money on parking."

"How can you think of money at a time like this?" asked Joe.

"It's a defence mechanism. Cold rationality," Martha joked.

She thought she saw Tayana shiver as they donned their coats to leave.

Martha dozed in a folding chair while Gordon fidgeted. Though he craved air, he craved nicotine even more, and he found himself repeatedly patting the front of his hospital gown in search of cigarettes and a lighter. This was the cruel irony of Dante's third circle, the particular hell of gluttons and addicts. Gordon couldn't go outside to smoke if his life depended on it, yet he felt as if his life depended on it. The automatic blood pressure cuff on his left arm tightened, marking another fifteen-minute interval of limbo.

"96 on 60. Let's hold off on the Lasix." The voice of an adolescent boy? Gordon looked toward a gap in the curtains. A short man in scrubs was looking past him at the monitor and speaking to someone out of eyeshot. Then he looked at Gordon. "Mr. Gray? I'm Dr. Najarian. How are you feeling?"

Martha jerked upright, jolted out of sleep, as Gordon replied, "Better."

"Good, good," the doctor murmured as he stepped toward the bed. "Mind if I have a listen?" Both Gordon and Martha tried to read his poker-faced expression as he assessed Gordon's chest with his stethoscope. "Um-hmm." He frowned at the monitor.

Now Martha stood, alert as a doe, as if ready to jump aside in case a crack ER team descended. Gordon wondered if she'd been watching too many hospital dramas.

"Mr. Gray, you're a very sick man," said Dr. Najarian.

"You don't say," wheezed Gordon.

Dr. Najarian ignored Gordon's sarcasm and spoke to Martha. "This is probably aspiration pneumonia in the setting of COPD and heart failure. He's fragile. He'll be in hospital for a few days on IV antibiotics. We'll clear the fluid from his lungs. Hopefully, he'll be home to ring in 2020."

"Thank you," said Martha.

"You're welcome. Porter will be by shortly to bring him up to our medical unit," said Dr. Najarian as he parted the curtains and left.

Gordon squawked, "That's it? I'm stranded here?"

"Looks like it," Martha said blankly.

"For crying out loud." He was trapped, like a rat behind a refrigerator at breakfast time in a greasy spoon. He desperately needed a smoke.

"Dad. You heard what the doctor said. Home by New Year's. That's good news."

"Duchess, I need a cigarette."

"What?"

"Don't ask 'what.' You wouldn't last a day in this joint without your gin." A dastardly comparison, but it delivered his point.

Martha looked weary rather than offended. She sighed and said, "Okay. Let's call the nurse. I'm sure you're not the first hardcore smoker they've dealt with. They can probably do something for you." Martha rang the call bell.

Something turned out to be a nicotine patch on his shoulder. Gordon still hankered for a cigarette but at least the symptoms of withdrawal were no longer driving him into murderous lunacy.

To his utter relief, Martha, Joseph, and Tayana had finally gone home. Now the sun was setting over the parking garage outside his window. He hadn't lifted so much as a pinky finger all day, yet he was exhausted. He'd sleep.

He'd sleep despite the sting of the IV whenever he bent his arm, the plastic mask pressing into his face, the giddy laughter of staff looking forward to shift change, the stench from the communal bathroom, and the regret of a ruined Christmas. He closed his eyes. He was aware of someone leaving a tray. He was too tired to thank the tray bearer for food he wouldn't eat.

Gordon drifted into an oddly tinted world in which a young Judy Steinman smiled and reached for him from a moving streetcar on a busy street. He ran as fast as the cars, but he couldn't catch up. He couldn't catch her.

While Martha soaked away the sour sweat from the endurance test of Elmington General, Joseph and Tayana lazed in the living room.

Tayana chawed on two pieces of Hubba Bubba, then blew an enormous bubble that Joe burst with a stab of his finger.

"Beat that," challenged Tayana.

"Nope. I can't," said Joe. "I'm chewing my pieces one at a time. Same as my liquorice allsorts. Conserving for the future."

"I've got to admit, your mom is super creative when it comes to stockings. Too bad we're not millionaires though. Imagine if we had a winning ticket. We could upgrade the bathrooms at Agape."

"Tayana, I'm wondering—"

"Uh-huh."

"Should I stay here and just you fly to Winnipeg for New Year's? Then meet back in BC, on the fifth as we planned?"

"What? That came out of the blue." Tayana's words were barbed with irritation. "Why change the plan? Don't answer that. I know your grandpa is sick, but your mom's here and she's more than capable of handling everything. I've told my family all about you. You have to come to Winnipeg. Matt and Josh are counting on it."

"Forget I suggested it," Joe said quietly. "It was a stupid idea."

"Damn right."

"Hey—you're not supposed to agree with me."

"But it was a stupid idea. It would be weird if my brand-new husband didn't come to meet my family."

"What do I care how things look, Tayana?"

"I'll forget you said that," she hissed.

Neither spoke for a few moments. Tayana blew bubbles and read the fashion magazine she'd found in her stocking. Joe read over her shoulder and wondered why she found tips on lipstick application so interesting. She didn't even use lipstick. He shifted back on the chesterfield, closed his eyes, and let his mind roam.

He had an idea. "Tayana, I'd feel better about leaving Elmington if we had a cell phone. So Mom can call me if Grandpa—"

Tayana threw her magazine onto the coffee table and turned

to Joe. "A cell phone? You know what Master Garuda says about that."

"Yeah, I've heard his lectures. Electromagnetic radiation, mind control — I get that. But look at Mom. Half the time she doesn't even know where her phone is. She's not addicted to it. She's not behaving like the zombie slave of an evil corporation. Her phone is just a tool for communicating. That's all."

"Okay. Perhaps she isn't addicted to it. But we'd get kicked out of the village if we got a phone."

"That's not exactly true. We'd get kicked out of the village if Master Garuda *found out* we got a phone."

Tayana shook her head and reached for her magazine. Her mouth was sealed into a tight, straight line.

"The silent treatment? I have a reasonable idea to give us peace of mind when we go home and you give me the silent treatment?"

"Fuck you, Joe. There. Now I'm not silent. When we joined the village, we swore an oath to renounce electronic devices. If you can't keep that minor vow, how can I trust you to keep the big ones?"

"That's not a minor vow. We don't have to worry about being manipulated by corporations because Master Garuda does it for them."

"I can't believe my ears. The answer is no, we shouldn't get a phone and yes, we should keep our promises. If that's too hard then—"

"Then what, Tayana?"

Tayana didn't reply. She got up, grabbed her coat, stamped her feet into her boots, and stomped off, slamming the door behind her.

"Everything okay?" called Martha from behind the bathroom door.

"Peachy," Joe called back.

Martha sat at the kitchen table, drinking a G and T, nibbling on sweets, and scrolling through the news on her laptop. Although it was only eight, the kids had gone to bed.

A raw turkey sat in the fridge. As she scrolled and sipped, Martha pondered the merits of squeezing the bird into the freezer or cooking it slowly overnight. Memories of chewing on dry meat verging on jerky in holidays past settled the matter. Freezer.

And she had a text to send. By now, the Wallis family celebration would be winding down.

Martha tapped:

> Merry Christmas, Imogen!

The reply was nearly instantaneous.

> Martha! Merry Christmas! How are festivities Chez Gray?

> Cancelled. Dad's in the hospital with pneumonia.

> What? That's terrible. Why the bloody hell didn't you tell me? I'm phoning, you poor, adorable bitch. Pick up.

Thursday, December 26th, 2019

While Joseph and Tayana shopped for Boxing Day bargains, Imogen and Martha made their way to Gordon's hospital room through a labyrinth of hallways, alcoves, and fire doors. As the

Telehealth nurse had predicted, the casualties of over-indulgence now dozed in stretchers and wheelchairs haphazardly lining the corridors. Gordon had a new roommate. A sixtyish man occupied the bed that had been empty the day before.

"He sleeps all the time. Just wakes to hork up gunk, then the sandman takes him again," said Gordon's roommate. "You the daughters?"

"She is," said Imogen. "I'm a friend."

"Bill here. Awful time to get sick. But there's no rule that states you can't expire on the day of the Good Lord's birth—or the day after."

Martha startled at the word "expire" and Bill quickly added, "Not that anyone's expiring just yet. But Gordon don't look too good. We made our acquaintance, then he went down for the count. The emphysema? Yup, I can tell by the wheeze. Had an uncle pass from that. They say it's like you're breathing through a straw. Me, I got the angina bad after supper yesterday. A knife right here." Bill thumped his sternum. "The nitro wouldn't stop it. The wife insisted I be seen to, and the rest is history. 'Holiday heart,' the doc called it. Now I'm hooked up to these wires. Chest looks like a switchboard. Can't complain though. Had a cousin took sick on holiday in Arizona without insurance—"

Gordon stirred under his tangled blankets and moved his hand in a beckoning gesture. Martha went to him, and he rasped, "Pull the curtain."

Imogen was already tugging the pale blue drape that hung from the rail between the beds and smiling an apology for cutting the conversation short. She peeked around the fabric edge and said gently, "Bloody nasty luck you've had, Bill. I hope you're better soon."

Somehow Gordon had slid in his bed with his knees drawn up and his head pitched forward. "Help," he wheezed. His face was a similar colour to the drapery, thought Martha. The colour of an old man on the threshold of death.

Imogen pressed the call bell.

"We can't wait for the nurses," Martha said. "We've got to sit him up. Grab hold of that pad underneath him and we'll slide him up the bed." Imogen's eyes searched Martha's and Martha explained, "That's what the nurses did when my mother was sick. On the count of three, we pull hard." She counted, and in an instant Gordon was repositioned.

"Thanks," Gordon wheezed. "Urinal."

Martha froze, not comprehending.

Imogen picked up a curved, plastic bottle from the side table. "This thing?" she asked.

"Yeah. Need help. Diaper," came Gordon's staccato reply.

Martha lifted Gordon's gown and saw his predicament at once. The old man was sitting in a sodden blue wad fixed in place by tabs.

"Turn around, Martha. I'll take care of this," said Imogen.

Martha did as she was told. For what seemed an epoch, she watched a flock of gulls circling over the parking garage and listened to the rustle of bed clothes, Imogen's soothing murmur, and the old man's cough. Gordon was too ill for modesty. Too ill to fend for himself even in this supposed haven. She should've stayed overnight.

"You're a pro, lass," wheezed Gordon. "Thanks."

Martha turned around.

Imogen smiled at the patient. "I'm crazy aunt to seven nieces and nephews. At least you're cooperative, Gordon."

A woman wearing a Santa-themed smock appeared at the foot of the bed. "Can I help you?"

"Too late," said Imogen. "He needed a urinal."

"I'll empty that. He's voiding a lot because of the IV," the nurse stated without apology.

"He was in a bloody mess when we got here," said Imogen. "We rang the bell ages ago. We had to clean him up ourselves."

"He wasn't breathing very well," Martha added.

"I'm sorry. We're over-capacity and we're doing our best."

Gordon grimaced and waved his hand as if directing a choir to lower the volume.

Martha had nothing to say anyway. Old people likely died every day in hospital beds under the noses of personnel who pleaded overwork. Though the institutional indifference to the old man's plight was infuriating, challenging the nurse's excuse was futile because there was no way to judge its truth. She'd just have to make sure the old man wasn't left by himself without advocate or aide.

Evidently, Imogen felt differently. Words sharp as icicles, she said, "Tell me, nurse, are dead patients easier to care for than live ones? He was almost fucking gone when we arrived. He couldn't breathe the way we found him."

Red-faced, the nurse backed away as Bill tossed in his two cents from the other side of the curtain. "Dead buggers don't ring the bell. That'd save a few steps."

Joe weighed the iPhone in his hand, eager to test its features.

"We agreed on a flip phone," said Tayana. "Texting and calling only. No data."

"I know. There's nothing wrong with staying abreast of new technological innovations."

"Staying abreast? Who even says that? You sound like your mother."

"Oh?" Joe shrugged but he didn't take his eyes off the phone.

A salesperson in a blue polo shirt approached and asked if they needed assistance.

Joe started to reply, but Tayana laid her hand on Joe's arm to stop him and said, "Not now. We're just looking today."

"Sale's on till the thirty-first, but we'll be out of stock on some items before then."

"Thanks. We'll keep that in mind," said Tayana.

After the salesperson turned away, Joe said, "Thank you for not humiliating me by asking about a flip phone."

"What?"

"The flip phone. It's like wearing orthopedic shoes."

"I heard what you said, but I don't understand your attitude. Yesterday, you said you didn't care what my family thought. Today you're worried what a salesclerk thinks if you don't buy a fancy phone. A stranger who you'll never see again."

Joe shook his head and scrolled through the menu of games on the screen.

"Joe, what does Master Garuda say about status envy?"

"I can't remember. I'm tired of living like a Mennonite, Tayana. I mean, look at this thing. Everything we do on the desktop in the library we can do on this little box, without Garuda's parental controls."

"You want to cruise porn sites?"

"Of course not. You're deliberately misunderstanding me."

"If Agape is too freaking restrictive for you, why did you join?"

Joe put the phone back on the rack, turned to Tayana, and said gently, "For you."

"For me?"

"Well, yeah. Garuda knows it too. He knew I wouldn't leave last fall because of you. He needs strong backs. Tiger and Wolfgang work half as fast as I do. The other guys are old. He married us in a hurry to make sure I'd return after winter break. Worked out well, I'd say."

"You'd say."

"Is there an echo?" Joe joked.

"No. A divorce." For the second time in as many days, Tayana stalked off—this time with Joe in pursuit wondering why his revelation made her so angry.

After assessing Gordon, Dr. Najarian guided Martha and Imogen to a tiny sitting room at the end of the corridor and bid them be seated.

"As you are aware, Gordon is very sick. He's marginally better today, and that's what we want to see—improvement, even incremental, day by day. He still needs the mask, but his oxygen saturation is stable. He's receiving a powerful antibiotic by IV, and diuretics and steroid treatments. We'll do a CT scan to check for malignancy or some other disease process, but I believe we're dealing with a simple, straight forward, aspiration pneumonia." Dr. Najarian paused and looked at Martha and Imogen to judge their level of comprehension. "It's not contagious," he added.

"You do expect him to get better?" asked Imogen.

"That is what we hope for. He's in the battle of his life. Usually, I'd transfer someone as sick as Gordon to ICU, but he declined that level of care. You understand that he does not want to be resuscitated if he stops breathing or if his heart stops beating. No tubes, no ventilator."

"He's a DNR," confirmed Martha.

Dr. Najarian smiled mildly. "Yes. Precisely."

"Can't you overrule him? For his own good?" asked Imogen.

Martha shook her head and Dr. Najarian replied, "That wouldn't be appropriate or legal. Gordon is of sound mind and that decision is his to make."

"But the ICU has one-on-one nursing care, right? Here, on the medical unit, he's lost in the shuffle," pleaded Imogen.

"It's okay, Imogen," said Martha.

"No, it's not. Dr. Najarian, when we got here today, Gordon was curled up at the bottom of his bed, wet with urine, struggling to breathe. He'd be better off in the ICU."

"That's terribly unfortunate," Dr. Najarian frowned. "I

advise you to report that to the charge nurse. I'll have a word with her myself."

For a moment, no one spoke. Dr. Najarian took advantage of the lull to stand and move toward the doorway. "Hopefully in three or four days, we can start planning for discharge in early January. When Gordon's stronger, physio will work with him, and the occupational therapist will determine his capabilities. That said, I don't foresee Gordon managing at home alone. It's not too soon to plan for that."

When Martha and Imogen returned to Gordon's room, they found Joe reading *Eat, Pray, Love* to the old man who was propped on a pillow, eyes closed, just breathing. Joe placed the book face down on the sill and looked up at Martha and Imogen.

"We just met with Dr. Najarian," said Martha. "Where's Tayana?"

"Resting," replied Joe. "What did the doctor say?"

"He said Grandpa's improving."

They careened from the garage in Imogen's Yaris hatchback into busy streets, speeding round corners and darting through gaps in the traffic. Martha grabbed the handgrip above the door to brace herself.

"There's no call for bloody theatrics, Lady MacBeth," said Imogen as she swerved around a truck. "This vehicle's engineered for city driving. On the remote chance anything hits us, we'll be safe in the interior of a marshmallow."

Or crushed under the bumper of a Hummer, thought Martha. She said, "It's you hitting someone else that worries me, Imogen. We're in no rush."

Imogen laid a reassuring hand on Martha's knee.

"Two hands on the wheel," squeaked Martha. "For safety."

"Let's grab coffee and go down by the lake. Hash things out,"

Imogen suggested. "Away from the drama of a marriage in trouble."

"What makes you say that?"

"*Resting?* Do you really believe Tayana's resting? You saw the hangdog look on Joe's face. She ditched him for the afternoon. Let's give her time alone."

"I won't pretend to know—"

"No. That's safer." Imogen took a Tim Horton's gift card from the visor and tossed it onto Martha's lap. "Won it at the holiday office party. Coffee's on me."

Hot drinks in cup holders, they parked on a dirt lot near a marina, facing over Lake Ontario. The snow and ice had melted, and waves crashed onto the gravel beach, tossing up freezing bullets of water.

"I never get tired of watching the lake." Imogen shifted her seat back and stretched her long legs.

"Me neither. Dad taught me to canoe not far from here."

"Your dad..."

Martha stared straight through the windshield. "Do you think he'll get better, Imogen?"

"Yes. This time."

"We didn't win a friend with that charge nurse. Dale Carnegie would be disappointed in us."

"Fuck Dale Carnegie. Gordon's life is worth more than the nurse's bloody feelings. Disapproval is a powerful motivator, and they know we're watching. The stick is mightier than the carrot. You can use that in your book."

"I'm not sure if that's true, Imogen. We don't want to make enemies of the people who are caring for Dad."

"Enemies, shnenemies. The sooner he's out of there the better."

"I'll cancel the support worker and Meals on Wheels tomorrow. I have an excuse to wiggle out of a New Year's Eve party I was dreading too."

"There you go, Martha. Lemonade from lemons."

They sipped their coffee and listened to the roar of the lake.

Imogen spoke first. "Do you want me to drive you back to the hospital tonight?"

"No, that's okay," answered Martha. "I'll have supper with the kids and go back myself. They're due to fly out on Saturday."

"And what about you? You can't go back to BC—"

"No, I expect not. I'll have to let the department head know. September all over again."

Imogen slipped her hand around Martha's and they watched the waves in silence.

Supper was a stiffly formal affair with conversation limited to requests for the saltshaker or the passing of butter. In the afternoon, Tayana had accepted a Meals on Wheels delivery from Sarah, who'd expressed her concern for Gordon and her good wishes to the household. Martha divided the roast beef supper three ways and added a salad and bread to extend the rations.

"I'll go grocery shopping in the morning," said Martha as Joe took his empty plate to the sink and grabbed a cookie from the sweet tray. He ate it in a single bite.

"And I'll do the dishes," said Tayana.

Joe picked up a tea towel, but Tayana refused his help. "Spend some time with your mom, Joe. I'd prefer to be alone," she said in a monotone.

Joe shrank away, and when Martha suggested they go for a walk, he headed for the door.

"Christmas lights don't look as nice without the snow," Joe said as they walked along a row of extravagantly decorated houses.

"Another green Christmas," said Martha. "But you'll have snow in Winnipeg."

"I don't know if I'll go."

"Oh?"

Joe kicked a stone up the sidewalk, then kicked it again when they reached it.

After the third kick, Martha said, "It's none of my business—whatever's happening between you and Tayana—but you should probably fix it instead of running away."

"Mom, I feel like I've made a huge mistake."

They walked in silence for half a block, then he continued, "I love Tayana, but I can't stand living at the Ecovillage and they're a package deal. I've been going along with everything for months . . . the crazy rules . . . everyone kissing Garuda's ass. We're fighting over buying a goddam cell phone."

"A cell phone?"

"Well, that and what the phone represents. I feel trapped."

"Trapped by Tayana?"

"No. Jesus, Mom. The community—Agape Ecovillage. It's smothering."

"There are some decisions that you're within your rights to make on your own."

"Okay."

"You don't need to consult your spouse on every detail of life. Tayana's your wife, not your mommy. If you want a phone, buy a goddam phone."

"You're quoting me."

"Yup."

"Where were you yesterday with that advice?"

"Attending the sickbed. You know, Joe, I'm always happy to talk. I really missed you when you were out of reach."

"I know."

"Are you okay for money?"

"Yes, Mom. Plenty in the bank from tree planting last spring. That's the only advantage of communal living. It's economical. Do you have time to walk all the way to the lake?"

"Absolutely," said Martha.

They cut through a park, then strolled down a street of century homes, chatting about this and that. The bare branches of massive maples and oaks clattered in a light breeze. Joe was leaving in two days and the old man was gravely ill and Martha still had to return to the hospital that evening, yet she felt happy. Ecstatically happy. For once she and Joe were simply mother and son, like normal people.

Friday, December 27th, 2019

Gordon's eyes fluttered open in the night. He coughed up a hamster-sized wad of phlegm, then felt around for a tissue box. For crying out loud. For want of this small necessary he had to lift his mask, spit into the corner of the sheet, then ball it up to hide the evidence.

He heard snoring. Beeps and bells. A big window, a bed next to his . . . what the? Hospital. Now he remembered. He ached from crown to toe, especially his neck from the crumby pillow. Breathing hurt.

"You awake, Gord?" A voice in the dark. "Gord? You okay?"

"Yes," Gordon rasped. "Elmington General. Christmas time. Six times seven is forty-two. The capital of Spain is Madrid."

"Well, aren't you a sharp bugger."

"Thanks. Remind me of your—"

"Bill. We're previously acquainted. You might've been addled by the delirium at the time."

"Bill, what day is it?"

"Friday, December the twenty-seventh. It's the middle of the night, 'bout three."

"Jeez. I think I lost a couple days."

"You won't miss them. They weren't nothing to write home about."

Gordon coughed again, then said, "Fill me in anyway, Bill."

"Okay. You've got the pneumonia. Was touch and go but looks like you're denying Jesus the pleasure of your company after all. Your daughter Martha went home about an hour ago. Said she loves you and she'll be back in the morning with the kids."

"You're a courtroom stenographer, Bill."

"No, Gord. Logistics. Long-haul trucking. Unless the doc takes my licence away."

"Don't you sleep?" Gordon asked, genuinely curious.

"Nope. I can't. I'm worried sick. I've gotta pay for my rig and the wife likes to shop. She's a collector. You name it—Beanie Babies, Peter Rabbit dishes, and what have you. Says they're an investment but I'm not convinced of the value. I'm in a shit-smeared pickle if I can't convince the doc I'm safe to drive."

"What's wrong with you?"

"A bum ticker and the diabetes. Clogged arteries. They're deciding how to fix them. Might need a bypass. Hey, Gord. Want a drink? Bedside service at this hotel, though it's a dry establishment. Some of the nurses are awful easy on the eyes. A distraction from life's troubles."

Gordon's tongue felt like sandpaper. "Sure. Juice," he said.

"I'll ring the bell," said Bill. "You're a sack of bones, Gord. Better ask for a snack too."

At nine am, Gordon was roused from a nap by a fit man who was a dead ringer for Ed Allen, from his Elvis-inspired haircut to his snugly tucked T-shirt and high-waisted polyester trousers.

"I'm Jason, the physiotherapist," he said. "Gordon Gray?"

Gordon nodded.

"Excellent. Today our focus is your breathing and mobility and our goal is for you to sit in the chair." Jason set his clipboard on the windowsill and clapped his hands twice. "Ready!"

"No jumping jacks?" wheezed Gordon.

"Not today. First, let's have you sit at the side of the bed and dangle your feet."

Gordon felt woozy as Jason elevated the head of the bed. "I'm weak as a kitten," Gordon muttered.

"That's because you're deconditioned." Jason frowned. "You've been allowed to lounge, muscles atrophying, strength diminishing. There's a saying. 'Use it or lose it.' This concept must be foremost in your mind during your rehabilitation." Jason used his forearm like a shovel under Gordon's knees and swung him around as if he were positioning a mannequin in a department store window. "There," Jason said with satisfaction.

The position change provoked a coughing fit. Jason placed a box of tissues beside Gordon. "Very good," he pronounced. "Balance, breathe deeply, and cough." He strode to the other side of the bed and pounded on Gordon's back. "Again," he commanded.

After enduring Jason's blows, Gordon pleaded exhaustion, but Jason wouldn't have it. "Gordon, remember what I said. Use it or lose it. Fifteen minutes in the chair."

"But coach . . ." Gordon whined. Jason had already produced a pair of yellow socks with non-skid stripes from his back pocket and was pulling them onto Gordon's feet.

"We will stand, pivot, and sit," said Jason.

"But there's only one chair," argued Gordon.

"You will sit," Jason clarified, missing Gordon's joke entirely. On the other side of the curtain, Bill laughed, prompting Gordon to smile like a class clown.

"Focus," Jason scolded. "On the count of three, push with your legs and stand up."

Jason counted and heaved Gordon to his feet, then deposited

him on the chair. "Well done, Gordon" he said. "I'm proud of you." After he tucked a blanket round Gordon's legs, he took a paper from his clipboard and handed it to Gordon. "This is your exercise program," said Jason. "Arm lifts, leg lifts, and foot circles. We'll go over each movement later."

Gordon fought a bubbling well of nausea. "Ten minutes?" he wheezed.

"Fifteen. Here's your call bell." Jason clipped the cord to Gordon's gown, then opened the curtain and strode away with his clipboard tucked under his arm.

Bill lay on his side facing Gordon's bed. "You won't achieve a shapely figure without effort, Gord," he deadpanned.

"Look who's talking," Gordon wheezed irritably.

The time came for good-bye. Joseph and Tayana were booked on an early flight the next morning and needed rest. Martha absented herself from the room on the pretext of buying a parking pass. Bill buried himself in a hunting magazine. A hush descended, broken only by an unintelligible conversation in the corridor and the rhythmic whoosh of the IV pump as it delivered the old man's evening dose of antibiotic.

"We'll come back as soon as we can, Grandpa," said Joe.

"You'd better. I'm on tenterhooks wondering if Elizabeth Gilbert will self-actualize."

"You're so funny, Grandpa." Tayana reached over the bedrail and squeezed Gordon's hand.

With unexpected strength, Gordon grabbed Tayana's wrist and pulled her in for a hug. "You too, Joe," he said.

Joe leaned in and wrapped the old man in his arms. Joe wouldn't cry, especially in front of an audience. "Promise me you'll get better," he whispered.

Gordon shook his head, then coughed to muster his breath

to continue speaking. "Promise me you'll take care of Tayana and your mother. They're smart, independent women and they'll tell you they don't need a man to watch out for them, but don't believe them. They need you."

Tayana argued, "I don't think we need—"

Gordon looked her in the eye and interrupted. "Martha would have a fifty percent chance of blowing herself up if she had to start a car with jumper cables."

With all the subtlety of a pufferfish, Joe squared his shoulders and vowed, "I'll take care of them, Grandpa. You don't need to worry about that."

"That's my Joe," Gordon said solemnly.

Tayana crossed her arms and rolled her eyes.

After Tayana and Joe left, Bill said, "That girl's a live wire, Gord. Your grandson will have his hands full with her."

"He won't be bored," Gordon concurred.

"She reminds me of my cousin, Nora. Tongue as sharp as a slice of Limburger. Has her husband wrapped around her finger like a dew worm on hook. One day, she saw a home decorating show on the TV, and she made him hang pink wallpaper in the rumpus room. Imagine playing pool with your buddies in a goddam field of roses and carnations. . . ."

Too exhausted to feel bereft from the parting, Gordon drifted into a dreamless sleep to the soundtrack of Bill's prattle.

Saturday, December 28th, 2019

Martha was jarred from a semi-comatose state by the ring of her cell phone. She reached over the coffee table and fumbled for it, grabbing it just on time. "Hello?" she answered.

"Are you alright, Mom?"

"I'm not your mom," protested Martha, voice hoarse from booze and sleep.

"True. Are you alright, sexy bitch? Because you don't sound alright."

"I'm fine, Imogen."

"Really? You sound fucking depressed. As if you're about to slash your wrists with a broken gin bottle . . . because you drank the whole thing and now it's empty just like your cold, empty heart and you won't see your precious boy till God knows when so you may bloody well pack it in—"

"Hold on. Are you trying to make me feel better?" asked Martha.

"Yup. Reverse psychology. Is it working?"

"Sort of," Martha conceded. "Actually, I'm not really blue. We had a good visit and the kids said they'd stay in touch. Dad seems to have turned a corner. Yes, I've been drinking. I was sober all week so tonight I'm scratching my itch. I won't apologize for it."

"I wouldn't dream of asking you to. Go on. Bottoms up. You deserve it."

"How was the movie?"

"*Jumanji*? The kids loved it. I binged on popcorn and Twizzlers."

"What's it about?"

"It's rather complicated. It's about a video game and—hey, Martha. I have an idea."

"Oh?"

"Why don't I come over and tell you all about it? I'll bring a bottle in case you're running low."

"Umm, I don't know. It's late."

"Precisely. It's grown-up time. The brats are back with their parents and I'm craving adult company."

"I guess . . ."

"Great," squealed Imogen. "See you in ten."

Martha put her phone on the coffee table and wondered what she'd agreed to.

Sunday, December 29th, 2019

Early the next morning, Martha still wondered. She awoke with a jackhammer headache and a stomach that felt like Krakatoa emerging from dormancy. She lay in her single bed, but she wasn't alone. Jesus. At least she was fully clothed. A bejewelled hand rested on her hip. She lifted the hand and its owner mumbled and turned over. Martha squinted and stole a dizzying glance over her shoulder. Thank God. In the dimness she saw that Imogen was fully clothed too.

Martha closed her eyes and tried to reassemble the pieces of her fractured memory. There'd been Chinese food, flirtation with an embarrassed delivery man, a lot more booze, a juvenile game of truth or dare, embarrassing confessions, and maudlin tears and comforting. A hug. Lots of hugs. A kiss? Had they kissed? Jesus. Had she let Imogen kiss her?

Martha suspected she had. She felt as if she'd suffocate if she breathed the same air as Imogen for even a second longer. She slipped out of bed as quietly as a profoundly hungover, arthritic, fat woman could, and crept to the kitchen for a glass of water and Tylenol. She leaned over the sink to collect herself.

She was used to the cycle of solo drinking—of hungry need, having just one, anxiety melting away, finishing the bottle, waking in panic, coping with aftermath, and vowing to be temperate. Wash, rinse, repeat, by herself. This felt very weird. She hadn't woken to a surprise bedmate since she was newly divorced. She had to figure out exactly what had happened and what to do about it.

Fortified by three extra strength tablets and warm tap water, she steadied her hand and wrote:

Good morning, Imogen,

Wasn't that a party? Might've been the gin, eh?

I feel awful so I've stepped out for some fresh air. I'll be gone a while. Help yourself to anything you want in the kitchen. Don't bother locking the door when you leave. Thieves don't steal on Sundays.

Martha

After a steadying espresso in a café and a penitential walk on the waterfront, Martha returned to 22 Roselea at eleven, relieved the Yaris wasn't in the driveway. The house was tidy. Take-out containers and empty bottles and cans filled the kitchen blue box. Glasses sparkled on the drainboard. Bits of food and sticky rings had been wiped away from the tabletops. Martha found the note she'd written on the coffee table. Below it, Imogen had scrawled a note in reply:

Hi Martha,

Hope you're not too tender from our party. As they say, "Drink in haste, repent at leisure." We had fun, so the pain's worth it.

Martha – You're a fucking cunt tease, but I'm a perfect gentlewoman so I'm trying my utmost not to pressure you. We cuddled like schoolgirls, and it was bloody fantastic, but I want more. I also want you in my life even if you don't want more. Just don't toy with me, okay?

I'll lay low for a few days to give you space.

Love,

Imogen X

Martha turned the note over and huffed, "Cunt tease." It was a wildly unfair epithet. Imogen had invited herself over, kept the booze flowing, and, with no green signal in sight, instigated whatever had happened. Imogen was the one who toyed and manipulated, not her.

Martha flopped onto the chesterfield, picked up the note,

and reread it. Then she read it again. Imogen wasn't victimizing her. She was expressing desire, issuing an invitation, and cautioning her that she felt vulnerable. Far from predatory, Imogen had lobbed a ball into her court, and Martha controlled play. She had to decide.

She rewound the fuzzy film of the previous night in her brain. When Imogen brushed some sauce off her cheek, she was revolted and attracted. Every time Imogen touched her, she felt ill and she longed for more. She didn't remember a kiss—not exactly—but she probably would've kissed Imogen back. Martha wasn't gay, but she was celibate, and the lifestyle was wearing thin—threadbare, actually—with nary a man to mend the holes.

Martha tore the paper into tiny flakes and let them flutter onto the carpet so she couldn't obsess over Imogen's note and no one else could ever find it and read it.

Monday, December 30th, 2019

Gordon sat in a wheelchair with a portable oxygen tank slung over its handle and a box of tissues on his lap. Martha sat to his right. Across the table the discharge planner, a prune-faced woman named Kay Smythe, presided over their meeting. A standard issue, institutional clipboard and a large binder with Gordon's name on its spine faced her at a right angle to the table edge. Gordon had come across Kay's type in budget meetings at city hall, and he was tempted to demand copies of all her papers so he wouldn't be at a disadvantage, but he decided against succumbing to paranoia.

"I'm afraid my colleagues have been remiss in not initiating the discharge process sooner," Kay said briskly.

"Dad was very sick," said Martha. "They couldn't have—"

Kay closed her eyes, tilted her head back, and sniffed, "We

begin planning for discharge at the time of admission. This is how we facilitate movement through the system."

An unwelcome association of fecal matter in bowels arose in Gordon's mind and he rasped, "When I arrived on Christmas Day, the discharge plan would've been a body bag and a hearse."

"Nevertheless," continued Kay, "Your file has not been handled in a timely manner and your progress through the care plan is lagging. Now, shall we review your current status, Mr. Gray?"

"Please call me 'Gordon'. Sure. Go ahead."

"Gordon." Kay perched a pair of reading glasses on her nose and opened a file. "We're at day five. Dr. Najarian switched you to an oral antibiotic and puffers yesterday. You're off the oxygen mask and back on nasal prongs. The dietician reports that you're eating poorly but you're taking fluids adequately by mouth. According to the therapists, you're able to sit for up to an hour in a chair, but you require one-person assistance with transfers, toileting, and care. You perform your exercises, including deep breathing and coughing, with prompting, not independently. And finally, your cognition is intact."

Gordon nodded. He felt oddly detached from this uncannily accurate assessment, as if he were submitting to a performance evaluation in a personnel office in dreamland.

"At this juncture, there is little the hospital can do for you," added Kay. "I've contacted Sonya Tam, the case manager in the community, and she informed me that you live alone, on one level, with three stairs at the entrance and that you're a smoker. Correct?"

"Yes," said Gordon.

Kay turned to Martha and said gently, "She also shared that you can't be expected to help too much."

"Well, I live in Vancouver," said Martha. "I'll help Dad as much as I can though."

Kay flashed a patronizing "there's a good girl" smile at Martha and turned back to Gordon.

"You meet the criteria for admission to a crisis bed in long-term care."

"Uh-uh. No way." Gordon's face turned a furious red. "I won't agree to that."

"Gordon, this could be a short-term admission to give you time to regain your mobility and stamina in a supportive environment."

Gordon wheeled his chair back and angled it away from the table. "Do you have a Plan B, Kay?"

"Yes, of course, though it's less than ideal. It's certainly not as safe." She gathered her papers into a neat pile. "You'd return to your home, and we'd arrange support through Sonya Tam. It's a lot for Martha to manage, and your smoking and noncompliance with therapy measures give us some pause."

"I'm taking time off work," offered Martha.

"Plan B. That's what I want," Gordon declared. "When can I go home?"

"That's up to Dr. Najarian," replied Kay. "January second is realistic if you're choosing to return to your own home. The New Year holiday delays the process somewhat and we'll need to resume services and have you fitted for a wheelchair."

"Plan B it is," said Gordon. "Thank you, Kay." He extended a knobby hand over the desk as if sealing a deal after lengthy negotiation at city hall.

Kay appeared to perform an infectious disease assessment on the proffered extremity, then, after a brief hesitation, she extended her own hand and shook.

After the meeting, as Martha pushed Gordon back to his room, he said, "I told her, didn't I, Duchess? What a tight-assed, officious, awful woman. She even threw her colleagues under the bus."

"I didn't think she was awful," soothed Martha. "She was just doing her job."

"So were the KGB, Duchess. So were the KGB."

Back at the room, they found Bill in his street clothes, also seated in a wheelchair. His belongings had been packed into two plastic bags and slung onto the chair handles in the manner of Gordon's oxygen tank.

"Doc just delivered my get out of jail card. I still have to go for a test, then Denise is picking me up at the front entrance. The porter should be here soon."

"No surgery, Bill?" asked Gordon.

"Surgery's next week, so I'll be on a conjugal visit rather than full parole." Bill winked suggestively, though Gordon doubted Denise would see any action. "Gord, you being a librarian, I thought you'd appreciate having some reading material so I left my magazines and a half-decent paperback on your bed. Enjoy."

"That's generous of you, Bill. Thanks," wheezed Gordon as Martha pushed him to his half of the room. "A Jack Reacher novel. That'll be fun."

"Denise didn't know I already read it when she brung it in last night. It's a good one. Jack has to stop a rogue nuclear physicist, who's secretly in cahoots with the North Koreans, from blowing up a nuclear power plant that's sitting smack dab on the San Andreas fault. While working security at a cocktail party thrown by the governor, Jack meets an Asian lady with a mysterious butterfly tattoo who's skilled in the art of Thai massage. The strange thing is, she doesn't even speak Thai. She has a Russian accent. Meanwhile...."

Martha ducked out of the conversation to find a washroom. She had a feeling the old man wouldn't have to read the book to know its every detail once Bill had finished outlining the plot.

After supper, Martha lay on the chesterfield, gazing at the Christmas tree. The needles had dried to a faded, military green due to its unquenched thirst. It was still pretty though. She'd leave it up till after the second so the old man could admire it one more time before it was transformed into mulch at the municipal garden waste depot. Other tasks took priority over cleaning up Christmas—some she dreaded.

On the surface, the dean would bubble with bromides when he heard of her predicament, and he'd grant her a leave of absence, but there'd be payback for inconveniencing him. A petty man, he could scuttle her pet grad course, "From Marx to Malthus: Victorian Bio-Economic Philosophy," or sentence her to Philosophy 101 until End Times. Her cell rattled on the table.

"Hello?" she answered.

"Martha. It's Sally. I got your email and I thought I'd check in."

"That's sweet of you. How was your Christmas?"

"Lovely. Obviously, yours wasn't. How's your father?"

"Much better. He's getting around in a wheelchair and flirting with the nurses. He'll probably come home on Thursday."

"That's wonderful news. The invitation still stands . . . for tomorrow night."

"I wish I could be there, but I don't think I can make it, Sally. As I mentioned in the email, I'll be at the hospital helping Dad."

"Well, drop by if you can. Come at midnight for the countdown. When are you returning to Vancouver?"

"I'm not. I'm taking time off to help Dad get stronger. Failing that, I'll have to move him into a place where he can get the help he needs."

"If there's anything I can do . . . Looking after old people is so stressful. Like toddlers except they don't grow out of it. Hey—I know." Sally giggled.

"Know what?"

"Yoga. It's a stress reliever. I'll bring you to my class."

"But I don't—"

"This time no 'buts,' Martha. You'll need to take breaks from caregiving. It's like on the airplane when it's heading for disaster and the oxygen masks drop down. They tell you to put one on yourself before you help someone else, even a baby. It's called 'caring for the caregiver.' Yoga is definitely the answer."

"I don't think I'd—"

"That's the doorbell. I've got to go. The caterer is dropping off the centrepieces and linen for tomorrow. Tootles."

Tootles? Jesus. Yoga? Martha hadn't participated in an exercise class in years. She lifted one leg to test her flexibility, then the other. Her limbs moved like the components in a rusty Swiss army knife. Maybe yoga would limber them up.

She was too rigid—physically, mentally, and emotionally. She wished she were spontaneous like Sally and Joseph and the old man and Imogen. Spontaneous and generous were a matched set and she was neither. It seemed as if every act of kindness she'd ever undertaken was preceded by a cost-benefit analysis.

Imogen was the polar opposite. No pretense, no premeditation, driven by instinct. Poor Imogen. She said she'd "lay low" and that likely meant she was waiting for a call, hanging by the phone like a lovesick teenager. After two days, it was high time Martha texted her.

> Hey

Imogen's reply lit the screen a couple minutes later.

> Hey yourself

> It's almost 2020. We should celebrate.

>> What do you suggest?

> New Year's Eve?

>> Sorry. I'm going to a party with some old chums and taking the brats skating on New Year's Day. Maybe later in the week. How's Gordon?

> Better. I'm bringing him home on Jan 2.

>> That's great! Maybe I'll catch up with you then. After work if I'm not too tired?

> OK.

Martha put her phone down. "If she's not too tired," Martha mocked bitterly. Unexpectedly alone for New Year's Eve. Damn, damn, damn. The tree wasn't pretty at all. It looked terrible. Dusty, dead, and shrouded in humiliating tinsel. The Christmas season was definitely over.

Thursday, January 2nd, 2020

Martha found the old man dressed, seated in a porter chair, and clutching a Manila envelope.

"You're late, Duchess. I was about to ask the charge nurse to phone in a missing person's report."

"Sorry, Dad. I slept in." Martha apologized as she attached an oxygen tank from home to Gordon's tubing. "What's in the envelope?"

"Basic 'care and keeping of Gordon' instructions," he rasped. "Prescriptions, phone numbers for homecare, which we have anyway, and a letter for Dr. Southey."

"I should thank the nurses."

"Don't bother, Duchess. I already have. Let's get out of here."

Martha helped Gordon into his winter coat. As she pushed the porter chair out of the room, Gordon saluted good-bye to the frail, elderly man who'd replaced Bill in the next bed.

Midway down the corridor, Gordon asked, "Did you remember to bring my cigarettes?"

"What?"

"Pardon. My cigarettes."

"Umm..."

"For crying out loud, Martha. Yesterday, that was the one thing I asked you not to forget and you even repeated it back to me. Twice."

Martha pressed the down button at a bank of elevator doors. "I'm sorry, Dad. You have your nicotine patch, and you can't smoke on hospital grounds anyway."

"A blatant falsehood. I've seen people smoking on the sidewalk out front."

Martha had too—even some smokers wearing hospital gowns under their jackets and pushing IV poles. She was fairly certain the tobacco fanciers were violating a "no smoking" edict, but to say so was to pour gasoline onto Gordon's smouldering annoyance. "Let's buy you a pack on our way home. I'll even let you smoke in the car with the windows open," she suggested.

"That's generous of you. Letting me smoke in my own car."

"Dad..."

"The Corolla is smoke free. I would never sully her in that way."

"Her?"

Gordon ignored Martha's comment. "Is the parking pass still valid?" he wheezed.

"Yes."

"Then kick it up a notch, Duchess, and get us the hell out of here. There's a convenience store on Lakeshore with parking right in front. We'll go there, then to Practi-Care Health for the wheelchair, and last to the pharmacy."

"I'm pushing the chair as fast as I can," said Martha.

"You'd be faster if you weren't hungover," goaded Gordon.

By 7:00 pm, Martha had already tucked the old man into bed for the night. Her headache was finally subsiding, so she brewed a cup of Earl Grey and set up a temporary workspace at the kitchen table. Tonight she'd be productive. Work was the only reliable antidote to the wheel-spinning misery of the last forty-eight hours. It was solace from self-inflicted, circular loneliness, disappointment, and worry. She typed a dozen versions of the first sentence of an introductory chapter for *It's All Your Fault*, but each slid around on the screen, offering no traction, no hook, for a hypothetical reader to fasten onto. She googled "writer's block" and diddled and dawdled for the better part of an hour when Imogen called.

"Hey," said Imogen.

"Hey yourself," replied Martha.

"So."

"So."

Silence.

"How's your dad?"

"Fine. Sleeping."

"So he's home."

"I told you he was coming home today," Martha said, sounding cooler than she'd intended.

More silence.

"How was your New Year?" Martha ventured.

"Okay. Great. Crappy. My old friend who used to be interesting is expecting her fourth kid. Her husband is teetotal in solidarity. He droned on and on about their genius progeny. How anyone can tell that a fetus is bloody brilliant by a blurry ultrasound image is beyond me and I told him so, which ruffled his cock feathers. The other couple has gone full frontal keto, and booze has too many fucking carbs for their sacred body temples. The conversation was as boring as a stats lecture. Did you know that hummus has six grams of carbs per serving? You're welcome. How was your New Year's?"

"Crappy also. I went on a two-day bender."

"Martha."

"I know. I know. I'm so stupid."

"Yes, you are," said Imogen. "Lovable and stupid."

Tears flooded Martha's eyes.

"Do you want me to come over?" asked Imogen.

Martha didn't answer. She didn't want Imogen to know she was crying.

"Martha, I'm coming over right now."

"I'm okay," Martha choked.

"I'll see that for myself, Martha fucking stupid Gray," said Imogen.

True to her word, she slipped into the house ten minutes later without ringing the doorbell. Martha had cleared the kitchen table so Imogen wouldn't see her papers and laptop and ask about her work. The fluorescent ceiling lamp flooded the room in a harsh light suited to needlepoint and police interrogation and the time felt much later than quarter past eight. Martha filled the kettle and set it to boil.

"Chamomile, peppermint, Earl Grey . . . something called

'Soul Balm'. They're what's left of my mother's tea stash," Martha said as she shuffled cellophaned boxes in the cupboard.

"Soul Balm. That sounds innocuously daring," said Imogen. "For the table of reckless ladies at the temperance tea."

Martha squinted at the fine print on the side of the box. "It's made of rosehips, lemon balm, lavender, elderflower, and orange peel."

"Revolting penance for the excesses of the season," said Imogen.

"Soul Balm it is." Martha took a teapot from the cupboard, rinsed it with hot water from the tap, and dropped in two teabags.

"I'm surprised at your mother's low standards. I thought Judith would've been a loose-leaf drinker."

"She was a utilitarian. Tea bags saved time and set her apart from the women in her family. The Steinman women brew their own concoctions from their herb gardens."

"Disowning her roots?"

"I suppose." Martha leaned back against the counter and crossed her arms. "Nothing she did was unintentional. Even buying tea."

"Were you ever close to your mom's family?"

"Not really," Martha shrugged. "Weddings and funerals. We exchange Christmas cards. Mom alienated her siblings in spectacular fashion. She let her sister, my Aunt Becky, come and help Dad when she was dying, and that was it. Mom's family attended her funeral and we promised to keep in touch . . . rekindle the annual summer picnic and get together at Christmas, but we never did. I went back to Vancouver, back to my life."

"And your dad's the last Gray standing, besides you and Joe."

"Yeah. They die young in Dad's family and the survivors are sprinkled across the Commonwealth." Just before the kettle whistled, Martha lifted it from the burner and filled the teapot. She put the kettle back and turned off the gas. "Living room?"

"Sure," Imogen agreed as she took two mugs from the drainboard.

They sat cross legged on the couch and Imogen regaled Martha with amusing stories of skating with her nieces and nephews.

Martha poured the tea, then picked up her mug and blew at the steam. The tea was too hot to drink. "Do you ever wish you had kids of your own, Imogen?" asked Martha.

"Now that's a pointy question," answered Imogen.

"Why?"

"I don't know why the fuck why. It's just one of those off-limit questions, like asking about someone's income or how many times a day they shit."

Martha sipped her tea and burnt her tongue.

Imogen sighed. "Since it's you who's asking, Martha, yes, I do bloody wish I had kids, but by the time I realized that it was too late. I only came to my senses a couple of years ago, after Sophie dumped me, hooked up with someone else, and they both got pregnant within months. Now I'm a jealous, forty-three-year-old crone. Anyway, I do have kids. My nieces and nephews and my familiar, Twinkle."

Martha didn't know what to say—what to say to someone who'd closed the door on what could have been her most important relationship. "You're not a witch," Martha tried, thinking of Twinkle.

"How do you know?" Imogen cackled, breaking the serious mood.

"Do you have any spells to cure dipsomania?"

Imogen grinned fiendishly. "Martha, my dear. It's really bloody simple. You replace a harmful addiction with a healthy one. You could take up philately or marathon running or workaholism, but that would make you a Nobel-prize winning bore. I suggest you try sex."

"Sex?" Martha laughed, relieved to have the old Imogen back.

"Yes. Let me be your gateway drug."

Martha stopped laughing so she wouldn't be misunderstood and said, "I won't say 'no, that's impossible,' Imogen. Will 'maybe' do? This is all . . . new."

"It will have to do," Imogen said wistfully. "I won't beg you. I don't understand your mindset though, Martha. I offer you love on the basis of chemistry, a strong, magnetic attraction, a mutual pull that you can't deny is there. You resist a healthy connection and run to the bottle and wind up battered and blue. In a dysfunctional death spiral."

"Ahh. Now you're venturing into psychobabble. Alcoholism as hysterical, Freudian, id-driven compulsion. Maybe the bottle represents a penis. Something you don't have, Imogen."

"Details. Fucking details, crazy lady. Healthy people love other people, not their genitals. Normal adults hook up with other consenting adults, male or female. It's not fucking 1982. Okay, I'm a pussy lover because I'm discerning, but you understand what I'm saying, and you know it's true."

"Shh. You'll wake Dad."

"You're shushing me?"

"No. Yes. I don't think we want him listening to this conversation, that's all."

"Fine. Whispering on quiet tippy toes. Gordon knows you drink too much and he's not homophobic so whatever. I'll shut the fuck up."

"Imogen."

"Martha."

They drank their tea, though neither of them actually tasted anything.

"Nice tree, if you like anorexic pines," said Imogen. "Twiggy."

"I forgot to water it," said Martha. "I'll take it down tomorrow."

"Library closes at five on Fridays. Do you want help?"

"Yes. I'd like that. We can try the peppermint tea. If it's not too stale."

Friday, January 3rd, 2020

Martha's phone pinged on her bedside table at seven am.

> Mom. I'm texting you on my new Galaxy. Now you have my number. Talk soon!

Martha replied with a thumbs up and a heart emoticon and went back to sleep. Blissfully, beautifully, deliciously sober sleep.

Part IV

Wednesday, February 12th, 2020

Martha struggled into downward dog in the "Yoga for Caring Spirits" class at Nirvana Garden, the popular yoga studio Sally and Mavis attended in a strip mall off Lakeshore. From her inverted vantage, she viewed herself in the wall of mirrors to her rear and saw an upside-down Basset hound in a pack of whippets and Afghan terriers. Her baggy trackpants and T-shirt weren't doing her any favours.

"Push your tail up, proudly, to the heavens," Jonquil commanded as she strode around the room. "Relax into the pose, through the sit bones. Release any tension you are holding there."

Dangerous advice. Someone passed wind. Martha suspected the culprit was the shirtless man with the ankh tattoo who'd humble bragged about cheating on his three-day fast by gorging on his girlfriend's kimchi. If Imogen were there, they'd have exchanged glances and burst out laughing.

"Excellent," pronounced Jonquil. "We are letting go of what

is no longer needed." She paused behind Martha. "This is me time. Time to integrate soul and body. Find your centre and when you are ready, lift your right leg up, pushing through your heel. Martha, dear heart. That's your left leg."

Martha quickly switched and nearly toppled over.

"Centre. Centre," Jonquil coached.

The class moved from warm-up through a series of sun salutations, into a crescendo of complicated abdominal exercises, and forty-five minutes later finished in corpse pose, flat on backs, eyes closed.

"*Savasana*. Dwell in the experience of being dead in body yet vibrantly alive in spirit," said Jonquil. "Whatever your challenges, as you move through your day, you may enter this state, this beingness, and find peace in your immortal spirit."

The room was so quiet, Martha worried she'd missed a cue. She opened one eye for reconnaissance. Jonquil loomed nearby, so she quickly shut it.

"We are far more than flesh and blood," Jonquil cooed maternally. "As caregivers you are called to entwine with other spirits, to lift the suffering other into your field of energy, in universal healing. Go in peace, dear hearts. *Namaste*."

"*Namaste*," repeated the class in unison.

Martha picked herself up and rolled her mat into a tight coil. Jonquil's advice was gibberish, yet kind and reassuring, and Martha left each class feeling better than when she'd arrived. She heard someone say her name. She tucked her mat under her arm and turned.

"I thought it was you, Martha."

"Joanne. What a coincidence. Dad told me you do yoga."

"I'm new to Nirvana Garden. They're installing new hardwood floors in the studio at the Elmington Club and it's closed for the month. I suppose you could call me a spiritual refugee."

"I'm new too. This is only my third class. I think you know Sally Dunfield."

"Of course," Joanne nodded. "We're in a book club together. She was at my Labour Day pool party, remember?"

"That's right. Forgetful me," said Martha. "She recommended this class as a stress reliever. What did you think of it?"

"I loved it. I'm often overwhelmed by caregiving. Michael comes home from the office with his shoulders in knots, bound with tension, and it falls on me to restore his balance with wholesome food, sometimes a massage. Don't let me get started on Ethan Michael...."

"Sons." Martha shook her head knowingly, though she couldn't imagine what mild, malleable Ethan would do or say that would send a mother to yoga class for emotional succour.

"Well, I'd better run," said Joanne. "I mustn't be late picking up Ethan."

"*Namaste*," said Martha. She had to hurry too. The old man panicked if he was left alone for more than a couple of hours and she wanted to buy a yoga outfit at Boldly Beautiful.

The boutique's angry Adele mannequin wore a valentine bikini with hearts resembling pasties. Harry Connick Junior swung from the speakers. Martha waved to Claire, then headed to the gym and yoga section. She was tired of dressing as if she were Rocky Balboa, running up the steps of the Philadelphia Museum of Art in a lather of sweat. She wanted something flattering, though not oppressively body-hugging. A garment of liberation.

Martha shifted hangers of stretchy clothes in a rainbow of pastels and jewel tones. Spaghetti straps were out. Frankly, anything sleeveless and requiring the prompt mowing of pit hair could be excluded. She searched for something swishy . . . a New Age drapery . . .

"For yoga or the gym?" Claire asked, sidling up like a ninja.

"Yoga," a startled Martha replied.

"I remember now. From last summer. You're the Barbara Ann ruffle bottom."

"I'm Martha, actually."

"Martha. I never forget a customer." Claire flashed a warm smile. "Unitards are popular this season."

"Oh?"

"Many curvy women think they can't wear clingy fabric, but that's a misconception. A unitard lengthens, streamlines, and delivers a high-quality yoga experience."

"I was thinking of something looser—" Martha perceived a shadow of disappointment in Claire's expression. "But I'm open to trying one on."

"As I recall, you prefer deeper, cooler colours. Perhaps a jewel tone?" Claire shuffled through the queenly section, extracted a few outfits, and laid them over the rack. "Himalayan Dawn from our Samsara collection. What do you think?"

"I think it's pink."

"Perhaps something darker . . . Smoldering Incense?"

"That's a nice purple. And I like that blue—"

"Temple Twilight," corrected Claire. She led Martha to the fitting rooms and handed her the outfits. "I'm nearby if you need anything."

Martha tried the unitard first. It fit like sausage casing. Even in a flattering mirror, she resembled a bratwurst sausage with a braided ponytail. She checked the tag. *Crimson Prayer Flag. Queenly. Made in Bangladesh. $94.95.* "Money well saved," she muttered.

Outfit after outfit disappointed and it was getting late. She settled on a pair of navy brushed-cotton leggings and a loose-fitting, dark purple top with empire pleats at the bra line. Queen of the studio for $74.65. Made in Mexico.

"Ah. A classic," Claire commented at the counter. "And such a regal shade."

"I'll fit in with the cool kids now," joked Martha.

"We have some nice yoga slippers—"

"I'm okay barefoot."

"A headband? It's a must for Bikram." Claire reached under the counter and presented several swatches of richly hued, patterned fabric. "They're 40 percent off during our Sweetheart Sales event."

Martha was vaguely aware of hot yoga and she wanted to appear knowledgeable. "Why not," she said. "A floral one."

"How about the Lotus Lily? It picks up the colour in your tunic and leggings and pulls your outfit together very nicely."

Martha agreed. She left Boldly Beautiful with a spring in her step.

The parking lot was bathed in the rosy glow of sunset. Rush hour. The drive home would be slow, and supper would be late.

Gordon paddled his wheelchair with his feet to smoke at the front door and watch for Martha. Though she didn't complain, he could tell she disliked being in a smoke-filled home, so he took care to hold his cigarette and exhale on the exterior side of the threshold. The gas bill would be a doozy, but that was the price of semi-independence. He didn't have to ask to be taken in and out of the house like a sick puppy.

Winter and weakness had made him a shut-in. He was too tired to read anything longer than a brief article. The banality of TV was worse than boredom. Every second of every day passed like a minute and every minute like an hour. The sun barely lingered in the southwest, yet Martha still wasn't back. He'd bite his tongue when she finally returned. She had a right to a life of her own.

They'd reached an impasse. Martha was marooned in Elmington, caring for him, and he was marooned in illness, neither improving nor declining. She stole snatches of time for writing and day parole from 22 Roselea; he stole her freedom.

Something had to give.

He had three options to break the logjam and all of them were crumby. He could try to convince Dr. Southey that he should be put out of his misery, a long shot given her dismissive attitude. He could kill himself but that took courage he didn't have. He could give Valhalla Terrace a try. This was the easiest option, a socially acceptable, slow death of bland food and dependence. Whatever he decided, he couldn't prevail upon Martha to keep him in his own house much longer.

Gordon put on his oxygen for a couple of minutes, then removed it and lit another cigarette. A crow flew from under the Kingsworth's birdfeeder into the Gilberts' spruce tree to roost for the night. At last, a pair of headlights shone onto the pavement and the Corolla turned into the driveway. Equilibrium restored. They'd have supper together, maybe listen to "As It Happens," and then Martha would help him settle in for the night. Gordon was an old crow too—roosting and hoping for a catastrophe to shake him off his perch.

Saturday, February 15th, 2020

"It's a long movie, Dad. Are you sure you'll be okay?" Martha asked.

"Sure I'm sure," wheezed Gordon. "Just help me to the bathroom and into bed and I'll stay put for the night."

Martha removed Gordon's plate from the table and scraped the remains of a tuna casserole into the bin.

"What time is Imogen picking you up?"

"Seven-fifteen." Martha rinsed the plate.

"What are you seeing?"

"*Parasite*. It's a Korean movie. A dark comedy thriller."

"Which one? A comedy or a thriller. Surely it can't be both, Duchess."

"Surely it can, Dad. Imogen says it's an Asian Tarantino meets Coen brothers flick with themes of class struggle. The proletariat rise against the bourgeoisie and everything turns out badly."

"Sounds like a documentary on the Cultural Revolution."

"I'll tell you all about it in the morning."

"Do I have time for a quick smoke?"

Martha glanced at the clock. "Yes." She wheeled the old man to the front door. "While you do that, I'll get ready."

"Get ready? It's just Imogen. It's not as if you're going on a hot date."

A half hour later, the old man's nightly ablutions complete, Martha stood by his bedside while Imogen waited at the front door.

"Your pillows are okay?" Martha asked.

"Yes," Gordon rasped.

"Your phone is here and set to speed dial if you need me."

Gordon nodded.

"Your oxygen is flowing."

"Tickling my nose as we speak."

"You have your panic button, Kleenex, glass of water, Ventolin, urinal, reading glasses, and your *Harpers*."

"Check, Duchess. Seat belt is fastened. Now skedaddle or you'll be late."

The Saturday evening audience tumbled from the cinema onto the sidewalk—shy couples on dates, chattering flocks of friends, and Martha and Imogen.

"That was bloody brilliant," Imogen proclaimed.

"It was very good," agreed Martha.

"Good? An unjustly trite word. Brilliant and nothing less. Theme piled on velvety rich theme like a fucking layer cake. This is a film to discuss."

Same set-up as on a straight date, Martha thought with amusement.

Imogen continued, "We could go out for a drink, but my place isn't far and it's quieter than a bar."

Well played. A or B? Face-saving or next level? Martha said, "Let's go to your place, Imogen."

Imogen shot Martha a sideways smile, and they headed for the municipal parking lot.

Gordon woke under a suffocating oppression, as if a monster were sitting on him. His chest heaved but barely moved air. His nasal prongs blocked his nostrils and delivered nothing. Zilch. He marshalled his strength to turn onto his side, to release his ribcage from the bondage of the monster's weight.

Had hypoxia stolen his senses? The clock radio was dark. The house was a soundless tomb. He could hear himself breathe though. Oh God. The power was off. No electricity meant no oxygen. He didn't have the strength to shout, but that wouldn't do any good anyway. He was alone. He patted his chest and feebly swept his hand through his blankets to find his panic button, but it was nowhere to be found. Gone. A fine, terrible end. Martha would never forgive herself.

He coached himself to hang on. In through the nose, out through the mouth, slow and deep. If he could go without oxygen while he smoked, he could go without it until help arrived. He remembered the full, portable oxygen tank standing sentry near the front door like a dress-up soldier standing guard with a fake bayonet—useless—useless unless he could get to it. He pulled himself up and damn near died with the effort. The tank could've been locked up in a vault in Fort Knox and the outcome would be identical. He'd never make it.

A tiny light shone a beacon in the darkness. The phone. Battery powered, for crying out loud. He need only press one button. One button to reach Martha.

Yaris at rest in its berth in the garage, they rode the elevator to Imogen's condo. Martha felt as anxious as a teenage girl on her first date. Her stomach flipped as the elevator halted, and her heart pounded as they walked down the poshly carpeted corridor. Imogen unlocked the door.

"My lair." Imogen beckoned Martha into an open concept room with a wave of her arm.

As they hung their coats, Imogen's cat wandered over and rubbed her face against Martha's leg. "This must be Twinkle," said Martha. She bent to scratch the creature behind her ear.

"My fur daughter," said Imogen. "Look at that. You've already bonded."

Martha followed Imogen into the living room, a jumbled space of mismatched furniture, pillows, books, and magazines.

"The couch is the most comfortable place to sit," said Imogen. "I have wine, tea, and soda water."

"Wine please," replied Martha. "Just a glass ... because I have to get home to Dad." Jeez. She was a fumbling adolescent.

"Well, I won't bring you the whole bottle then," Imogen laughed as she went to the kitchen. "Red or white?"

"Surprise me."

A moment later, Imogen returned with two sensible glasses of red.

"To friendship," Imogen toasted. "Martha the Marxist, notwithstanding your nutty politics, I've loved you from the moment you walked into the library six months ago."

Martha nervously sipped her wine.

Imogen took the glass from Martha's hand and set it beside her own on the coffee table. Then, she brushed a lock of hair from Martha's face and kissed her.

Martha savoured the sweet taste of wine ... the softness of Imogen's mouth on hers. Tongues mingled and danced, arms clung, bodies pulled together. Martha was achingly aroused yet confused by the hungry intensity of the encounter. She craved more, skin on skin, flesh melding with flesh, but she needed to regain control ... to think. Or not. No thinking, no fear, lying back ...

As Imogen fumbled with the buttons on Martha's blouse, Martha's phone rang.

"Leave it." Imogen commanded in a husky whisper.

"I can't."

"You can."

Martha pushed Imogen away. "It might be Dad. I have to check it."

Imogen sat back while Martha fished the phone from her pocket.

"It's him," Martha muttered. "Hello? Dad?"

The voice on the other end was barely intelligible, more wheeze than word. "Power's out ... No oxygen ..."

"We're coming. Just sit forward and breathe. We'll be there soon."

Martha looked at Imogen.

"I heard, Martha. Let's go."

In that instant, in that singular turn of time, Martha realized she loved Imogen back.

Imogen sped down an ink-black Roselea Drive with only headlights to illuminate the way. They screeched to a halt in the driveway and Martha ran into the house with Imogen on her heels. Martha knew the house by instinct, and she got to the old man's room in seconds. She couldn't see how poorly he was until Imogen used her phone as a flashlight.

Gordon was slumped forward, breathing like a broken accordion. "Porta... wheeze... porta..."

"Portable oxygen. Right!" yelped Martha. She stumbled by Imogen, retrieved the tank, put the tubing and prongs on Gordon's face, and turned the knob to maximum.

Gordon breathed in and out for a few minutes before he could spit out a full sentence. He gasped, "Turn it down. We'll run out."

"Don't we have another tank?" Martha asked.

He shook his head.

At once Martha recalled that they'd used it to go to the clinic for the old man's follow-up X-ray the previous afternoon. As she thought of calling 911, the lights flickered on, the clock radio flashed zeroes, and the concentrator roared into duty.

"Thank holy fucking God," said Imogen.

Martha switched the reading light on and changed Gordon's oxygen tubing back to the concentrator.

Gordon smiled weakly, slack jawed.

"You're as blue as a Smurf, old man," Imogen exclaimed.

"Ventolin." Martha grabbed Gordon's aero-chamber and gave him two puffs of medication, then stood back and scrutinized her patient. "Your colour's improving now, Dad."

"Thanks, Duchess," wheezed Gordon.

After several minutes, Martha said, "I think we're out of the woods."

"Do you want me to hang around for a while? Just in case?" asked Imogen.

"In case of what?" said Gordon. "You saved my life. You can sleep now, Wonder Woman."

"If you're sure, I'll be on my way," said Imogen. She winked at Martha. "I'll call you in the morning."

"Not too early, lass," said Gordon. "We'll all need our beauty sleep."

Sunday, February 16th, 2020

Martha and Gordon sat in the living room, sipping coffee. Martha scrolled though the local news on her laptop while Gordon relaxed in the La-Z-Boy, a break from his wheelchair.

"Says here it was a fault in a transformer. According to Elmington Hydro, the power was out for about five thousand customers for over an hour," said Martha.

"The power stayed on in the cinema?"

"Yes."

"That teaches us a lesson, Duchess."

"What's that, Dad?"

"I should be living in a place that has an emergency generator."

"I don't think we should make decisions on one-off events," said Martha. She savoured the bitter richness of the day's first cup of coffee, then she spoke thoughtfully. "I suppose we could buy a generator."

"Or I could move into Valhalla Terrace."

"Dad. You don't mean that. You're building your strength."

"Am I?"

Martha didn't answer.

"I'm exactly where I was when you brought me home from the hospital a month ago. Progress? A big, round blimp of a zero. And you're tired."

"You'd miss this house."

"Not really. It's four walls, a roof, and your mother's ghost. She'll move with me. Stephen King gets it all wrong."

"How?"

"Ghosts. They haunt people, not places. Specifically, they haunt the people who remember the dead. *The Shining* was a crock. Kubrick was slightly closer in the uncut version of the movie. Whither thou goest, they will go."

Martha gazed through the window and tried to remember the street of her childhood. Judith haunted her too. She had a fuzzy recollection of the 1970s streetscape, but a technicolour memory of being slapped when Gordon wasn't present. She hadn't forgotten the sting of judgement, how Judith wielded her twisted "truth" as a weapon of control. "I'll try to leave her here," said Martha.

"I hope you can, Martha. I'm sorry I didn't stop her."

"Hey—I'm okay."

"I turned a blind eye."

"You didn't want a fuss. I get it. And I forgive you. I didn't blame you in the first place."

A tear rolled down the old man's cheek. He dabbed it discreetly with a tissue, as if hoping Martha wouldn't notice, so she pretended she didn't.

She said, "It's the same reason you're thinking of moving into Valhalla Terrace. To avoid a fuss."

"Is that so, Duchess?"

"Yes."

"I suppose you're right."

They drank their coffee in companionable silence, until the old man broke it. "Will you call Sonya Tam tomorrow?"

"Only if it's what you really want," replied Martha.

"It is," said Gordon.

Imogen called late in the morning and asked after Gordon.

"He's back to his usual decrepit yet feisty self," said Martha as she closed her bedroom door and sat on her bed. "He wants to go into a nursing home."

"It's about time," said Imogen.

"I don't know. I thought we were doing okay here."

"Martha, he's running you ragged. You don't have a bloody life."

"We went out on Saturday night."

"And then we went home, didn't we?"

Martha didn't know if Imogen was referring to her apartment or 22 Roselea so she said vaguely, "Yes, we did," and added, "I won't be needed in Ontario if he's in a nursing home."

Dead air. Martha was about to fill the void when Imogen asked, "When can I see you ... alone?"

"I don't know. Soon."

"Soon," Imogen repeated. "After Saturday night, all you can say is fucking 'soon'."

Martha disliked a quarrel. She said, "Imogen, I want to see you too. Please be patient with me."

"I could come over."

"And I'd sneak you into my room as if we're horny teenagers?"

No answer.

Martha continued, "I'm not ready to be open about us and the logistics are complicated. Soon." She steered to safer water. "Are you working tomorrow?"

"Yup," Imogen said sharply. "And it's the last place I want to be. I got an email from Simon this morning, on the fucking Sabbath. The tinpot dictator doesn't rest. He marked the bloody message as 'urgent'."

"And?"

"And he's cancelling the debate I arranged for next week. I had introductory speakers and a moderator coming from out of town and the debating club was super keen."

"What? You mean 'Transgenderism versus transracialism'?"

"Yes."

"Is it hypocritical to accept gender fluidity yet condemn a person who changes his or her racial or ethnic identity?"

"Yes, that debate. Nowadays it's 'their', Martha. Not 'his or her'."

"I'm linguistically old-school."

"Prehistoric."

"Why does he want to cancel?"

"Because of complaints from some busybodies who can't have 'Their Truth'—capital letters and air quotes—held under the cold light of rational examination."

"Hmm. What are you thinking, Imogen?"

"I don't know. I was hoping the debate would help me grapple with the subject."

"I mean about the cancellation. Are you going to fight it?"

"I can't. I'm on fucking probation, remember?"

"It's not like you to back down," said Martha.

"You're right. I'm not backing down. Fuck the debate. I'm off on Thursday, so come by my place, Martha. Maybe you can spare some time while you're out grocery shopping or whatever."

"Okay."

"Okay?"

"Yes. Okay, Imogen. I'll make it work."

Thursday, February 20th, 2020

The interview dragged on longer than Martha had expected it would. From her perch on the chesterfield, Sonya Tam spoke slowly and repetitively, as if Martha and the old man had a weak grasp of English. After assessing Gordon's mobility and mental state and how they were managing, Sonya asked Gordon if he had any goals for his health.

"Yes. I have one. Death—the sooner the better," said Gordon.

Sonya peered over her laptop, expression like a startled rabbit, hands stilled over her keyboard.

"Aren't you going to type that into your form?" he asked.

Sonya stammered, "It's an umm, an unusual goal. It doesn't have a category. I mean, umm . . ."

"Dad, do you have another goal for Sonya?" asked Martha.

"I'd like to give Martha her freedom," Gordon said to Sonya.

Martha suggested, "You could put down something about safety. Not falling and hurting himself or slipping in the bathroom. Something that ticks a box for long-term care."

Sonya's face relaxed and she nodded. "Yes. Those are excellent goals. Thank you, Gordon."

Gordon shrugged.

Sonya frowned into her screen and typed rapidly. When she finally looked up, Gordon asked, "So, lass, do I qualify for Valhalla Terrace?"

"Well, yes and no," replied Sonya. "You qualify for long-term care, specifically a crisis bed because Martha is burning out."

Martha started to object but Gordon silenced her with a fierce glare.

"However, the waiting list for Valhalla is two years. If we consider Oakview Lodge . . . it has similar amenities but it's an older facility. The waiting list is typically a month or two, though a bed offer might come through before the end of the month. For a private room. They're more expensive, you see."

"Dad's insured," said Martha. "Though I really don't think it's that urgent. I don't feel as if we're in crisis, as if we need to deprive someone of a bed whose needs are more pressing."

Gordon broke in, "Semantics, Martha. If Sonya, with her expertise and wise judgement, has deemed me a crisis case, who are we to argue?"

"I would never label anyone a 'crisis'," said Sonya. "It's the situation—how a client manages in their context and home environment."

"A crisis situation then," Gordon said flatly. "Indeed, this is a crisis." He waved a wizened hand at the orderly living room. "Sonya, please put me down for a crisis bed at Oakview Lodge."

"But Dad. Don't you want to see the place first?"

"Nope. My decision is firm," Gordon declared.

Martha had deliberately let the supply of milk and Nescafe run low as an excuse to grocery shop. After running her errand, she pressed the buzzer code for "I. Wallis" at the front entrance of Imogen's building and waited.

Imogen's voice crackled on the intercom, "Hello?"

"It's me."

"Martha. How quaint. Most visitors text me. I'll buzz you in."

Martha felt disembodied, as if she were observing a stranger ride the elevator, walk down the hallway, and knock. Imogen opened the door, their eyes locked, and the feeling vanished.

"I can't stay long," said Martha.

"I know," said Imogen.

"A half hour. No more."

Imogen didn't say anything. She took Martha's hand and led her to the living room, where they fell together in a clumsy hug. Imogen's edges met Martha's curves; angles enfolded over pliant flesh. Martha felt Imogen's breath on her neck, then a nuzzle, and they returned to the Eden of Saturday night, arms and legs entwining, mouth eagerly seeking mouth, heavy clothing falling away.

Martha gave in to Imogen's touch—tentative and gentle, then insistent and carnal, hands and mouth exploring breasts and belly and scar. They descended onto the couch. Martha's self-consciousness melted away and she allowed Imogen to take her to a place she hadn't been to in a very long time.

Afterward, Imogen raised herself over Martha and they rolled face to face in a tender embrace. Martha moved to return Imogen's attention.

"It's okay, Martha," Imogen whispered, stopping her. "Our half hour's up."

Wednesday, February 26th, 2020

The old man's phone rang while he was in the bathroom, so Martha answered Sonya Tam's call.

"I have good news, Martha," said Sonya. "Oakview Lodge is offering Gordon a bed. A private room. Gordon has until Friday to decide whether to accept or refuse it."

"He'll accept it," said Martha. "When can he move in?"

"Monday, though I'll confirm that with the director of care. She'll be in touch shortly with a list of things for you to bring and all the details for Gordon's admission."

"Thank you," said Martha.

After they ended the call, Martha flopped onto the chesterfield, mind whirling like an eggbeater. It was good news. Of course it was good news. She had two months until the summer term started, ample time to move the old man into Oakview Lodge and sell his house. She'd be back in Vancouver by the end of April. It was terrible news.

Monday, March 2nd, 2020

Moving day arrived. Gordon surveyed the sprawling 70s façade of Oakview Lodge from the passenger seat of the Corolla while Martha fetched his wheelchair from the trunk. A half circle of smokers sat in the shelter of a long porch. A pair of dirty, knee-high snowbanks flanked a salt-stained sidewalk, marking the route from driveway to front door, from ordinary life to institutional purgatory. Hades' waiting room, thought Gordon. He heard the trunk slam shut so he pushed his door open, stuck his feet out, and pulled himself up by the passenger door frame.

"Ready for this, Dad?" Martha asked from behind the wheelchair.

"I think so, Duchess," he wheezed as he sat down.

Martha hooked Gordon's tank onto the handle and pushed the wheelchair over ridges of ice, up the walk, and in through two sets of sliding glass doors. They entered a large atrium furnished with washable armchairs and Thomas Kincaid prints. Old people were everywhere, some slouched in wheelchairs, some dozing in recliners, others pacing aimlessly. Gordon felt as if he'd stumbled into a bizarre high school reunion for the elderly graduates of Living Dead Collegiate.

"You're new." A skinny, bald man resembling a turtle appeared from behind an artificial fig tree.

"Hello yourself," said Gordon.

"I'd apologize for being rude, but I've given up good manners for Lent, so I won't bother. Name's Frank." The man paddled over in his wheelchair. "Frank Vanstone."

"I'm Gordon Gray and this is my daughter, Martha."

"Welcome to Bedlam."

"Frank, do you know where the director's office is?" Martha asked.

"You mean Diane? Over there."

Frank's gesture was too vague to interpret, so Martha excused herself and went to find a directory or arrow or some other signpost of officialdom.

"Are you the greeting party?" Gordon asked.

"Yup. Me, myself, and I," replied Frank. "I was you six months ago. Dumped off in a state of bewilderment by my well-meaning kids. You get used to the place. The living's pretty easy. Heck, you don't even need to chew your food or wipe your ass."

"Lucky me," said Gordon.

"Just watch out for Rita. That old magpie there. If she gets into your room, she'll steal your stuff to feather her nest." Frank flung his arm toward a group of three women, each with snow-white perms. "Most of the folks here are addled but harmless. You still have your wits though. I can tell by the look of you."

"Thanks, I guess," Gordon wheezed.

"And you're a smoker. Me too."

Gordon ignored a sudden, urgent tobacco craving and asked, "You're a detective?"

"And you're a joker. I'm an accountant, actually. Until I retired."

"I'm a retired librarian."

Frank nodded an acknowledgment. "Want to go out for a smoke?"

"I thought you'd never ask," Gordon replied in a falsetto that provoked a cough.

"This way, my dear," said Frank.

Gordon trailed behind Frank in a sedate, two-wheelchair procession to the front door.

"We have to press in the code to go out," Frank explained as he batted at a keypad. A sign displaying the pertinent numbers hung next to it.

"That doesn't seem secure," said Gordon.

"Keeps the wandering confused in, and lets the merely forgetful out," Frank worked on opening the door. After several tries, the sliders opened, and the old men headed into the frigid, delightfully subversive freedom of smoking on an institutional porch in winter.

An odour of industrial-grade cleanser and fried breakfast had assaulted Martha's nose as she pushed the old man into the overheated building. How odd that her first impression of Oakview Lodge was olfactory rather than visual.

Martha habitually underestimated how long it took to pack up and transport Gordon to appointments and today was typical —they were running late. She'd always been prompt— especially eager to make a first impression of trustworthiness on teachers, bankers, health care professionals—anyone with a hand in one's fate. She'd been rude to Frank, rushing away from his warm welcome, but it was already quarter past, and the appointment was set for ten, damn it.

As she crossed the atrium, Martha spotted a sign next to a plate glass window. "Diane Stefano, Director of Care." She knocked on the glass, and a smartly dressed woman with a helmet of stiff, curly hair rose from the desk and opened the door.

After quick self-introductions and accepting Martha's apology for delay, Diane pulled out a chair and invited Martha to sit, then seated herself behind a massive desk stacked with papers and files. "Where's Gordon?" she asked.

"He met a fellow named Frank so I left him in the atrium," Martha replied.

"Ah, yes," Diane smiled. "When I read Gordon's profile, I immediately thought of Frank and I told him about Gordon. He's been waiting near the door since nine-thirty to meet our new resident."

"That explains the friendly ambush," Martha smiled in return.

"Most of our residents have dementia and the residents who are cognitively normal often form close bonds," said Diane. "We don't need Gordon here for most of the paperwork. We might as well get started and find him later." Diane pulled a thick file of forms from one of her piles.

As Diane confirmed Gordon's demographic and financial particulars, Martha felt the boulder of oppressive responsibility lift from her shoulders. The old man would be okay at Oakview Lodge.

Gordon sat in his wheelchair by his window and waited for someone to come and help him get ready for bed. He didn't want to rush the girls by pressing his call bell. They'd come when they could. They had plenty on their plate, for crying out loud. Next door was Nelda, a zeppelin of a woman who gobbled her food at supper as if starving and worried for her next meal. She'd need to be hoisted from chair to bed with the crane from the hallway. On the other side were the Lee sisters. He could hear the staccato of a Cantonese newscast through the wall. And across the hall was Frank, legs as sturdy as overcooked spaghetti noodles, arms barely stronger.

Martha hadn't noticed the soupy, nondescript beige of the walls. Imogen would see them and want to paint them a brighter colour to cheer him. He'd dissuade her. He didn't bargain on a long tenancy anyway. Martha had done her best to make the room homey though. His La-Z-Boy and tray table sat in the corner, along with his phone, iPad, and a few favourite novels, and his clothes hung in the closet. She'd put some framed family photos on the dresser and paintings that Judith bought decades ago on the walls. Over the foot of the bed, Martha had draped a couple of quilts. Long ago—August 1965 to be exact—they'd come from Judith's hope chest and the quilting frame of her aunts before that. Were there girls who tucked away linen and china for marriage these days? Unlikely.

Gordon looked at his concentrator, same size as a cedar chest. The move into Oakview Lodge marked his passage from late life to end of life. The room was a museum case for a decaying relic, and that was okay.

Martha had weighed the merits of abstention, in case the old man needed her on his first night in the nursing home, versus a few celebratory drinks. The latter won, partly because she'd forgotten how to fill time when no one called for help in the bathroom or needed encouragement at meals, and partly because she could drink her fill. Imogen was away at a conference. Now dressed in pajamas, Martha sat sideways on the chesterfield, legs carelessly crossed at her ankles, an icy G and T and a few airy self-help books on the coffee table in a weak nod to work.

First, she texted Joseph to update him on the old man's move and new contact information. She didn't expect a quick response as Joe kept his phone off most of the time to keep peace with Tayana.

Then she texted Imogen.

> Mission accomplished.

Imogen replied at once.

> Well done. How did it go?

Well. The staff are friendly and helpful. Dad has a pleasant room and a new friend named Frank. How's the conference?

> Boring. Afternoon session was on open-source scholarship.

But that sounds interesting.

> It was a fucking snooze. Zzzz. Tomorrow I'm attending Libraries as Tools of Empowerment. I'll pick up some literature for you.

For me or for my book?

> You choose. What are you doing on your first night of freedom?

Having a drink.

> Cheers and easy does it.

Cheers!

> Soon networking and cocktail hour. I'd better get ready. If the conversation turns to databases, I'll text you again. XO.

XO.

Martha set her phone on the coffee table and took a

satisfying gulp of her drink. Then she picked up a book by Fearne Cotton. *Calm*. "How aspirational," Martha murmured as she opened the candy-coloured cover. Five pages later, she was fast asleep, and she didn't wake until the sun dazzled the snow on Tuesday morning.

Tuesday, March 3rd, 2020

Gordon sat across from Frank in the dining room, bowls of oatmeal with cream and generous scoops of brown sugar in front of them, "to fatten us up," explained Frank. Across the room, a woman howled in her tilting chair. The racket ceased as she gummed down the spoonfuls of goop a support worker shovelled into her mouth, and then she was back at it. Fuel in the maw of a noisy boiler, thought Gordon.

He sipped his coffee and watched Frank try to keep his spoon level. Frank's drinks, lukewarm decaf and juice alike, were presented in plastic sippy cups with straws poking through their tops. Ingenious. Frank's clumsiness would not be allowed to disturb the repose of the dining room by causing spillage from dishes or the breakage of glass.

A stocky support worker with the biceps of a longshoreman detoured by their table on her way to the kitchen with a tray of dirty dishes. "I'm Theresa," she said. "And you must be Gordon."

"Indeed I am, lass." Gordon flashed what he hoped was an endearing smile.

"Welcome to Oakview." Theresa looked at Gordon's full bowl. "Not hungry today?"

"I'm not a breakfast eater."

"I could get you some toast."

"No thanks, Theresa." Gordon shook his head. "I'm fine."

"Got to keep your strength up. There's a trivia contest in the atrium this morning."

"I'm okay," Gordon insisted. "I eat better at lunch."

Theresa nodded and hurried off.

"They always try to do that. Push you to eat," said Frank. "If I finish my oatmeal, they look disappointed if I don't ask for eggs."

"Are you going to the trivia contest?" asked Gordon.

"No. I'll skip it. The questions are too easy. 'What colour is a banana? And what is the hottest season?' I'd have a cigarette on the porch though."

"You're on," said Gordon.

Martha stood in the hallway as Mavis and Sally surveyed the bedrooms and bathroom. She'd called Sally that morning to enquire about appraisal, and Sally lined up the appointment with Mavis straight away.

"It's a charming, basic, post-war bungalow," Mavis commented as she switched on the ceiling light in Martha's room. "Like a time-capsule. Your parents didn't change any walls or put on an addition."

"No. It was just the three of us. We didn't need the space," said Martha.

"The carpet, wallpaper, and drapes scream velour jumpsuits and ashtrays and variety shows with Kraft commercials," Sally laughed.

Martha shrugged and led Mavis and Sally back to the living room. After Martha had poured coffee and they were seated, Mavis enthused, "I love this little house. But—"

"But—" echoed Martha. Here we go.

"But it's worth the same whether you invest in fresh paint and flooring or not. Most buyers will see this house as a gut and redo, or a teardown. People don't see the potential, the magic, in modest homes."

Sally piled on, "There's no place for a dishwasher, let alone an island or peninsula in a mid-century kitchen. And a household needs two bathrooms at a minimum."

Martha had no wish to debate whether a bathroom for each occupant was a need or want. She asked, "What's the bottom line?" and then wondered about the strange language coming from her mouth.

"Eight, perhaps nine, depending on timing. You'll likely have a bidding war," said Mavis.

Martha's face was impassive, yet Sally still read her mind. "Eight hundred thousand, silly. Not eighty. Martha—your father is sitting on a million-dollar property if he lists with Mavis."

"Oh, I see," Martha said slowly, numbers finally registering. Her heart thumped with excitement. How odd that the lure of money could transform sentimentality into greedy calculation so quickly. "I'll drop by to speak with Dad this afternoon and get back to you after that," she promised.

As Martha had expected, Gordon readily agreed to list 22 Roselea with Mill Realty. Martha called Mavis with the news and Mavis replied with a request to meet Gordon for signatures and an emailed list of tasks for Martha such as decluttering all rooms and clearing the snow from the back deck. The idea, Mavis said, was to transform the bungalow from an old man's cramped home into an airy house of unlimited potential with the backyard as a jewel in its crown.

Now it was late afternoon, crisp and cold. Martha decided to go for a walk to clear her mind for planning. The goal was simple —makeover 22 Roselea into an elderly debutante, ready for claim. On the other hand, the steps to achieving this were complex, akin to the lunar landing. Would she begin in one corner and work out, or start in the basement and work her way up? Would she rent a storage locker? A dumpster? Sell the contents or give them away? What of papers and documents? And how would she dodge Judith's ghost?

Martha went down to the lakeshore to clear her head and strategize. She looked out over moraines of gravel-pocked ice to the grey water beyond, the horizon a smudge in the dwindling light. She remembered holding hands with Imogen, just up the shore, on a winter afternoon of high winds and crashing waves before the ice had formed. Imogen would be back on Thursday. As a librarian, she'd know a thing or two about organization.

Martha buttoned the collar of her coat and turned to walk home. Home since December, though not for much longer.

When Martha returned, she found a folded sheet of pink paper caught in the letter slot. She shook her boots off her feet, hung her coat, and took the paper into the kitchen. It read:

Martha,

Forgive the terribly short notice!! I don't know why I didn't think of it before –

Would you like to join us for book club tonight??? It's my turn, so just next door at 8:00 pm.

We're discussing "Educated" by Tara Westover, tho you needn't have read it to join in. Sally and Mavis will be here, along with a couple of other keen bookworms.

Please come!!!

Joanne

A summons. With Sally's fingerprints all over it. Martha wouldn't go. She was being asked as a charity case. Poor Martha Gray, all alone in her sick father's house, probably eating a TV dinner and watching "Wheel of Fortune," maybe peeking through the bay window and noticing Mavis's BMW parked in the driveway of 24 Roselea. This was obviously instigated by Sally in conversation with Mavis after they left. A tale of pity would've been transmitted to Joanne, who'd issued the invitation with the smug satisfaction of a do-gooder. If Joanne had wanted Martha to attend, she would've phoned. She didn't expect Martha to actually show up.

Martha felt irritated by the late, obligation-driven invitation and by hunger. She opened the fridge door and took stock—bottles and jars of condiments, a quarter tub of cottage cheese, a dried-up slice of salami, three eggs, and some wilted cabbage. She looked at her laptop on the kitchen table and sighed with boredom.

Why not? Why not attend book club? If the hostess was disappointed when she appeared on her doorstep, at least Sally and Mavis would welcome her. She'd read *Educated*. A glass or two of wine and some cheese and crackers would make a fine supper.

It was seven. Martha put her coat and boots back on. She'd buy a bottle of pinot grigio for the hostess, change her clothes, and arrive at a fashionable 8:05.

Martha spied Mavis parking her SUV and dashed over to 24 Roselea to time her arrival with her old friends.

"You came!" Sally called as she stepped out of the vehicle.

"I knew it. You asked Joanne to invite me, didn't you," said Martha as they waited for Mavis to organize herself and join them.

"We should've invited you sooner, Martha. I don't know why we didn't," said Sally.

"Except we didn't. Forgive us, Martha," Mavis admitted as they walked to the front door. "We should've connected the dots and invited you in February."

"January, Mavis. We could've invited her in January," said Sally. "It was my turn to host, but her father was sick, and—"

Martha had no chance to dismiss the need for apology before Mavis had rung the bell and the door swung open to the chimes of Big Ben.

Ten minutes later, all three were seated in Joanne's living room, introductions completed, wine glasses at hand, copies of *Educated* tucked beside laps. Amy, a tanned, statuesque holistic lifestyle coach, was the common link in the group. Everyone present except Martha had been her client at one time or another. Jenn, a high school English teacher with a severe black bob and thickly framed glasses, completed the circle.

"Selena sends her regrets," Joanne said. "Her girls are sick. She told me it could be that awful Wuhan flu. There's a Chinese girl on Zoe's badminton team and—"

Jenn interrupted, "We can't blame Asian people every time someone catches a sniffle."

"It's not a sniffle," Joanne protested.

"Selena bails on us whenever she hasn't read the book, or she has a bad hair day. We're at her place in April so she'll have to pull herself together."

"Compassion," Joanne sang. "We don't all work a regular teacher's schedule."

"Or at all," Jenn sang back.

Touché. Martha sipped her wine and enjoyed the spectacle of barely concealed hostility until the oven buzzer called Joanne to the kitchen. Jenn mockingly raised her glass to Joanne's back and took a slug from her glass.

The conversation shifted to admiration of Amy's YouTube channel. "It's a way to reach people who I can't coach directly," Amy explained. "I keep my content short, fifteen minutes tops, and try to inspire viewers to take better care of themselves. Relationships, nutrition, skin care, fashion—"

"Sex," Sally giggled.

"It's an important health topic," Amy said earnestly.

Joanne returned and set a platter of baked brie, red pepper

jelly, and crackers and a platter of mini quiches and bite-sized sausage rolls on the coffee table. Martha was nearly finished her first glass of wine and she was ravenous. She popped a sausage roll into her mouth and bit into spongy matter that tasted like flavoured tofu.

"Martha is interested in self-help too," said Mavis.

"Oh?" said Amy.

All eyes tracked to Martha as she swallowed the pastry lump. "Umm, from an academic perspective, actually. I'm exploring how the self-help industry bolsters neoliberal economic and social structures. The genre's orthodoxy is that one should find contentment by changing oneself rather than the systems that exploit."

"Exploit whom?" asked Jenn.

"Well, the readers of self-help for a start. The thread that runs through the literature is that happiness and the accumulation of material wealth are attainable for readers if they follow a formula or a set of rules. Human agency is exaggerated within a weird vacuum, disassociated from systemic injustice."

Three pairs of eyes glazed over while Jenn leaned in. "Your research sounds fascinating, Martha. I think you've just helped me to identify why I've always hated self-help and why I didn't like *Educated* either."

Three voices rose in protest with Joanne's prevailing. "I happened to love the book," she said as she refilled everyone's glass. "How Tara Westover survived her childhood at all is miraculous. I can't imagine Ethan coping with such deprivation and danger. A creative child is a sensitive orchid, not a dandelion like Tara."

"I admire the way she taught herself math," Mavis added.

Jenn adopted a southern accent. "It's an inspirational, true-blue memoir on radical bootstrapping. From rags and scrap metal to Oxbridge U."

"You don't believe her?" Mavis asked.

"No," Jenn replied. "Not really. I think she stretched the truth."

"Even if it's only half true, you have to admire how she survived all the accidents and violence," said Sally.

Martha sank deeper into her overstuffed chair, defences falling away in the warmth and banter of the room. She noticed that her glass was emptying faster than the others', but she couldn't slow down, and she didn't object when Joanne filled it a third time. She curled up and listened to the conversation, unpressured to contribute.

Martha's mind drifted to Judith and her own escape from her calloused hand, dirt under nails, hyper-religious childhood—a world of predictable domestic rhythm, hard labour, corporal punishment, and the Bible. She'd scaled the walls of the ivory tower too. What manner of memoir would Judith have written if she'd dared acknowledge her roots? What kind of self-help book? Martha imagined a few titles— "Success through Radical Discipline" or "The Steinman-Gray Method: Raising Children Who Won't Embarrass You."

She was swallowing the last drops of her fourth glass when Amy stretched and announced that she had to wake early the next morning for a CrossFit workout before meeting a client at the gym. Moments later, they were donning coats and thanking Joanne for the evening.

"Hold on a minute!" Sally's screech reverberated under the Union Station-like ceiling of the front hall. "I've forgotten what we're reading for April."

"*We Have Always Been Here*," replied Jenn. "Another memoir to inspire and delight."

Martha finished the evening with a nightcap on the old man's chesterfield.

Wednesday, March 4th, 2020

Gordon sat on the side of his bed while Dr. Katherine Southey completed his admission physical. She pressed her fingertips into the top of his left foot. She'd dropped in to see her Oakview Lodge patients before clinic. It was an ungodly hour to be prodded. Not even eight o'clock—before coffee and a cigarette, for crying out loud. Even after a night's rest, Gordon's feet were swollen and the pressure from Katherine's fingers left dimples in his skin.

"Hmm," she said as she stood and squirted her hands with sanitizer.

"Hmm?" asked Gordon.

"I wonder if I should increase your Lasix. . . ."

"You want my opinion, Katherine?"

She laughed. "No Gordon. I'm just thinking aloud. Your chest isn't bad, all things considered. Let's have you put your feet up when you can. I think you should wear compression stockings to help with your circulation. I'd rather not add more pills . . . at least until I see your blood work."

"You mean pantyhose?" Gordon rasped.

"Yes. Well, no. Not pantyhose. They're similar but they only go up to your thigh and you can wear them under your pants. On in the morning, off at night."

Gordon had no intention of wearing a tight ladies' garment of any sort, though he wouldn't waste time on objections. She was already backing toward the door and he had to stop her. "Umm, Katherine?" he asked. "There's something on my mind. Do you have a minute?"

She glanced at her watch and forced a thin smile. "Sure. A minute."

"You can sit in my wheelchair if you'd like."

She eyed the wheelchair as if checking for cooties, then sat facing Gordon. "Well?"

"As I said last fall, I'd like to have a referral for MAID."

Katherine shook her head as if shocked by the request. "But you just moved in here. You should give yourself time to adjust."

"I only want to know if I qualify and to have the option open."

"Well, there are legal guidelines to determine who qualifies for it." She pulled her phone from her pocket, tapped in a query, and read aloud, "The patient must be capable of making healthcare decisions; have a grievous and irremediable medical condition; and natural death must be reasonably foreseeable."

"Okay," Gordon said quickly. "I believe I tick those boxes. Capable? Check. Grievous medical condition? I have dozens, therefore check. Every day I foresee my death, which is reasonable given my age. Again check."

Katherine crossed her legs, settling into the discussion. "Let's set aside the question of whether you're eligible for assisted death for a moment, Gordon. Remind me why you want to consider it at all."

"Two words. 'I'm tired.'"

"Okay. You're tired."

"I'm in a state of advanced, terminal, stage four, metastatic decrepitude. You can diagnose me at a glance."

Katherine nodded slowly.

She wouldn't be corralled into any promises, but he'd make his case, as he'd rehearsed for weeks. "Apologies to the great poets, Katherine, but I'm soon ready to go gentle into that good night. My life is no longer wild or precious. My life's work is behind me. Regression to Pablum and Pampers lie ahead."

"Incontinence isn't inevitable, Gordon."

"But decline is. To channel Monty Hall, which would *you* choose, Katherine? Behind door number one is a booby prize, a goat. We open the door to reveal the former physician and triathlete, Dr. Southey, now deaf, blind, and chair-bound in her dotage. And then there's door number two, a black door marked with a skeletal, robed figure holding a scythe. Perhaps there's a prize behind door number two. Perhaps oblivion. No one in the audience knows. Not even Monty Hall knows. Wouldn't you gamble on door number two?"

"Okay. You've laid out your logic, Gordon. But there was always a third door in 'Let's Make a Deal', wasn't there? The choice needn't be binary."

"Of course, it's binary," challenged Gordon. "It's 'to be or not to be.' Crappy life versus death."

"How's your mood?"

"I'm not depressed if that's what you're asking. My request is rational and life-affirming. Why ruin a wonderful, seventy-eight-year trip with a sojourn in a flea-bag motel at the end? I want off the bus when I ring the bell."

"You're unhappy at Oakview Lodge?"

"No, not at all. My room is nice, the food's adequate, and the people are friendly. I speak metaphorically. It's my senescence that's flea infested and unbearable."

"Alright. For now, let's set aside your claim that you're not depressed. Gordon, I'll be honest. I don't think you even qualify for an assisted death."

"Why not?"

"Because your health is stable. You're better than you were in January."

Tears of frustration pooled in Gordon's eyes. His predicament was obvious to both of them, but Katherine wouldn't acknowledge it. She passed Gordon a Kleenex. He mashed the tissue against his eyes, cleared his throat, and prepared to hear more rationalizations for her stonewalling.

"Gordon, you're not even eighty. You have chronic illnesses that could get better if you quit smoking. No practitioner would predict your death to be reasonably foreseeable."

"I wouldn't survive without modern healthcare," argued

Gordon. "My current existence is unnatural. I rely on medication and the everyday heroism of the staff."

"And you're not suffering. You told me yourself that you don't have pain."

"Ah, Katherine. I'm disappointed that you have the blinkered perspective of the empiricist. My suffering is not physical. It's existential. I'm not depressed; I'm realistic and I want to die when I choose."

Katherine tented her fingers and frowned. Gordon's plea hung in limbo between them. Finally, she said, "I acknowledge that you're suffering, Gordon. Down the road, there may be a route to your wish. However, as your doctor, I'm duty-bound to address any mental health issues before we even consider this request. I'd like to start you on a mild antidepressant."

No way. He wouldn't let her smother his will with pharmaceuticals. "All I have left is my brain and I won't take anything that will diminish my capacity to think," said Gordon.

"But—"

"Save your counsel. I did some research into antidepressants after I saw Tanice last fall. They all have side effects."

"Consulting Dr. Google, eh?"

"Sensible self-education."

A crash of dishes from the dining room reminded them both that breakfast was underway. Katherine's first patients of the day were probably filling her clinic waiting room already.

"I'll order the stockings. Keep your feet up, Gordon, and cut back on the smoking. I'll see you again in a couple of weeks. We'll revisit the issue of your mood then. In the meantime, google 'Remeron'. It's a light antidepressant, well tolerated in the elderly, and it might just turn that frown upside down."

"Thanks," Gordon said blankly.

Gordon decided to skip breakfast. Even coffee didn't appeal. The staff were occupied in the dining room, so he shoved his feet into his slippers and transferred himself to his wheelchair. He pulled a quilt around his shoulders, changed his oxygen tubing to his portable tank, and paddled out to the porch.

The air was still under a china-blue sky. He took off his oxygen and lit a cigarette, drawing a smooth puff of pleasure over his tongue, a balm for the soul. If heaven existed, there would be cigarettes there. And Judith. A childish fantasy yet comforting, nonetheless.

A squirrel scampered across the slender branch of a cherry tree. The pliant wood bent under the animal's weight and he clung on desperately. Comical self-rescue. The squirrel regained the branch and leaped to a thicker one, then ran along it and jumped to the roof of the bird feeder. A blue jay squawked in protest from another tree and a pair of chickadees flew away. Gordon marvelled at this active community of creatures. What did people know of the lives of animals? Of the lives of other people?

Katherine thought she knew best, but a woman of forty who ran marathons couldn't fathom his situation, and his longing to take control of his fate. Even Martha and Imogen understood more about life and death than Katherine Southey MD.

"Not hungry this morning?" Frank wheeled up beside Gordon and turned his chair to look over the garden too.

"Not really. I'll have a coffee later." Gordon lit Frank's cigarette for him.

Frank took a deep drag, nodded his thanks, and said, "I saw a redwing blackbird yesterday. Just over there, on the dogwood. Beautiful song."

"A sure sign of spring," said Gordon.

They smoked and watched the birds until a delivery van rumbled up the driveway and scared them off.

"Do you think birds and animals know about death?" Gordon asked.

"I think they're smarter than most people credit them," answered Frank. "Besides, what does anyone know about death? Gertrude, that Bible thumper who always says grace before meals, claims she's ready for Jesus to call her to heaven. He's called her a few times, but she hasn't gone. Instead, she goes by ambulance to Elmington General. She seems as reluctant to test her certainty as anyone else."

Gordon extinguished his cigarette on the edge of a concrete planter and put his oxygen back on. "I'm not a believer, but I've soon had enough of life."

"Me too," Frank admitted. "I've had a good life. Four kids and a baseball team worth of grandkids. Despite what people think of accountants, an interesting career. Carol and I globetrotted before the cancer took her. I'm ready to go anytime." He took a long drag.

"Have you ever thought of deciding yourself when the time is right . . . to go?" asked Gordon.

"What—like suicide?" asked Frank.

"Yeah. Doctor assisted or on your own."

"That's a mortal sin," Frank joked.

Gordon shrugged.

"You're serious." Frank's voice crackled with surprise.

"Why not? Save a lot of hassle. You get to choose the time and date."

"I see now. A convenient date," said Frank.

Gordon elaborated. "You can go to the bathroom beforehand, so it's not messy. Choose nice clothes and music, some poetry."

"You lost me on the poetry. They wouldn't need to drug me. That would push me over the edge."

"Philistine."

Frank crushed out his cigarette. "It's something to think about."

"What? Whitman or Dickinson?"

Frank laughed. "I'm going in before I catch pneumonia."

"And I'll have another smoke and hope I do," said Gordon.

Frank turned back and paddled away. He'd listened and didn't think the idea was crazy. That was something.

Gordon was napping in his room when he heard a familiar voice calling, "Mr. Gordon!"

For crying out loud. Was there a fire or something? Gordon opened his eyes and looked up. "Angelo!" he squawked, straightening in his recliner. "What are you doing here?"

"Working," Angelo entered the room. "This is my other job."

"Sit, sit," Gordon urged.

"Okay, just a little. My shift starts in ten minutes." Angelo sat on the foot of the bed.

"It's been a month and more. How are you?" asked Gordon.

"Keeping out of trouble."

"And Marisol and Pedro?"

"Keeping mama out of trouble. My wife will be extra busy because we're expecting another baby in August."

"Angelo, you devil. That's wonderful news. When did you have time to—" Gordon stopped himself. It was an impertinent question.

"I went to Manila for my auntie's funeral, remember?"

"Yes, I remember. Your favourite aunt."

"So sad, Mr. Gordon. I tell myself God needed another angel in heaven to watch over the children on earth, then I'm happy again. If the baby's a girl, we name after my aunt. Maricar."

"Maricar and Marisol. Two peas in a pod."

Angelo smiled broadly and stood. "I better get to work, Mr. Gordon. I'm glad you're here instead of Valhalla."

"Me too," Gordon agreed. "I'm glad you're here too."

After Angelo left, Gordon put his head back and closed his eyes again—in vain. Though his English was basic, the sage from Manila had expressed a profound truth. The old made way for the young. Ashes to ashes, the plough of fate turning every life into death in its furrow. The planet was both a nursery and a compost bin, and lamenting and clinging and renting of garments were acts of the foolish. In a minute, he'd take up that quarrelsome iPad and search for a doctor who would help him.

"Dad?"

Gordon opened his eyes again. Martha carrying a small yet heavy-looking cardboard box. "Duchess. What have you there, pray tell?"

"Some leftover bottles of Ensure. You can keep them here, in your room, in case you're hungry and the kitchen's closed."

"The kitchen never closes."

"Still. I won't drink them, and we have to clear out the house."

Gordon's eyes narrowed as Martha bent gingerly and put the box in his closet. "Are you unwell, Duchess?" He could diagnose a hangover at a glance.

"I'm fine," replied Martha. "I was at Joanne's book club last night. May have eaten a sausage roll that was off."

"Or had a glass too many," Gordon added.

"Yeah," Martha admitted. "Fortunately, hangovers are self-limiting."

Though Gordon was careful never to scold, Martha quickly changed the subject. "We talked about that memoir, *Educated*."

"The one about the girl who grew up with home-schoolin' End Timers and got her PhD?"

"That's it. Have you read it?"

"Didn't have to. I lived with it. It's your mother's story,

Martha. Except tooting her own horn in a memoir would've been impossible for her. She wasn't humble, but she was modest, all Mennonite in her marrow."

Martha looked at the photo on the dresser of a young, dark-eyed, dark-haired Judith seated on a gingham picnic blanket and holding a fat baby on her lap, willow branches as frame and backdrop.

Gordon continued. "She let her achievements speak for themselves. Including you."

"She was ashamed of me, Dad."

"No, she wasn't. She was proud of you. She just couldn't let herself show it. She didn't know how."

"She had a freaking PhD in psychology."

"Exactly. She knew she was flawed. She studied hard, for years and years, and she tried to change but she couldn't."

Martha appeared to force back angry tears. She wasn't ready to see Judith as anything but a monster. He had to back off. Voice gentle, Gordon said, "She gave you her brains, curiosity, and wit. At least grant her that."

"No," objected Martha. "She gave me her neuroticism. If I have any wit, and that's an open question, I got it from you."

They were spinning their tires. Time to shift gears . . . go easy. He said, "I suppose you're right, Duchess. I gave you my outstanding wit and my modesty."

Martha chuckled weakly. "I'll get us some ginger ale."

"Let's have it al fresco," suggested Gordon. "It's time for my afternoon smoke."

Thursday, March 5th, 2020

"Come on, Gordon. Show us some leg." Anita, a late-career nurse, bent over the footrest of Gordon's recliner and tugged and pushed at his trouser cuffs.

"You're on a fool's errand, lass. I don't intend to wear stockings anyway," said Gordon.

"Dr. Southey ordered them," Anita declared, as if no more need be said on the subject.

"Fine. She can wear them," said Gordon.

"They're comfortable once you get used to them. They push the blood up from your lower legs. Keeps the swelling down . . . prevents muscle fatigue and blood clots."

"Do you wear them?" asked Gordon.

"No, but I have normal circulation," replied Anita as she measured the circumference of Gordon's legs. She jotted the numbers down in a note pad she kept in her patch pocket. "If I order them today, we'll have them by early next week."

"Is that a promise or a threat?"

"You decide, Gordon." Anita sighed. She went to the cart she'd parked outside Gordon's door, and returned with his inhaler, a tiny cup of medication, and a glass of water. "Puffer first," she ordered.

Gordon saluted and inhaled on command, then coughed as the powder hit his throat.

"Pills." Anita handed him his medication.

"Remind me what's in here, lass," Gordon rasped. His breathing always got worse before it got better after using the inhaler.

"Lasix, Eliquis, digoxin, and Norvasc," answered Anita. "Hey, are you quizzing me?"

"Damn right I am. I want to make sure Dr. Southey didn't change anything without telling me."

Anita stuck an oximeter on Gordon's finger. "Ninety-two

percent. Acceptable. Gordon, I'm curious. How do you manage to go without oxygen when you smoke? I mean, you're borderline with it going at three litres—"

"I just take the tubing off for a couple minutes at a time. Have a smoke, then put it right back on."

"What?" Anita looked startled. Her words gushed out like a torrent from a firehose. "Gordon, that's extremely dangerous! You could catch fire. Start the building on fire. You can't be out there with your oxygen and an open flame. I can't believe what I'm hearing."

"I've been doing it for months. No harm," countered Gordon.

"Not anymore, you're not. That's a very dangerous thing to do. From now on, you ask someone to take you out to smoke without the tank. And if I see you smoking on the porch with your tank, I'll haul you back inside and take your cigarettes away."

"You can't do that," objected Gordon. "That's forcible confinement and theft."

"I can and I will—for your own safety." Anita strode back to the hall.

"Wait a—"

"I have to go," she interrupted as she pushed the cart away. "You're not my only resident, you know."

Gordon was furious. How dare she. How dare she decide what he could and couldn't do.

War had been declared.

Friday, March 6th, 2020

Martha read aloud from the attachment on a text she'd received from Mavis:

Shy Elmington Charmer

Great opportunity in desirable neighbourhood, walking distance to lake, quiet street, close to schools. Cute single-family home, 2-bedroom, one bath, eat-in kitchen, attached garage, generous lot. Add your own touches or start afresh. $875,900. Act fast!

"That's how she wants to list the house. What do you think?"

"It's fine," replied Imogen. "Makes the house sound like a precocious fifteen-year-old girl in pigtails and pinafore, ready for finishing school, but you say she knows what she's doing."

"She's a pro. She wants Sally to come by for photos on Monday and put the listing up on MLS ahead of the spring rush."

"When?"

"The photos? Monday. With a sign on the lawn and showings starting Tuesday."

"Monday? No fucking way, Martha. We've barely started packing." Imogen plunked herself down on a crate, next to a box of dishes from the corner cabinet, and crossed her arms, on strike. "We'll need weeks at the rate we're going," she whined.

"We don't have to pack everything. We just have to get rid of the clutter. If a prospective buyer opens a closet, stuff shouldn't fall off shelves or spill out."

"Or bury them in an avalanche."

"Right."

Imogen returned to the task of wrapping fragile things and tucking them into cardboard boxes. She said, "These are pretty dishes. They seem out of character for your mother." She held a saucer with a floral wreath running round its edge up to the window light, then turned it over and whistled. "Royal Doulton."

"Yeah. We never used the china. I think those were a wedding gift from an aunt on Dad's side."

"Pity," said Imogen affecting a posh English accent.

"Not really. I would've been the dishwasher, and if I'd broken one . . . Anyway, Judith never entertained here at the house. If she had to hold a party, she'd rent a room at a restaurant. She said that a professional woman should never relegate herself to a domestic role such as hostess if she wanted to be taken seriously. Even among friends."

Martha's tone mocked, yet Imogen agreed. "She was right, Martha. The bearer of birthday cakes and the buyer of collective retirement gifts gets no respect. Menial errands are for low-status lightweights. People pleasers. Many a woman has killed her career by running around the office getting signatures on a card."

"The advice seems so calculating, though, Imogen. If you want to cook for your friends, you should cook for your friends. Throw away the rule books and live as you wish. That is true feminism."

Imogen cocked an eyebrow as if to say, "True feminism?" then returned to her task.

"What now?"

"Martha, you button your shirt all the way to the freaking collar. You do not throw away rule books. You adore them. You are completely and utterly captivated by rule books."

"I read as a scholar, sure. I have to understand the dynamic."

"Uh-huh? A scholar, eh? That's cover. You read self-help as a survivor. You were raised by an abusive army commandant and an indulgent anarchist with no middle ground and no siblings to help you figure things out. Now you careen between the two extremes and you never find the middle."

"Whatever," Martha said, irritated.

"Oh, that is so adolescent. Is that the best you can do?" Imogen paused work and crossed her arms.

"Yes," Martha said sharply.

The silence hung as thick as the dust in the air until Imogen balled up a sheet of the newspaper she'd been using as wrapping and threw it at Martha's back. "I'm sorry."

Martha dropped a pile of magazines in the blue box and turned. "For what?"

"For psychoanalyzing you."

"Imogen, you know you're right so don't apologize, and for God's sake, don't gloat." Martha threw a phone book into the bin, on top of the magazines. She sensed Imogen's gaze on her back, felt her sympathy. Jesus. Gross.

However, when Imogen spoke, she said exactly the right thing. "We need a break, Martha. Want to drink some gin from a china teacup?"

Martha turned again. "You mean, strike a balance? The middle road? Be genteel and reckless at the same time?"

"Sure. We can toast Judith's ghost and send her off. Hold a compassionate, nonviolent exorcism."

Martha laughed. "Why not."

"Afterward, we can figure out how to pull you out of the fucking closet. You're a dusty old prom dress and you need your freedom," Imogen added.

"Baby steps, Imogen," called Martha as she went to the kitchen to fetch the booze. Not a cruel "no," though that was the real answer. There was only so much change Martha could handle, least of all her identity, and Imogen had to understand that.

Imogen departed to run errands ahead of her Saturday shift, leaving Martha alone in the bungalow for the evening. She swept out the garage and then piled boxes of clothing and houseware awaiting dispersion along its cinder block wall. At last, she felt as if she'd accomplished enough to break for the evening and check her email.

The background chatter of the pandemic rising in Asia, sweeping across the globe, began to infect her inbox. Updates from the university, missives from the dean, what-if speculations from friends and colleagues—and a message from Diane Stefano, Director of Care, Oakview Lodge. Like an anxious parent finding a note from the principal in her child's backpack, Martha clicked on that message first:

Dear Friends and Family of the Residents of Oakview Lodge,

As you may be aware, COVID 19 is a contagious infection that causes pneumonia, especially in vulnerable populations such as the elderly and immunocompromised people. The residents at Oakview Lodge are at risk of severe illness from COVID 19. Currently, case numbers are rising in Canada, a concerning situation for all in the Oakview community.

To protect your loved ones, we ask that you avoid visiting Oakview if you show any signs of illness, including fever, cough, runny nose, sore throat, or fatigue. Additionally, we will be screening visitors at the door and you will be turned away if you show any signs of infection. Lastly, we ask that you limit your visits. From Saturday, March 7th, 2020, we will have a policy of one visitor per resident only.

Please understand that we truly appreciate our Oakview Lodge community and that these measures are being taken out of an abundance of caution and care for your loved ones.

Our policies including infection control and visiting can be found on our website at . . .

Martha clicked delete out of irritation over new, petty, institutional rules, then rethought her hasty dismissal and retrieved the message. She had to pay attention to this . . . phenomenon? The gathering clouds of pestilence and doom? "One visitor only." At a time? Or total? Martha decided that Diane meant "at a time." Imogen would be visiting after work on Saturday. "One only" didn't make any sense. It was unreasonably strict.

Hoping for more information, Martha clicked on the link, but the bullet-pointed webpage only restated the content of Diane's letter. She felt as if walls were falling in around her. As she skimmed through article after article, she realized she hadn't been keeping up with the emerging crisis. She had to see the old man. Right away. Check out the situation for herself.

Martha made it to Oakview Lodge by eight pm. Frank sat alone on the porch. He greeted her with a sombre, "Hi Martha. Your father's inside tonight." She started to reply, but Frank continued. "He's banished from the smoking area because he's on oxygen. Not too happy about it. Can't say I blame him. I miss his company. That's for sure."

"Thanks for warning me, Frank. I'd better get in there," said Martha.

As she passed through the double doors she was confronted by a self-serve screening and decontamination centre consisting of a table with sanitizer and a new sign that stood as tall as an NBA player and was printed in bold red and black lettering. She cleaned her hands, wrote her name in the binder to declare her good health, and headed to Gordon's room.

She found the old man sitting on his rollator by the window, knocking the ash from his cigarette on the edge of the sill.

"Dad?"

"Duchess. Close the door—quick!"

She did as she was told then crossed the room. "What are you—"

"Taking matters into my own hands," wheezed Gordon. He took a final puff, extinguished the butt in a Dixie cup of water, and stuck it in its pack of origin. Then he put his oxygen back on.

"You're taking a big risk." Martha settled onto the armrest of the recliner to face him.

Gordon caught his breath, then spoke. "What can they do? Expel me? I leave the window open—it doesn't open wide but it's enough—and the smoke clears with the ventilation blowing all the time."

"What if someone comes in and catches you?"

"A couple of them have. Angelo and Theresa. But they don't do anything because it's more work for them. They'd have to take me outside . . . monitor me."

"Jeez, Dad. What if Diane found out, or one of the nurses?"

"I know my rights. They can take my cigarettes away, but they can't throw me out. I don't have a home to go to anymore. I'd be homeless." Gordon grinned conspiratorially. "And you'd smuggle in more cigarettes."

"We could ask for nicotine patches."

"Absolutely not. Patches are to smoking what porn is to real sex. Sorry, Duchess. I'm embarrassing you."

Martha shook her head to dismiss his apology. "You should have called me. When they changed the rules on you."

"You're cleaning out the house. You have enough to do without fighting a losing battle here. Policies are policies. The best approach is to work around them."

"Smoking here seems more dangerous than the porch though."

"You have a better idea?" When Martha didn't reply he asked, "Is Imogen back?"

"Yes, Dad. She'll visit you tomorrow after work. Just her. It's one visitor at a time now because of COVID 19."

"They're scared we'll all catch it. Meanwhile, half of us hope we will, fatally, and the other half don't know their undies from their dinner plate."

"You can't speak for the other residents, Dad, and Oakview has a duty to keep you safe. The rules do seem strict though."

"Have you heard from Joseph?"

"Only that short email with the photo of Tayana and him in the greenhouse."

"Yeah. I saw it too. Among the seedlings. They look happy."

Martha nodded.

"Best anyone can hope for," Gordon said wistfully. "Martha, I asked Dr. Southey about MAID."

"What?" The old man turned conversational corners faster than she could follow.

"M.A.I.D. Medical assistance in dying," said Gordon.

"Okay?" She knew death was his major preoccupation, but he was only settling into nursing home life.

"I want to have the option. Not right away, just for when I choose. For when I'm really fed up, once and for all."

"What did Dr. Southey say?"

"In a word, 'no,' because I'm not sick enough. So I called the number on the MAID hotline and left a message."

Martha gazed out the window. Everything always happened before she was ready. Decisions made, world changing, people disappearing. She clung to the flagpole while tornadoes blew by and left her to sort out her life, alone in their aftermath. "Have you heard back?"

Gordon spoke softly, as if his words would be easier to process at low volume. "Not yet, Duchess. As I said, I only want to keep the option in my back pocket."

Martha kept her composure. What the old man was telling

her wasn't exactly a surprise. What came next surprised her though.

"Just in case the MAID doctor declines my request, I'm keeping my digoxin tablets here. In case, Martha." Gordon paddled over to his dresser, pulled the top drawer open, and pulled out a silver cigarette case, a gift from Judith that he used for odds and ends such as business cards and matches because it was too precious and too dandyish for cigarettes.

"You're not taking your pills?"

"I take everything but the digoxin. The nurses usually leave my pills on my tray table as I'm 'mentally capable', and I've started tucking the digoxin away. It's digitalis, Martha. In a large dose it stops the heart. The muscle squeezes and doesn't let go."

Once again, Martha found herself horrified and curious at the same time. "How many have you saved, Dad?"

"Only one, so far. I started this morning." His eyes shone with pride at his own cleverness.

"Aren't you afraid your CHF will get worse if you don't take them?"

Gordon dismissed the concern with a scowl, as if to imply the question was daft.

Martha muttered, "No, I suppose you aren't," and dropped the subject.

They talked of other things—the packing of the house, the weather, and other trivial matters—until Gordon removed his oxygen and pulled his cigarettes from his pocket.

"I'm getting out of here," said Martha. "I don't want to be caught red-handed with you smoking."

"Nighty-night then, Duchess."

"Good night, Dad." She kissed the top of his head and fled.

As she joined the light Friday evening traffic, she ruminated on Diane's message, the news of the day, and the old man's shrinking world. He was boxed into a jail cell because he couldn't follow the rules. He couldn't follow other people's rules. Only his own. And again, she was his lifeline. When she went back to BC, as soon as she was out of the picture, he'd — well — he'd probably pull his own plug.

She pulled into the driveway of 22 Roselea and texted Joe.

Saturday, March 7th, 2020

The snow was melting, leaving a gritty filth on Elmington's roads, sidewalks, and parking lots. Fed up with the stale gloom of the house, Martha stepped outside with a broom. A sweater was all she needed for warmth. The sunshine caressed her shoulders and energized her soul. What a fine afternoon. Only those who bore the huddled inconveniences and minor discomforts of a long Canadian winter without a beachside holiday could revel properly in the first warm days of spring. On such a day as this she almost felt sorry for snowbirds. The winter weather would return, but on this day the streets of Elmington belonged to cheerful joggers, parents pushing strollers, and kids on skateboards and bikes.

First Martha tidied the back deck, sweeping with single-minded purpose. The regular yoga sessions had paid off. She felt strong and unstoppable, like the bunny with the drum kit in those old battery commercials. By late afternoon, she'd finished the deck and the front porch and she was moving down the driveway, raising plumes of dust with each stroke, revealing asphalt under the dirt, cigarette butts, and the detritus of winter.

She didn't hear Imogen park her little car on the street and sidle up behind her for the noise of the broom and her intense focus. She did feel Imogen's arms encircle her and pull her in and Imogen's kiss on her neck. Martha stepped away and spun around. "Not here," she hissed.

Imogen's smile crumpled into hurt. "I was only—"

"Someone could've seen us," said Martha.

"Who?" A single bewildered syllable.

"Anyone. The neighbours. Joanne Kingsworth."

"Joanne Bloody Kingsworth. You don't even like the woman. What would it matter if she saw us, Martha?"

"She'd tell Sally and Mavis and—"

"Oh. So that's it. You're afraid of gossip. You don't want anyone to know about us. Bloody hell, Martha."

"It's not like that, Imogen," Martha protested.

"Oh? What's it like then?"

Martha ignored the taunting question and began sweeping with angry vigour until Imogen snatched the broom away. "What's going on, Martha?"

"I'm not ready to—"

"You're ashamed of us, aren't you?"

"Keep your voice down, Imogen. People will hear us."

"No, they won't, Martha. Because I'm leaving."

"Let's go into the house and talk."

"No. You're sweeping." Imogen tossed the broom back to Martha. "Call me when you're ready to be honest. When you're ready to stop treating me like your fucking dirty little secret." She left the driveway in swift strides, started the Yaris, and roared away.

Martha leaned against the broom and stared at the place where Imogen's car had been parked. Imogen wasn't coming back. She picked up where she'd left off, grimly determined to finish the job. As the sun set, an icy chill rolled up from the lake. She'd looked forward to spending the evening with Imogen . . . ordering food, huddling under blankets, and laughing and talking and not running out of things to say. Never running out of things to say. Damn her.

Saturday evening. After a hot bath, Martha sat in a lawn chair with a G and T and a bowl of potato chips and surveyed the living room. Only yesterday she and Imogen had pushed the furniture into a corner and built a pyramid of empty boxes at the former site of the old man's recliner. The broadloom was dingy and worn in paths and show-room fresh where furniture had protected it. She had a DIY carpet cleaning machine reserved for Sunday afternoon. The walls needed a proper scrub too. She'd taken down pictures for the old man's room at Oakview. Now bright, off-white rectangles decorated the yellow-beige walls at eye level. And the curtains! The house proclaimed with trumpets and banners and a malodorous punch in the nose that a smoker had lived in it. Maybe it would be easier to paint the walls than wash them. She could have the curtains dry-cleaned. Imogen would know what to do.

A drink first. Let the Beefeater drown her pride and self-pity in a moderate glass, then find an angle, a key, and approach Imogen contritely. Win her over—literally. Imogen in her little car, driving over, all understanding and forgiveness, laughter and affection. If Martha could find the right words.

She went back to the kitchen, fixed another drink at the counter, and picked up her phone. A simple message was best.

> I'm sorry.

Imogen always answered right away. Tonight she did not. A few minutes later, Martha tried again.

> Hey Imogen. Can we talk? I have all-you-can-eat junk food here. Or we can go upscale with Mumbai Gourmet.

No reply. Fine. Whatever. She had to get back to work. She filled a bucket with warm water and Pine-Sol, stirred up a sudsy froth, and tackled the walls with a rag. Great streaks and arcs of light beige appeared under each pass of her arm. The bucket water turned the colour of a mud puddle. Slow progress. She needed help.

She texted Imogen again.

> Hi Imogen. I'm cleaning the walls now. Barrel of laughs but would be even more fun with you.

A moment later, Martha's phone rattled. Finally. Now they could talk things out. Get back to normal. Martha opened Imogen's message.

> Martha. I love you but I can only continue with you and me being us if you acknowledge our relationship publicly. If your answer is yes, I'll come over right away.

An ultimatum. Martha didn't make decisions under duress. Imogen was playing with fire. Acting as if one's identity was an emergency, which it was not. Jesus. This was all she needed . . . soul-searching, emotionally-charged discussions in the middle of —Martha looked at the striped wall—this upheaval. If that's what it took to get some help, then game on. She replied:

> Imogen, I love you too. Can we talk about this? Come on over. I'm sorry about what happened in the driveway.

> If you're sorry and you want me in your life, then answer yes.

> Let's talk.

> No. Let's not. You take, take, take, Martha. I ask for one little thing, and you say let's talk. No. Fucking no. Good night and good-bye.

Jesus. "One little thing?" It wasn't "one little thing." It was a huge, enormous, gigantic life-changing thing. An entire identity wasn't an unfashionable dress that you replaced on a whim. And to insinuate that she was selfish at a time like this! Imogen's accusation was way off base. The timing was horrible. Imogen was the selfish one.

Martha refilled the bucket and continued washing the walls. It was miserable work.

Sunday, March 8th, 2020

The old man was resting in his recliner when Martha arrived with a box of summer clothes at mid-morning. His hair was pasted onto his scalp in a ducktail and he was freshly shaven, doused in cologne, and dressed in crisply pressed clothes. Martha made a mental note to ask about a barber.

"Who did your hair, Dad?" she asked as she set the box on the bed.

"Theresa. Gave me a jacuzzi bath too. She's handy with a comb and a dab of Brylcreem," wheezed Gordon.

"I'd say she missed her calling."

"Perhaps, Duchess. She runs a fine bath. A Jill of all trades. What's in the box?"

"Your summer clothes. Cotton shirts, shorts, sandals . . ."

"You have high hopes," said Gordon.

"To look at you this morning, I think you'll need these

clothes," said Martha as she began transferring Gordon's summer wardrobe from box to closet.

"How did you and Imogen make out with the house last night?"

"Well. The outdoor sweeping is finished, and the walls are washed. I'm picking up a carpet cleaner this afternoon."

"Sounds adventurous," deadpanned Gordon. "The intelligentsia cavorting with the proletariat."

"A machine. Not a man," Martha clarified.

Gordon shook his head, as if disappointed she hadn't laughed at his joke. "Good," he said. "It'll keep you and Imogen busy and her mind off work. I thanked her yesterday and told her she didn't have to help, but she said she was having fun polishing the 'bloody tarnish off the silver teapot that is 22 Roselea.' Her words. I'm not one to swear."

"She's a hard worker," said Martha.

"Damn right she is. Simon doesn't know how lucky he is to have her on staff. He repays her people skills and creativity in the kids' department by reviewing her expenses from the conference. She's back one day and the officious pinprick trots into the library, on a Saturday for crying out loud, to deliver censure. A final warning, no union rep present."

Martha shook her head as if Imogen's predicament had been troubling her all night.

The old man continued, "The committee made a huge mistake when they hired that rule obsessed, nitpicking, people hater. If she loses her job over this—"

"She'll be okay, Dad," Martha said reassuringly. "She always finds a way to hang on." Why hadn't Imogen said anything? Oh, right. Because she'd rejected her before Imogen had a chance to tell her.

"Yeah. Nine lives," Gordon agreed. "Hey, are those my swimming trunks?"

"I believe they are," replied Martha, relieved to change the subject. She held up a garment printed with pink flamingoes on an indigo background for the old man's appraisal.

"Last time I wore those, your mother and I were up on the Bruce Peninsula."

Grateful for diversion from the matter of Imogen, Martha continued unpacking and listening as the old man prattled down memory lane. She left an hour later and phoned Imogen from the parking lot, but her call went directly to a full voice mailbox.

Gordon was finishing his second cigarette of the afternoon when his phone rang. Joseph's voice shouted into his ear over the rumble of vehicles and the blast of a truck horn.

"Grandpa?"

"Joe! Where are you?"

"At the co-op. I'm filling the van and picking up our bulk food order."

"Ah, that explains the racket. Doesn't sound like Shangri-La."

"Agape," Joseph corrected, laughing. "I've left utopia to run errands in town."

"How's Tayana?"

"Fine. We're both fine. And you, Grandpa?"

"Fine too. I'm at Oakview Lodge. But you know that. You called me on my new number."

"Yeah. Mom texted me and told me to call you. She made it sound like it was an emergency, but you sound pretty good, compared to last Christmas."

"Thanks . . . I guess. I'm adjusting to the communal lifestyle. Any tips, Joe?"

"For living in community? It's not easy. Umm . . . let's see. Obedience is easier than resistance?"

"Never mind," said Gordon. "Your mother fervently believes

in collectivism, but a week at Oakview would fix her idealism in a jiffy."

"You could move back to the house."

"No, Joe. I'm here for the count. Your mom and Imogen have been getting the house ready for sale. I'm where I belong."

"That's okay then," said Joe. "I'd like to move. I'm tired of ridiculous rules and all the hassle of living in a crowd, but Tayana loves it here."

"And you love Tayana."

"Yeah, so I'm stuck. Maybe in the fall, after harvest, we'll go back to Winnipeg for a visit."

"I hear Winnipeg is especially lovely in winter," Gordon teased.

"Her family gives Winnipeg an edge over Siberia and hopefully Agape. Maybe we can visit you too."

"I'd like that," said Gordon. "Now you should phone your mom. Not a text, a real call. She'd love to hear your voice."

"I will," Joe promised. "I'd phone more often, but the signal's spotty on the farm and Master Garuda is basically the NSA."

"That's utopia for you," said Gordon. "Now shoo. You have another call to make."

After he hung up, Gordon sat contentedly for a few moments and thought of Martha, Joseph, Tayana, and Imogen—his people. Whatever problems they faced, they had each other. Each of them would be okay if they stuck together after he was gone.

For the last time, Martha flicked the toggle on the carpet cleaner to silence its roar. She hauled the machine into the kitchen and dumped the final round of dirty water from its reservoir into the sink. The rental was worth every penny.

What a difference some sudsy water, a rotating brush, and a powerful vacuum made. If Imogen had come over, they could've moved more of the furniture . . . cleaned more thoroughly.

Martha checked her phone, hoping the ice had melted. Two missed calls from Joe. Joe! Jeez. He'd texted too.

> Hi Mom. I'm in town so tried to call. Going back to the farm now. Sorry I missed you. Talked to Grandpa. He sounds good. I'll call again when I can.

Martha tapped a response with no idea when Joe would receive it.

She tried Imogen's number, and again she reached a full voice mailbox. Imogen would see the missed calls, so Martha didn't text. The situation was too delicate. She had to find the right combo of words to crack the safe. Send the wrong message and everything would blow up in her face and ruin her life again.

Monday, March 9th, 2020

Sally climbed down from the stepladder she'd brought and zipped her camera into its case. "I'll have plenty to work with, Martha. The magic happens at my desk. I can even out tones, straighten lines, brighten everything up."

"Like Photoshopping a mugshot for a dating profile," said Martha.

"Exactly. Good-bye, receding hairline, adios, crow's feet, au revoir, double chin. I should have the photos ready by tonight if you want a preview."

"That's okay, Sally. You're busy enough."

"It doesn't take any time. I'll cc you when I send them to Mavis."

Martha nodded, "Okay."

"Where will you stay when the house is sold?"

"Hopefully back in my condo in Vancouver. In the meantime, I plan to stay in my bedroom, here, in one room, so the house can be shown without me in the way." She mentally added, *I'd planned to stay with my girlfriend, but we had a relationship-ending blowup, so now I'm a refugee in the old man's house.*

"That's fine. Mavis will warn you when she's arranged a showing, so you can tidy up and you aren't underfoot."

"Underfoot?"

"Yes, silly. Real estate is like sausage making. You don't want to witness it. Buyers can be downright mean. Mocking other people's taste, sniffing about the décor, complaining about proportions, closet size, you know . . ."

"It's nothing personal, though, is it? I don't think hearing criticism would bother me."

"Until it does, Martha. Believe me. You don't want to know what people think of your precious little house. You only want an unconditional offer with a quick close."

"Okay," agreed Martha. "I'll make myself scarce. Mavis said the listing and sign would go up tomorrow?"

"That's another thing. We might want to wait a week or two. I'm not supposed to say anything because it's all hush-hush, but Mavis heard through her grapevine that the government might be shutting down business for a week or two. She doesn't want to put up the listing and create a buzz only to press pause. You want a sold sign up, pronto—not a sad looking 'for sale' sign, stuck in the lawn for weeks, crying to the world, 'no one wants me'—even if the reasons are beyond anyone's control. Anyway, she's working the phones today, calling her contacts in government, so she can be ahead of the curve."

"I can't believe property sales would be shut down."

"Neither can I," said Sally, "and I said that to Mavis. She told me to pay attention to what's happening in China, in Europe . . . all those people dying in Italy. The government might shut down everything—stores, schools, gyms, even Nirvana Garden. People are scared. Anyway, when Mavis knows what's up, she'll finalize the plan."

"Thanks, Sally."

"No problemo, Martha."

After Sally left, Martha flipped open her laptop and caught up on the news.

Tuesday, March 10th, 2020

Diane Stefano summoned Martha to her office as a matter of urgency, and now they sat across from each other at her desk, occupying the same chairs as they had a week prior.

"I'll come straight to the point," said Diane. "Gordon is finding the adjustment to Oakview Lodge difficult."

"How do you know that?" asked Martha.

"Well, he exhibits several signs. He stays in his room a lot. He's oppositional. He violates rules and routines and claims ignorance and surprise when he's called on his behaviour."

"He seemed happy when I visited on Sunday."

"Oh, I'm not saying Gordon isn't happy. In fact, he seems quite pleased with himself— pushing buttons, testing boundaries. The staff have been coping admirably, but this morning matters came to a head."

Came to a head, like an over-ripe, pus-filled zit. Martha detested that phrase. Now annoyed, she couldn't stifle her instinct to defend the old man. "He's not used to following anyone's routine but his own and he's only been here a week," she said stiffly.

"That's true," agreed Diane. "We expect to encounter some challenges as the staff learn about a new resident and the resident finds their place in Oakview, especially when the resident is confused. However, that isn't the case with Gordon. He is fully cognizant of the rules."

Such as not smoking in his room, thought Martha. A predictable, justified, heat-seeking missile of an allegation was on its way. Best listen with angelic innocence, hear Diane out, and empathize. "He can be difficult," said Martha, hoping she came across as understanding.

"Difficult and dangerous."

Martha frowned. Surely characterizing the old man as "dangerous" was a tad over the top. He weighed all of 130 pounds and moved at the speed of a Model T with a broken axle.

Diane continued. "This morning the nurse caught him smoking in his room. We suspected he'd been engaging in this behaviour, but he wouldn't admit it, even when asked directly. He was quite manipulative and evasive."

"I hope he didn't lie."

"No, he didn't. He didn't tell the truth either. Anita had to pop into his room after she'd already given him his medications to catch him by surprise."

Martha imagined the dramatic, high-conflict scene as if it were an episode on a true crime show— 'Take-Down at Oakview Lodge.' "Then what happened?" she asked.

"Anita removed Gordon's cigarettes and lighter from his person. We have a smoking contract and we've drafted rules for Gordon. I thought we should have your input before we present them to him."

A smoking contract would go over like a lead balloon trailing an anchor. Martha chuckled nervously.

Diane picked up on her hesitancy. "Martha, in my experience, the elderly need structure. We'll lay out the rules clearly so there can be no misunderstanding and no debate. As part of Gordon's circle of care, we'd like your buy-in . . . for unity."

"Does Dad get any input?"

Diane shook her head. "I'm afraid he's not interested in contributing to the conversation."

"Oh?"

"He transferred himself to bed right after Anita confiscated the hazardous items and he's been lying there ever since, facing the wall and refusing to eat or drink. He says we've stolen his personal property."

"Well, haven't you?"

"No. They're his cigarettes. If he abides by the rules, he'll have access to them. We've explained that to him."

They had to get beyond definitions . . . beyond debating the meaning of words such as "personal property" and "stolen". Martha said, "Alright. What rules do you have in mind?"

Diane pushed a stapled, two-page document across the desk. "The first page is our standard smoking contract. We introduce that if we run into problems."

"Like Dad."

"Like your dad's behaviour. The contract stipulates that he must follow the rules. Failure to comply will result in loss of smoking privileges. The rules are on the next page."

Martha flipped the first leaf over and read:

Gordon's Rules for Tobacco Use
   I agree to:

1. *Always ask politely for a staff member or family member to take me outside to smoke.*
2. *Never smoke in my room or any place other than the designated outdoor smoking area.*

3. *Never borrow cigarettes from Frank or any other resident.*
4. *Always keep <u>all</u> of my smoking products including cigarettes, matches, and lighter with the nurse and ask for them politely when I want to use them.*
5. *Never use foul or abusive language when communicating.*

Martha pushed the document back to Diane. "Is Dad aware that you've drafted these rules?"

"Yes. Umm, not exactly. As I mentioned, he refused to participate in a discussion on safe smoking. Of course, I did inform him that we'd be taking steps."

Taking steps. A flaming red matador's cape. No wonder the old man was catatonic with rage. Meanwhile, the writing was on the wall in bold, six-foot-tall capitals. Diane managed an institution housing some two hundred frail elderly people. She couldn't compromise on safety. Martha sighed with resignation. "These rules are actually nonnegotiable, correct?"

"Correct," Diane nodded slowly.

"Very well. May I make a couple of minor suggestions?"

"Please do."

"If you could replace the word 'never' with a simple 'not'. And Dad would be insulted by rule number five. He's normally chivalrous to a fault. You could add that rule if his standards slip, but I'd leave it off for now. You don't need to use the adverb 'politely' either."

"He wasn't polite to Anita," argued Diane. Martha frowned and Diane quickly added, "But we can omit that word if you feel Gordon will respond better."

Martha nodded in return. "I'll talk to him, Diane, before you lay down the law again. And I'll take him outside for a smoke. If you could let Anita know . . . I'll need his hazardous items."

Wednesday, March 11th, 2020

Smoking on the porch with supervision sucked. Gordon didn't say so out loud because he didn't want to seem ungrateful, and anyway, he had to concentrate on breathing between puffs, not complaining. Per the Rules, Martha left his oxygen inside the building, and he couldn't stick it on to catch his breath. He was locked into a perverse ritual. Ask nicely to smoke, escalate to begging, be taken outside like a puppy being housebroken, smoke—quickly—and be pushed back indoors for his oxygen. The procedure left him breathless and grumpy and pining for release.

Martha vowed to visit daily, but she could only come for a couple hours, and by mid-April, she'd be back in BC. Most of the time, he had to bother staff who were busy and disapproving. That morning even Angelo ducked into a broom closet when he saw him coming down the hall. The support workers and nurses didn't have time to indulge his addiction. They didn't understand that smoking was not a pleasure; it was a necessary ordeal.

"Like old times, eh, Gordon," said Frank, parked next to him on the porch.

Gordon nodded and drew a puff on his cigarette.

Martha spoke for him. "Dad enjoys your company, Frank. Better than being in your room, isn't it, Dad?"

Weak shrug.

She went on. "Especially now that the worst of winter is behind us. You two will really enjoy this porch when the flowers come up."

Flowers? For crying out loud. As if he and Frank would want to talk about flowers and kittens and unicorns . . . if he could even muster his breath to talk. He stared grimly at the matted, brown lawn and shook his head. Flowers . . .

"There was quite a show last fall, Martha," said Frank. "The gardener put in some mums and late-blooming crocuses and those weird purple and white cabbages. Carol would've loved to see them."

Judith would've too.

"Mom would've too. Isn't that right, Dad?" said Martha.

Gordon forced a gruff "yes" and took a final drag on his cigarette.

"I'd better get Dad inside, Frank. See you later," said Martha as she turned the wheelchair.

"See you at supper," said Frank.

Gordon briefly raised his hand off the armrest in response.

Just past the double doors, Martha retrieved his tank from behind a potted palm and put the tubing back onto his face. Gordon took a few breaths, in through the nose, out through the mouth. He felt marginally better.

"I'll keep your hazardous items, Dad, and take you out again in an hour or so," she said.

Hazardous items. Their twisted, dark joke. Gordon smirked and wheezed, "Thanks, Duchess." Now she'd want to talk about the sale of the house. He didn't care about the house. He'd sign on the dotted line when the time came, whatever the price, terms, and conditions.

He didn't care anymore. He really didn't care.

Martha flopped onto her back and stared at the lunar landscape of her bedroom ceiling. The irony of the situation wasn't lost on her. She longed for Imogen, but she couldn't talk to Imogen. She longed to talk about Imogen, but she couldn't talk about Imogen

—not with anyone. Intense emotion and secrecy were a poisoned cocktail.

In the ceiling, jagged plaster hills cast shadows across valleys as the sun set. Martha found herself reciting the 23rd Psalm, memorized long ago, when she was about eight and Judith had decided she should learn the "foundational mythologies of western culture." The psalm was beautiful, comforting poetry, spoken at funerals in grave murmurs, and it soothed her.

If she were Catholic, she could get herself to a confessional. Blurt out everything to the priest between sobs. Say the requisite "Our Fathers" and "Hail Marys" and be grateful that someone knew about Imogen even if he didn't approve. Someone who wasn't Imogen. She could call a helpline, but the judgement would be worse. People who worked at helplines wouldn't understand her need to shelter her relationship with Imogen from other people's prying interest. They were the sort of people who would label her a closeted, homophobic dyke in denial . . . like a fundamentalist pastor devoted to "shepherding" young gay men. She'd be a "case" in their minds.

She was alone. More alone than when Brian had left her. At least then she had Joseph to take care of and friends to lean on. She hugged herself and the tears came again.

After a long time, she rolled onto her side and stared at the pyramid of self-help books on her bedside table. She pulled the chain on her lamp. She wouldn't read anything tonight. The books' advice was predictable, futile, one-size-fits-all nonsense—face the situation. Confront the problem. Live "authentically"—whatever that meant.

One last time. She'd try one last time. She picked up her cell and called Imogen. This time her call didn't go to voicemail. Another woman, not Imogen, answered the phone. Martha hung up.

Friday, March 13th, 2020

Gordon's phone rang as he dozed in his recliner. He shook himself awake and answered it.

"Gordon Gray?" A young, female voice, clear as a crystal bell. A stranger.

"Yes."

"My name is Lauren Cardinal. I'm a nurse practitioner with the assisted dying program."

"Oh, yes," Gordon replied. He cleared the sleep from his throat. "Yes. I was hoping to hear from you."

"First off, my apologies. You called a week ago, but we've had delays because of the coronavirus."

Gordon couldn't comprehend why a virus should matter to the terminally ill, though he didn't say so.

"Perhaps you could give me some background," said Lauren. "Tell me a little about yourself. We can stop if you get tired. There's no rush."

She wanted to hear his story. She had compassion. Gordon told Lauren about his life, his predicament, and his wish for a metaphorical trapdoor with a lever he could pull so he'd fall into oblivion at the time and date of his choosing.

"That's a good way to put it, Gordon. MAID is just like that," said Lauren. "I sense that you're not quite ready yet . . . to pull the lever. You have matters to attend to, such as your house sale and making sure Martha's okay."

"But I do qualify?" asked Gordon.

"By our conversation today, I believe you do. I can't see any reason why you wouldn't qualify for a medically assisted death. I'd like to visit you."

"When?" asked Gordon.

"In a week or two? I could come sooner if you prefer."

"That would be fine, lass. In a week or two. I'm always here. At Oakview Lodge."

Lauren wished Gordon well. He basked in the thought of Lauren's warmth and civility for the rest of the day.

Saturday, March 14th, 2020

After enduring a wickedly horrid week, Martha stumbled into Saturday.

Mavis had recommended postponing the house sale, citing market instability. Apparently buyers didn't fall in love with their ideal properties when contagion lurked. Like herpes, coronavirus was a passion-killer. "Wait," Mavis advised. "By mid-April, business should return to normal."

Meanwhile, the university administration issued daily, contradictory edicts on April exams and plans for the summer term and Daniel pleaded for her return to help deal with the queues of worried undergrads outside the office doors.

And there was Imogen. She phoned the old man but she didn't visit him. Imogen was avoiding her, which meant that she was suffering too. Cold comfort.

Martha drove to Oakview Lodge. The old man needed her and this morning, she needed him.

She parked the Corolla in the strangely vacant parking lot and walked up to the front entrance. The door was locked. A large sign covered its window:

No Visitors Permitted
 Due to community spread of COVID-19, Oakview Lodge is closed to All Visitors.
 For more information, please visit www...

No warning. No consultation with families about appropriate measures. Nobody to answer questions. Martha walked over the sodden lawn to the old man's window and peered in, but the curtains were drawn. She rapped on the glass, but no one answered. She returned to 22 Roselea with the sensation of having tripped into a malevolent parallel universe.

Gordon woke. His joints ached. His pillow had slipped from behind his head and he laboured to breathe. Still alive. Seventy-eight years of mornings and alive every time. He fumbled for the remote to raise the head of the bed but only succeeded in knocking it onto the floor. He needed help, again, as he would all day. He pressed the button.

Theresa crossed the room, flicked on his light, and chirped a cheery "Good morning, Gordon."

No breath, no answer, only wheeze.

"Let's get you up." Theresa retrieved the remote from the floor and elevated the head of the bed.

He could breathe better but the involuntary repositioning jarred his neck and hips, and a spasm of pain raced through the length of his spinal column. Coughing, an act necessary to life, hurt like the dickens. Theresa gave him a tissue.

"There. That's better, isn't it?" She dropped the remote on his lap. "That what you were calling for, Gordon?"

He nodded and half-smiled his gratitude.

"Good. I'll be back in fifteen with some towels and warm water and we'll get you up for breakfast. Saturday morning. Pancakes!" If ever a woman bustled, it was Theresa. She vanished from the room in a plump blur.

Alone again. Alone with the concentrator. The machine hissed and pumped incessantly, rhythmically. Pushing oxygen and memories into his nose, infusing his brain. A fanciful notion.

What was that noise? A rap on the window. The curtains

were drawn. He couldn't see. He couldn't tell what had made the noise. Likely a squirrel. The squirrels chased each other round the garden and one of them must've scampered onto the sill.

He'd ask Theresa to open the curtains once he was decent.

Wednesday, March 18th, 2020

Mavis answered her phone while she was driving. "I'm hands-free," she said smoothly when Martha asked her if she shouldn't pull over. "I can't run a real estate business if I don't use my vehicle as an office."

"If you say so," said Martha.

"I'm quite capable of multitasking," Mavis said, words clipped with defensive annoyance. "Not much traffic anyway for a weekday."

Often a pedestrian, seldom a driver, Martha had witnessed the same dangerously distracted driving in Bluetooth users as furtive cell holders, but now was not the time to deliver a lecture on safety. She asked, "Have you been to Valhalla Terrace? To see your mother?"

"No. Not for a couple of weeks. Why?"

"Dad's home is closed to visitors. 'Locked down' in the parlance of journalists. I tried to visit on Saturday, but the doors were locked. All Dad knows is that they're in quarantine and no one on staff has any more information. I've called and called the office, but no one answers the phone. No managers, no nurses, no receptionist."

"Come to think of it, I did read an email from Valhalla—you bastard! Let me in, damn you! I think it's all the nursing homes, Martha. The Ministry of Health . . . public health . . . northern Italy . . . not enough ventilators . . . all those old people . . . New York City!"

Martha heard the blast of a horn. She wouldn't prolong the call only to hear metal crumple, glass shatter, and the thump of a cyclist on the hood. She said, "Let's talk later, Mavis. I'm sure you're as concerned for your mother as I am about Dad. I'll try to get more information and I'll let you know if I find out anything."

"Thanks, Martha. And don't worry. The oldsters are safer in their nursing homes with twenty-four-hour care than they would be with us."

"Maybe," said Martha, and she disconnected the call.

Gordon and Frank were not hungry at lunch, a meal presented in lumpy, grey hills of meatloaf, overboiled broccoli, mashed potato, and banana custard. Derek, the meal server, set their plates before them, then ducked away in the manner of a terrorist who'd set a bomb with a short fuse. Gordon wouldn't complain anyway. A three-star Michelin extravaganza wouldn't have held any greater appeal. He only wanted a cigarette.

Frank poked the meatloaf with his fork, tentatively, as if teasing a sleeping weasel. "A bit of ketchup would give some colour," he said. "You mind?"

Gordon squeezed a dollop of lurid scarlet over the mass on Frank's plate.

Frank tasted the meat. "Beef," he announced. "Menu confirmed with real-world testing."

"Want mine?" asked Gordon.

Frank interpreted the question as rhetorical and continued on his conversational track. "Father raised Herefords. Roast beef every Sunday . . . short ribs, steak, brisket . . . we never wanted for a good meal."

"Food used to taste better," Gordon agreed.

"Mama always laid out a big spread. Meat, potatoes, pickles, fresh bread and butter, bit of veg . . . cake and pie. Cheddar and fruit. Fresh in summer, canned in winter. We had an orchard too."

Gordon, Toronto born and raised, idealized farm life and in fleeting, fanciful moments wondered if the fates had mixed up Judith and him at birth.

"I think this is broccoli," said Frank. "Some people throw the trunks away, but I don't mind them if they're cooked right. Now this—I'd say it's overcooked."

Understatement of the day, thought Gordon. "Did you miss the farm when you left?"

"Yeah, though I liked accounting too. Set Carol and me up nicely and we could afford a big house, put the kids through university, weddings for the girls, travel." Frank tried a morsel of potato.

"You'll be missing the kids with these crazy rules," Gordon ventured.

Frank swallowed. "You betcha. It's stupid, isn't it? The commands from on high. 'Lock up the vulnerable. Punish the old, inconvenient buggers. Keep them safe for their own damned good.' No consultation. Anyone ask you if you want to be locked up, Gordon?"

"No."

"No. You're damn right. No, they did not. Mark my words, some of us are going to die with no good-bye from our families. It's, it's—"

"Stalinist?" Gordon offered.

"I was going to say 'draconian'," said Frank. "But Stalinist isn't off the mark." He scooped some potato onto his spoon. "This is edible if you enjoy the taste of mucilage."

"I'll pass." Gordon gazed through the window. Across the lawn, at a wing perpendicular to theirs, a young woman held a baby, about six months old and bundled in a purple snowsuit, up to the window. The woman guided the baby's little hand to wave to someone Gordon couldn't see, inside. She put the baby back in its stroller and held a cell phone up to her ear. Clever. The human will for connection had not withered under threats from the COVID boogieman altogether. "Look at that, Frank," he said, pointing. "That lady with the baby at the window. Maybe you *can* see all your grandkids. Can't hug them, but that's something, isn't it?"

"Like in that movie, 'The Boy in the Striped Pyjamas.'" said Frank.

"You have the idea," said Gordon. The comparison with a Holocaust scenario was a mile too far, but Frank understood the concept. Even better if you could manage a visit while out for a smoke. You wouldn't need the phone. He'd call Martha. Desperate times called for desperate creativity.

Friday, March 20th, 2020

Although Martha wouldn't bend the rules, Imogen would and readily agreed to come to Oakview Lodge when Gordon asked her to visit. She snuck up to the porch and asked Angelo to make himself scarce.

"I'm sure you have better things to do. If you hook the codger up to his oxygen, I'll watch him and make sure he doesn't smoke another cigarette. I'll stay on the grass. Brownie promise," she said, saluting with two fingers.

Angelo checked his watch. It was after five and the managers had left for the weekend. "Okay, miss. Ten minutes. Then it's supper time. But don't come on the porch. If someone catch you, act surprised that you break the rule. Don't say my name."

As soon as Gordon had his oxygen on and Angelo had left, Gordon hunted in his pocket for his cigarettes.

"No way," Imogen scolded. "I promised Angelo you

wouldn't do that. Conversation is all you get." Gordon started to object but Imogen talked over him. "As a former elf in the Elmington Heights Brownie troop, I must keep my Brownie honour."

Gordon acquiesced. Time, relative as ever, hurtled forward and they couldn't squander a single second. He wheezed, "I haven't seen Martha. She only phones. She's scared to come. Scared to get caught by the staff."

Imogen feigned interest in the snowdrops that had emerged through the grass with the mid-March thaw.

"I worry about her, Imogen. She only has her work and that's not a substitute for a husband. Joseph might as well be in Antarctica studying snow fleas for all she hears from him. Her friends seem more like frenemies—except for you."

"Frenemies? Bloody hell," said Imogen.

"That's the current terminology in like-hate female relationships, isn't it?" rasped Gordon.

"Yeah, but it sounds weird when you say it," said Imogen.

They fell silent for a moment. Imogen's irritation puzzled him. Gordon searched her face for clues to why she was hostile. She looked wan, thinner than gaunt, and her eyeliner had crept into the creases that radiated from the corners of her eyes. "You okay, lass?"

"Yes. Why shouldn't I be?" Imogen said irritably.

"Because you're not," said Gordon. "You look sick."

"I suppose the COVID is getting to me. If I hear someone utter the phrase 'new normal' again I shall have to shove a bloody sock in their mouth. A stinky wool sock covered in burrs."

"Whoa."

"Oh, I have more phrases I detest, old man. 'Social distancing . . . an abundance of caution . . . flatten the curve . . . we're all in this together.' Bloody hell!"

"Bloody hell?"

"No. I'll keep that one. It's bloody useful. Especially these days."

Gordon nodded. Imogen was on a cathartic tear and his only job was to listen.

"There's a silver lining though. Simon's germophobic and I'm expendable—cannon fodder. He won't fire me now. I'll be the first person he'll call back when the library reopens. I miss the brats though. And people. I miss living, breathing people." Imogen's gaze fell again to the snowdrops.

"I miss people too," said Gordon. "Martha only phones because she won't bend the rules and visit. And I miss freedom. I hardly get out to smoke."

The lass stiffened and seemed to suppress a scowl as he edged toward his request. Odd.

He continued. "I'm going to take off my oxygen and have a cigarette, and you're going to be my lookout." Gordon was already pulling his cigarettes and lighter from his pocket.

"Well . . ." Imogen hesitated, then relented, "Okay. Make it quick though. We don't want to get Angelo in trouble."

"Maybe you should go. I can handle Angelo. I don't want to get *you* into trouble."

"Alright, old man."

"Imogen? Before you go—how's Martha? She doesn't say much on the phone. I'm worried about her."

Imogen shook her head and looked away.

"You don't know?" Gordon squawked.

"No. I don't," replied Imogen.

Gordon lit his cigarette, took a deep drag, and stared at Imogen, eyes narrowed. He exhaled smoke like a wise old dragon. "Now I get it. You've had an argument." He took Imogen's silence as admission. "Sisters shouldn't fight. Whatever happened, don't let it come between you. Not now. Not with the world the way it is."

Imogen shrugged. "Martha isn't easy to get along with, Gordon. She can be difficult. A fucking cactus."

"Difficult," Gordon repeated, expression quizzical. "Since when has 'difficult' stopped you from friendship?"

"I'd better go." Imogen turned and walked away.

"Okay. Bit of advice?" said Gordon.

Imogen paused, back turned to him.

"Don't be stubborn. When you get my age, you realize that 99 percent of the fights you had were pointless, ego-driven nonsense. I'd say the same to Martha, but she isn't here to nag."

"Consider me advised." Imogen started for the parking lot.

Gordon watched her drive off. She drove too fast. He finished his cigarette, replaced his oxygen, and waited for Angelo. He'd saved two weeks' worth of digoxin and he'd arranged a consultation for early April with Lauren Cardinal, but he wouldn't do anything until Imogen and Martha were sorted out. They had to sort themselves out. He'd have to scold Martha too.

Saturday, March 21st, 2020

Gordon requested that his curtains stay open night and day in case anyone dropped by and tapped on the glass. No one did. Still, when he woke at odd hours, he could watch the shadows of tree limbs dancing on the walls and see the moon rise over the parking lot, depending on time and phase. He observed a crescent moon in the east between the trees, whittled to a sliver. It rose later each night. Past midnight then. No need for a clock if you paid attention to the sky. He didn't read much anymore, had no interest in the inanity of TV. The sky was his entertainment now.

His breath felt heavy and stale in his lungs. He had to sit up. He reached for the remote to adjust the bed. Damned hand. For crying out loud. His right hand wouldn't move. Must've rolled on it. Nope. There it lay, limp, inert. Disobedient as a dead donkey. Oh. God. This was why the "F" word was invented. For situations like this.

Gordon tried his left hand. Squeeze, release, wiggle the fingers. All digits in working order. He understood and he felt queasy. He pressed the call bell. A moment later a circle of light shone in the room and over the bed. A flashlight with a human holding it.

"Yes, Gordon?"

Who was that? Impossible to remember the names of the night staff, so seldom had he needed them. "Aargh." What the—? No words. No words. His tongue wouldn't cooperate. He tried again. "Aargh . . . aargh."

Lights on. He squinted.

"Gordon? Gordon?" The young female voice cried. "Oh my God. I think you've had a stroke." Phone to her ear. "Mary Beth. Come quick. I think Gordon Gray has had a CVA."

A minute later, Mary Beth raised the head of his bed. She shone a light into his eyes, told him to stick out his tongue, now a disobedient, flaccid slab of flesh. "Aargh . . ."

Mary Beth said to the young nurse, "Go to the nurses' station, Tracy. Crush four baby Aspirin. Then come right back."

She stuck a blood pressure cuff on Gordon's arm and pestered with questions. At least the lass had the sense to stick with the "yes-no" sort.

"Gordon, I think you've had a stroke."

Nod.

"I'd like to send you to hospital."

Head shake. Eyes wide with fear.

"Do you wish to stay here?"

Nod.

"You understand, the stroke could get worse? You could die."

Nod.

"I'll ask again. Do you wish to go to hospital?"

Head shake.

"I'll call Dr. Southey and your family."

Nod.

"If your heart stops, do you want me to do CPR and call an ambulance?"

Shake. As vigorous as Gordon could manage.

"It's about three in the morning, Gordon, so I don't know if the doctor will come right away. We'll crush some Aspirin and give it to you. It might help. When Tracy returns, I'm going to ask you the questions again, so your wishes are understood with a witness. Then we'll make you comfortable."

Bother. Eye roll. So tired.

And so it went. He choked down the spoonful of sour goop Tracy shovelled into his mouth and then everything—the poking, the prodding, the do this and do that, the bizarre game of Simon Says—was repeated all over again. Mary Beth jotted some notes on a pad of paper. The girl nurses, for that is what they were, pulled him up in bed, and positioned his right hand on a pillow like a corpse lying in state.

Mary Beth said, "You're breathing okay, Gordon. Do you think you can sleep? It might help."

Nod. Yes.

"We'll keep checking on you."

The girls switched off the light. Alone again. Exhausted. Yes, he could sleep. For hours and hours, days and days, forever . . .

The ring of her cell jolted Martha awake. Jesus. Middle-of-the night calls were never good news. Answer, answer . . . phone on bedside table . . . find it . . . come on . . . futile taps and swipes. At last, the phone obeyed her vague commands, and a young, female voice spoke through the darkness.

"Is this Martha Gray?"

"Yes."

"My name is Mary Beth Horton. I'm the night nurse at Oakview Lodge. I'm sorry to wake you."

Martha sat up, suddenly very awake. She pushed her hair from her face.

The girl continued. "Gordon is unwell. He's stable. His vital signs are fine and he's comfortable."

So how was he unwell? Jeez. Would she get to the point?

"I'm not a doctor, so I'm not qualified to diagnose but it looks as if he's had a stroke. His right side is weak. His speech is garbled. He's resting now."

"A stroke," Martha repeated. He should've kept taking those digoxin tablets. Maybe she should say something—

Mary Beth continued, "I'm calling you for guidance. Gordon has indicated that he does not want to go to hospital. We've given him aspirin to control blood clotting and we've settled him, but obviously this is a change in condition and you're his power of attorney."

"Do you think he understands what has happened?" Martha asked, voice husky from sleep.

"Yes, though I can't be 100 percent sure," answered Mary Beth. "And his advance directives state, 'Treat at Oakview Lodge' but, of course, we can change that if you wish because you're his POA."

"No. Dad has been clear all along. No hospital."

"Fine. That's my thinking too," Mary Beth agreed. "No ambulance. I'll call Dr. Southey instead."

"When?"

"Now."

"Mary Beth, I should be there. I should be with my dad, right? I mean, he'll be scared and—"

"I'm sorry. You can't. Due to the quarantine. We have a 'no visiting' policy right now."

A verbal door slam in the face. Martha's voice broke with incredulity. "Even for a stroke?"

"Yes, even a stroke. I'm sorry." Mary Beth delivered her awful message with robotic empathy, like the computer in *2001*.

"But he could get worse, couldn't he? Is there no special policy for residents who get really sick?" Martha pleaded.

"No." Pause. "You could ask Diane Stefano. She's the only one with authority to bend the rules."

"I will," said Martha. "Mary Beth?"

"Yes, Martha?"

"Is he okay? He won't—"

"Gordon's okay now. He's not out of the woods but he's sleeping comfortably. We're checking on him frequently and we'll call you right away if we see any change."

"Thank you. When he wakes up, tell him I love him."

"I will," Mary Beth promised. "I will tell him just that."

A familiar voice, his name called over and over as if from the top of a well—this pulled Gordon from a deep, dreamless sleep. He fought to concentrate, to open his eyes. Daylight . . . blurry colour.

"There you are. Gordon? Open your eyes again. It's Katherine Southey."

Eyes. Open eyes. Katherine hovering over him. Bright green T-shirt. Halo of hair. Another flashlight.

"Gordon, stay with me for a minute or two, and then you can go back to sleep."

"Aargh." No words . . . the stroke . . . new normal. Try again. "Aargh."

"That's okay, Gordon. You don't have to talk. You've had a stroke. Is it okay if I examine you?"

No. No poking. Sleep. She would poke anyway. And did.

"Gordon, the nurses tell me you want to stay here, at Oakview."

Nod. Try again. Nod.

"If I send you to hospital, we can get a CT scan to see what's happening. A stroke is a brain injury, and I could find out how to treat you. Consult with neurology."

Hospital? Head shake. No, no, no. Sleep and never wake up. Close eyes and ignore.

"I'll call Martha."

Martha. She knows. The answer's "no". Martha will say "no."

"You rest now, Gordon. Sleep is healing after a stroke."

Alone. Light streaming through the window. Morning. No need to get up. Just sleep. Martha would refuse her. He could sleep.

Martha wouldn't agree to anything until she could see the old man herself and this was arranged. Dr. Southey and Diane Stefano spoke as if she were requesting approval for a cold war summit of nuclear powers. Her visit would violate emergency policy, and besides, other families couldn't visit, could they? Surely she understood? But they relented, agreeing in medical mumbo-jumbo that benefit outweighed risk. Martha was ushered to Gordon's bedside that afternoon—a Saturday, of all days, when a senior health professional should've been home, spending time with family, "recharging batteries" in Diane's words, rather than dealing with a recalcitrant power of attorney.

Now Martha sat with the old man. His breath was even and quiet, considering his COPD, and his face placid. Thin before, now he was skeletal, sallow skin stretched over skull and shoulders, all bony peaks and hollow valleys. She hadn't noticed the extent of his diminishment, hidden as he'd been under sweaters and trackpants on previous visits. Her incredible shrinking father.

Dr. Southey had informed Martha by telephone that the old man couldn't speak and was paralyzed on his right side. She urged transfer to hospital if only to discover the extent of his "brain attack," the term she'd used to explain what had happened inside the old man's skull. When asked if this knowledge would change the outcome of his stroke, she admitted that was unlikely. "Wouldn't it be better to know for sure?" Dr. Southey had asked. The woman seemed unaccustomed to hearing the word "no." Martha could visit with the tacit understanding that they'd get to "yes".

They wouldn't.

The old man wouldn't want it. And now he stirred. Heavy lids opened, cloudy eyes fought to focus, breathing quickened.

"Dad? Dad? It's me. It's Martha. I'm right here with you." She squeezed his limp hand.

"Aargh, aargh."

"You don't need to talk, Dad. Just rest. It's okay."

"Aargh . . ." Eyes closed again. And a couple minutes later, open and wild. The eyes of a fox caught in a leghold trap. "Aargh."

He understood. Okay then. "Dad, be calm. I'm right here."

Nod.

"Dad, Dr. Southey wants you to go to hospital. For a scan. Do you want to go to the hospital?"

Wild fox eyes again. A panicked "aargh."

"Do you want to stay here? At Oakview?"

Nod.

"Okay. It's settled. You'll stay here."

He slept again, for three or four minutes, then woke suddenly. The eyes again. Staring, struggling to communicate something. Martha followed the track of the old man's eyes to the top drawer of his dresser. "Aargh."

"The drawer? Look inside? You want me to—" Martha rose and went to the dresser. "Yes?"

Nod.

Martha pulled open the drawer. So obvious. The silver cigarette case. She opened it. Among bits and bobs was a folded Kleenex, a couple weeks' worth of pills hidden in its creases.

"Aargh . . . aargh!"

No way. She couldn't. No hospital transfer? Fine. Murder the old man with pills? No way. No way. Jesus. Martha refolded the Kleenex and tucked it inside the case. "I can't, Dad."

Hand lift. Silent benediction and head shake and "Aargh!"

"Something else?"

Nod.

"This paper?"

Nod.

"Yes?" Martha unfolded the scrap. Wobbly, spider writing, angled forward, message clear despite the uneven pressure of the pen. She read aloud, "'Lauren Cardinal. Discuss MAID. April 10th in am'. And a phone number. That's it?"

Nod.

"Alright. I'll call her. You told me about her. I remember. I'll call her from the parking lot," said Martha. She put the paper in her pocket and returned to her bedside vigil as the old man lapsed back into sleep.

Afternoon sunshine streamed through the windshield. Martha had to cup her hand around the screen of her phone to see its tiny keyboard. She considered what she should say. The old man was literally half alive and half dead, able to hear but not speak, left side operating in obeyance of brain, right side impervious to command. He would never again tease his family or gently rebuke them or impart paternal advice. Joseph and Imogen had to be informed sans sugar-coating. Martha texted two simple telegram-style messages. Then she called Lauren Cardinal, or rather, her voice mail and listened to a recorded message that informed callers she was away and would return to work on Monday, April 6th.

Martha turned the key in the ignition, put the car into gear, and started back to Roselea Drive. She dreaded the claustrophobia of the empty house, and after travelling several blocks through a drab commercial district, found herself steering toward the lake instead. There she could think. Her phone pinged repeatedly during the journey. She parked, then found a sunny, wind-still bench and read her messages.

Joseph first. He "couldn't get away . . . ecovillage preparing for collapse of civilization . . . Tayana frightened of virus, refuses to travel. Grandpa always gets better—"

Martha wasn't surprised. Joe was a glass-over-flowing optimist. He needed time to process bad news.

Ping. Imogen had texted again. One, two, three texts.

> Not fair, Martha. Dump horrible news on me and vanish

said the fourth. Then:

> I'm calling. Pick up.

The cell rang and Martha answered it. After she relayed the horror of the last twelve hours, Imogen said, "Come to my place. You can't do anything tonight now that Gordon's locked up in that fucking fortress. I'm on the wagon again and there's no booze, but you don't need that right now anyway. You need to eat. I made a pot of beef barley soup."

Martha accepted the meal, and afterward, a night in Imogen's bed, and there was no further mention of the battle royale that had driven them apart.

Tuesday, March 24th, 2020

Diane permitted Martha to visit the old man on Sunday and Monday, "on compassionate grounds, in case of a turn for the worse." Today Diane unlocked the front door and walked alongside Martha so they could "have a quick word," before she saw him.

Diane was brisk. "Your father is stable now. We've transferred him to a tilt chair. Dr. Southey was in early this morning and ordered IV fluids for hydration, to perk Gordon up until he's eating more. She's ordered physiotherapy as well."

"Oh," said Martha, blindsided by the sudden change in plans. "Have you asked Dad what he wants? He's always been clear that he wants as little medical intervention as possible."

"Well, no, we haven't, Martha, and with good reason. Dr. Southey has deemed Gordon incapable of making his own decisions. The stroke has affected his cognition and he lacks insight into his condition. You're POA. Part of the care team. We'd like your buy-in."

"I see. I'll talk to Dad," said Martha, shrugging away Diane's patronizing tone.

Diane ignored Martha's subtle resistance. "We can't expect full recovery, but given time, Gordon will probably be able to feed himself, build up function in his non-dominant side. That brings me to another matter."

"Which is?"

"Your visits. Please understand, I don't make the rules. The government has banned nonessential visits at all long-term care homes, including Oakview. I'm afraid we'll have to ask you to make this your last visit, while we're in lockdown."

They arrived at the old man's door. Martha turned, "Ask or order, Diane?"

"I'm just the messenger, Martha. We're regulated the same way as every other nursing home in Ontario."

"But Dad's not out of the woods yet. He's so fragile. As you said, he's not eating—"

"Oh, he's eating. Not much, of course, but Theresa fed him this morning and he ate."

Like a French goose with a funnel in its gullet, thought Martha. Jeez. "I thought Dr. Southey would order palliative care for Dad."

"That's premature, Martha. The stroke is fresh. We're still in 'wait and see' mode, and he deserves a chance to recover, even if only partially, with active treatment, don't you think?"

Martha shrugged. She didn't know what to think. Yesterday they'd told her the old man was likely dying and today he was recovering, and she doubted his condition had changed at all. He stood on the fulcrum of an existential teeter-totter, tipping neither this way nor that. She had to see him to decide. If it was their last visit during lock-down, she'd make it a long one. She peered through the doorway and the old man stared back at her. He'd heard half their conversation.

Gordon sat in a firm chair that was tilted back as if he were an astronaut ready for lift-off. Days and nights were jumbled and if he were asked what day it was, he'd have had a one in seven chance of guessing correctly. He'd thought his world couldn't shrink anymore. Wrong again. His universe had collapsed to a near singularity of sleep, the swallowing of mush, a pervasive nausea, and diaper changes. In flights of fancy, he stood at the edge of a cliff, a swirling, mysterious abyss before him, beckoning him to dive. He couldn't dive. He was paralyzed. He needed to be pushed.

He heard voices, felt warmth on his skin. A blinding light

flooded through his eyelids. Right. East window. Morning. Martha's voice and who? Who? A woman's voice with a sharpness that revealed a desire to control. Diane. It was Diane. *Visiting prohibited . . . active treatment . . .* Not good. No push. Bed and torture chair. That was the master plan.

Martha sounded hesitant. He understood. She didn't like the plan. He had to reach her. Convince her to push him.

Martha exhausted all of the topics she could think of—the weather, politics, Joseph, Imogen, the pandemic, watching Ethan skateboard, the price of maple syrup, and a fifty-year trip down memory lane. The old man punctuated her narrative with odd, guttural sounds to let her know he was with her. He was tired now, drifting into sleep.

She sat back and watched him. The oxygen concentrator hissed and pumped in the corner. The smell of sour sweat permeated the air. Humans could adapt to almost any crappy situation and go on living. If you didn't pay attention, you stopped hearing ambient noises, smelling odours, sensing walls closing in. You put up and shut up. The room used to feel cozy; now it felt like a jail cell. She'd stay till the staff kicked her out. Read a little, nap a little, keep the old man company, and think. Figure things out.

A half hour later, Theresa appeared with a tray. "Martha? Gordon? Lunch time," she called. "We're supposed to take Gordon to the dining room, but I think you want to spend time here today. Because of—"

"Our last visit during lockdown," Martha finished. "You're busy, Theresa. I can feed him."

"You sure?" Theresa was already setting the tray on the bed.

"Yes. I'll take my time. Small spoonfuls. Like you do."

"Thanks, Martha." Theresa rushed away.

Gordon's eyes had fluttered open as the new voice registered in his consciousness. He looked at the tray and his lip half curled in disgust.

"Can't say I blame you," said Martha. Three rows of mush, a pastel tricolour flag of orange, white, and green, filled the plate and a sippy cup of pink sludge stood to the side. "Try a little?"

Head shake and "Aargh."

Martha's eyes met the old man's. His eyes pleaded, begged.

"I don't know what you want, Dad. Should I change your position?" She rose to adjust the angle of his chair.

Head shake. Eyes looking away.

If only she were telepathic, she'd put her hand to his face in a Vulcan mind meld. "Are you wet?"

Head shake. Eyes back to hers, this time insisting she hold his gaze, then darting to the top drawer of the dresser and back to her eyes. *Drawer, Martha, drawer, Martha.* She knew. She sat down again and watched him. His eyes kept pleading. He wouldn't let her off the hook. When she left, he'd be trapped. Unless—

"If I put your digoxin in your food, will you eat?" Martha ventured.

Nod. A strong yes.

Tears filled their eyes.

"I love you, Dad," said Martha. She couldn't agree to his demand in words. She could only act. She made her decision and there was no turning back. Everything they had to say had been said. The staff would be occupied in the dining room for a half hour at most. It was now or never.

Martha stood again and closed the door. A long hug and more tears. "You are the best father a duchess could ever have," Martha said, words choked with sobs.

Gordon half smiled. Tears tumbled over his cheeks. Happy eyes.

Once begun, the task was easy. Martha took Gordon's

cigarette case from the drawer, removed and unfolded the tissue, and dropped thirteen tiny, white tablets onto a spoonful of mashed potato. Vision blurred by emotion and tears, she didn't see the fourteenth tablet bounce from the tray to the quilt, hidden under the tray's edge. The old man opened his mouth like a fledgling seeking nourishment for flight and Martha delivered the last spoonful of food he would ever swallow.

Gordon closed his eyes. Martha kissed him on the cheek and left.

Anita stopped by Gordon's room a half hour later to discuss the plan for Gordon's rehabilitation with Martha. She saw the tray of untouched food, sensed stillness in the room, and immediately knew something was wrong. Gordon lay inert in his tilt chair, his skin the plasticine, greyish yellow of the dead despite the concentrator pumping oxygen into his nose. Indeed, he was dead. She checked for heart tones with her stethoscope anyway—absent—then flicked the toggle on the concentrator to stop its racket.

This wasn't an emergency. The hospital wouldn't welcome the likes of Gordon Gray at the best of times, much less during a pandemic, and his advance directives precluded heroic measures. Besides, dead was dead. Modern medicine couldn't work miracles, and Gordon wasn't a modern-day Lazarus. The old man had been on borrowed time and in her unsolicited opinion, the rehab plan wouldn't have helped him anyway. He'd have gone on for months, years even, in a state of suspended animation. His death was a blessing.

Anita looked at her watch. 13:12. She'd record the numbers for officialdom.

She looked at the tray of food. Life was strange, wasn't it? A few minutes ago, daughter fed father. Martha had made a start anyway. The spoon had a bit of potato on it; the serviette was crumpled. And now, no daughter, dead father. Too strange?

She rang the call bell. It was more efficient to have Gordon in bed for transfer to the undertaker's gurney and she'd need help with that. Then, she lifted the tray. A single, white pill on a blue patch of quilt caught her eye. Gordon took his meds crushed in apple sauce now. How had that little thing ended up there? And where was Martha? She said she'd be available all afternoon to discuss the rehab plan. If she was in the washroom, she'd have left her coat.

Anita felt her breath change. She was hyperventilating. Intuition outpaced conscious thought in situations like this. Best leave Gordon where he lay and set the tray where she'd found it. She called Diane on her portable phone. A few minutes later, Diane called Dr. Southey and the coroner.

When Anita phoned Martha to inform her of her father's death, she wished she'd thrown the pill away and given the Grays a modicum of peace.

Part V

Tuesday, March 24th, 2020

Martha felt as if she was trapped in a dream, the kind she got when sunlight hit her eyelids and it was too bright to see the imaginary world her brain had conjured. Scarcely aware of herself, she drove down streets made empty by order of public health to the driveway of 22 Roselea. Her universe was scrubbed of people and shadow and noise—everything shimmered in white light and the neighbourhood was still save for the birds squabbling at the Kingsworths' feeder. Reality didn't register until she stepped over the threshold and entered the bungalow, the faint odour of cigarette smoke and Pine-sol acting like smelling salts in her nostrils.

Without taking off her shoes or turning on the lights, she went to the kitchen, half-filled a plastic cup with gin and took it to the lawn chair in the living room. She toasted the air with a "Rest in peace, Dad," gulped a finger of the molten liquid and tried to think. The old man was dead and she assumed she was still the only one who knew it. It might be an hour or two before anyone checked on him. If she called the funeral home, a hearse might appear at Oakview's door before the staff called her. As Tayana would say, "Awkward!"

Martha set the cup on a crate and tried Joseph's number, but her call went straight to voice mail so she thumbed a message. "Hi Joe. Sad news. Grandpa passed away about a half hour ago. He's at peace now." Too callous? She added a heart emoji.

Next she phoned Imogen who answered on the third ring with "Hey, girlfriend."

After a bowl of soup and some fence mending on Saturday night, was that what she was? "Hi Imogen," she replied, her own voice echoing oddly in her ears.

"What's wrong?"

Having to say a thing made it real. Vocal cords garroted by the shock of what she'd done, Martha lost her words and Imogen said, "Oh. Oh no. Gordon. He's—"

Martha managed to whisper, "Yes."

"I'm so sorry."

Salty rivulets spilled from Martha's eyes. An alert that someone else was calling sounded in her ear but the caller hung up after three rings. She couldn't have answered coherently anyway.

Now Imogen's voice was breaking too. "I'm babysitting my nephews. Their parents are essential workers and they'd freak if you came here. I'll come over to your place at eight, okay?"

"Okay. Eight."

Martha ended the call and took another gulp of gin, its bitterness tethering her to earth and staunching her tears. A few minutes later, Joseph's name lit her phone screen. "Joe," she answered.

"Mom," and then a strangled sobbing. "I can't believe it. I didn't realize when you said Grandpa was so sick. I should've come to Ontario and I didn't. Now he's gone."

Joseph needed her to be strong, so she forced herself to use the same script she'd followed when Judith died. "He's at peace now Joe. It's what he wanted." When Joe didn't reply, she added, "He lived a good life."

"Jesus, Mom. He's gone and he won't come back. You sound so unemotional. Like you're announcing a sale on shovels or something."

"I'm sad. Of course I'm sad. I loved him too, but I saw him every day, Joe, and I watched him struggle. He told me over and over he wanted to die. I'm sad but I'm also relieved because he doesn't have to suffer anymore."

"I should've been there."

"I told you he was—" No. An 'I-did-tell-you' would be cruel. Martha exhaled heavily and said, "You were with him at Christmas and that meant a lot to him. The nursing home's closed to visitors so you couldn't have seen him anyway."

"I could've phoned him."

"He couldn't talk."

"I should be there for you."

"I'm okay, Joe."

"You're always okay. Normal people gather when someone they love dies." Joe was crying again.

Normal people? She glanced at the red plastic cup and shrugged away the criticism. "I want that too, but it's probably not a good idea to fly right now."

"I'm not afraid of a stupid virus."

"Neither am I, but the government is and everything's closing up. We can get together and do something in Grandpa's memory after the pandemic's over."

She heard quiet sobs and the sound of wind.

"Joe?"

"I can't believe he's gone. He was the best grandpa."

"Yeah. He was."

"I gotta go, but I'll call you soon, okay, Mom?"

"Soon."

Martha ended the call without telling Joseph that she loved him. She was too wrung-out to say those simple yet important words. She finished her drink and returned to the kitchen for the bottle, then hurried back when her phone rattled and rang on the crate.

Oakview. "Hello?"

"Hello. This is Anita from Oakview Lodge. Am I speaking with Martha?"

"Yes."

"Martha, I'm sorry to have to tell you that your father has passed away."

"Oh."

"I found him shortly after lunch. He looked peaceful and I don't believe he suffered."

"I'm glad—glad he looked peaceful." What a daft thing to say.

"Unfortunately, with the new rules, you can't come into the building, so we'll call the funeral home and pack Gordon's belongings for you to collect at the loading dock. Today's Tuesday so we're looking at Thursday for his things."

"Harrison's."

"Pardon?"

"Harrison's. That's the funeral home."

"Alright. Thank you. Uh, one more thing."

Martha didn't miss Anita's hesitation, her effort to sound matter-of-fact. "Yes?"

"The coroner is following up—routine when a death is unexpected—so the body may go to autopsy."

Martha's stomach flipped and her heart galloped. Residents died every week at Oakview. They were alive one day and they left in a casket with an honour guard the next. Anita was lying. There was nothing routine about the involvement of a coroner or the possibility of an autopsy.

"We'll miss your father, Martha," Anita said gently. "He was such a lovely man."

"Do you think so?" Before she could stop herself, Martha laughed, "I'll bet you say that to all the families."

Anita gasped. "Are you joking?"

"No." What a time to crack up. "Yes," she corrected. "I'm sorry, Anita. I guess I'm in shock with this news. Thank you. I appreciate everything you've done for Dad. Please thank all the staff for me."

"I will."

As Martha ended the call, a cold sweat broke over her forehead and she shivered in the cool, dim room so like a movie-set interrogation cell. People in authority would have questions and she'd have to answer them sensibly. Contacting a lawyer would be an admission of guilt so she was on her own.

Dr. Katherine Southey's Dictated Progress Note, 24 March 2020:

Gordon Gray found vital signs absent at approx. 13:15 in his room at Oakview Lodge, nurse pronounced death. DNR, no effort to resuscitate made. Nurse noted pill on bed, absence of daughter who had been visiting at time of patient's probable death. Upon examination, no signs of trauma or choking. Due to patient's history, stability, and suspicious behaviour of daughter (advocating for MAID despite patient's lack of capacity), body left in situ and death referred to coroner.

"You want the details?" Martha asked Imogen after they'd had a good cry and Imogen had driven her from the barely furnished bungalow to the comfort of sofa and condo.

"Only what you want to tell me," replied Imogen, sitting cross-legged next to her.

The gin was wearing off, and Martha felt pressure building in her temples. It was easier to tell Imogen everything. If she couldn't hire a lawyer, confessing to an intelligent ally, albeit one with shaky judgement, might help her negotiate the next few weeks. Two heads were better than one. When Martha had finished her account, Imogen leaned back against the armrest and cocked her head to the side, eyebrows peaked in inverted Vs.

She whistled lightly and said, "Basically, you did what people say they would do in that situation but never have the nerve to do."

"Basically."

"And everything would be fine except Gordon's corpse is now evidence in a murder case."

"Jeez, Imogen. Do you have to say it like that? Maybe they won't find anything amiss."

"They've decided his death is irregular, but there are no bumps or bruises or stab wounds. At least none that you're aware of. On CSI, the pathologist would take samples for toxicology. Stat."

"Holy shit," muttered Martha, mind racing to inevitable conclusions. "Maybe I could pretend I didn't even know he was on digoxin. If they think the nurses gave him the wrong dose—"

"Wow! Pin it on the nurses and let them take the fall. That's immoral."

Imogen was right. If the staff got into trouble, she'd have to confess. Suppressing panic, Martha said, "I can't just admit everything. I think I should wait and see what happens."

Imogen bolted upright. "Your phone."

"What?"

"Your phone, Martha. You have to erase everything."

"Why?" she asked as she pulled it from her pocket. "There's

nothing incriminating—"

Imogen cut her off. "Remember you said you didn't call the funeral parlour because it would be weird for a hearse to show up at Oakview out of the blue, before they told you? Don't you think it's odd that you texted Joe before the nurse called you? You have to erase everything in your log—just in case."

"In case of what?"

"In case the police ask to see it."

Martha's fingers were already brushing across the screen. "I definitely need a lawyer."

"No. Not yet anyway," declared Imogen. "You need a highly perceptive girlfriend to inform you when toilet paper is stuck to your shoe. Someone to save you from yourself."

"I could jot down a few names and numbers," Martha said miserably. "As you said, 'just in case.'"

"Don't, Martha, for the same reason you've erased your call log. If you're searching for lawyers online and the police seize your computer, won't that look suspicious?"

Imogen was trying to help, but every sentence she uttered landed like a bucket of ice water over Martha's head, washing away her alcohol buzz and revealing her circumstances in sharp relief. She must have looked awful because Imogen hugged her. "Don't worry Martha. We're in this together."

Except they weren't. She'd floated into a whirlpool and Imogen was standing on the bank holding a frayed rope. Imogen could shout suggestions, but she couldn't rescue her.

"We should plan Gordon's funeral," said Imogen, releasing her embrace. "We'd both feel better if we took positive action and behaved normally."

"There isn't much to plan," said Martha. "I checked Harrison's website. They allow ten mourners per service, and they live stream on Zoom. I don't even want to bother. Dad wanted to be cremated, so I'll arrange that through Harrison's and we can scatter his ashes at the lakeshore."

"That's it?"

"That's it."

"Fucking brutal, Martha. If I were a cop—"

"You said we should behave normally. Well, that's my normal. It might look suspicious, like I'm going to very little effort for my beloved father, but I don't have the energy to do more. I used it all up when Dad was alive."

Imogen gave a little shrug. "A fancy funeral might be too 'Lady MacBeth' anyway. Unconvincing. Like when a woman goes missing and her husband or boyfriend appears on the news begging for her return. Ninety-nine percent of the time he turns out to be the killer."

Martha shivered. "I think I'm off the hook for a funeral because of the pandemic, but we should write an obituary to post on Harrison's website."

"Want me to do it? Just the facts, nothing fancy."

"Yes, thank you," Martha nodded. "I suppose I should dig out the photo albums from storage. Dad would want a picture from when he was young."

"I have some oldies I rescued from the library when Simon was on a decluttering campaign," said Imogen, brightening. "I think I have something we could use." She went to a sagging bookshelf by the window and returned with a candy-striped box.

For the next hour, Martha and Imogen sifted through old pictures, laughing and crying in turns. Before they tired of their task, they found the ideal image of Gordon Gray, handsome in a rumpled corduroy jacket, a snifter balanced on his lectern and a cigarette in his fingers as he introduced an author at a literary event circa 1975. Decades after the photo was taken, the author won a Nobel Prize. Martha and Imogen agreed that the old man would've been pleased with their choice.

Thursday, March 26th, 2020

After Martha collected her father's belongings from the nursing home and deposited them in the storage locker, she returned to the bungalow to set about the grim task of informing the world of his death. Imogen convinced her to run the obituary in the *Toronto Star*, but it was the page on Harrison's website where Martha lingered, Nick Harrison having posted it that morning.

> *Gordon Stuart Gray, 12th of July, 1941 – 24th of March, 2020*
>
> *Gordon was born in Toronto and attended East York Collegiate where he excelled in football and drama, playing the role of Petruchio in* The Taming of the Shrew. *His love of English literature swept him into the University of Toronto, where he completed his BA in 1963 and his MA in 1965. While at university, Gordon met the love of his life, Judith Steinman (d. 2016), whom he married the year he graduated.*
>
> *Gordon worked at Elmington Public Library from 1966 until his retirement in 2007. He welcomed everyone who entered the doors of the library, from reluctant readers to bibliophiles, with humour and old-fashioned graciousness. Many librarians benefited from his patient mentorship and sardonic wit. Over his four-decade tenure, he transformed the library from rooms of hushed gloom to vibrant halls of literary discovery and community.*
>
> *Gordon is survived by his daughter Martha, his grandson Joseph, and Joseph's wife Tayana. In lieu of flowers, donations of remembrance may be made to Friends of the Library and the Children's Book Bank.*

The obituary was the work of a colleague, not a daughter, with Imogen's admiration for her boss shining through the bare-bones demographics of his life, but it served the purpose of notifying the world of the old man's death. A handful of notes of condolence appeared under the post, all former colleagues and library patrons whom Imogen had contacted. Still no family or friends because they hadn't been informed yet and that was up to her.

Martha gazed through the curtainless window. The Kingsworths' vehicles seldom left the driveway since lockdown, and there was precious little chance of getting their voicemail. Email. That was the solution. Everyone all at once, from the Steinman relatives to Sally, Mavis, Daniel and her colleagues, with a link to the obituary. Moments later, task complete, she closed her laptop, stood, and stretched. The only people she really cared to talk to were Joseph and Imogen, but it was Sally who called her first.

"Oh my God, Martha! At a time like this! I'm so sorry," Sally cooed into her ear.

"Well, Dad was very sick—"

"It wasn't, you know, like New York City?"

New York City. 9-11? What was she taking about?

"Those nursing homes with the virus," Sally spluttered. "They send sick residents home from the hospital and it gets in and boom—"

"No, nothing like that," Martha interrupted. "Dad had that stroke, and he took a bad turn."

"That's a relief. I mean, Mavis's mom is in Valhalla. It's a huge worry. But your dad! He was such a nice man. We'll all miss him."

"Thank you, Sally."

"Oh, Martha. If we weren't in lockdown, I'd drive right over and give you a big hug."

"You're very kind, Sally. If it wasn't so dangerous, I'd appreciate that."

"Um, Mavis will be in touch. She'll have to pause the sale

until your dad's estate is settled." Sally giggled softly, and Martha guessed she was nervous.

"The sale?"

"The house."

"I understand," said Martha, impatient for the conversation to end. "I guess I'll have to find someone to look in on it when I'm back in Vancouver."

"That's a tomorrow problem, Martha. Today, you take care of you, Sally's orders. Okay?"

"Okay," Martha repeated blankly.

"Hugs!" And Sally was gone.

Martha stared at her phone. Unless she took action, awkward conversations like that would plague her for days. She set her mind to figuring out how to silence all incoming calls except for those from Joseph and Imogen.

Wednesday, April 1st, 2020

The sun was cheerful, but the wind prickly—poetic weather for an April Fool's lakeside service to honour the old man. After Imogen parked, Martha buttoned the collar of her sweater and lumbered out of the car to retrieve the waxy cardboard box containing Gordon's cremains from the backseat. The wind carried the smell of rotting fish from the choppy water. Imogen and Martha picked their way over loose stones to a gabion of limestone rock.

"Here?" suggested Imogen. "We're more or less sheltered, and the same principle applies with ashes as pee when it comes to wind."

Agreeing, Martha set the box on the mesh of the gabion and pulled out her phone to connect with Joseph and Tayana via Zoom. After a fumbling persistence, they connected.

Martha raised her voice over the wind. "Can you see us?"

"No. Only your silhouettes," Joe shouted back. "And you're breaking up."

"Story of my life," Martha muttered in self pity. They couldn't see Joe or Tayana on the screen in the bright afternoon sunlight either, so Imogen seized the phone from Martha's hands, disconnected Zoom and reconnected them on speaker phone.

"Better," said Joe. "Now we hear you clearly."

"We'd better get started before the Stasi notice us," said Imogen. "The beach is closed and they've been ticketing people."

"Even for scattering ashes?" asked Tayana.

"When people are afraid, common sense is the first casualty," Martha said ruefully. "Imogen?"

"Could you hold the phone, Martha?" Imogen returned the device and cleared her throat. "Um, your mom asked me to lead, but feel free to break in as we go. First a song from the Byrds. It was popular when Gordon married Judith." Imogen found her own phone and played a rock version of the immortal wisdom of *Ecclesiastes*.

Martha's throat tightened with the poignancy of hearing the voices of the young men, now elderly themselves, and the simplicity of their twanging guitars, drums, and tambourine. She wiped away tears with her sleeve and turned her face to the bracing wind. Imogen made no move to comfort her, thank God.

Joe and Tayana sobbed softly, but Imogen stiffened her back and cleared her throat. "If I don't carry on, I'll be a bloody mess like you three. At this point, I'd like each of us to say a few words and share what Gordon meant to us." She stage-whispered to Martha, "Do you want to go first?"

"Sure," said Martha. "I'll go." She took a deep breath to master herself. "I never doubted that my father loved me from the day I was born until the day of his death. He made living with my mother tolerable by running interference, acting as co-

conspirator, and arguing my case whenever I ran against Mom's crazy rules—and that happened a lot. Dad was the one person Mom listened to, and he was also the one person who listened to me. Besides teaching me to ride a bike, paddle a canoe, drive a car—the usual things fathers teach their daughters—he taught me to think for myself. His lessons were never pedantic. If I suffered some minor calamity, he'd roll a consoling lesson into a story featuring my alter-ego and deliver it at bedtime with cookies and milk and a hug. Everyone loved Dad—well, almost everyone—and he deserved people's love because he was kind. That's all."

"Joe?" Imogen prompted.

"Okay," Joe's voice quavered over three time zones. "I'll speak on behalf of both of us. We never had the chance to say good-bye and Tayana and I will always regret it because Grandpa was more than a grandfather. He was my idol, my friend—"

His words gave way to gut-clenching sobs and Tayana broke in, bitter as the wind. "Joe is suffering because Grandpa's end was sudden and he passed to the next realm alone, no human warmth to comfort him, no prayers to guide his soul. We're bidding good-bye to nothing . . . to dust in a jar because he left us without—"

"Wait," Martha broke in. "That's not exactly true. I told Joe that he was sick—"

Grasping Martha's sleeve, Imogen shook her head, then spoke at the phone. "Where do you think Gordon is now, Tayana?"

"He's in Bardo."

"So he's only gone for a while and he'll come back?" said Imogen. "He'll be reincarnated, right?"

Martha rolled her tear-filled eyes but Imogen ignored her cynicism and peered at the phone.

"Yes. Technically that's true," replied Tayana. "His soul will animate another, yet unborn body and he'll live on."

"Then maybe we're only saying good-bye for a while," said Imogen.

What a fake, thought Martha, though she had no better words to soothe Joe's grief.

"I guess it's my turn," said Imogen. "Gordon was a rare bird—a fearless librarian who stirred the pot. He was my mentor, my confidante, and my ally in fighting the good fight against censorship and petty rules. Gordon Gray was the antonym of banality. And the opposite of evil. He was goodness. I can't believe he's really dead. He had too big a personality to be mortal. Gordon, wherever you are, God speed, old friend."

But he was dead, thought Martha, and Imogen knew it. Obviously she was bridging two thousand miles and a generational divide with pseudo-spiritual claptrap. There was no point in objecting, in putting forth her own materialist views. "Shall we scatter Dad's ashes now?" she asked.

Imogen nodded and they ambled to the water's edge. "We'll chant a prayer," said Tayana.

"Ready," said Imogen.

A monotonic baritone and soprano hummed incomprehensible syllables through the cell phone. Martha set her phone on a rock, eased the top off the box, and removed the Ziplock bag. Now the old man had more in common with goldfish crackers than a human being. She opened the seal and upended the bag over wave-lapped pebbles. Fine grey ash blew across the water. Done. The bag was empty and so was she.

Imogen gave her a weak smile and opened a PDF on her screen. "In closing I'd like to read a poem," she said. Joe and Tayana fell silent, and Imogen continued. "Gordon was proud of his Scottish roots, so I chose a Burns poem titled 'Epitaph on a Friend'." She read the poem's single, short verse.

"Thank you, Imogen," said Martha. "And thank you, Joe and Tayana."

"Mom—for God's sake, don't thank us. We're mourning

with you," said Joe.

"Yes, well, I'm glad you're here. You know what I mean."

They ended the call and Imogen took her elbow. Martha stuffed the plastic bag back in the box and threw it in the garbage can on their way back to the car, oblivious to the black Crown Vic driving a slow circle in the parking lot.

Thursday, April 2nd, 2020

"Martha Gray?" called a man from behind her.

Assuming the voice belonged to a neighbour relieving the boredom of lockdown with a walk, Martha turned. "Yes?" She didn't recognize the middle-aged man who wore sunglasses, a bomber jacket, and baggy beige pants.

"I'm sorry about your father."

"Thank you. I'm terrible with faces—"

"Paul Thurlow, Elmington Police." The man drew a plastic badge from his breast pocket and flashed it. "Mind if we walk together?"

A sick despair rose in Martha's throat and her legs felt like jelly. "I don't mind," she replied.

Thursday, June 18th, 2020

The Crown Attorney's offices faced north. Though midday, Jim Bryant sat in gloom with a thick file labelled "R. v. Gray – Notes" and a synopsis of *R. v. Latimer* before him under a puddle of lamplight. He leaned back in his swivel chair, provoking an ominous groan from its springs, and absently scratched the two-day stubble on his chin.

Jim didn't have to keep up appearances. The COVID bogie man had chased the hysterically risk-averse staff from the building into virtuous self-isolation in their homes. Since March, Jim had assumed peripheral duties such as copying, printing, making pots of horrible coffee, and absenting himself from the torture of Zoom meetings on slim pretexts. The government's draconian pandemic measures were an affront to the *Charter of Rights and Freedoms,* but the legal community largely obeyed the zealots in public health with compliant clicks of their heels, cheered on by the propagandist media. Jim was quite alone.

He'd prosecute Gray to the best of his abilities, though this case would be a grim affair. Martha Elizabeth Gray had confessed to ending her father's dismal life. Autopsy and witness testimony corroborated her confession. But where was the real crime in a case like this? The Crown Attorney wanted first-degree murder —purportedly on ethical grounds—justice for the weak and defenceless and blah, blah, blah, though Jim suspected that heightened drama and a rise in public profile with a first-degree charge was the pompous asshole's real motivation. Jim would take no joy in getting a conviction.

Save *R. v. Latimer*, there was precious little by way of precedent. Almost three decades ago, Robert Latimer had been charged with first-degree murder for killing his severely disabled daughter who'd lived in intractable pain. He was convicted of second-degree murder and spent nearly a decade in prison. Martha Gray stated she'd ended her father's life out of mercy and love. The parallels were obvious.

Jim leaned forward again, propped an elbow on his desk, and returned to the file. He'd highlighted witness statements, underlined discrepancies, jotted notes in the margins. The Crown Attorney smelled blood and, truth be told, he did too, though a less severe, second-degree murder charge better matched the circumstances. He took a swig of coffee, found it cold and bitter, and pushed his mug aside.

The autopsy report stated that the cause of Gordon Gray's death was cardiac arrest secondary to digoxin toxicity, the blood levels of the pertinent medication so high the overdose had to have happened on purpose . . . like the babies in that hospital case back in the 80s, though nurse Susan Nelles was only guilty of being in the wrong place at the wrong time, her name dragged through the mud, career ruined, and the real infanticidal maniac never identified.

In this case, the evidence lined up with Martha's statement: Gordon Gray wanted to die, had been saving up medication to kill himself, and when he couldn't carry out his plan due to his condition, she acted for him at his request.

And yet—

How had a man who had lost the power of speech made such a request? How was she so sure that death was what he wanted?

Furthermore, Martha Gray had a financial motive to kill her father. Private rooms in nursing homes were expensive and the longer Gordon lived, the less Martha would inherit. As soon as she'd installed Gordon in Oakview, she'd emptied his house in the hope of a swift sale to the tune of nine hundred grand. The real estate ladies, Mavis Mill and Sally Dunfield, stated that Martha was keen to dump the place. She wanted to get back to Vancouver, incidentally the most expensive city in the country, and she seemed disappointed when Mavis delayed the listing due to lockdown. There was a son who lived on a squalid commune in BC. Kids grew up slowly these days. Maybe he needed cash and Martha had helped him to an early inheritance.

Jim drew his index finger down a list of credit card transactions. Martha wasn't a shopaholic apart from some pricey purchases at the fat ladies' bathing suit shop and her yoga lessons, but she burnt through money on booze and take-out. She had the appetite of King Henry the Eighth. Like the gluttonous monarch, was she a murderer too?

Doctor Katherine Southey seemed to think so. In formal

statements, she primly cited her duty to maintain confidentiality, then told the interviewer that Gordon could have lived for years under her tender care. A model patient, he'd bonded with other residents, quit smoking, seemed to rally after his stroke. The smell of bullshit wafted from her words, but she'd be a credible witness. Same with the nursing home director, Diane Stefano. They'd present themselves to the jury as caring professionals who were helping Gordon to recover from his stroke.

The best hope for the defence was Gordon's former colleague, Imogen Wallis, and good luck with that. Even Jim's jaded eyes burned when he read her statements, swear words peppering the sentences like chilis in a Mexican stew. When Martha was arrested, Wallis emerged from the dusty stacks of Elmington Public Library to give her story as "Gordon's protégé and friend." She painted a portrait of the Grays as a loving, caring family—Gordon as doting father and Martha as devoted daughter. However, Wallis's strangeness and volatility would be the undoing of the defence.

Even with fuzzy gaydar, Jim detected the affair. Joanne Kingsworth, the hawk-eyed, civic-minded, duty-bound neighbour who'd helped poor, dear Gordon in his year of need, filled in the blanks. Imogen Wallis loved Martha more than she loved Gordon and that made her an unreliable, highly combustible witness. Cross examination would be a cakewalk. He wouldn't go too far, definitely wouldn't bully a member of the marginalized alphabet community, but he'd take her down by planting a seed in the jury's mind—as Martha's lover, Imogen Wallis would have benefited from Gordon's death. Kingsworth told the police that she suspected the lovers of verbally and physically abusing the old man. Jim jotted a reminder by her name to follow up.

Evidence and witnesses were clicking into place like pieces of a preschooler's jumbo jigsaw puzzle, though first-degree murder seemed a cruel stretch. This one was second-degree and a decent defence lawyer could get her off of that charge too, no skin off his nose. The cell phone chimed from wherever he'd left it. In his briefcase? On a filing cabinet? After several rings, he located it in his drawer and barked a hasty hello.

Finally. Elmington Municipal Marina. They'd launch The Legal Beagle in an hour and a berth near the southern gap had come open, just right for a 32-foot sloop. Could he come down?

You betcha. Only two months behind schedule thanks to viral paranoia sweeping land and sea. He'd be there in half an hour. Jim locked the files in his desk drawer and forgot about the unfortunate Gray family for the rest of the day.

Entry in the Diary of Claire Posner, Tuesday, November 23rd, 2021

Today Martha Gray was found guilty of the second-degree murder of her father, Gordon Gray. I'm disappointed but not surprised. The crown prosecutor was a pit bull, and Martha had confessed to the police.

The media portrayed her as a sideshow freak – too smart, too weird, too aloof – a witch for the ducking stool. The mob wanted blood and they got it. Most people can't handle things that happen on the hazy margins of right and wrong. They want a clear border and punishment for anyone who crosses it. Courtrooms reflect society.

Martha came across as cold, but she's only shy. When you help a woman choose a bathing suit, you get a sense of her soul. Boldly Beautiful has lost an interesting client to the vagaries of prison.

Lesson learned: Follow the rules or else! The government gives its blessing and money to doctors who put old, sick people out of their misery, but don't you dare try it yourself. Don't you dare take matters into your own hands. DIY euthanasia isn't a courageous act of care and love, dear diary – it's murder!!

This fascinates me. The tension between the moral ambiguity of real life and the black and white certainty of the law. Which reminds me, I have to work on my application and finish Jake's sweater. The deadline for the master's criminology program at U of T is next week and Christmas is only a month away.

Wednesday, November 24th, 2021

She couldn't be with Martha, but she could try to descend into her hell. The more Imogen clicked and watched and clicked and read, the more she suffered—which was precisely the bloody point. She made herself face the breathless, know-it-all articles, the spittle-sprayed commentary, the lazy judgement of Joe Q. Public. The webpages featured crude, hastily rendered pastels of the judge frowning over half-moon glasses, of the jury's solemn, blurred faces, and of Martha, a solitary lump in an ill-fitting blouse—ugly, distorted, unrepentant, and alone as the verdict was read. Guilty of second-degree murder. For weeks Martha had been a spectacle in the infotainment arena, a lamb-toy for the lions, and Imogen could do fuck all to stop the torture.

Martha would be locked up for a decade, separated from anyone who gave a damn, and she, Imogen Wallis, was to blame. The only thing she could do was punish herself. Click, look, turn the psychic knife in her belly. It was all her fault. She'd let Bryant twist her words. The harder she'd resisted his badgering, the tighter he'd gripped until she spewed a bloody, sordid, scandalous emesis of testimony. Her words had sealed Martha's fate.

A relentless cramp gripped her shoulder. Twinkle prowled around her feet. Imogen glanced to the corner of her screen. Two am. Past time for bed. She checked the visiting rules for Grand

River Women's Penitentiary. Hold on. A Facebook notification. From Sophie. Sophie!

"Hey girl. Bad luck, huh? Call me if you think it would help."

No. Imogen wouldn't call. Not now. No way.

"All the news that's fit to print, Angelo?" Frank asked as he accepted the *Globe and Mail*.

"And plenty that isn't, Mr. Frank." Angelo backed away, then paused and sat on a low table near Frank's wheelchair.

"The Gray trial . . ."

Angelo nodded gravely.

"A terrible way to find one's fifteen minutes of fame."

Angelo cocked his head to the side quizzically.

Frank explained, "There was this artist from New York who said—" Then he shook his head. "Never mind. It's just a saying and a bad joke. Anyway, Martha Gray is infamous, not famous, and guilty of murder no less."

"Do you think she's really guilty?" Angelo repeated the question he and Frank had mulled for the past year and a half.

"She's only guilty of acting impulsively and bravely. She should be given a medal, not a prison sentence, poor girl. Gordon wanted to die. He would've turned to dust slowly and painfully in that blasted recliner if she'd walked away. Remember Angelo, they locked us up that week, no visitors for months. Somehow she understood the stakes — what had to happen."

"But murder is a mortal sin."

"So is torture."

"We weren't torturing Mr. Gordon."

Frank shrugged in mild challenge. "You weren't, but the system was. Imagine yourself trapped in Gordon's body. You can't walk, can't move, can't talk. You need to pee, but you can't tell anyone, so you have to go in your drawers. You can't even scratch your ass let alone have a smoke."

Angelo nodded, as if bidding Frank to continue convincing him.

"You're kind, Angelo, but not everyone is. Some are rough and mean. Like that one they fired. Ashley . . ."

"She quit."

"Okay. Compelled to quit. Imagine you're helpless and Ashley is looking after you."

A pained expression darkened Angelo's face.

Frank leaned forward and shook a bony finger. "God above knows what was in Martha's heart—and what Gordon was going through. It's the justice system that couldn't differentiate between mercy and sin."

"I think of my own parents. I can never do what she did."

"I couldn't either. Few of us could. Doesn't make it wrong, does it?"

Angelo smiled slightly. "Do I ever tell you about the first time I meet Mr. Gordon?"

"No," replied Frank, happy to change the subject.

"We're not supposed to talk about patients, but he's in heaven now."

"He is indeed. Reciting poetry to the angels."

"I'll tell you the story if you keep it here." Angelo pursed his lips and patted his chest. Frank nodded and Angelo settled into his reminiscence. "I went to his house to give him a shower. . . ."

Tuesday, December 7th, 2021

Sally arranged the furniture for the reconvening of book club. They'd need six chairs if Selena came, seven if Emma joined them instead of sulking in her room. Four months since Sam broke off the engagement. Never mind. Six chairs at most. She shifted the rocking chair so it wouldn't hit the rosewood cabinet or the wall. That was the trouble with a rocker. So soothing but such a threat to freshly papered walls.

Next she checked the essentials. Napkins on the coffee table. Fan them just so and the little reindeer faces with cute red noses peeked out. A smart print. You never knew what you'd find at Winner's. Eight Santa plates beside the napkins. They looked like a matching set, though the plates had come from an outlet store in the States. Maybe the dish of holiday wine glass charms should go on the coffee table instead of the cart. They weren't needed, but no one could admire them if they were stuck by the ice bucket. Emma always chose the angel. . . .

Canapes and fruit and cheese tray covered in Saran on the alcove counter, eggnog in the fridge, wine on the cart, glasses spotless. What was missing? Christmas carols. Nice and low. Instrumental was best at a social occasion. Set the tone without distracting. Kenny G? Whatever Mavis's opinion on saxophone music, Kenny G would be perfect. They'd talk about Martha and no one would really hear "Winter Wonderland," but it would lighten the atmosphere. This month's book was a downer too.

Doorbell. Sally spotted Joanne's brand-new Escalade in the driveway. She smiled into the mirror over the mantel, crinkled her eyes just so. Ready. To the door.

Joanne was wearing a surgical mask. She'd take it off for food and drink, wouldn't she?

Moments later they were seated with glasses of wine, Joanne in the rocker and Sally in the leather upright. She and Martha sat in the same chairs a few days before Christmas nearly two years ago. Poor old Martha.

Joanne didn't feel the same way and said so. "She's really guilty of first-degree murder, Sally. She killed Gordon in cold blood. You shouldn't feel sorry for her. If anything, she's lucky. The justice system is far too lenient."

"She said she did it to end his suffering," Sally said quietly to test the strength of Joanne's opinion.

"And you believe that?"

"Well—"

"Don't. She's a psychopath. Period. She manipulates people into feeling sorry for her. She almost got away with murder with that ridiculous confession." Joanne mocked, "Poor Martha Gray. So misunderstood. Persecuted by a heartless system." Her voice hardened. "For murdering her father in his bed. She took the life of a helpless, gentle, sweet old man. Ethan is traumatized by this whole ordeal."

Sally sipped her wine. Joanne drove her opinions as if she were driving a Hummer. She was too intimidating to challenge directly. She'd never warmed to Martha. Now Sally realized that Joanne actually hated Martha. Usually the peacemaker, Sally felt a duty to defend her old friend.

"She confessed—that's true, Joanne. No one will ever know what really happened though. Except Martha. If we take her at her word—"

"Sally, I can't believe my ears. You can't take her at her word. She's a liar and a psychopath. She's sick."

"Well, if she's sick, shouldn't we help her?"

"Depends on who you mean by 'we'. The prison therapists, maybe. Maybe not. Definitely not us."

Sally said nothing. She'd support Martha with a kind letter, a care package . . . whatever the prison allowed.

Joanne continued, "Dr. Southey testified that Gordon was recovering when Martha killed him. Gordon wasn't her only victim, Sally. Since he died, Ethan has been severely anxious and withdrawn. Now he's refusing to talk to me about his trauma."

"Ethan," Sally repeated softly. "Gordon loved kids. He took a real interest in them, never a cross word. He always had time for a joke and a laugh."

At once Joanne looked as if she were about to cry. "Martha

robbed us, Sally. She took him from us. Karma put her in jail, and I pray that karma will see justice done."

On this assertion, Sally wouldn't argue. How could she? Joanne was wrong about Martha, but she was too unbalanced by Gordon's death to be challenged. Joanne shielded her vulnerability with her strong opinions and her precious, over-protected son, poor kid.

Sally saw the flash of headlights as another vehicle turned into the driveway. She'd have to warn Mavis to watch what she said about Martha when she greeted her at the door.

Thursday, December 16th, 2021

Katherine plunked herself down in the chair opposite Diane and accepted a mug of tea, blew the steam away, and took a sip. "Thanks. This hits the spot."

How things had changed, thought Diane. The simple act of blowing on a hot beverage cradled in one's hands or extinguishing candles on a birthday cake were viewed as dangerous and irresponsible acts by many. "You're welcome," she said. "It's such a crazy time of year. I'm glad you have time to spare today."

"Geoff agreed to do a week of hospital rounds in exchange for getting Christmas off," said Katherine. "Five for one. A fair deal. We never ski till January anyway. Are you taking any time off?"

"Not yet. We're always short-staffed through the holidays. I'm exhausted, so I will eventually. When public health lets up with their demands. When the pandemic is finally over, I'm going to think about my future. Re-evaluate."

"I get that. We've all been through the wringer, though I'd hate to see Oakview lose a good nurse."

"Which is why I asked you to stop in. You've stuck by us here through thick and thin and I thought we should debrief. Decompress. Lay our thoughts and feelings bare so we can move on."

"Diane—"

"I don't know about you, Katherine, but that trial was an ordeal for me. We were all on trial. Media sniffing around for blood. First the Wettlaufer inquiry, then the first wave of the pandemic, then the Grays. The reporters circled like sharks looking for an angle, a scandal, someone to scapegoat. They've pinned the blame on management for practically every friggin' nursing home death for the past five years. It's always the nurses' fault. Whenever anything happens, they blame the nurses."

"At least this time it wasn't the nurses they cared about," said Katherine.

"Wasn't it?" Diane asked rhetorically. She shifted to a mocking tone, imitating the precise speech of a cross-examining lawyer. "Shouldn't Gordon Gray have gone to hospital after his stroke? Is it common nursing practice to deprive the elderly of emergency care? Didn't you see the signs that Martha Gray was unstable? Homicidal? Is it usual to let family members feed residents who are at risk of choking? Without supervision?"

"You had an answer every time, Diane," soothed Katherine. "And doctors feel the heat too."

"I suppose, though look what happened to Sonya Tam. Sure, she shouldn't have spoken to the media, especially after Martha was charged, but she admitted her mistake and apologized and they still kicked her to the curb for breaking patient confidentiality. Now she's in trouble with the College of Nurses and to what end? Everything came out at the trial anyway."

"It was a dumb thing to do. No one in her right mind talks to the media and she did it repeatedly," Katherine countered. "A doctor would've had to answer for that too. Especially before the trial of the year."

"The century."

Katherine set her mug on the desk, recklessly close to the edge in Diane's opinion, and said, voice low, "Since the trial, I can't look Dr. Najarian in the eye. The guy gives me the creeps. Second-guessing my judgement . . . claiming Gordon was end-stage COPD and I should've followed through on his request for MAID. Did he do a pulmonary function test when Gordon was under his care? Assess him for depression? Follow him month after month after month? The nerve of the guy. Lauren Cardinal's testimony I could understand. MAID is her bread and butter and anyone with a common cold and a death wish is fair game for her, but a hospitalist? I saw him cycling on Lakeshore the other day."

Diane didn't want to imagine why this was significant to Katherine. The comment seemed sinister, so she ignored it and said evenly, "We did our best for Gordon. There will always be differences in opinion on how to treat patients and those discussions belong on rounds or in the nurses' station, not in a court room."

"Here, here," said Katherine. "We can put all of this behind us now. Martha Gray is in prison where she belongs. Everything could have been avoided if she'd dealt with us honestly and openly."

"That's what bugs me, Katherine. What if Dr. Najarian and Lauren Cardinal were right? What if we should have tried harder to communicate with Gordon? So things didn't spin out of control with Martha?"

"You trust my clinical judgement, don't you, Diane?"

"Of course."

"Then believe me when I tell you that Gordon did not have the mental capacity to make life and death decisions after his CVA. My conscience is clear, whatever that creep Najarian says, and yours should be too. You're a good nurse. I did my job, and you did yours."

"Thank you, Katherine," Diane said, as if receiving a priestly blessing. "That means a lot to me."

Katherine looked at her watch, took a final swig from her mug. "I'd better run. It's time for clinic. The traffic's only getting worse the closer we get to the holidays, and Tanice will be wondering where I am."

Sunday, December 19th, 2021

When he was fast asleep, he was easier to love. In the pale glow of the full moon just before dawn, he was easier to love. A curl of hair tumbled over his forehead. His beard was finally filling in . . . catching up with his age. His mouth held a smile even in sleep. Innocent as a choir boy. He never woke with the predawn crow of the rooster or the racket of pots and pans in the kitchen. He probably wouldn't wake to the cry of a baby either.

The arguments were exhausting. When he'd married her, he'd married the community. All this talk of leaving had to stop. Joe had to stop it. They needed stability now. The thought of getting on a bus, breathing recirculated air through a mask and sitting on sticky upholstery made her queasy. She rolled over and reached for the glass of ginger tea she'd prepared the night before. A few sips to dampen the nausea.

The duvet came with her, and Joe's back was exposed to a wintery draft. His eyes fluttered open. "Hey, Tayana," he murmured affectionately, arms stretched for her and the new day, yesterday's fight forgotten.

"Joe." She nestled her chin in the hollow of his shoulder. "Umm easy, okay? I feel a little sick."

"What's wrong?"

"I went to see Grace yesterday, while you were chopping

wood with Tiger." Come on. Courage. Out with it. "And, umm, you're going to be a father."

"What?"

"I said—"

"A father. A dad! Tayana... You're—how?"

A question too daft to answer. "I'm due in July."

"Jesus." Arms tightened. A whoop of joy with a blast of hot breath in her ear. "That's fantastic. We're fantastic." Joe arched back, smiled broadly, and beheld her as if she was a goddess. Like old times.

"You're happy... about the baby?"

"Of course, I'm happy. I'm ecstatic. You know what this means. We have to get out of here. We'll have to go to Winnipeg. Find an apartment. I'll get a job. You'll need your mom. Your real family."

Was he suddenly playing the freaking opposite game? Why did she have to continually correct him? All the time. "Grace is here. I need Grace to help me through this. She went with me to speak with Master Garuda, and he said we can move into the stone cabin. We'll have more space that way."

"What? You told Garuda before you told me?"

"Well..."

"Holy fuck, Tayana." Joe turned onto his back and stared straight up. "Why?"

To avoid the argument over where they'd live when the baby came, though fat lot of good that did, evidently. She couldn't say that though. "It was Grace's idea," she lied.

"Grace. Okay, so I'm the third to know. The fourth counting you."

"Grace only gave me the test yesterday."

Joe slid his arm under the small of her back and held her again. Mollified.

"Why didn't you tell me last night?" he asked softly.

"I guess I needed to process everything... to think things

over," she replied, looking into his eyes. They were fine when they connected on this primal level, when they didn't overthink things and they followed the pattern of the community. Joe was always going on about freedom, but living simply at Agape was freedom too. He had to understand that.

"If it's a boy, we'll call him Gordon," he declared.

Before she could object to a name that would only bring ill fate to its bearer, the stench of scorched eggs escaped from the kitchen and engulfed their room. Another wave of nausea welled from Tayana's belly. Ginger tea wouldn't do. She swept out of bed and ran. They had seven months to negotiate the baby's name, but she had mere seconds to get to the toilet before she hurled.

Wednesday, March 24th, 2022

Martha sat cross-legged on her cot and picked at the pills on her brown blanket, wishing her interlocuter would vanish so she could order her thoughts. Two years. It'd been two years since she walked out of the old man's room and into . . . what? Jesus. If the woman would only shut up, Martha could try to figure things out all over again, but new women often talked too much, eager to establish alliances, ease loneliness, ward off the crazy voices echoing inside their skulls. New women either talked too much or not at all.

"Bet you didn't think you'd get caught. Prob'ly thought they'd chalk it up to a heart attack, right?"

Martha stared blankly at the tiny mountain of polyester fluff balls she'd created.

"Gotta give 'em credit. The cops dig and dig like starving rats in a junkyard. Don't get me wrong—I hate the cops—but credit where credit's fucking due, right?"

Martha's noncommittal sigh had the effect of throwing a birch log onto the conversational fire.

"And innocent until proven guilty, my arse. They fucking decide and they find the evidence to back the charge, irregardless of the real truth."

The woman obviously wanted her to confess or deny. Most people couldn't tolerate ambiguity. Martha offered silence.

"Whether you did it or not is none of my bee's wax so don't tell me nothing if you don't want to. I get it. I seen at dinner you're not a gabber."

Martha returned to her task.

"Me? Talking's therapy. Not talking to the fucking headshrinker, but friends, you know?"

Martha nodded politely.

"Since you're asking, I'm in for manslaughter. Brandi had it coming. Sniffed around my man like a bitch in heat. Tight shorts and top down to here. I ain't blaming Ryan. Men are weak. All prick and no fucking brains. I had to send a message. Gave her plenty of warning. Told her to fucking back off. Would've been aggravated assault, but the bitch up and died."

Martha abandoned her project and looked warily at the woman sprawled on the cell's other cot. She was soft, as if she were made of pillows, yet she'd just admitted to killing another human being. The woman was a noisy, giant, Boston crème donut with violent impulse oozing from her core.

"The cops blamed me. The legal aid lawyer was a swinging dick who pissed off the judge. A lady judge. She hated my guts, and I didn't stand a chance. Prob'ly had husband troubles herself that she didn't have the guts to solve. End of fucking story."

Silence could provoke as surely as a clumsy word. Martha spoke gently, as if steadying a nervous horse. "And now you're here. Welcome to Grand River Women's Penitentiary."

"Welcome?" the woman brayed. "You the fucking bellhop at the Hilton?"

Martha laughed along defensively.

"Thanks anyway." The woman yawned and stretched. "First day is always fucking long. I'm going to sleep." She rolled over and faced the wall.

"Good night," said Martha.

Seconds later, the timer switched off the lights. It occurred to Martha that no one had introduced the woman and they hadn't exchanged names. She brushed her fabric mountain away and laid back to savour the darkness. Names were for tomorrow. Now she had silence.

At night silence flooded this small room and her small life. Silence was infinitely more than an auditory void—it was a black canvas with no edges, a horizon, a bottomless vessel. She had to think carefully or the silence filled with intruders and ugliness, monsters materializing from nowhere and attacking the order of her mind. On good nights, she sank into the silence, weighing and sorting and boxing her memories, and she felt better for it.

A system of thousands of moving parts and little minds had put her here. Nothing personal. No good deed goes unpunished. The greatest of deeds is punished in spectacular fashion. Whenever anyone asked if she'd do it again, her answer came swiftly. Yes. She would. She hadn't had a choice. She had to do what her father had asked of her. She wasn't happy with the outcome but at least she wasn't a coward. This particular monster, the do-over monster, was easy to dispatch. Less so, her self-pity.

Self-pity was a monster of another colour entirely. Cut it here and it grew there. It changed shape and face and never, ever went away. You had to starve it if you ever hoped to kill it. Hers was unbridled, uncontained, and amply fed by petty nuisances and outrageous injustices. Cold showers, slimy meatballs, library books with missing pages . . . the crushing uncertainty of the appeal process . . . Imogen.

Betrayal had a name, and it was Imogen Wallis.

Martha played the Imogen film reel backward and forward in an infinite loop, emotion shifting with each memory. The facts had been stated simply in a brief phone call: Imogen was helping Sophie and her two children now. "Laterally promoted" from under Simon's thumb in early February, she also had to fix a withering branch library. She had no time to write or call or visit. Sophie needed her. Sophie's kids needed her. The Thistledown Community Library needed her. Twinkle, neurotic and cranky in her new home, needed her. With so much need and so little time, Imogen had nothing left to give to Martha and she wanted nothing more from Martha. "I guess this is good-bye then," Martha said before she hung up for the last time.

She hid her hurt from the predators, licked her wounds under the cloak of night, and tried to figure out why, when she'd been so confident of their connection, Imogen had abandoned her. Martha developed and discarded theories based on her own unworthiness, Imogen's fear, vulnerability, and her need to be needed, and Sophie's obvious advantages to explain the betrayal, but nothing quite fit. There was no logic to love and the death of love. Affairs ended every day, all around the planet. Experience, that most cruel of teachers, had taught Martha that she would suffer, would tire of suffering, and eventually the film would wear out and she would heal.

She still had Joseph. He and Tayana were going to be parents. Martha greeted this news with joy. She loved Joseph with all her heart. A parent's love for a child was a pure, golden thread that ran through generations, and Joe was about to discover it. Maybe fatherhood would repair their connection, despite the prison walls.

Judith visited the silence too, though in a diminished form. Prison seethed with women like Judith—angry, narcissistic, and dangerous—and these women defanged her. A spectre paled against actual threat. The memory of slaps and biting criticism held nothing on the looming possibility of kicks and punches.

The ghost of Judith haunted Martha only when she had the luxury of safety to indulge it and prison was "no fucking cocktail party at the Ritz"—as one of the square-trousered, briskly hair-styled guards put it.

Indeed. Prison was definitely not a cocktail party. It was as dry as a temperance picnic in the Gobi Desert and Martha was healthy and clearheaded for it. Gordon would've been proud of her sobriety.

He would've been proud of her book sales too. Her academic career was over, but *Pacifiers for the Proletariat* sold well enough to warrant a modest second print run at Christmas with fresh cover art, a flattering introduction, and a new editor and publicist. In a handwritten letter, Philip at Merganser Press floated the idea of a memoir, if it wouldn't be too painful to write. It wouldn't. She had a lot to say about taming monsters.

As she considered her answer to Philip's letter, she heard a hoarse whisper.

"Martha? You still awake?"

"Yes," Martha whispered back. "Sorry. I don't know your name yet."

"Tina."

"Tina," Martha repeated. "Pleased to meet you."

The woman giggled softly and in a disastrous attempt at a royal accent replied, "Enchanted, I'm fucking sure." After a moment, she asked, "Do you ever have nightmares?"

"Yes. Sometimes," said Martha.

"Me too. Can we make a deal?"

"Yes, Tina."

"If either of us gets scared in the night, we can wake the other up?"

"Sure," agreed Martha. "It's a deal."

About the Author

Renee Lehnen is a registered nurse by profession and a writer by passion. Her short stories have been published in the anthologies *Dark Secrets* and *Murder! Mystery! Mayhem!* Her pen name for her recently released romance novel is "Renata North." In addition, Renee was the 2019 winner and 2020 runner-up of Stratford Rotary's short story contest. For more information about her work, please visit www.lehnen.ca Renee lives in Stratford, Ontario with her husband.

Also by Renee Lehnen

What Love Demands

(as Renata North)

Manufactured by Amazon.ca
Bolton, ON